SANCTUS

In 2007 Simon Toyne quit his job and moved to France to fulfil a long-held desire to write a thriller. After a sleepless night crossing the Channel, he and his family abandoned a planned eight-hour drive to their new home and limped instead to the city of Rouen. It was the sight of the sharp spire of Rouen Cathedral piercing the pre-dawn sky that gave birth to the fictional Citadel of *Sanctus*.

Sanctus, his first novel, became an immediate bestseller. To date it has been translated into 25 languages and published in 40 countries.

thesancti.com

simontoyne.net

COMING SOON
SPRING 2012

THE KEY

The exciting sequel to the

Sunday Times bestseller *Sanctus*

Read an exclusive preview now…

SANCTUS

SIMON TOYNE

HARPER

Harper
An imprint of HarperCollins*Publishers*
77–85 Fulham Palace Road,
Hammersmith, London W6 8JB

www.harpercollins.co.uk

This paperback edition 2011
1

First published in Great Britain by HarperCollins*Publishers* 2011

A catalogue record for this book is available from the British Library

ISBN: 978 0 00 739158 5

Printed and bound in Great Britain by Clays Ltd, St Ives plc

MIX
Paper from
responsible sources
FSC
www.fsc.org **FSC C007454**

To K
For the adventure

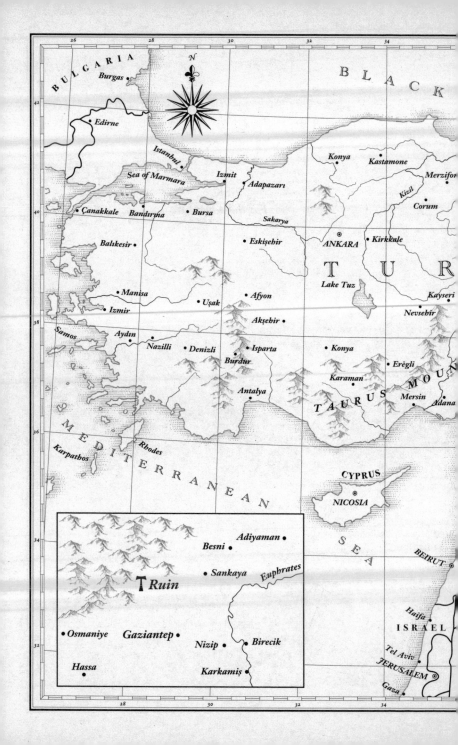

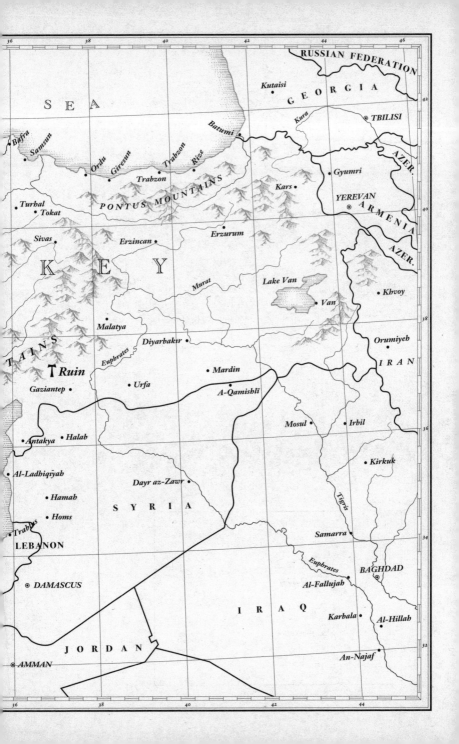

I

A man is a god in ruins

<small>RALPH WALDO EMERSON</small>

1

AL-HILLAH, BABIL PROVINCE
CENTRAL IRAQ

The desert warrior stared through the sand-scoured window, goggles hiding his eyes, his *keffiyeh* masking the rest of his face. Everything out there was bleached the colour of bone: the buildings, the rubble – even the people.

He watched a man shuffle along the far side of the street, his own *keffiyeh* swathed against the dust. There weren't many passers-by in this part of town, not with the noon sun high in the white sky and the temperature way into the fifties. Even so, they needed to be quick.

From somewhere behind him in the depths of the building came a dull thud and a muffled groan. He watched for any indication the stranger may have heard, but he just kept walking, sticking close to the sliver of shade provided by a wall pockmarked with automatic weapon fire and grenade blasts. He watched until the man melted away in the heat-haze then turned his attention back to the room.

The office was part of a garage on the outskirts of the city. It smelled of oil and sweat and cheap cigarettes. A framed photograph hung on one wall, its subject proudly surveying the piles of greasy paperwork and engine parts that covered every surface. The room was just about big enough for a desk and a couple of chairs and small enough for the bulky air-conditioning unit to maintain a reasonable temperature.

When it was working. Right now it wasn't. The place was like an oven.

Another grunt of pain snapped him to attention. He began emptying drawers, opening cupboards, hoping he might quickly find what he was looking for so they could vanish back into the desert before the next patrol swung past. But the man who had taken it clearly knew its value. There was no trace of it here.

He took the photograph off the wall. A thick black Saddam moustache spread across a face made featureless by prosperity; a white *dish-dash* strained against his belly as his arms stretched around two shy-looking girls who had unfortunately inherited their father's looks. The three of them were leaning against the white 4x4 now parked on the garage forecourt. He looked over at it, heard the tick of the cooling engine, saw the shimmer of hot air above it, and a small but distinctive circle low down in the centre of the blackened glass of the windscreen. He smiled and walked towards it, the photo still in his hand.

The workroom took up most of the rear of the building. It was darker than the office and just as hot. A vivid slash of sunlight from a couple of narrow windows high in the back wall fell across an engine block which dangled on thin chains that looked far too slender to keep it aloft. Below it, lashed to the workbench with razor wire, was the same fat man who had smiled out of the photograph in the front office. He wasn't smiling now. His nose was bloodied and broken and one of his eyes had swollen shut. Crimson rivulets ran from where the wire touched his sweat-slicked skin.

Another man in dusty fatigues stood by him, gripping a tyre iron, his face also obscured by *keffiyeh* and goggles.

'Where is it?' The interrogator raised the weapon.

The fat man said nothing, merely shook his head, his breathing growing more rapid in the anticipation of fresh pain. He screwed up his one good eye. The tyre iron rose higher.

1

A flash of light filled his skull as it struck the rock floor.

Then darkness.

He was dimly aware of the heavy oak door banging shut behind him and a thick batten sliding through iron hasps.

For a while he lay where he'd been thrown, listening to the pounding of his pulse and the mournful wind close by.

The blow to his head made him feel sick and dizzy, but there was no danger he was going to pass out; the agonizing cold would see to that. It was a still and ancient cold, immutable and unforgiving as the stone the cell was carved from. It pressed down and wrapped itself round him like a shroud, freezing the tears on his cheeks and beard, chilling the blood that trickled from the fresh cuts he himself had inflicted on his exposed upper body during the ceremony. Pictures tumbled through his mind, images of the awful scenes he had just witnessed and of the terrible secret he had learned.

It was the culmination of a lifetime of searching. The end of a journey he had hoped would lead to a sacred and ancient knowledge, to a divine understanding that would bring him closer to God. Now at long last he had gained that knowledge, but he had found no divinity in what he had seen, only unimaginable sorrow.

Where was God in this?

The tears stung fresh and the cold sank deeper into his body, tightening its grip on his bones. He heard something on the other side of the heavy door. A distant sound. One that had somehow managed to find its way up through the honeycomb of hand-carved tunnels which riddled the holy mountain.

They'll come for me soon.

The ceremony will end. Then they will deal with me . . .

He knew the history of the order he had joined. He knew their savage rules – and now he knew their secret. They'd kill him for sure. Probably slowly, in front of his former brothers, a reminder of the seriousness of their collective, uncompromising vows: a warning of what would happen if you broke them.

No!

Not here. Not like this.

He pressed his head against the cold stone floor then pushed himself up on all fours. Slowly and painfully he dragged the rough green material of his cassock back over his shoulders, the coarse wool scouring the raw wounds on his arms and chest. He pulled the cowl over his head and collapsed once more, feeling his warm breath through his beard, drawing his knees tightly under his chin and lying clenched in the foetal position until the warmth began to return to the rest of his body.

More noises echoed from somewhere within the mountain.

He opened his eyes and began to focus. A faint glow of distant light shone through a narrow window just enough to pick out the principal features of his cell. It was unadorned, rough-hewn, functional. A pile of rubble lay strewn across one corner, showing it was one of the hundreds of rooms no longer regularly used or maintained in the Citadel.

He glanced back at the window; little more than a slit in the rock, a loophole carved countless generations earlier to give archers a vantage point over enemy armies approaching across the plains below. He rose stiffly to his feet and made his way towards it.

Dawn was still some way off. There was no moon, just distant stars. Nevertheless when he looked through the window the sudden glare was enough to make him squint. It came from the combined light of tens of thousands of street lamps, advertising hoardings and shop signs stretching out far below him towards the rim of distant mountains surrounding the plain on all sides. It was the fierce and constant glow of the modern city of Ruin, once the capital of the Hittite Empire, now just a tourist destination in southern Turkey, on the furthest edge of Europe.

He looked down at the metropolitan sprawl, the world he had turned his back on eight years previously in his quest for truth, a quest that had led him to this lofty, ancient prison and a discovery that had torn apart his soul.

Another muffled sound. Closer this time.

He had to be quick.

He unthreaded the rope belt from the leather loops of his cassock. With a practised dexterity he twisted each end into a noose then stepped to the window and leaned through, feeling the frozen rock face for a crag or outcrop that might hold his weight. At the highest point of the opening he found a curved protrusion, slipped one noose around it and leaned back, tightening it, testing its strength.

It held.

Tucking his long, dirty blonde hair behind his ears he gazed down one last time at the carpet of light pulsating beneath him. Then, his heart heavy from the weight of the ancient secret he now carried, he breathed out as far as his lungs would allow, squeezed through the narrow gap, and launched himself into the night.

2

Nine floors down, in a room as grand and ornate as the previous one was meagre and bare, another man delicately washed the blood from his own freshly made cuts.

He knelt in front of a cavernous fireplace, as if in prayer. His long hair and beard were silvered with age and the hair on top of his head was thin, giving him a naturally monastic air in keeping with the green cassock gathered about his waist.

His body, though stooped with the first hint of age, was still solid and sinewy. Taut muscles moved beneath his skin as he dipped his square of muslin methodically into the copper bowl beside him, gently squeezing out the cool water before dabbing his weeping flesh. He held the poultice in place for a few moments each time, then repeated the ritual.

When the cuts on his neck, arms and torso had started to heal he patted himself dry with fresh, soft towels and rose, carefully pulling his habit back over his head, feeling the strangely comforting sting of his wounds beneath the coarse material. He closed his pale grey eyes, the colour of parched stone, and took a deep breath. He always felt a profound sense of calm immediately after the ceremony, a sense of satisfaction that he was upholding the greatest tradition of his ancient order. He tried to savour it for as long as possible before his temporal responsibilities dragged him back to the earthbound realities of his office.

A timid knock on the door disturbed this reverie.

Tonight his beatific mood was obviously going to be short-lived.

'Enter.' He reached for the rope belt draped over the back of a nearby chair.

The door opened, catching the light from the crackling fire on its carved and gilded surface. A monk slipped silently into the room, gently closing the door behind him. He too wore the green cassock and long hair and beard of their ancient order.

'Brother Abbot . . .' His voice was low, almost conspiratorial. 'Forgive my intrusion at this late hour – but I thought you should know immediately.'

He dropped his gaze and studied the floor, as if uncertain how to continue.

'Then tell me *immediately*,' growled the Abbot, tying the belt round his waist and tucking in his Crux – a wooden cross in the shape of the letter 'T'.

'We have lost Brother Samuel . . .'

The Abbot froze.

'What do you mean, "lost"? Has he died?'

'No, Brother Abbot. I mean . . . he is not in his cell.'

The Abbot's hand tightened on the hilt of his Crux until the grain of the wood pressed into his palm. Then, as logic quickly allayed his immediate fears, he relaxed once more.

'He must have jumped,' he said. 'Have the grounds searched and the body retrieved before it is discovered.'

He turned and adjusted his cassock, expecting the man to hurry from the room.

'Forgive me, Brother Abbot,' the monk continued, staring more intently at the floor, 'but we have already conducted a thorough search. We informed Brother Athanasius the moment we discovered Samuel was missing. He made contact with the outside and they instigated a sweep of the lower foundations. There's no sign of a body.'

The calmness the Abbot had enjoyed just a few minutes previously had now entirely evaporated.

Earlier that night Brother Samuel had been inducted into the Sancti, the inner circle of their order; a brotherhood so secret only those living within the cloistered halls of the mountain knew of its continued existence. The initiation had been carried out in the traditional manner, finally revealing to the groomed monk the ancient Sacrament, the holy secret their order had been formed to protect and maintain. Brother Samuel had demonstrated during the ceremony that he was not equal to this knowledge. It was not the first time a monk had been found wanting at the moment of revelation. The secret they were bound to keep was powerful and dangerous, and no matter how thoroughly the newcomer had been prepared, when the moment came it was sometimes simply too much. Regrettably, someone who possessed the knowledge but could not carry the burden of it was almost as dangerous as the secret itself. At such times it was safer, perhaps even kinder, to end that person's anguish as quickly as possible.

Brother Samuel had been such a case.

Now he had gone missing.

As long as he was at liberty, the Sacrament was vulnerable.

'Find him,' the Abbot said. 'Search the grounds again, dig them up if you have to, but find him.'

'Yes, Brother Abbot.'

'Unless a host of angels passed by and took pity on his wretched soul he must have fallen and he must have fallen nearby. And if he *hasn't* fallen then he must be somewhere in the Citadel. So secure every exit and conduct a room-by-room sweep of every crumbling battlement and bricked-up oubliette until you find either Brother Samuel or Brother Samuel's body. Do you understand me?'

He kicked the copper bowl into the fire. A cloud of steam erupted from its raging heart, filling the air with an unpleasant metallic tang. The monk continued to stare at the floor, desperate to be dismissed, but the Abbot's mind was elsewhere.

As the hissing subsided and the fire settled, so it seemed did the Abbot's mood.

'He must have jumped,' he said at length. 'So his body *has* to be lying somewhere in the grounds. Maybe it got caught in a tree. Perhaps a strong wind carried it away from the mountain and it now lies somewhere we have not yet thought to look; but we need to find it before dawn brings the first coachload of gawping interlopers.'

'As you wish.'

The monk bowed and made ready to leave, but a knock on the door startled him afresh. He looked up in time to see another monk sweep boldly into the room without waiting for the Abbot to bid him enter. The new arrival was small and slight, his sharp features and sunken eyes giving him a look of haunted intelligence, like he understood more than he was comfortable with; yet he exuded quiet authority, even though he wore the brown cassock of the Administrata, the lowliest of the guilds within the Citadel. It was the Abbot's chamberlain, Athanasius, a man instantly recognizable throughout the mountain because, uniquely among the ritually long-haired and bearded men, he was totally bald due to the alopecia he had suffered since the age of seven. Athanasius glanced at the Abbot's companion, saw the colour of his cassock and quickly averted his eyes. By the strict rules of the Citadel the green cloaks – the Sancti – were segregated. As the Abbot's chamberlain, Athanasius very occasionally crossed paths with one, but any form of communication was expressly forbidden.

'Forgive my intrusion, Brother Abbot,' Athanasius said, running his hand slowly across his smooth scalp, as he did in times of stress. 'But I beg to inform you that Brother Samuel has been found.'

The Abbot smiled and opened his arms expansively, as if preparing to warmly embrace the news.

'There you are,' he said. 'All is well again. The secret is safe and our order is secure. Tell me, where did they find the body?'

The hand continued its slow journey across the pale skull. 'There is no body,' he paused. 'Brother Samuel did not jump from the mountain. He *climbed* out. He is about four hundred feet up, on the eastern face.'

The Abbot's arms dropped to his sides, his expression darkening once more.

In his mind he pictured the granite wall springing vertically from the glacial plain of the valley, making up one side of the holy fortress.

'No matter.' He gave a dismissive wave. 'It is impossible to scale the eastern face, and there are still several hours till daybreak. He will tire well before then and fall to his death. And even if by some miracle he does manage to make it to the lower slopes, our brethren on the outside will apprehend him. He will be exhausted by such a climb. He will not offer them much resistance.'

'Of course, Brother Abbot,' Athanasius said. 'Except . . .' He continued to smooth down hair that had long since departed.

'Except what?' the Abbot snapped.

'Except Brother Samuel is not climbing *down* the mountain.' Athanasius's palm finally separated itself from the top of his head. 'He's climbing *up* it.'

3

The black wind blew through the night, sliding across the high peaks and the glacier to the east of the city, sucking up its prehistoric chill with fragments of grit and moraine freed by the steady thaw.

It picked up speed as it dipped down into the sunken plain of Ruin, cupped like a huge bowl within an unbroken ring of jagged peaks. It whispered through the ancient vineyards, olive groves and pistachio orchards that clung to the lower slopes, and on towards the neon and sodium glow of the urban sprawl where it had once flapped the canvas and tugged at the red-and-gold sun flag of Alexander the Great and the *Vexillum* of the fourth Roman legion and all the standards of every frustrated army that had clustered in shivering siege round the tall dark mountain while their leaders stared up, coveting the secret it contained.

The wind swept on now, keening down the wide straight highway of the eastern boulevard, past the mosque built by Suleiman the Magnificent and across the stone balcony of the Hotel Napoleon where the great general had stood, listening to his army ransacking the city below while he stared up, surveying the carved stone battlements of the dark dagger mountain that would remain unconquered, piercing the flank of his incomplete empire and haunting his dreams as he later lay dying in exile.

The wind moaned onwards, cascading over the high walls of the old town, squeezing through streets built narrow to hamper the charge of armoured men, slipping past ancient houses filled to the beams with modern mementoes, and rattling tourist signs that now swung where the mouldering bodies of slaughtered enemies had once dangled.

Finally it leapt the embankment wall, soughed through grass where a black moat once flowed and slammed into the mountain where even it could gain no access until, swirling skywards, it found a lone figure in the dark green habit of an order not seen since the thirteenth century, moving slowly and inexorably up the frozen rock face.

4

Samuel had not climbed anything as challenging as the Citadel for a long, long time. Thousands of years of hail and sleet-filled wind had smoothed the surface of the mountain to an almost glassy finish, giving him virtually no hold as he worked his way painstakingly to its summit.

Then there was the cold.

The icy wind that had smoothed the rock over aeons had also chilled its heart. His skin froze to it on contact, giving him a few moments' valuable traction, until he had to tear it free again, leaving his hands and knees bloody and raw. The wind gusted about him, tugging at his cassock with invisible fingers, trying to pluck him away and down to a dark death.

The rope belt wrapped around his right arm rubbed the skin from his wrist as he repeatedly threw it high and wide toward tiny outcrops that were otherwise beyond his reach. He pulled hard each time, closing the noose around whatever scant anchor he had snagged, willing it not to slip or break as he inched further up the unconquerable monolith.

The cell he had escaped from had been close to the chamber where the Sacrament was held, in the uppermost section of the Citadel. The higher he managed to get, the less he risked coming within reach of other cells where his captors might be waiting.

The rock which had up to this point been hard and glassy became suddenly jagged and brittle. He had crossed an ancient geological stratum to a softer layer that had been weakened and split by the cold that had tempered the granite below. There were deep fissures in its surface, making it easier to climb but infinitely more treacherous. Foot- and handholds crumbled without warning; fragments of stone tumbled down into the frozen darkness. In fear and desperation he jammed his hands and feet deep into the jagged crevices; they held his weight but were lacerated in the process.

As he moved higher and the wind strengthened, the cliff face began to arch back on itself. Gravity, which had previously aided his grip, now wrested him away from the mountain. Twice, when a sliver of rock broke away in his hand, the only thing that stopped him from plummeting a thousand feet was the rope bound to his wrist and the powerful conviction that the journey of his life was not yet over.

Finally, after what seemed like a lifetime of climbing, he reached up for his next handhold and felt only air. His hand fell forward on to a plateau across which the wind flowed freely into the night.

He gripped the edge and dragged himself up. He pushed against crumbling footholds with numb and shredded feet and heaved his body on to a stone platform as cold as death, felt the limits of the space with his outstretched hands and crawled to its centre, keeping low to avoid the worst of the buffeting wind. It was no bigger than the room he had so recently escaped, but whilst there he had been a helpless captive; up here he felt like he always had when he'd conquered an insurmountable peak – elated, ecstatic, and unutterably free.

5

The spring sun rose early and clear, casting long shadows down the valley. At this time of year it rose above the red Taurus peaks and shone directly down the great boulevard to the heart of the city where the road circling the Citadel picked out three other ancient thoroughfares, each marking a precise point of the compass.

With the dawn came the mournful sound of the muezzin from the mosque in the east of the city, calling those of a different faith to prayer as it had done since the Christian city had fallen to Arab armies in the seventh century. It also brought the first coach party of tourists, gathering by the portcullis, bleary-eyed and dyspeptic from their early starts and hurried breakfasts.

As they stood, yawning and waiting for their day of culture to begin, the muezzin's cry ended, leaving behind a different, eerie sound that seemed to drift down the ancient streets beyond the heavy wooden gate. It was a sound that crept into each of them, picking at their private fears, forcing eyes wider and hands to pull coats and fleeces tighter round soft, vulnerable bodies that suddenly felt the penetrating chill of the morning. It sounded like a hive of insects waking in the hollow depths of the earth, or a great ship groaning as it broke and sank into the silence of a bottomless sea. A few exchanged nervous glances, shivering involuntarily as it swirled around them, until it finally took shape as the vibrating hum of hundreds of deep male voices intoning sacred words in a language few could make out and none could understand.

The huge portcullis suddenly shifted in its stone housing, making most of them jump, as electric motors began to lift it on reinforced steel cables hidden away in the stonework to preserve the appearance of antiquity. The drone of electric motors drowned out the incantations of the monks until, by the time the portcullis completed its upward journey and slammed into place, it had vanished, leaving the army of tourists to slowly invade the steep streets leading to the oldest fortress on earth in spooked silence.

They made their way through the complex maze of cobbled streets, trudging steadily upwards past the bath houses and spas, where the miraculous health-giving waters of Ruin had been enjoyed long before the Romans annexed the idea; past the armouries and smithies – now restaurants and gift shops selling souvenir grails, vials of spa water and holy crosses – until they arrived at the main square, bordered on one side by the immense public church, the only holy building in the entire complex they were allowed to enter.

Some of the dopier onlookers had been known to stop here, gaze up at its façade and complain to the stewards that the Citadel didn't look anything like it did in the guidebooks. Redirected to an imposing stone gateway in the far corner of the square, they would turn a final bend and stop dead. Grey, monumental, immense, a tower of rock rose majestically before them, sculpted in places into ramparts and rough battlements, with the occasional stained-glass window – the only hint at the mountain's sacred purpose – set into its face like jewels.

6

The same sun that shone down on this slowly advancing army of tourists now warmed Samuel, lying motionless more than a thousand feet above them.

The feeling crept back into his limbs as the heat returned, bringing with it a deep and crucifying pain. He reached out and pushed himself into a sitting position, staying that way for a moment, his eyes still closed, his ruined hands flat against the summit, soothed by the primordial chill from the ancient stone. Finally he opened them and gazed upon the city of Ruin stretched out far below him.

He began to pray, as he always did when he'd made it safely to a peak.

Dear God our Father . . .

But as his mouth began to form the words, an image surfaced in his mind. He faltered. After the hell he'd witnessed the previous night, the obscenity that had been perpetrated in His name, he realized he was no longer sure who or what he was praying to. He felt the cold rock beneath his fingers, the rock from which, somewhere below him, the room that held the Sacrament had been carved. He pictured it now, and what it contained, and felt wonder, and terror, and shame.

Tears welled up in his eyes and he searched his mind for something, anything, to replace the image that haunted him. The warm, rising air carried with it the smell of sun-toasted grass, stirring a memory; a picture began to form, of a girl, vague and indistinct at first, but sharpening as it took hold.

A face both strange and familiar, a face full of love, pulled into focus from the blur of his past.

His hand shifted instinctively to his side, to the site of his oldest scar, one not freshly made and bloody, but long-since healed. As he pressed against it he felt something else, buried in the corner of his pocket. He pulled it out and gazed down upon a small, waxy apple, the remains of the simple meal he had not been able to eat earlier in the refectory. He had been too nervous, knowing that in a few short hours he would be inducted into the most ancient and sacred brotherhood on earth. Now here he was, on top of the world in his own personal hell.

He devoured the apple, feeling the sweetness flood into his aching body, warming him from within as it fuelled his exhausted muscles. He chewed the core to nothing and spat the pips into his lacerated palm. A splinter of rock was embedded in the fleshy pad. He raised it to his mouth and yanked it away, feeling the sharp pain of its extraction.

He spat it into his hand, wet with his own blood, a tiny replica of the slender peak he now perched upon. He wiped it clean with his thumb and stared at the grey rock beneath. It was the same colour and texture as the heretical book he had been shown in the depths of the great library during his preparation. Its pages had been made from similar stone, their surfaces crammed with symbols carved by a hand long since rendered to dust. The words he had read there, a prophecy in shape and form, seemed to warn of the end of things if the Sacrament became known beyond the walls of the Citadel.

He looked out across the city, the morning sun catching his green eyes and the high, sharp cheekbones beneath them. He thought of all the people down there, living their lives, striving in thought and deed to do good, to get on, to move closer to God. After the tragedies of his own life he had come here, to the well-spring of faith, to devote himself to the same ends. Now here he knelt, as high as it was possible to get on the holiest of mountains –

– and he had never felt further from Him.

Images drifted across his darkened mind: images of what he had lost, of what he had learned. And as the prophetic words, carved in the secret stone of the heretical book, crawled through his memory, he saw something new in them. And what he had first read as a warning now shone like a revelation.

He had already carried knowledge of the Sacrament this far outside the Citadel; who was to say he could not carry it further? Maybe he could become the instrument to shine light into this dark mountain and bring an end to what he had witnessed. And even if he was wrong, and this crisis of faith was the weakness of one not fit to divine the purpose of what he had seen, then surely God *would* intervene. The secret would remain so, and who would mourn the life of one confused monk?

He glanced up at the sky. The sun was rising higher now – the bringer of light, the bringer of life. It warmed him as he looked back down at the stone in his hand, his mind as sharp now as its jagged edge.

And he knew what he must do.

7

Over five thousand miles due west of Ruin, a slim blonde woman with fine, Nordic features stood in Central Park, one hand resting on the railing of Bow Bridge, the other holding a letter-sized manila envelope addressed to Liv Adamsen. It was crumpled from repeated handling, but not yet opened. Liv stared at the grey, liquid outline of New York reflected in the water and remembered the last time she'd stood there, with him, when they'd done the touristy thing and the sun had shone. It wasn't shining now.

The wind ruffled the lake's burnished surface, bumping together the few forgotten rowing boats tethered to the jetty. She pushed a strand of blonde hair behind her ear and looked down at the envelope, her sharp, green eyes dry from staring into the wind and the effort of trying not to cry. The envelope had appeared in her post nearly a week previously, nestling like a viper among the usual credit-card applications and pizza-delivery menus. At first she'd thought it was just another bill, until she spotted the return address printed on the lower corner. She got letters like this all the time at the *Inquirer*, hard copies of information she'd requested in the pursuit of whatever story she was currently working on. It was from the US Bureau of Vital Records, the one-stop store for public information on the Holy Trinity of most people's lives: birth, marriage and death.

She'd stuffed it into her bag, numb with the shock of its discovery, where it had been buried ever since, jostled by the receipts, notebooks, and make-up of her life, waiting for the right moment to be opened, though there never, ever could be one. Finally, after a week of glimpsing it every time she reached for her keys or answered her phone, something whispered in her mind and she took an early lunch and the train from Jersey to the heart of the big anonymous city, where no one knew her and the memories suited the circumstances, and where, if she lost it completely, nobody would bat an eyelid.

She walked now from the bridge, heading to the shore-line, her hand dipping into her bag and fishing out a slightly crushed pack of Lucky Strikes. Cupping her hand against the steady wind to light a cigarette, she stood for a moment on the edge of the rippling lake, breathing in the smoke and listening to the bump of the boats and the distant hiss of the city. Then she slid her finger under the flap of the envelope and ripped it open.

Inside was a letter and a folded document. The layout and language was all too familiar, but the words they contained were terribly different. Her eyes scanned across them, seeing them in clusters rather than whole sentences:

> . . . *eight year absence* . . .
> . . . *no new evidence* . . .
> . . . *officially deceased* . . .

She unfolded the document, read his name, and felt something give way inside her. The clenched emotions of the past years flexed and burst. She sobbed uncontrollably, tears born not only of the strangely welcome rush of grief, but also of the absolute loneliness she now felt in its shadow.

She remembered the last day she'd spent with him. Touring the city like a couple of rubes, they'd even hired one of the boats that now floated, cold and empty, nearby. She tried summoning the memory of it but could only manage fragments: the movement of his long, sinewy body uncoiling as he pulled the oars through the water; his shirt sleeves bunched up to his elbows, revealing white-blonde hairs on lightly tanned arms; the colour of his eyes and the way the skin around them crinkled when he smiled. His face remained vague. Once it had always been there, conjured simply by uttering the spell of his name; now, more often than not, an impostor would appear, similar to the boy she had once known but never quite the same.

She struggled to bring him into focus, gripping the slippery substance of his memory until a true image finally snapped into place; him as a boy, struggling with oversized oars on the lake near Granny Hansen's house in upstate New York. She'd cast them adrift, hollering after them, 'Your ancestors were Vikings. Only when you conquer the water will I let you come back . . .'

They were on the lake all afternoon, taking it in turns to row and steer until the wooden boat felt like a part of them. She'd laid out a victory picnic for them in the sun-baked grass, called them Ask and Embla after the first people carved by Norse gods from fallen trees found on a different shore, then thrilled them with more stories from their ancestral homeland, tales of rampaging ice giants, and swooping Valkyries, and Viking burials in flaming longships. Later, in the dark of the loft where they waited for sleep, he had whispered that when he died in some future heroic battle he wanted to go the same way, his spirit mingling with the smoke of a burning ship and drifting all the way up to Valhalla.

She looked down at the certificate again, spelling out his name and the verdict of his official demise: a death not by spear or sword or selfless act of incredible valour, but simply by a period of absence, clerically measured and deemed substantial enough. She folded the stiff paper with practised creases, also remembered from childhood, squatted by the edge of the lake and placed the makeshift boat on its surface. She cupped her hand round the pointed sail and fired up her lighter. As the dry paper began to blacken and burn, she pushed it gently out towards the centre of the empty lake. The flames fluttered for a moment, searching for something to catch hold of, then sputtered out in the cold breeze. She watched it drift until the lapping of the gun-metal water eventually capsized it.

She smoked another cigarette, waiting for it to sink, but it just lay flat against the reflected image of the city, like a spirit caught in limbo.

Not much of a Viking send-off . . .

She turned and walked away, heading to the train that would take her back to Jersey.

8

'Just take a moment to listen, ladies and gentlemen,' the tour guide implored his glassy-eyed charges as they stared up at the Citadel. 'Listen to the babble of languages around you: Italian, French, German, Spanish, Dutch, different tongues all telling the history of this, the oldest continually inhabited structure in the world. And that same jumble of languages, ladies and gentlemen, brings to mind the famous Bible story of the Tower of Babel from the book of Genesis, built not for the worship of God, but for the glory of man, so God became angry and "confounded their language", causing them to scatter throughout the nations of the earth, leaving the tower unfinished. Many scholars believe this story refers to the Citadel here at Ruin. Note also that the story is about a structure that was not built in praise of God. If you look up at the Citadel, ladies and gentlemen,' he swept his arm dramatically upward at the massive structure filling everybody's vision, 'you will notice that there are no outward signs of religious purpose. No crosses, no depictions of angels, no iconography of any kind. However, appearances can be deceptive and, despite this lack of religious adornment, the Citadel of Ruin is undoubtedly a house of God. The very first bible was written inside its mysterious walls and has served as the spiritual foundation stone upon which the Christian faith was built.

'Indeed, the Citadel was the original centre of the Christian church. The shift to the Vatican in Rome happening in AD 26 to give the rapidly expanding church a public focus. How many of you here have been to Vatican City?'

A smattering of reluctant hands rose up.

'A few of you. And no doubt you would have spent your time there marvelling at the Sistine Chapel and exploring St Peter's Basilica, or the papal tombs, or maybe even attending an audience with the Pope. Sadly, even though the Citadel here is reputed to contain wonders the equal of them all, you will not be able to see any of them, for the only people allowed inside this most secretive and sacred of places are the monks and priests who live here. So strict is this rule that even the great battlements you see carved into the solid stone sides of the mountain were not constructed by stonemasons or builders, but by the inhabitants of the holy mountain. It is a practice that has not only resulted in the uniquely dilapidated appearance of the place, but has given the city its name.

'Yet despite its appearance, it is no Ruin. It is the oldest stronghold in the world and the only one that has never been breached, though the most infamous and determined invaders in history have tried. And why did they try? Because of the legendary relic the mountain supposedly contains: the holy secret of Ruin – the Sacrament.' He let the word hang in the chill air for a second, like a ghost he had just conjured. 'The world's oldest and its greatest mystery,' he continued, his voice now a conspiratorial whisper. 'Some believe it to be the true cross of Christ. Some that it is the Holy Grail from which Christ drank and which can heal all wounds and bestow eternal life. Many believe the body of Christ Himself lies in state, miraculously preserved, somewhere within the carved depths of this silent mountain. There are also those who think it just legend, a story with no substance. The simple truth is, ladies and gentlemen, no one really knows. And, as secrecy is the very cornerstone upon which the Citadel's legend has been built, I very much doubt that anyone ever will.

'Now, if anyone has any questions,' he said, his brisk change of tone communicating his sincere wish that nobody did, 'then ask away.'

His small, darting eyes pecked the blank faces of the crowd staring up at the huge building, trying to think of something to ask. Normally nobody could, which meant they would then have a full twenty minutes to wander around, buy some souvenirs and take bad photos before rendezvousing back at the coach to head off somewhere else. The guide had just drawn breath to inform them of this fact when a hand shot up and pointed skywards.

'What's that thing?' a red-faced man in his fifties asked in a blunt northern British accent. 'That thing as looks like a cross?'

'Well, as I've already mentioned, the Citadel has no crosses anywhere on its –'

He stopped short. Squinted against the brightening sky. Looked again.

There above him, clearly visible on the famously unadorned summit of the ancient fortress, was a tiny cross.

'You know, I'm not . . . sure what that is . . .' He trailed off again.

No one was listening anyway. They were all straining their eyes to get a better glimpse of whatever was perched on top of the mountain.

The guide followed suit. Whatever it was wavered slightly. It looked like a capital letter 'T'. Maybe it was a bird, or simply a trick of the morning light.

'It's a man!' Someone shouted from another group standing nearby. The guide looked across at a middle-aged man, Dutch by his accent, staring intently at the fold-out LCD screen of his video camera.

'Look!' The man leaned back so others could share his discovery.

The guide peered at the screen over the jostling scrum. The camera had been zoomed in as far as it would go and held unsteadily on a grainy, digitally enhanced image of a man dressed in what looked like a green monk's habit. His long, dark-blonde hair whipped round his bearded face, blown by the higher winds, but he stood perfectly still at the summit's edge, his arms fully outstretched, his head tilted down, looking for all the world like a human cross – or a lonely, living figure of Christ.

9

In the foothills rising to the west of Ruin, in an orchard first planted in the late Middle Ages, Kathryn Mann led a group of six volunteers silently across the dappled ground. Each member of the group was dressed identically in an all-over body smock of heavy white canvas with a wide-brimmed hat dripping black gauze on every shoulder and shading every face. In the early morning light they looked like an ancient sect of druids on their way to a sacrifice.

Kathryn arrived at an upright oil drum covered with a scrap of tarpaulin and began removing the rocks holding it in place as the group fanned out silently behind her. The buoyant mood that had filled the minibus as it threaded its way through the empty, pre-dawn streets had long since evaporated. She removed the last of the weights. Someone held up the smoker for her. Usually the warmer the day the more active the bees became, and the more she needed to subdue them. Despite the building heat, Kathryn could already tell this hive was the same as the others. No hum sounded inside it and the dry red brick that served as a landing pad was empty.

She pumped a few cursory puffs of smoke into the bottom of the hive then lifted the tarp to reveal eight wood battens spaced evenly across the rim of the open drum. It was a simple top-bar hive; they could be made out of almost any old bits of salvage, as this one had been. The expedition to the orchard had been intended as a practical demonstration of basic beekeeping, something the volunteers could put into practice in the various parts of the world they would be stationed in for the next year. But as dawn had broken and hive after hive was found and checked, the expedition turned into a first-hand encounter with something much more disturbing.

As the smoke cleared Kathryn lifted a side batten carefully from the drum and turned to the group. Hanging beneath it was a large, irregular-shaped honeycomb almost empty of honey; the hive had been successful and prosperous until very recently. Now, despite a handful of newly hatched worker bees crawling aimlessly across its waxy surface, the hive was deserted.

'A virus?' a male voice asked from under one of the shrouds.

'No.' Kathryn shook her head. 'Take a look . . .'

They formed a tight circle around her.

'If a hive is infected by CPV or APV, chronic or acute bee paralysis virus, then the bees shiver and can't fly so they die in or around the hive. But look at the ground.'

Six hats dipped and surveyed the spongy grass growing thickly in the shade of the apple tree.

'Nothing. And look inside the hive.'

The hats rose, their wide brims pushing against each other.

'If a virus had caused this then the bottom of the hive would be deep with dead bees. They're like us; when they feel sick they head home and hunker down until they feel better. But there's nothing there. The bees have just vanished. There's something else here too.'

She held the batten higher and pointed at the lower section of the honeycomb where the hexagonal cells were covered with tiny wax lids.

'Un-hatched larvae,' Kathryn said. 'Bees don't normally abandon a hive if there are still young to be hatched.'

'So what happened?'

Kathryn slotted the comb back into the silent hive. 'I don't know,' she said. 'But it's happening everywhere.' She began walking back to the boarded-up cider-house at the edge of the orchard. 'Same thing's been reported in North America, Europe, even as far east as Taiwan. So far no one's managed to work out what's causing it. The only thing everyone does agree on is that it's getting worse.'

She pulled off her gauntlets as she reached the minibus and dropped them into an empty plastic crate. Everyone followed suit.

'In America they call it Colony Collapse Disorder. Some people think it's the end of the world. Einstein said that if the bee disappeared from the face of the earth then we'd only have four years left. No more bees. No more pollination. No more crops. No more food. No more man.'

She unzipped her gauze face protector and slipped off her hat revealing an oval face with pale, clear skin and dark, dark eyes. She had an ageless, natural air about her that was vaguely aristocratic and was regularly the object of the young male volunteers' fantasies, even though she was older than many of their mothers. She reached up with her free hand, unclipped a thick coil of hair the colour of dark chocolate and shook it loose.

'So what are they doing about it?' The enquirer – a tall, sandy-haired boy from the American Mid-West – emerged from beneath a bee smock. He had the look most volunteers had when they first came to work for Kathryn at the charity: earnest, un-cynical, full of health and hope, shining with the goodness of the world. She wondered what he would look like after a year in the Sudan watching children die slowly from starvation, or in Sierra Leone persuading starving villagers not to plough fields their great-grandfathers had worked because guerrillas had sown them with landmines.

'They're doing lots of research,' she said, 'trying to establish a link between the colony collapses and GM crops, new types of nicotinoid pesticides, global warming, known parasites and infections. There's even a theory that mobile phone signals might be messing around with the bees' navigational systems, causing them to lose their bearings.'

She shrugged off her smock and let it fall to the ground.

'But what do you think it is?' Kathryn looked up at the earnest young man, saw the beginnings of a frown etching itself on to a face that had barely known a moment's concern.

'Oh, I don't know,' she said. 'Maybe it's a combination of all these things. Bees are actually quite simple creatures. Their society is simple too. But it doesn't take much to upset things. They can cope with stress, but if life becomes too complex, to the point where they don't recognize their society any more, maybe they abandon it. Maybe they'd rather fly off to their deaths than stay living in a world they no longer understand.'

She looked up. Everyone had stopped squirming out of their smocks and now stood with worried expressions clouding their young faces.

'Hey,' Kathryn said, trying to lighten the mood, 'don't listen to me; I just spend too much time on Wikipedia. Besides, you saw it's not happening to all the hives; more than half of them are buzzing fit to burst. Come on,' she said, clapping her hands together and immediately feeling like a nursery teacher leading a bunch of five-year-olds in a sing-song. 'Still got lots to do. Pack away your smocks and start breaking out the tools. We need to replace those dead hives.' She flipped the lid off another plastic crate lying on the grass. 'There's everything you need in here. Tools, instructions on how to make a basic top-bar hive, bits of old boxes and lengths of timber. But remember, in the field you'll be building hives from whatever you can scavenge. Not that you'll find much lying around where you'll be going. People who don't have anything in the first place don't tend to throw anything away.

'You can't use anything from the dead hives. If some kind of spore or parasite *did* cause the colony to fail, you'll just import disaster to the new one.'

Kathryn pulled open the driver's door. She needed to distance herself from the volunteers. Most of them came from educated, middle-class backgrounds, which meant they were well-meaning but impractical and would stand around discussing the best way of doing something for hours rather than actually doing it. The only way to cure them was to throw them in at the deep end and let them learn by their own mistakes.

'I'll check how you're doing in half an hour. If you need me, I'll be in my office.' She slammed the door shut behind her before anyone could ask another question.

She could hear the dull clatter of tools being sorted and the first of many theoretical discussions. She turned on the radio. If she could hear what they were talking about, sooner or later the mother in her would compel her to assist and that wouldn't help anybody. She wouldn't be there for them in the field.

A local radio station drowned out the noise of the volunteers with traffic news and headlines. Kathryn reached over to the passenger seat and picked up a thick manila file. On the cover was a single word – *Ortus* – and the logo of a four-petal flower with the world at its centre. It contained a field report detailing a complex scheme to irrigate and replant a stretch of desert created by illegal forest clearances in the Amazon Delta. She had to decide today whether the charity could afford it or not. It seemed that every year, despite fundraising being at an all-time high, there were more and more bits of the world that needed healing.

'And finally,' the radio newscaster said with that slightly amused tone they always reserve for novelty items at the end of the serious stuff, 'if you go down to the centre of Ruin today you're sure of a big surprise – because somebody dressed as a monk has managed to climb to the top of the Citadel.'

Kathryn glanced up at the slim radio buried in the dashboard.

'At the moment we're not sure if it's some kind of publicity stunt,' the newscaster continued, 'but he appeared this morning, shortly after dawn, and is now holding his arms out to form some kind of a . . . a human cross.'

Kathryn's insides lurched. She turned the keys in the ignition and jammed the minibus into gear. She drew level with one of the volunteers and wound down her window.

'Got to go back to the office,' she called. 'Be back in about an hour.'

The girl nodded, her face registering mild abandonment anxiety, but Kathryn didn't see it. Her eyes were already fixed ahead, focusing on the gap in the hedge where the track fed out on to the main road that would take her back to Ruin.

10

Halfway between the gathering crowds and the Citadel's summit, the Abbot, tired from a night spent awaiting further news, sat by the glowing embers of the fire and looked at the man who had just brought it.

'We had thought the eastern face to be insurmountable,' Athanasius said, his hand smoothing his pate as he finished his report.

'Then we have at least learned something tonight, have we not?' The Abbot glanced over at the large window, where the sun was beginning to illuminate the antique panes of blue and green. It did nothing to lighten his mood.

'So,' he said at length, 'we have a renegade monk standing on the very summit of the Citadel, forming a deeply provocative symbol, one which has probably already been seen by hundreds of tourists and the Lord only knows who else, and we can neither stop him nor get him back.'

'That is correct.' Athanasius nodded. 'But he cannot talk to anyone whilst he remains up there, and eventually he must climb down, for where else can he go?'

'He can go to hell,' spat the Abbot. 'And the sooner that happens, the better for us all.'

'The situation, as I see it, is this . . .' Athanasius persisted, knowing from long experience that the best way to deal with the Abbot's temper was simply to ignore it. 'He has no food. He has no water. There is only one way down from the mountain, and even if he waits for the cover of night the heat-sensitive cameras will pick him up as soon as he gets below the uppermost battlements.

We have sensors on the ground and security on the outside tasked to apprehend him. What's more, he is trapped inside the only structure on earth from which no one has ever escaped.'

The Abbot shot him a troubled glance. 'Not true,' he said, stunning Athanasius into silence. 'People have escaped. Not recently, but people have done it. With a history as long as ours it is . . . inevitable. They have always been captured, of course, and silenced – in God's name – along with everyone unfortunate enough to come into contact with them during their time outside these walls.' He noticed Athanasius blanch. 'The Sacrament must be protected.'

The Abbot had always considered it regrettable that his chamberlain did not possess the stomach for the more complex duties of their order. It was why Athanasius still wore the brown cassock of the lesser guilds rather than the dark green of a fully ordained Sanctus. Yet so zealous was he, and dedicated to his duty, that the Abbot sometimes forgot he had never learned the secret of the mountain, or that much of the Citadel's history was unknown to him.

'The last time the Sacrament was threatened was during the First World War,' the Abbot said, staring down at the cold grey embers of the fire as if the past was written there. 'A novice monk jumped through a high window and swam the moat. That's why it was drained. Fortunately he had not been fully ordained so did not yet know the secret of our order. He made it as far as Occupied France before we managed to . . . catch up with him. God was with us. By the time we found him the battlefield had done our job for us.'

He looked back at Athanasius.

'But that was a different time, one when the Church had many allies, and silence could easily be bought and secrets simply kept; before the Internet enabled anyone to send information to a billion people in an instant. There is no way we could contain an incident like that today. Which is why we must ensure it does not happen.'

He looked back up at the window, now fully lit by the morning sun. The peacock motif shone a vibrant blue and green – an archaic symbol of Christ, and of immortality.

'Brother Samuel knows our secret,' the Abbot said simply. 'He must not leave this mountain.'

11

Liv pressed the buzzer and waited.

The house was a neat new-build in Newark, a few blocks back from Baker Park and close to the state university where the man of the house, Myron, worked as a lab technician. A low picket fence marked the boundaries of each neighbouring plot and ran alongside the single slab pathways to every door. A few feet of grass separated them from the street. It was like the American dream in miniature. If she'd been writing a different kind of piece she would have used this image, conjured something poignant from it; but that wasn't why she was here.

She heard movement inside the house, heavy footfalls across a slippery floor, and tried to arrange her face into something that didn't convey the absolute loneliness she'd felt since her lunchtime vigil in Central Park. The door swung open to reveal a pretty young woman so heavily pregnant she practically filled the narrow hallway.

'You must be Bonnie,' Liv said, in a cheerful voice belonging to someone else. 'I'm Liv Adamsen, from the *Inquirer.*'

Bonnie's face lit up. 'The baby writer!' She threw her door wide open and gestured down her spotless beige hallway.

Liv had never written about babies in her life, but she let that slide. She just kept the smile burning all the way into Bonnie's perfectly coordinated kitchenette where a fresh-faced man was making coffee.

'Myron, honey, this is the journalist who's going to write about the birth ...'

Liv shook his hand, her face beginning to ache from the effort of her smile. All she wanted to do was go home, crawl under her duvet and cry. Instead she surveyed the room, taking in the creaminess and the carefully grouped objects – the scented tea-lights blending the smell of roses with the coffee, the wicker boxes containing nothing but air – all sold in matching sets of three by the IKEA cash registers.

'Lovely home . . .' She knew that's what was expected. She thought of her own apartment, choked with plants and the smell of loam; a potting shed with a bed, one ex-boyfriend had called it. Why couldn't she just live like regular folk, and be happy and content? She glanced out at their pristine yard, a green square of grass fringed with Cypress leylandii that would dwarf the house in two summers unless pruned drastically and often. Two of the trees were already yellowing slightly. Maybe nature would do the job for them. It was her knowledge of plants, and their healing properties in particular, that had landed Liv this gig in the first place.

'Adamsen, you know about plants and shit,' the conversation had started prosaically enough when Rawls Baker, proprietor and editor at large of the *New Jersey Inquirer* cornered her in the elevator earlier in the week. The next thing she knew she'd been cut from the crime desk, her usual beat on the darker side of the journalistic street, and charged with producing two thousand words under the heading 'Natural Childbirth – as Mother Nature Intended?' for the Sunday health pullout. She'd moonlighted before with the occasional gardening article, but she'd never done medical.

'Ain't a whole lot of medicine involved, far as I can see,' Rawls had said as he marched out of the elevator. 'Just find me someone relatively sane who nevertheless wants to have their baby in a pool or a forest glade without any pain relief bar plant extracts and give me the human interest story with a few facts. And they'd better be a citizen. I don't want to read about any damned hippies.'

Liv found Bonnie through her usual contacts. She was a traffic cop with the Jersey State Police, which took her about as far from being a hippy as you could get. You couldn't practise Peace and Love when dealing with the daily nightmare of the New Jersey turnpike. Yet here she was now, radiant on her L-shaped sofa, clutching the hand of her practical, lab scientist husband, talking passionately about natural childbirth like a fully paid-up earth mother.

Yes – it was her first child. Children, actually; she was expecting twins.

No – she didn't know what sex they were; they wanted it to be a surprise.

Yes – Myron did have some reservations, working in the scientific field and all, and *yes* – she had considered the usual obstetric route, but as women had been giving birth for generations without modern medicine she strongly felt it was better for the babies to let things take their natural course.

She's having the baby, Myron added in his gentle, boyish way as he stroked her hair and smiled lovingly down at her. *She doesn't need me to tell her what's best.*

Something about the touching intimacy and selflessness of this moment pierced the armour of Liv's good cheer and she was shocked to feel tears coursing down her cheeks. She heard herself apologizing as Bonnie and Myron both rushed to comfort her and managed to pull herself together long enough to finish the interview, feeling guilty that she had brought the dark cloud of her unhappiness into the bright sanctuary of their simple life.

She drove straight home and fell fully clothed into her unmade bed, listening to the drip of the irrigation system watering the plants that filled her flat and ensured, in the loosest sense, that she shared her life with other living things. She picked through the events of the day and wrapped herself tightly in her duvet, shivering with cold as if the solid ice of her loneliness could never be melted, and the warmth of a life like Bonnie and Myron's would never be hers.

12

Kathryn Mann swung the minibus into a small yard behind a large town house and brought it to a standstill amid a cloud of dust. This segment of the eastern part of the city was still known as the Garden District, though the green fields that gave it that name were long gone. Even from the back, the house had an aura of faded grandeur; the same flawless, honey-coloured stone that had built the public church and much of the old town peeped through in patches from beneath blackened layers of pollution.

Kathryn slipped out of the driver's seat and headed past an empty cycle-rack built on the site of the well that had once provided them with fresh water. She fumbled with her jingling key ring, heart still hammering from the stress of the several near misses she'd had while driving distractedly through the thickening morning traffic, found the right key, jabbed it into the lock and twisted the back door open.

Inside, the house was cool and dark after the glare of the early spring sunshine. The door swung shut behind her as she punched in the code to silence the alarm. She hurried down the dim hallway and into the bright reception area at the front of the building.

A bank of clocks on the wall behind the reception desk told her the time in Rio, New York, London, Delhi, Jakarta – everywhere the charity had offices. It was a quarter to eight in Ruin, still too early for most people to have started their working day. The silence that drifted down the elegant wooden staircase confirmed she was alone. She bounded up it, two steps at a time.

The five-storey house was narrow, in the style of most medieval terraces, and the stairs creaked as she swept up past the half-glazed office doors that filled the four lower floors of the building. At the top of the stairwell another reinforced door with thick steel panels hung heavily on its hinges. She heaved it open and stepped into her own private quarters. Crossing the threshold was like stepping back in time. The walls were wood-panelled and painted a soft grey, and the living room was filled with exquisite pieces of antique furniture. The only hint of the current century was offered by a small flat-screen TV perched on a low Chinese table in one corner.

Kathryn grabbed a remote from the ottoman and fired it in the direction of the TV as she headed towards a bookcase built into the far wall. The shelves stretched from floor to ceiling and were filled with the finest literature the nineteenth century had to offer. She pressed the spine of a black calfskin-bound copy of *Jane Eyre* and with a soft *click* the lower quarter sprang open to reveal a deep cupboard. Inside was a safe, a fax machine, a printer – all the paraphernalia of modern life. On the lowest shelf, resting on top of a pile of interior-design magazines, was the pair of binoculars her father had given her on her thirteenth birthday when he'd first taken her to Africa. She grabbed them and hurried back across the painted floorboards towards a skylight in the sloping ceiling. A roost of pigeons exploded into flight as she twisted it open and poked out her head. A blur of red roof tiles and blue sky smeared across her vision as she raised the binoculars then settled on the black monolith half a mile away to the west. The TV flickered into life behind her and started broadcasting the end of a story about global warming to the empty room. Kathryn leaned against the window frame to steady her hand and carefully traced a line up the side of the Citadel towards the summit.

Then she saw him.

Arms outstretched. Head tilted down.

It was an image she'd been familiar with all her life, only

carved in stone and standing on top of a different mountain halfway across the world. She had been schooled in what it meant from childhood. Now, after generations of collective, proactive struggle attempting to kick-start the chain of events that would change mankind's destiny, here it was, unfolding right in front of her, the result of one man acting alone. As she tried to steady her shaking hand she heard the newsreader running through the headlines.

'In the next half-hour we'll have more from the world summit on climate change; the latest round-up of the world money markets; and we reveal how the ancient fortress in the city of Ruin has finally been conquered this morning – after these messages . . .'

Kathryn took one last look at the extraordinary vision then dipped back through the skylight to find out what the rest of the world was going to make of it.

13

A slick car commercial was playing as Kathryn settled into an ancient sofa and glanced at the time signal on the TV screen. Eight twenty-eight; four twenty-eight in the morning in Rio. She pressed a speed-dial button and listened to the rapid beeps racing through a number with many digits, watching the commercial play out until, somewhere in the dark on the other side of the world, someone picked up.

'¿Ola?' A woman's voice answered, quiet but alert. It was not, she noted with relief, the voice of someone who had just been woken up.

'Mariella, it's Kathryn. Sorry for calling so late . . . or early. I thought he might be awake.'

She knew that her father kept increasingly strange hours.

'Sim, Senhora,' Mariella replied. 'He has been for a while. I lit a fire in the study. There is a chill tonight. I left him reading.'

'Could I talk to him please?'

'Certamente,' Mariella said.

The swishing of a skirt and the sounds of soft footsteps filtered down the line and Kathryn pictured her father's housekeeper walking down the dark, parquet-floored hallway towards the soft glow of firelight spilling from the study at the far end of the modest house. The footsteps stopped and she heard a short muffled conversation in Portuguese before the phone was handed over.

'Kathryn . . .' Her father's warm voice drifted across the continents, calming her instantly. She could tell by his tone that he was smiling.

'Daddy . . .' She smiled too, despite the weight of the news she carried.

'And how is the weather in Ruin this morning?'

'Sunny.'

'It's cold here,' he said. 'Got a fire going.'

'I know, Daddy, Mariella told me. Listen, something's happening here. Turn on your TV and tune it to CNN.'

She heard him ask Mariella to turn on the small television in the corner of his study and her eyes flicked over to her own. The shiny station graphic spun across the screen then cut back to the newsreader. She nudged the volume back up. Down the line she heard the brief babble of a game show, a soap opera and some adverts – all in Portuguese – then the earnest tones of the global news channel.

Kathryn glanced up as the image behind the newsreader became a green figure standing on top of the mountain.

She heard her father gasp. 'My God,' he whispered. 'A Sanctus.'

'So far,' the newsreader continued, 'there has been no word from inside the Citadel either confirming or denying that this man is anything to do with them, but joining us now to shed some light on this latest mystery is Ruinologist and author of many books on the Citadel, Dr Miriam Anata.'

The newscaster twisted in his chair to face a large, formidable-looking woman in her early fifties wearing a navy blue pinstripe suit over a plain white T-shirt, her silver-grey hair cut short and precise, in an asymmetrical bob.

'Dr Anata, what do you make of this morning's events?'

'I think we're seeing something extraordinary here,' she said, tilting her head forward and peering over half-moon glasses at him with her cold blue eyes. 'This man is nothing like the monks one occasionally glimpses repairing the battlements or re-leading the windows. His cassock is green, not brown, which is very significant; only one order wears this colour, and they disappeared about nine hundred years ago.'

'And who are they?'

'Because they lived in the Citadel, very little is known about them, but as they were only ever spotted high up on the mountain we assume they were an exalted order, possibly charged with protection of the Sacrament.'

The news anchor held a hand to his earpiece. 'I think we can go live now to the Citadel.'

The picture cut to a new, clearer image of the monk, his cassock ruffling slightly in the morning breeze, his arms still stretched out, unwavering.

'Yes,' said the newsreader. 'There he is, on top of the Citadel, making the sign of the cross with his body.'

'Not a cross,' Oscar whispered down the phoneline as the picture zoomed slowly out revealing the terrifying height of the mountain. 'The sign he's making is the *Tau.*'

In the gentle glow of firelight in his study in the western hills of Rio de Janeiro, Oscar de la Cruz sat with his eyes fixed to the TV image. His hair was pure white in contrast to his dark skin, which had been burnished to its current leathery state by more than a hundred summers. But despite his great age, his dark eyes were still bright and alert and his compact body still radiated restless energy and purpose, like a battlefield general shackled to a peacetime desk.

'What do you think?' his daughter's voice whispered in his ear.

He considered her question. He had been waiting for most of his life for something like this to happen, had spent a large part of it trying to make it so, and now he didn't quite know what to do.

He rose stiffly from his chair and padded across the floor towards French doors leading on to a tiled terrace that dimly reflected the moonlight.

'It could mean nothing,' he said finally.

He heard his daughter sigh heavily. 'Do you really believe

that?' she asked with a directness that made him smile. He'd brought her up to question everything.

'No,' he admitted. 'No, not really.'

'So?'

He paused, almost frightened to form the thoughts in his head and the feelings in his heart into words. He looked across the basin toward the peak of Corcovado Mountain, where *O Cristo Redentor*, the statue of Christ the Redeemer, held out its arms and looked down benignly upon the still-sleeping citizens of Rio. He'd helped to build it, in the hope that it would herald the new era. It had indeed become as famous as he had hoped, but that was all. He thought now of the monk, standing on top of the Citadel, the gesture of one man carried around the world in less than a second by the world's media, striking an almost identical pose to the one it had taken him nine years to construct from steel and concrete and sandstone. His hand reached up and ran round the high collar of the turtleneck sweater he always wore.

'I think maybe the prophecy is coming true,' he whispered. 'I think we need to prepare.'

14

The sun was now bright over the city of Ruin. Samuel watched the shadows shorten along the eastern boulevard, all the way to the fringe of red mountains in the distance. He barely felt the pain burning in his shoulders despite the strain of holding up his already exhausted arms for so long.

For some time now he had been aware of the activity below, the gathering crowds, the arrival of TV crews. The murmur of their presence occasionally drifted up to him on the rising thermals, making them sound uncannily close. But he only thought about two things. The first was the Sacrament, the second, the face of the girl in his past. As his mind cleared of everything else, they seemed to merge into a single powerful image, one that soothed and calmed him.

He glanced now over the edge of the summit, past the overhang he'd had to scramble up what seemed like days ago. Way down to the empty moat, over a thousand feet below him.

He slipped his feet into the slits he had cut just above the hem of his cassock then hooked his thumbs through two similar loops cut in the ends of each sleeve. He shuffled his legs apart, felt the material of his habit stretch tightly across his body, felt his hands and his feet take the strain. He took one last look down. Felt the updraught from the thermals as the morning sun heated the land. Heard the babble of voices on the strengthening breeze. Focused on the spot he had picked out just past the wall where a group of tourists stood beside a tiny patch of grass.

He shifted his weight.

Tilted forward.

And launched himself.

It took him three seconds to fall the same distance it had taken him agonizing hours to climb the night before. Pain racked his exhausted arms and legs as they strained against the thick woollen material of his cassock, fighting to keep it taut against the relentless rush of air. He kept his eyes fixed on the patch of grass, willing himself towards it.

He could hear screams now through the howl of the wind in his ears and pushed down hard with both arms, increasing the resistance, trying to tilt his body upwards and correct his trajectory. He saw people scattering from the patch of ground he was heading for. It hurtled towards him. Closer now. Closer.

He felt a sharp tug at his right hand as the loop ripped apart. The sudden lack of resistance twisted and threw him into a forward spin. He reached for the flapping sleeve, pulled it taut again. The wind immediately ripped it free. He was too weak. It was too late. The spin worsened. The ground was too close. He flipped on to his back.

And landed with a sickening crump five feet past the moat wall, just short of the patch of grass, arms still outstretched, eyes staring upwards at the clear blue sky. The screams that had started as soon as he stepped off the summit now swept through the crowd. Those closest to him either turned away or looked on in fascinated horror as dark blood blossomed beneath his body, running in rivulets down fresh cracks in the sun-bleached flagstones, soaking through the green cloth of his tattered cassock, turning it a dark and sinister shade.

15

Kathryn Mann gasped as she watched it happen, live on TV. One moment the monk was standing firmly on top of the Citadel; the next he was gone. The picture jerked downwards as the cameraman tried to follow his fall then cut back to the studio where the flustered anchorman fiddled with his earpiece, struggling to fill the dead air as the shock started to register. Kathryn was already across the room, raising the binoculars to her eyes. The starkly magnified view of the empty summit and the distant wail of sirens gave her all the confirmation she needed.

She ducked back inside and grabbed the phone from the sofa, stabbing the redial button as numbness closed round her. The answer machine cut in; her father's deep, comforting voice asked her to leave a message. She speed-dialled his mobile, wondering where he could have gone so suddenly. Mariella was obviously with him or she'd have picked up instead. The mobile connected. Cut straight to voicemail.

'The monk has fallen,' she said simply.

As she hung up, she realized she had tears in her eyes. She had watched and waited for the sign for so long, like generations of sentries before her. Now it seemed as if this too was just another false dawn. She took one last look at the empty summit then replaced the binoculars in the concealed cupboard and tapped a fifteen-digit sequence into the keyboard on the front of her safe. After a few seconds there was a hollow click.

A box the size of a laptop computer and about three times as thick lay behind the blast-proof titanium door, encased in moulded grey foam. Kathryn slid it free then carried it to the ottoman in front of the sofa.

The incredibly tough polycarbonate resin looked and felt like stone. She released the hidden catches holding the lid in place. Two fragments of slate lay inside, one above the other, each with faint markings etched on its surface. She looked down at the familiar pieces, carefully split from a seam by a prehistoric hand. All that remained of an ancient book, the carved symbols predated those of the Old Testament and could only hint at what else it might have contained. Its language was known as Malan, of the ancient tribe of Mala – Kathryn Mann's ancestors. In the gloom she looked at the familiar shape the lines made.

It was the sacred shape of the Tau, adopted by the Greeks as their letter 'T' but older than language, symbol of the sun and the most ancient of gods. To the Sumerians it was Tammuz; the Romans called it Mithras, to the Greeks it was Attis. It was a symbol so sacred it had been placed on the lips of Egyptian kings as they were initiated into the mysteries. It symbolized life, resurrection and blood sacrifice. It was the shape the monk had formed with his body as he stood on top of the Citadel for all the world to see.

She read the words now, translating them in her head, matching their meaning with the heady symbolism and the events of the past few hours.

The one true cross will appear on earth
All will see it in a single moment – all will wonder
The cross will fall
The cross will rise
To unlock the Sacrament
And bring forth a new age

Beneath this last line she could see the tips of other beheaded symbols but the jagged edge of the broken slate drew an uneven line across them, preventing further knowledge of what they might have said.

The first two lines were easy enough to reconcile.

The true sign of the cross was the sign of the Tau, older by far than the Christian cross, and it had appeared on earth the moment the monk had spread his arms.

All had seen it in a single moment via the international news networks. All had wondered because it was extraordinary and unprecedented, and no one knew what it meant.

Then she faltered. She knew the text was incomplete, but she could not see a way past what remained.

The cross had indeed fallen, as the prophecy had foretold; but the cross had been a man.

She looked beyond the window. The Citadel was about eleven hundred feet from base to peak, and he had fallen down the sheer eastern face.

How could anyone possibly rise from that?

16

Athanasius clutched the loose bundle of documents to his chest as he rapped on the gilded door of the Abbot's chambers. There was no reply. He slipped inside and found, to his great relief, that the room was empty. It meant, for the moment at least, he did not have to converse with the Abbot about how the problem of Brother Samuel had now been solved. It had brought him no joy. Brother Samuel had been one of his closest friends before he had chosen the path of the Sancti and disappeared forever into the strictly segregated upper reaches of the mountain. And now he was dead.

He arrived at the desk and laid out the day's business, splitting the documents into two piles. The first contained the daily updates of the internal workings of the Citadel, stock-takes of provisions and schedules of works for the constant and ongoing repairs. The second much larger pile comprised reports of the Church's vast interests beyond the walls of the Citadel – anything from the latest discoveries at current archaeological digs worldwide; synopses of current theological papers; outlines of books that had been submitted for publication; sometimes even proposals for television programmes or documentaries. Most of this information came from various official bodies either funded or wholly owned by the Church, but some of it was gleaned by the vast network of unofficial informers who worked silently in every part of the modern establishment and were as much a part of the Citadel's tradition and history as were the prayers and sermons that made up the devotional day.

Athanasius glanced at the top sheet. It was a report submitted by an agent called Kafziel – one of the Church's most prolific spies. Fragments of an ancient manuscript had been discovered in the ruins of a temple at a dig in Syria and he recommended an immediate 'A and I' – Acquisition and Investigation to learn and neutralize any threat they may contain. Athanasius shook his head. Another piece of priceless antiquity would undoubtedly end up locked in the gloom of the great library. His feelings on this continued policy was no secret within the Citadel. He had argued, along with Brother Samuel and Father Thomas – inventor and implementer of so many improvements within the library, that the hoarding of knowledge and censorship of alternative ideas was the sign of a weak church in a modern and open world. The three of them had often talked in private of a time when the Citadel's great repository of learning might be shared with the outside for the greater good of God and man. Then Samuel had chosen to follow the ancient and secretive path of the Sancti and Athanasius could not help but feel that all their hopes had died with him. Everything Samuel had been associated with during his life in the Citadel would now be tainted.

He felt tears prick the corners of his eyes as he looked down at the day's documents and imagined the news they would bring in the weeks to come: endless reports regarding the monk who had fallen, and how the world perceived it. He turned and headed back to the gilded door, blotting his eyes with the back of his hand as he slipped from the Abbot's chambers and back into the mountain labyrinth. He needed to find somewhere private, where he could allow his emotions to run free.

Head down, he marched purposefully through the crisply air-conditioned tunnels. The wide, brightly lit thoroughfares narrowed into a dimly lit staircase leading to a narrow corridor beneath the great cathedral cave, lined on each side by doors to small private chapels. At the far end of the passage a candle burned in a shallow depression cut into the rock by one such door, denoting that the room beyond it was already occupied. Athanasius stepped inside. The few votive candles that lit the interior flickered in the wash of the closing door and light shimmered across the low, soot-stained ceiling and the T-shaped cross standing on a stone shelf cut into the far wall. A man in a plain black cassock was hunched in prayer before it.

The priest began to turn, but Athanasius did not need to see his face to know who it was. He dropped to the floor beside him and gripped him in a sudden and desperate embrace, the sounds of his sobs muffled by the thick material of his companion's robes. They held each other like this for long minutes, neither speaking, locked in grief. Finally Athanasius drew back and looked into the round white face and intelligent blue eyes of Father Thomas, his black hair receding slightly and touched with grey at the temples, his cheeks glistening with tears in the candlelight.

'I feel like all is lost.'

'We are still here, Brother Athanasius. And what we three discussed in this room; that is not lost.'

Athanasius managed a smile, warmed by his friend's words.

'And we can at least remember Samuel as he truly was,' Father Thomas said. 'Even if others will not.'

17

The Abbot stood in the centre of the *Capelli Deus Specialis* – the Chapel of God's Holy Secret – high in the mountain. It was a small, low-ceilinged space, like a crypt, though it was so dark it was hard to make out how big it was. It had been cut by hand out of solid rock by the founders of the Citadel and remained unchanged ever since, the walls still bearing the crude marks of their primitive tools. The Abbot could smell the metallic tang of blood hanging in the air from the previous night's ceremony, rising from grooves cut in the floor that shone wetly in the weak candlelight. He traced the channels towards the altar where the outline of the Sacrament could just be seen rising out of the darkness.

At the foot of the altar he noticed a twist of new growth curling from the rock floor, the thin tendril of a blood vine, the strange red plant that grew around the Sacrament, springing up faster than it could be rooted out. There was something about the sheer fecundity of the plant that disgusted him. He was about to move towards it when he heard the deep rumble of the huge stone door rolling open behind him. The thick air inside the chapel stirred as two people entered. The candles shuddered in their molten pools of tallow and light danced across the sharp instruments that lined the walls. The door rumbled back into place and the candle flames settled, hissing softly as tallow bubbled against hot wicks.

Both men wore the long beards and green cassocks of the Sacramental order, but there was a subtle difference in their bearing. The shorter of the two stood slightly back, his eyes fixed on the other, his hand resting on the T-shaped Crux tucked into his rope belt; the second stood with his head slightly down, eyes lowered, shoulders stooping as if the weight of the cassock itself was still too much to bear.

'Well, Brothers?'

'The body landed beyond the boundaries of our jurisdiction,' the shorter monk said. 'There was no way we could secure it.'

The Abbot closed his eyes and exhaled deeply. He had hoped the news would lift his mood, not worsen it. He opened his eyes again and regarded the Sanctus who had not yet spoken. 'So,' he said, in a voice that was soft yet full of threat, 'where is he now?'

'The city morgue.' The monk's eyes did not rise above the Abbot's chest. 'We think they are performing a post-mortem.'

'You *think* they are performing a post-mortem,' the Abbot spat. 'Don't *think* they are doing anything; *know* it, or say nothing. Do not come into this room and bring me your thoughts. When you come in here, you bring only the truth.'

The monk fell to his knees.

'Forgive me, Father Abbot,' he pleaded. 'I have failed you.'

The Abbot looked down at him in disgust. Brother Gruber was the man who had thrown Brother Samuel into the cell from which he had subsequently escaped. It was Gruber's fault the Sacrament had been compromised.

'You have failed us all,' the Abbot said.

He turned and gazed once more upon the secret of their order. He could almost feel the eyes of the world turning towards the Citadel, burning through the rock like X-rays in an unquenchable search for what lay within. He was tired from the long night's wait, and irritable with it, and the cuts ached beneath his cassock. He'd begun to notice that, even though his ceremonial wounds healed as quickly as they always had, they pained him for longer and longer each time. Age was creeping up on him – slowly maybe, but gaining ground.

He didn't want to be angry with the cowering monk. He just wanted this situation to pass and the fickle gaze of the world to move on to something else. The Citadel had to weather the siege, as it always had.

'Stand up,' he said gently.

Gruber obeyed, his eyes still lowered so he didn't see the Abbot nod to the monk standing behind him, or the man remove his Crux and pull the top away to reveal the bright blade of the ceremonial dagger sheathed within.

'Look at me,' the Abbot said.

As Gruber raised his head to meet the Abbot's gaze the monk slashed quickly across his exposed neck.

'Knowledge is everything,' the Abbot said, stepping back to avoid the fountain of arterial blood pumping from Gruber's neck.

He watched the look of surprise on Gruber's face turn to confusion as his hand fluttered up to the neat line across his throat. Saw him sink back to his knees as the life flooded out of him and into the channels in the floor.

'Find out exactly what has happened to the body,' the Abbot said. 'Contact someone in the city council, or the police division, someone who has access to the information we require and is prepared to share it with us. We need to know what conclusions are being drawn about Brother Samuel's death. We need to know where the events of this morning may be leading. And above all we need to get Brother Samuel's body back.'

The monk stared down at Gruber, twitching feebly on the floor of the chapel, the rhythmic spurts from his neck weakening with every beat of his dying heart.

'Of course, Brother Abbot,' the short monk said. 'Athanasius has already begun to deal with press enquiries through his outside intermediary. And I believe – I mean, I *know* there has been some contact from the police.'

The Abbot felt the muscles tighten in his jaw as he sensed the eyes of the world upon him once again.

'Keep me informed,' he said. 'And send Athanasius to me.'

The monk nodded. 'Of course, Brother Abbot,' he said. 'I will pass word that you wish to see him in your chambers.'

'No.' The Abbot stepped over to the altar and wrenched the blood vine out at the root. 'Not there.'

He glanced up at the Sacrament. His chamberlain was not a Sanctus so did not know its identity, but if he was going to be effective in containing the current situation he needed to be more aware of what they were dealing with.

'Get him to meet me in the great library.' He moved towards the exit, dropping the vine on Brother Gruber's corpse as he stepped over it. 'He will find me in the forbidden vault.'

He grabbed a wooden stake set into the door and heaved against it. The rumble of stone over stone echoed through the chapel as the cool sweet air of the antechamber spilled through the opening. The Abbot looked back to where Gruber lay, his face pallid against a pool of blood in which the reflected candles danced.

'And get rid of that,' he said.

Then he turned and walked away.

18

The city coroner's office was housed in the cellars of a stone building which had, at various periods in its history, been a gunpowder store, an ice house, a fish locker, a meat store and briefly, for a short time in the sixteenth century, a prison. Its robust security and subterranean coolness were perfect for the new department of pathology the city council decided to create at the tail end of the 1950s. Here in these retro-fitted, vaulted cellars, on the middle of three old-style ceramic post-mortem tables, the broken body of Brother Samuel now lay, starkly illuminated and under the scrutiny of two men.

The first was Dr Bartholomew Reis, the attendant pathologist, the white lab coat of his profession worn loose over the black clothes of his social tribe. He had arrived from England four years previously on an international police exchange programme, his Turkish father and dual nationality easing the paperwork. He was supposed to stay for six months, but had never quite managed to leave. His long hair was also black, thanks more to chemistry than nature, and hung on either side of his thin, pale face like a pair of partly opened curtains. Despite his sombre appearance, however, Reis was renowned throughout every division of the Ruin police force as being the most cheerful pathologist anyone had ever met. As he often said, he was thirty-two, earning good money, and while most Goths only dreamed of making a living amongst the dead, he was actually doing it.

The second man appeared much less at ease. He stood slightly behind Reis, chewing on a fruit-and-nut breakfast bar he'd found in his pocket. He was taller than Reis but looked crumpled somehow, his summer-weight grey suit hanging loosely from shoulders that drooped under the weight of nearly twenty years' service. His thick, dark hair, shot through with silver, was pushed back from an intelligent face that managed to appear both amused and sad, a pair of half-moon tortoise-shell glasses halfway down his long, hawkish nose, completing the image of a man who looked more like a tired history professor than a Homicide detective.

Inspector Davud Arkadian was something of an oddity within the Ruin police force. His undoubted abilities should easily have raised him at this advanced stage of his career to the rank of chief inspector or beyond. Instead he'd spent the larger part of his life as a police officer watching a steady procession of lesser men get promoted above him, while he remained lumped in with the general raft of anonymous career detectives marking the days until their pensions kicked in. Arkadian was much better than that, but he'd made a choice early in his career that had cast a very long shadow over the rest of it.

What he'd done was meet a woman, fall in love and then marry her.

Being a happily married detective was rare enough, but Arkadian had met his wife while working vice as a sub-inspector. When he met his bride-to-be she was a prostitute preparing to testify against the men who had trafficked her from what was then the Eastern Bloc, then enslaved her. The first time he saw her he thought she was the bravest, the most beautiful and most scared person he'd ever met. He was detailed to look after her until the case came to trial. He often joked that he should bill for all the overtime because, twelve years later, he was still doing it. In that time he'd helped her kick the drugs they'd hooked her on, paid for her to go back to school to gain her teacher's diploma, and restored her to the life she should have been leading in the first place. In his heart he knew it was the best thing he'd ever done, but his head also knew the price that came with

59

it. High-ranking police officers couldn't be married to ex-prostitutes, no matter how reformed they were. So he remained a mid-level inspector, where the public scrutiny was less, occasionally picking up a case worthy of his abilities, but often catching the tricky ones no one more senior wanted to touch.

He looked down now at the monk's crumpled form, the lenses in his glasses magnifying his warm brown eyes as he assessed the details of the corpse. The forensics team had swept the body for trace evidence but had left it clothed. The rough green habit was dark with cold coagulated blood. The arms that had stretched out for so long making the sign of the cross were now arranged by his sides, the double loop of rope around his right wrist coiled into a neat pile by his ravaged hand. Arkadian took in the grisly scene and frowned. It wasn't that he didn't like autopsies – he'd certainly been to enough of them; he just wasn't sure why he had been specifically asked to attend this one.

Reis tucked his lank black hair into a surgical cap, logged on to the computer on the mobile stand by his side and opened a new case file. 'What do you make of the noose?' he said.

Arkadian shrugged. 'Maybe he was going to hang himself but decided it was too mundane.' He launched the balled-up wrapper of his fruit bar across the room, where it bounced off the rim of the bin and skittered underneath a workbench. It was clearly going to be one of those days. His gaze flicked to a TV monitor on the far wall, tuned to a news channel and showing footage of the monk on the summit.

'This is a new one on me.' Arkadian retrieved his wrapper. 'First watch the TV show. Now dissect the corpse . . .'

Reis smiled and angled the flat computer screen towards him. He unhooked a wireless headset from the back of the monitor, slipped it over his head and twisted a thin microphone in front of his mouth before pressing a red square in the corner of the screen. It started to flash; an MP3 file had begun to record directly into the case file.

19

Oscar de la Cruz sat near the back of the private chapel, his habitual white turtleneck sweater worn under a dark brown linen suit. His head was slightly lowered as he offered up a silent prayer for the monk, not knowing he was already dead. Then he opened his eyes and looked around at the place he had helped build over seventy years before.

There were no adornments in the chapel, not even windows; the soft light emanated from a network of concealed lamps that gradually brightened the higher you looked – a piece of architectural sleight of hand intended to draw the eye upwards. It was an idea he had stolen from the great gothic churches of Europe. He figured they'd taken much more from him and his people.

Oscar could see another twenty or so people holding their own private vigils; other night owls like himself, people of the secret congregation who had caught the news and been drawn here to pray and reflect on what the sign could mean to them and their kind. He recognized most of them, knew some of them pretty well, but then the church wasn't for everyone. Few people even knew of its existence.

Mariella sat nearby, wrapped in her own private contemplation, uttering a prayer in a language older than Latin. When she finished she caught Oscar's eye.

'What were you praying for?' he asked.

She smiled quietly and looked towards the front of the chapel where a large Tau was suspended above the altar. In all the years they'd been coming here, she had never once told him.

He remembered the first time he'd met the shy eight-year-old girl who'd blushed when he spoke to her. The chapel had been young then and the statue it was built inside had carried the hopes of their tribe. Now a man halfway round the world held them in his outstretched arms.

'When you built this place,' Mariella whispered, dragging his attention back to the silent room, 'did you really believe it would change things?'

Oscar considered the question. The statue of Christ the Redeemer had been built at his suggestion, and with the help of money he had been instrumental in raising. It had been sold to the people of Brazil as a great symbol for their Catholic nation but was in fact an attempt to bring the ancient prophecy of a much older religion to pass.

> The one true cross will appear on earth
> All will see it in a single moment – all will wonder

When it was finally revealed to the assembled world media, after nine years of construction, images of it appeared on newsreels and in papers around the world. It wasn't quite a single moment, but all did see it and the gushing encomia testified to their wonder.

But nothing happened.

In the years that followed, its fame had grown. But still nothing had happened; at least not what Oscar had hoped. He had succeeded in creating nothing more than a landmark for the Brazilian tourist board. His one consolation was that he'd also succeeded in building a secret chapel in the foundations of the huge statue, carved into the rock in another neat reflection of the Citadel, a church within a mountain.

'No,' he said, in answer to Mariella's question. 'I *hoped* it would change things, but I can't say I believed it would.'

'And what about the monk? Do you believe he will?'

He looked at her. 'Yes,' he said. 'Yes, I do.'

Mariella leaned forward and kissed him on the cheek. 'That's what I was praying for,' she said. 'And now I will pray that you are right.'

There was a sudden disturbance at the front of the church.

A small group of worshippers were huddled by the altar, their intense conversation whispering through the chapel like a strengthening breeze. One broke away and began walking up the aisle towards them. Oscar recognized Jean-Claude Landowski, the grandson of the French sculptor who had built the structure in which they all now prayed. He paused by each worshipper and whispered solemn words.

Oscar watched the body language of the recipients of Jean-Claude's news, and felt Mariella's hand grab his. He did not need to hear the words to know what was being said.

20

'OK,' Reis began in his best bedside manner. 'Case number one-eight-six-nine-four slash "E". The time is ten-seventeen. Attending are myself, Dr Bartholomew Reis of the city coroner's office, and Inspector Davud Arkadian of the Ruin City Police. The subject is an unidentified white Caucasian male, approximately thirty years of age. Height –' he withdrew the steel tape measure that was built into the table and extended it sharply '– six feet two inches. First visual assessment is commensurate with eyewitness reports, detailed in the case file, of a body that has sustained major trauma following a substantial fall from height.'

Reis frowned. He tapped the flashing red square to pause the recording.

'Hey, Arkadian,' he called in the general direction of the coffee pot, 'why'd they kick this in your direction? This guy threw himself off a mountain and wound up dead. Not much detecting called for, far as I can see.'

Arkadian exhaled slowly and slam-dunked the balled-up wrapper emphatically into the waste basket. 'Interesting question.' He poured two mugs of coffee. 'Unfortunately, this wasn't one of those "sneak off and do it in private" kind of suicides.' He grabbed the milk carton and poured most of its contents into one of the mugs. 'And our man here didn't just throw himself off *a* mountain; he threw himself off *the* mountain. And you know how much the people in charge hate it when anything, how shall we say, "un-family friendly" happens there. They think it might put people off coming to this beautiful city of ours, which will impact distressingly on sales of Holy Grail T-shirts and "True Cross of Christ" bumper stickers – and they don't like that. So they have to be seen to be doing everything they can to respond to such a tragic incident.'

He handed Reis a very white coffee in a very black mug.

Reis nodded slowly. 'So they throw an inspector at it.' He took a slurp of his homemade latte.

'Exactly. This way they can hold a press conference and announce that, having brought all the expertise and diligence of the police force to bear, they have discovered that a guy dressed as a monk threw himself off the top of the Citadel and died. Unless, of course, *you* discover otherwise . . .'

Reis took another long gulp of his tepid coffee and handed the mug back to Arkadian.

'Well,' he said, hitting the red button to restart the audio file. 'Let's find out.'

21

Kathryn Mann sat in her office on the second floor of the townhouse surrounded by piles of paperwork in a variety of languages. As usual her door was open to the hallway and through it she heard the footfalls on wooden floors, phones ringing and fragments of conversation as people drifted in to start the working day.

She'd sent someone back to the orchard to pick up the volunteers. She wanted to be alone with her thoughts and feelings for a while, and right now she just couldn't face another earnest discussion about dead bees. She thought of the empty hives in the light of the monk's death and it made her shudder. The ancients had been big on the omens contained in the uncharacteristic behaviour of animals. She wondered what they would have made of the supernatural events that were taking place in the world today: melting ice caps, tropical weather in formerly temperate zones, unprecedented tidal waves and hurricanes, coral reefs poisoned by acidic seas, disappearing bees. They would have thought it was the end of the world.

On the desk in front of her lay the field report she'd rescued from the passenger seat of the minibus. It had done little to lighten her mood. She'd only read half of it and already knew that it was going to be too expensive to fund. Maybe this was just one more bit of the world they were going to have to let wither and die. She stared hard at the carefully annotated diagrams and charts outlining initial building costs and projected tree growth, but in her head she was seeing symbols etched on to fragments of slate, and the shape made by the monk before he fell.

'Did you see the news?'

Startled, Kathryn looked up into the bright, clear face of a willowy girl beaming at her from the doorway. She tried to remember her name but the turnover of people in the building was so rapid she never trusted herself to get it right. Rachel maybe – or was it Rebecca? Here on a three-month placement from an English university.

'Yes,' Kathryn replied. 'Yes, I saw it.'

'Traffic's rammed out there. That's why I was late getting in.'

'Don't worry about it.' Kathryn dismissed the confession with a wave and returned to the dossier. The morning's news, which hung so heavily around her, was clearly just an inconvenience for most people – something to be gossiped over, wondered at and then forgotten.

'Hey, you want a coffee?' the girl asked.

Kathryn looked back up at her fresh, untroubled face and suddenly remembered her name. 'That'd be great, Becky,' she said.

The girl's face lit up. 'Cool.' With a whip-crack of auburn ponytail she turned and ran down to the kitchen.

Most of the work carried out by the organization was done by volunteers like Becky; people of all ages, giving freely of their time, not because of any religious obligation or national pride, but because they loved the planet they lived on and wanted to do something to look after it. That's what the charity did: brought water to places that had dried out; planted crops and trees in land that had been blighted by war or poisoned by industry; though this was not how Ortus had started, and it was not the work it had always done.

Her desk phone rang.

'Ortus. Can I help you?' she said, as brightly as she could manage.

'Kathryn,' Oscar's warm voice rumbled in her ear. Instantly she felt a little better.

'Hey, Daddy,' she said. 'Where've you been?'

'I was praying.'

'Did you hear?' She didn't quite know how to frame the question. 'Did you hear that he ... that the monk ...'

'Yes,' he said. 'I heard.'

She swallowed hard, trying to hold back the emotion.

'Don't despair,' her father said. 'We should not give up hope.'

'But how can we not?' She glanced up at the door and lowered her voice. 'The prophecy can no longer be fulfilled. How can the cross rise again?'

The crackle of the transatlantic line filled the long pause before her father spoke again.

'People have come back from the dead,' he said. 'Look in the Bible.'

'The Bible is full of lies. You taught me that.'

'No, that I did not teach you. I told you of specific and deliberate inaccuracies. There is still much in the official Bible that is true.'

The line went silent again save for the rising hiss of long-distance interference.

She wanted to believe him, she really did; but in her heart she felt that to carry on blindly hoping everything was going to be OK was not much different from closing your eyes and crossing your fingers.

'Do you really believe the cross will rise again?'

'It might,' he said. 'It's hard to believe, I admit. But if you'd told me yesterday that a Sanctus would appear from nowhere, climb to the top of the Citadel and make the sign of the Tau, I would have found that equally hard to believe. Yet here we are.'

She couldn't fault him. She rarely could. It was why she wished he had been around to talk to when the news had first broken. Maybe then she wouldn't have thought herself into such a melancholic state.

'So what do you think we should do?' she asked.

'We should watch the body. That is the key. It is the cross. And if he does rise again, we need to protect him from those who would do him harm.'

'The Sancti.'

'My belief is they will try and reclaim the body as soon as possible, then destroy it to end the prophetic sequence. As a Sanctus he will have no family, therefore no one will step forward to claim him.'

They both lapsed into silence as they contemplated what might happen if this came to pass. Kathryn imagined him lying in a dark, windowless room somewhere inside the Citadel as somehow, miraculously, his broken body began to mend. Then out of the shadows hooded figures started to emerge, green-clad men with daggers drawn and other instruments of torture to hand.

On the other side of the world her father pictured similar images, though his were not drawn from imagination. He had witnessed with his own eyes what the Sancti were capable of.

22

Athanasius had a profound dislike for the great library.

There was something about its trapped, anonymous darkness and labyrinthine chambers he found deeply claustrophobic and sinister. Nevertheless it was there the Abbot had summoned him, so it was there he now made his way.

The library occupied a system of caves about a third of the way up the mountain, chosen by the original architects of the Citadel because they were sufficiently dark and well ventilated to prevent sunlight and damp fading or corrupting the ancient scrolls and manuscripts. As the caves had filled with more and more priceless texts, it was decided that the preservation of such treasures could no longer be left simply to the darkness and a dry breeze, so a schedule of improvements had begun. The library now occupied forty-two chambers of varying sizes, and contained easily the most valuable and unique collection of books anywhere in the world. There was a standing, somewhat bitter joke among international religious scholars and academics that it was the greatest collection of ancient texts no one had ever seen.

Athanasius approached its solitary entrance with his usual feeling of gnawing unease. A cold blue light swept across his palm as the scanner checked and verified his identity before a door slid open, allowing him into an airlock. He stepped inside and heard the door slide shut behind him. His claustrophobia deepened. He knew it would not leave him until he had exited the library. A light blinked above a second scanner, indicating that the airlock was doing whatever it needed to do to ensure no tainted air accompanied him into the hermetically sealed world beyond the final door. He waited. Felt the desiccated air already sucking moisture from the back of his throat. The light stopped blinking. A second door slid open and Athanasius stepped into the library.

The moment he passed through into the darkness, a circle of light grew and enveloped him. It extended just a few feet in every direction and matched his movements exactly, keeping him at its centre as he strode across the reception hall towards the archway leading into the main body of the library. As well as the carefully controlled climate – a constant sixty-eight degrees Fahrenheit and thirty-five per cent relative humidity – the lighting was a marvel of modern engineering. It too had been progressively updated over the generations, with guttering candles making way for oil lamps, which in turn made way for electricity. The system of lighting it now utilized was not only the most advanced in the world, it was the only one of its kind. Like most of the recent technological improvements, it had been devised and engineered by one man: Athanasius's great friend, Father Thomas.

From the moment Father Thomas had entered the Citadel over a decade previously he had been treated differently from the usual intake. Like most of the inhabitants of the mountain, his past was unknown, but whatever he had done in his life outside, it became immediately clear that he was an expert in the preservation of ancient documents and a genius with electronics. In his first year he had been given special authority, by the Prelate himself, to totally overhaul and update the library. It was a task that took him nearly seven years to complete, the first year alone spent purely on experimenting with different light frequencies and studying their effect on various inks and writing surfaces. The lighting system he had then designed and built was brilliant in its simplicity and had been inspired by the very first scholars who'd walked through the library with a single candle illuminating only their immediate surroundings, whilst leaving the rest of the collection in total darkness.

Using a system of movement, pressure and heat sensors, Father Thomas had created an environment in which anyone entering the library was tracked by a central computer that provided a narrow column of light, sufficient to illuminate no more than their immediate surroundings. This light would then follow them throughout the library, constantly pushing away the darkness as they walked through it, without contaminating any area in which they were not working. The system was so sensitive that each monk could be identified by tiny differences in their body temperature and slight fluctuations in air displacement due to their unique size and weight. It meant the computer could not only monitor the movement of each visitor, it also knew who they were and where they went, so acted as an added security measure policing the monks' usage of the library.

Athanasius left the entrance hall now, following the thin filament of dim guide lamps set into the floor, marking the way through the darkness. Occasionally he came across other scholars flitting around like fireflies, trapped in their personal haloes of light, each one dimmer the further he progressed into the great library.

Father Thomas's other great innovation had been to zone the library according to age, ink and paper types, and to adjust the lighting in each area to suit their particular properties. So, as Athanasius ventured deeper into the places where increasingly older and more fragile texts were kept, so his own circle of light became gradually more muted and orange. It was as if he were walking backwards through time, experiencing the same conditions that would have illuminated the documents when they had first been written.

Furthest from the entrance was the smallest and darkest chamber of all. The oldest, most delicate and most precious texts were housed here. Scraps of vellum worn thin by time and ancient words scratched lightly on brittle stones. The glow in the forbidden vault, on the very rare occasions it shone at all, was the deep and sombre red of the embers of a dying fire.

Only three people had perpetual right of entry to this room: the Prelate, the Abbot and Father Malachi, the chief librarian. Others could be granted special authority by any of these three to enter the vault, but it happened rarely. If someone entered the space without the correct authorization, either by design or mistake, the lights would remain off and a silent alarm would alert the guard permanently stationed by the entrance who would surge through the dark halls to deal with the intruder.

Punishment for entering the forbidden vault was traditionally harsh, always public, and served as the greatest single deterrent for ever being inclined to do so. In the past transgressors had been brought before the fully assembled college of priests and monks to have their eyes put out, in order to cleanse them of whatever they may have seen; their tongue torn out with red-hot pincers, so they could not repeat anything they had inadvertently learned; and molten lead poured into their ears, to burn away any forbidden words that had been whispered therein.

The offender's broken body was then expelled from the Citadel as a warning to others of the dangers of disobedience and the pursuit of restricted knowledge. It was from this gruesome ritual that the phrase 'See no evil, hear no evil, speak no evil' sprang. There was a fourth, lesser known part of the saying which advised that you should also 'Do no evil unto others', a line which seemed somewhat irreconcilable when held up against the history of its origin.

Like everyone in the Citadel, Athanasius had heard the stories of what happened to those who strayed into the forbidden vault, but to his knowledge no one had been subjected to the punishment for hundreds of years. This was partly because the world had turned and such displays of barbarity were no longer tolerated, but mostly because no one dared enter without the requisite authority. He had been inside it only once before, when he had been appointed chamberlain, and had hoped he would never have cause to visit it again.

As he trudged dutifully through the gloom, his eyes fixed on the gossamer-thin filament embedded in the floor, he began to wonder about the purpose of his summons and whether there had been some terrible new discovery. Perhaps Samuel had somehow managed to gain access to the library between his escape and his doomed climb. Or made his way to the forbidden room and stolen or vandalized one of the sacred and irreplaceable texts . . .

Up ahead the thread of floor lights turned sharply right and disappeared behind the unseen upright of a stone wall. It marked the point where the pathway turned into the final corridor leading to the furthest vault. Whatever the reason the Abbot had summoned him, he would discover it soon enough.

23

'The victim shows signs of recent laceration and trauma to hands and feet,' Reis said as he continued his preliminary examination of the body. 'The cuts are numerous. Deep. Down to the bone in some cases. Also irregular and torn. There are fragments of what look like rock embedded in some of the wounds. I'm removing them and bagging them for analysis.'

He held his hand over the microphone on the headset and turned to Arkadian.

'He climbed up there before he jumped, didn't he?'

Arkadian nodded. 'There's no ancient lift in there, far as we know.'

Reis turned back and looked at the ravaged hands and feet of the monk, picturing the monumental height of the Citadel in his mind. 'Tough climb,' he said quietly, before releasing his hand from the microphone and continuing.

'The cuts to the victim's hands and feet, though recent, show signs of significant blood coagulation, suggesting the injuries were sustained a good few hours ante-mortem. There's scar tissue forming on some of the smaller cuts, in some cases grafting over the fragments of rock. I'd say, going purely on the extent of healing, that he'd been up there a few days before he jumped.'

He lowered the hand on to the cold ceramic table and examined the exposed arm.

'The length of rope attached to the victim's right wrist has also rubbed extensively on the skin, removing the epidermis. The rope is a rough, hemp-like weave, tough, and abrasive.'

'It's his belt,' Arkadian said. Reis looked up and frowned.

'Look at the cassock, around his waist.'

Reis switched his gaze to the middle of the dark, stained garment and spotted a thick leather loop stitched roughly to the cloth on one side and a tear on the other where its twin should have been. He'd noted other rips in the cassock, two above the hem and two by the wrists, but he'd missed this one.

'The rope may be the victim's belt,' Reis stated for the record. 'There are some leather loops round the middle of his cloak, though one appears to be missing. Again I will bag everything and send it across the hall for analysis.'

Arkadian reached behind Reis and pressed the flashing red square to pause the recording.

'In other words,' he said, 'our guy climbed up the mountain using his belt as a makeshift rope, cut his hands and feet on the rocks in the process, hung around on the summit long enough for them to start healing, then threw himself off as soon as there was a big enough crowd to ruin my morning. Case closed.

'Now, much as I'd love to hang around, I've got some less glamorous but nevertheless deserving cases to pursue. So, if you don't mind, I'll just borrow that phone over by the coffee pot and try to get on with some real police work.' He turned and disappeared beyond the harsh white light of the examination table. 'Just holler if you find any clues.'

'Oh, I will.' Reis reached for a pair of heavy-duty shears. 'You sure you don't want to watch? I'm about to cut his cloak off. Not every day you get to see a naked monk.'

'You're a sick man, Reis.' Arkadian picked up the phone and wondered which of his six active cases he should catch up on first.

Reis looked down at the corpse and smiled. 'Sick!' he muttered to himself. 'You try doing this every day and staying normal.'

He opened the shears, slipped them over the collar of the monk's cassock and started to cut.

24

Athanasius followed the filament of light in the floor round the corner and into the long dark corridor where the forbidden vault lay waiting. If there was anyone there ahead of him he couldn't see them. The blood-red light in the chamber was not designed to carry far. He hated the darkness, but he hated the fact that you couldn't hear anything even more. He'd heard Thomas explaining it to Samuel once – something to do with a constant low-frequency signal, inaudible to the human ear, which disrupted all sound waves and prevented them from carrying further than the circle of light that surrounded you. It meant you could be ten feet from someone and still have no idea what they were saying. It ensured that all forty-two chambers, even when full of scholars passionately arguing theological points, remained in a permanent state of librarian silence. It also meant that, despite his rapid and purposeful march through the Bible-black corridors, Athanasius could not even draw comfort from the sound of his own footfalls.

He was halfway down the corridor when he saw it. Briefly, at the edge of his light. A white spectral flash in the dark.

Athanasius sprang backwards, scanning the blackness. Trying to glimpse again what he thought he had seen. Something smacked into his back and he whirled around. Saw the stone upright of a bookcase. Whipped his head back to try and penetrate the ominous darkness.

He saw it again.

At first, just the faintest of outlines, like a web drifting in the dark. Then, as the thing advanced, it began to solidify into the gaunt and shuffling shape of a man. His body was thin and bony, barely looking strong enough to support the cassock that hung around him like partially discarded skin, and his long, sparse hair hung down in front of sightless eyes. Despite the ghastly appearance of the slowly advancing monk Athanasius felt his whole body relax.

'Brother Ponti,' he breathed. 'You gave me quite a start.'

It was the caretaker, an old monk specifically chosen for the task of cleaning and maintaining the great library because his blindness meant he needed no illumination to work by. He twitched his head in the direction of the voice, staring straight through Athanasius with his milky gaze. 'I'm sorry,' he rasped, his voice parched by the arid air. 'I do try and keep to the walls so as not to bump into folk, but this section's a bit on the narrow side, Brother . . .?'

'Athanasius.'

'Ah yes,' Ponti nodded. 'Athanasius. I remember you. You've been in there before, haven't you?' He waved in the direction of the vault.

'Once,' Athanasius replied.

'That's right.' Brother Ponti nodded slowly, as if agreeing with himself. 'Well,' he said, turning stiffly towards the exit, 'don't let me keep you. You'll find it's already occupied. And if I were you, Brother, I wouldn't keep him waiting.'

Then he turned once more and melted into the blackness.

25

It took Reis several minutes to slice through the saturated material of the monk's cassock. He cut from collar to hem, then down each arm, careful not to disturb the body beneath. Rolling the corpse slightly, he then removed the garment and placed it in a steel tray ready for separate analysis.

The guy was in pretty good shape.

At least he would have been before he fell a thousand feet on to solid rock.

Reis tapped the red square on the computer screen with his knuckle and restarted the recording.

'First impressions of the subject's body match what one would expect to see following a fall from a great height: massive trauma to the torso, shards of fractured rib jutting out through several places on both sides of the thorax, totally in keeping with the types of compression fracture caused by the extraordinary deceleration of a body in freefall coming into contact with the ground.

'The body is covered in thick, dark, coagulated blood from numerous puncture wounds. Both clavicles are fractured in several places, and the right one protrudes through the skin at the base of the neck. There also appears to be . . .'

He looked more closely.

' . . . some kind of historical, uniform incision running horizontally across the neck from shoulder to shoulder.'

He took hold of the retractable hose arching over the examination table and squeezed the handle, directing a jet of water on to the neck and chest of the corpse. The sticky, dark film began to wash away.

'Jesus Christ,' Reis muttered.

He moved the spray across the rest of the body: first the chest, then the arms, then the legs. He paused the recording once more.

'Hey, Arkadian,' he called over his shoulder, still transfixed by the livid body on the slab. 'You said you wanted a clue. How does this grab you?'

26

Athanasius stopped at the door, aware that he did not possess the right to enter the restricted room, and more than slightly fearful of what might happen if he did.

He looked inside.

The Abbot stood imposingly in the confined space, the red light seeming to radiate from him as if he were a demon glowing in the darkness. His back was to the door, so he could not see Athanasius. His eyes were fixed on a grid of fifteen apertures carved into the far wall, each containing a receptacle made from the same material as aircraft black box data recorders. Athanasius recalled Father Malachi telling him how they were strong enough to protect their precious contents even if the whole mountain fell upon them; that did little to comfort him now.

He glanced down at the invisible line on the floor and contemplated stepping boldly into the room, but the phrase 'See no evil, hear no evil' rose unbidden into his thoughts and he remained where he stood until the Abbot, either sensing his presence or wondering at the lack of it, turned and looked straight at him. Athanasius noted with relief that his master's face, despite its unsettling crimson pall, did not display the glower of a man on the warpath but the thoughtfulness of one with a problem to solve.

'Come in.' The Abbot removed one of the boxes from its recess and carried it to the lectern in the centre of the room. Sensing Athanasius's continued reluctance to step inside, he said, 'I spoke to Malachi on my way through. You may enter the vault – for an hour at least.'

As Athanasius obeyed, a second red glow accompanied him across the vault, confirming that – for the time being – his presence was legitimate.

The lectern stood in the centre of the room, facing the entrance but with the reading surface angled away from it. Anyone standing at it would be warned of an approach by the tell-tale sign of the advancing light, and any book placed there could not be seen from outside.

'I summoned you here,' the Abbot said, 'because I wish to show you something.'

He unlatched the box and gently opened it.

'Do you have any idea what this might be?'

Athanasius leaned forward, his aura joining the Abbot's to illuminate a book, bound with a single panel of slate with a bold symbol etched on to its surface – the symbol of the Tau.

His breath caught in his throat. He knew at once what it was, as much from descriptions he had read as the circumstances in which he was now discovering it.

'A Heretic Bible,' Athanasius said.

'No,' the Abbot corrected. 'Not *a* Heretic Bible. *The* Heretic Bible. This is the last remaining copy.'

Athanasius gazed down upon the slate cover. 'I thought they had all been destroyed.'

'That is what we wish people to believe. What better way to prevent them from searching for something than to persuade them that it does not exist?'

Athanasius considered the wisdom of this. He had barely spared a thought for the legendary book in years, because he thought it was exactly that – a legend. Yet here it was, close enough to touch.

'That book,' the Abbot said through clenched teeth, 'contains thirteen pages of outrageous, poisonous and twisted lies; lies which dare to contradict and pervert the very word of God as recorded and set down in our own true Bible.'

Athanasius stared down at the innocuous-looking cover. 'Then why spare this copy?' he asked. 'If it's so dangerous, why keep even one?'

'Because,' the Abbot replied, jabbing his finger at the box, 'you can destroy books, but their contents have a way of surviving; and in order for us to confound and defeat our enemies it helps if we first know their minds. Let me show you something.'

He placed a finger on the edge of the cover and opened it. The pages inside were also made of slate, held by three leather thongs. As the Abbot turned them, Athanasius felt an overwhelming temptation to read what was scratched on their surfaces. Unfortunately the rate at which the Abbot was proceeding, coupled with the nebulizing quality of the red light, made it virtually impossible. He could see that each page contained two columns of dense script, but it was several moments before he realized they were written in Malan, the language of the first heretics. With his brain now attuned he managed to pick up just two fragments as the pages flipped over. Two fragments, two phrases – both of which added to his already considerable state of shock.

'There,' the Abbot announced as he reached the final page. 'This is part of what equates to their version of Genesis. You are familiar with their bastard tongue, I believe.'

Athanasius hesitated, his mind still trembling with the forbidden words he had just read.

'Yes,' he managed to say without his voice betraying him. 'I have . . . studied it.'

'Then read,' the Abbot said.

Unlike the previous pages, the final tablet of slate contained only eight lines of text. They were arranged as a Calligram forming the sign of the Tau – the same textual symbol Kathryn Mann had gazed upon two hours previously. This one, however, was complete.

The one true cross will appear on earth
All will see it in a single moment – all will wonder
The cross will fall
The cross will rise
To unlock the Sacrament
And bring forth a new age
Through its merciful death

Athanasius looked up at the Abbot, his mind racing.

'This is why I brought you here,' the Abbot said. 'I wanted you to see with your own eyes how Brother Samuel's death may be interpreted by our enemies.'

Athanasius studied the prophecy again. The first three lines read like a description of the extraordinary events of the morning; it was the last four that made the blood drain from his cheeks. What they suggested was something incredible, unbelievable, momentous.

'This is why we kept the book,' the Abbot said solemnly. 'Knowledge is power; and knowing what our enemies believe gives us the advantage. I want you to keep a close and watchful eye on Brother Samuel's body. For if these twisted words contain any truth, and he is the cross mentioned here, then he may yet rise up – and be seen by our enemies as a weapon to use against us.'

27

Reis and Arkadian stared down at the body. Criss-crossing the skin was a complex and elaborate network of livid white scars; some old, some more recent – all deliberate. In the macabre setting of the autopsy room they gave the impression that the monk was some kind of gothic monster, stitched together from the component parts of a number of men.

Reis restarted the recording.

'The subject shows significant and uniform scarring over much of his body, the result of cuts made repeatedly by a sharp, clinical instrument such as a scalpel or a razor, possibly during some kind of ritual.'

He began the grisly inventory.

'Starting at the head . . . An old, healed scar entirely circumscribing the neck where it connects with the torso. Similar scars circumscribe both arms at the shoulder and both legs at the groin. The one at the top of the upper left arm has been recently re-opened, but already shows signs of healing. This incision is also straight-edged and extremely neat, surgically precise even, from a highly sharpened blade.'

'Also on the left arm at the junction of the upper bicep and tricep is a T-shaped keloid scar, thicker than the others, caused by repeated heat trauma.' He glanced across at Arkadian. 'Looks like this boy's been on the receiving end of a cattle brand.'

Arkadian stared at the raised 'T' on the monk's upper arm, all thought of his other cases now forgotten. He picked up Reis's camera. Its LCD screen displayed a miniature version of the monk lying on the autopsy table. With a press of a button it was transmitted wirelessly to the case file.

'There's another scar running along the top of the ribcage, and one bisecting it, down through the sternum to the navel.' Reis paused. 'In shape and size it resembles the Y-cut we make to remove major organs during a post-mortem.

'Radiating from the areola of the left nipple are four straight lines arranged at right angles to form the shape of a cross. Also not recent, each is approximately...' Reis produced his tape again ' . . . twenty centimetres long.' He took a closer look. 'There's another cross on the right side of the torso, level with the base of the ribcage; different from the rest; roughly thirteen centimetres laterally, like a Christian cross lying on its side; evidence of stretch marks on the skin surrounding it; must have happened a long time ago. It also hasn't been subjected to ritualistic re-opening, so maybe it isn't as significant as the others.'

Arkadian took another snap then examined the scar close up. It did look exactly like a fallen cross. He pulled back, searching for meaning in the pattern of incisions. 'Have you seen anything like this before?'

Reis shook his head. 'My guess is some kind of initiation thing. But most of these scars aren't fresh, so I don't know how relevant they are to his jumping.'

'He didn't just jump,' Arkadian said.

'What do you mean?'

'With most suicides, death is the principal objective. But not with this guy; his death was somehow . . . secondary. I think his primary motive lay elsewhere.'

Reis's eyebrows disappeared beneath his hair. 'If you throw yourself off the top of the Citadel, death has got to be *fairly* high on your agenda.'

'But why climb all the way to the top? A fall from almost any height would have been enough.'

'Maybe he was scared of winding up crippled. Lots of half-hearted suicide bids end up in the hospital rather than in here.'

'Even so, he didn't need to struggle to the very top. He also didn't need to wait. But he did. He sat there, for God knows how long, in the freezing cold, bleeding from multiple wounds, waiting for morning. Why did he do that?'

'Maybe he was resting. A climb like that is going to wipe anyone out; he would have been losing blood all the way up. So maybe he got to the top, collapsed from exhaustion, and the sun eventually revived him. Then he did it.'

Arkadian frowned. 'But that's not how it happened. He didn't just wake up and topple off the mountain. He stood there with his arms outstretched for at least a couple of hours.' He mimicked the pose. 'Why would he do that if he just wanted to end it all? I'm pretty sure the public nature of his death is significant. The only reason we're standing here having this conversation is because he waited until there was an audience. If he'd pulled this little stunt in the middle of the night I doubt whether it would even have made the news. He knew exactly what he was doing.'

'OK,' Reis conceded. 'So maybe the guy didn't get enough attention when he was a kid. What difference does it make? He's still dead.'

Arkadian considered the question.

What difference did it make?

He knew his boss wanted the whole thing dealt with quickly and painlessly. The politic move would be to ignore the natural curiosity he'd been born with and stop asking difficult questions. Then again, he could just turn in his badge and sell holiday apartments or become a tour guide.

'Listen,' he said, 'I didn't ask to be put on this case. Your job is to establish how someone died. Mine is to work out why, and in order to do that it's important to try and understand this guy's mindset. Jumpers are usually victims – people who can't cope any more, people who take the path of least resistance to death. But this guy had courage. He wasn't a classic victim, and he damn sure didn't take the path of least resistance. Which makes me think his actions meant something to him. Maybe they meant something to someone else too.'

28

Athanasius hurried up the corridor after the Abbot, their personal haloes brightening with every step they took.

'So tell me,' the Abbot said, without breaking stride, 'who has made contact from the investigation?'

'An Inspector Arkadian has been assigned to the case,' Athanasius replied breathlessly. 'He has already requested an interview with someone who might have information on the deceased. I told our brothers on the outside to say that the death was a tragedy and we would do everything we could to assist.'

'Did you say whether he was known to us?'

'I said there were many people living and working inside the Citadel and we would endeavour to discover if any of them were missing. I wasn't sure whether or not we wanted to claim him as ours at this point, or whether you would prefer us to remain distant.'

The Abbot nodded. 'You did well. Inform the public office to maintain the same courteous degree of cooperation, for now. It may be that the question of Brother Samuel's body will resolve itself without our interference. Once the authorities have completed the post-mortem and no family members come forward to claim the body, we can step forward and offer to take it as a gesture of compassion. It will show to the world what a loving and caring church we are, one prepared to embrace a poor, wretched soul who sought to end his life in such a lonely and tragic way. It will also bring Brother Samuel back to us without our having to admit kinship.'

The Abbot stopped and turned, fixing Athanasius with his sharp, grey eyes.

'However, in the light of what you have just read we must also be vigilant. We must leave nothing to chance. If anything unusual is reported, anything at all, then we must be ready to get Brother Samuel's body back immediately, and by any means necessary.' He stared at Athanasius from beneath his beetled brows. 'That way, if some miracle does come to pass and he rises again, he will at least be in our custody. Whatever happens, we cannot let our enemies take possession of his body.'

'As you wish,' Athanasius replied. 'But surely if what you have just shown me is the only remaining copy of the book, who else would know of the . . .' he hesitated, not quite sure how to describe the ancient words scratched on the sheet of slate. He didn't want to use the word 'prophecy' because that would imply that the words were the will of God, which in itself would be heresy. 'Who else could know the specifics of the . . . prediction . . .?'

The Abbot nodded approvingly, picking up on his chamberlain's caution. It confirmed to him that Athanasius was the right man to handle the official side of the situation; he had the political sophistication and the discretion for it. The unofficial side he would handle himself. 'We cannot simply trust that the destruction of all the books and the people who carried them has also destroyed the words and thoughts they contained,' he explained. 'Lies are like weeds. You can grub them up, poison the root, burn them away to nothing – but they always find a way to return. So we must assume that this "prediction", as you wisely refer to it, will be known in some form to our enemies, and that they will be preparing to act upon it. But do not worry, Brother,' he said, laying a hand heavy as a bear's paw on Athanasius's shoulder. 'We have withstood far more than this in our long and colourful history. We must simply do now as we have always done: stay one step ahead, pull up the drawbridge and wait for the outside threat to withdraw.'

'And if it does not?' Athanasius asked.

The hand tightened on his shoulder. 'Then we attack it with everything we have.'

29

Reis reached across the monk's body to a point at the top of the sternum, pressed down firmly with a long-handled scalpel and drew the blade smoothly down through the flesh, clear to the pubic bone, carefully following the line of the existing scar. He completed the Y-incision by making two more deep cuts from the top of the one he had just made to the outer edge of each of the monk's shattered collarbones. Finally he cut away the skin and muscle from the monk's chest and folded it open, revealing the ruined ribs beneath. At this point he would usually need surgical shears or the Stryker saw to cut through the cage of bone that protected the heart, lungs and other internal organs, but the massive impact of the landing had done most of the work for him. With just a few ligament cuts he managed to gain access to the chest cavity.

'Tap the square for me, would you,' Reis said, nodding towards the monitor. 'Got my hands full here.'

Arkadian looked at the bloody section of ribs Reis was clutching and restarted the recording.

'OK,' Reis said, the jaunty tone back in his voice, 'first impressions of the internal organs are that they are surprisingly well preserved, considering the impact. The ribs clearly did their job, even if they were all but destroyed in the process.'

He laid the ribcage down in a stainless-steel tray then made some well-practised cuts inside the body cavity to detach the larynx, oesophagus and ligaments connecting the major organs to the spinal cord before lifting the entire block out in one piece and transferring them to a wide metal container.

'The liver shows some evidence of haemorrhaging,' he said, 'but none of the major organs are particularly pale so he didn't bleed out. The subject probably died of systemic organ failure following massive trauma, which I'll confirm once I've run the tox and tissue tests.'

He carried the container to an examination bench by the wall and started taking routine measurements of the liver, heart and lungs, as well as tissue samples from each.

Arkadian looked up at the TV in the corner and was once again confronted by the eerie sight of the man now lying in pieces in front of him standing proud and very much alive on the summit of the Citadel. It was the footage all the networks were now using. It showed the monk shuffling towards the edge. Glancing down. Tipping forward, then suddenly dropping from view. The camera jerked downwards and zoomed wide as it tried to follow the fall. It tightened back in, losing focus as it found him again and struggled to keep him in frame. It was like watching the Zapruder film of the Kennedy assassination, or the footage of the planes hitting the Twin Towers. There was something momentous about it, and deeply terrible. He couldn't take his eyes off it. At the last moment the camera lost him again and pulled wide just in time to reveal the base of the mountain and the crowds of people on the embankment recoiling in shock from where the body had hit the ground.

Arkadian dropped his gaze to the floor. He replayed the sequence in his head over and over, piecing together the glimpsed fragments of the monk's fall . . .

'It was deliberate,' he whispered.

Reis looked up from the digital scales currently displaying the weight of the dead monk's liver. 'Of course it was deliberate.'

'No, I mean the *way* he fell. Suicide jumps are usually pretty straightforward. Jumpers either flip over backwards, or launch themselves forward and tip over head first.'

'The head's the heaviest part of the body,' Reis said. 'Gravity always pulls it straight down – given a long enough fall.'

'And a fall from the top of the Citadel should be plenty long enough. It's over a thousand feet high. But our guy stayed flat – all the way down.'

'So?'

'So it was a controlled fall.'

Arkadian went to the stainless-steel tray holding the cassock. He grabbed a set of tongs and peeled open the stiff material until he found one of the sleeves. 'Look. Those rips you found at the wrists? They were for his hands. It meant he could pull his robe tight against his body – like a kind of wing.' He dropped the sleeve and sorted through the grisly folds until he found the other cuts a few inches above the hem. 'And these were for his feet.' He dropped the material back down and turned to Reis. 'That's why he didn't fall head-first. He didn't jump off the mountain – he flew off it.'

Reis looked across at the broken body under the examination lights. 'Then I'd say he really needs to work on his landings.'

Arkadian ignored him, following this new thought. 'Maybe he thought he could reduce the speed of the fall enough to survive it. Or maybe . . .'

He pictured the monk again, his arms stretched out, his body tilted down, his head held steady, as if focusing on something, as if he was . . .

'Aiming.'

'What?'

'I think he was aiming for a specific spot.'

'Why on earth would he do that?'

It was a good question. Why aim somewhere if you were going to die wherever you landed? But then, death wasn't his primary concern, it wasn't nearly as important as . . . witnesses. 'He was aiming because he wanted to land in our jurisdiction!'

Reis's brow furrowed.

'The Citadel is a state within a state,' Arkadian explained. 'Anything that side of the moat wall belongs to them; anything this side is our responsibility. He wanted to make sure he ended up on our side of the wall. He wanted all this to happen. He wanted public investigation. He wanted us to see all these cuts on his body.'

'But why?'

'I have absolutely no idea. But whatever it is, he thought it was worth dying for. His dying wish, literally, was to get away from that place.'

'So what are you going to do when some big religious cheese comes calling, asking for his monk back? Give them a lecture on jurisdiction?'

Arkadian shrugged. 'So far they haven't even admitted he's one of theirs.'

He glanced over at the gaping body of the monk, the body cavity now empty, the surgically precise scars round his neck, legs and arms still visible. Maybe the scars were some kind of message, and whoever came forward to claim the body would know what they meant.

Reis picked up a cardboard container from underneath the examination table, restarted the recording, and began squeezing the contents of the monk's stomach into it. 'OK,' he said. 'The major intestine contains very little, so our friend's last supper wasn't exactly a banquet. Looks like the last thing he ate was an apple and maybe some bread a while before that, which I'll label and send for analysis. The stomach contents appear to be largely undigested, suggesting that his digestive system had wholly or partially shut down, indicating a high degree of ante-mortem stress. Wait a minute,' he said, as something shifted inside the slippery membranes between his fingers. 'There's something else here.'

Arkadian stepped over to the table as something small and dark dropped into the soup of apple pulp and gastric juices. It looked like a curled-up strip of overcooked beef. 'What on earth is that?'

Reis picked it up and moved across to the sink, knocking the long arm of the tap with his elbow and holding the object under the stream of water.

'It appears to be a small strip of leather,' he said, laying it down on a tray lined with a paper towel. 'It was rolled up, maybe to make it easier to swallow.' He took a set of tweezers and started opening it out.

'He was missing a belt loop from his cassock, wasn't he?' Arkadian whispered.

Reis nodded.

'I think we just found it.'

Reis moved it alongside a centimetre scale etched into the surface of the tray. Arkadian sent another picture to the case file. Reis flipped it over so he could photograph the other side and all the air seemed to be sucked from the room.

Neither of them moved.

Neither of them said anything.

Arkadian raised the camera.

The click of the shutter snapped Reis out of his trance.

He cleared his throat.

'Having unrolled and cleaned the leather object, something appears to be scratched on its surface.'

He glanced up at Arkadian before continuing.

'Twelve numbers, seemingly random.'

Arkadian stared down at them, his mind already racing. The combination for a lock? Some kind of code? Maybe they referred to a chapter and verse from the Bible and would spell out a word or a sentence that might shed light on things, possibly even the identity of the Sacrament. He checked the numbers again. 'They're not random,' he said, reading the sequence from left to right. 'Not random at all.'

He looked up at Reis.

'That's a telephone number,' he said.

II

Unto the woman he said, I will greatly
multiply thy sorrow and thy conception;
in sorrow thou shalt bring forth children;
and thy desire shall be to thy husband,
and he shall rule over thee.

Genesis 3:16

30

The primal screams echoed round the bright room with a desperate, animal quality that seemed out of place in the sleek modern setting of the New Jersey hospital.

Liv stood in the corner, watching Bonnie's face contort in pain. Her phone had woken her a little after two in the morning, dragging her out of bed, into her car, and south on I-95 with all the empty trucks making their way out of New York City. It had been Myron; Bonnie's waters had broken.

Another lung-deep scream tore through the room and she looked across at Bonnie squatting naked in the centre of the room, howling so hard that her face had gone purple and the cords in her neck stood out like high-tension cables. Myron held on, supporting one arm, while the midwife held the other. The howl ebbed slightly, making way for the incongruous sound of waves lapping against a beach. They flowed gently from a portable boom box in the corner.

In Liv's nicotine-starved mind the supposedly soothing sounds of the seashore morphed into the tormenting crackle of cellophane being ripped off a fresh pack of Luckies. She craved a cigarette more than she had ever desired anything in her life. Hospitals always had that effect on her. The very fact you were expressly forbidden to do something made it almost irresistible to her. She was the same in churches.

Bonnie's scream rose again, this time something between a moan and a growl. Myron stroked her back and made shushing noises like he was trying to calm a child who had woken from a terrible nightmare. Bonnie turned to him and in a low voice made raw from screaming panted a single word: 'Arnica.'

Liv reached gratefully for her notebook to log the request and the time it was made. Arnica was also known as wolf's bane or mountain tobacco and had been used since the dawn of time as a herbal remedy. Liv often used it herself to reduce bruising; it was also thought to alleviate the trauma of a long drawn out and painful childbirth. She found herself sincerely hoping this would prove to be true as she watched Myron fumbling with a small vial containing the tiny white sugar pills. The screaming started again and rose in pitch as another contraction arrived.

For God's sake, take the Pethedine, Liv thought.

An advocate of the healing properties of plants she may have been; a masochist she most definitely was not. Bonnie's screaming soared to a new zenith and her hand shot out to grab Myron, knocking the entire contents of the blue box on to the shiny vinyl floor.

Liv's cell phone rang in her pocket.

She felt for the 'off' button through the thick cotton of her cargo pants and pressed hard, hoping to catch it before it rang again. No one gave the slightest indication they even remembered she was there. She fished the phone out and glanced down at the scratched grey screen, made sure it was definitely off, then returned her attention, just in time, to the unfolding story in the room.

Bonnie's eyes rolled back in her head and her heavily pregnant form crumpled to the floor, despite the best efforts of Myron and the midwife to keep her upright. Instinctively, Liv dived for the emergency cord dangling by her side and pulled as hard as she could.

Within seconds the room filled with orderlies fluttering around Bonnie like moths, crunching homeopathic pills underfoot. A trolley appeared from nowhere and she was wheeled from the room, away from Liv and the gentle music of the shoreline, down the hallway to another room full of the latest drugs and clinical equipment.

31

Ruin Homicide shared office space with the Robbery Division on the fourth floor of a new glass block built behind the carved stone façade of the original police building. The office was open-plan and noisy. Men in shirtsleeves perched on the edge of desks and tipped back in chairs as they talked loudly into phones or with each other.

Arkadian sat at his desk with his hand clamped to his ear, trying to listen to the answer-phone message on the number he'd just called. A woman's voice. American. Confident sounding. Direct. Late twenties or early thirties. He hung up rather than leaving a message. You never got any information by leaving messages. Best just to keep on trying until whoever you were calling got curious and picked up.

He dropped the handset into its cradle and tapped the space-bar on his keyboard to banish the screensaver. The photos from the examination table appeared. With his eyes he traced the neat scars snaking across the dead monk's body, strange lines and crosses that ultimately formed one giant question mark.

Since the post-mortem, the mystery of the monk's identity had deepened. The Citadel still hadn't claimed him as one of their own, and all the regular methods of victim identification had so far drawn a blank. His fingerprints had come back unknown. Ditto his dental records. His DNA swabs were still working their way through the labs, but unless the dead man had been arrested for a sex crime, a homicide or some kind of terrorist activity it was unlikely he was going to show up on any of those databases either. And Arkadian's boss was starting to lean on him for some kind of progress report; he wanted to draw a line under this thing. So did Arkadian, but he wasn't going to whitewash it. The monk belonged to someone. It was his job to find out whom.

He glanced at the clock on the far wall. It was now a little after one in the afternoon. His wife would just be getting in from the school where she helped out three days a week. He dialled his own number and clicked on the lower left corner of his computer screen to open up a browser window while he listened to it connecting.

His wife picked up on the third ring. She sounded breathless.

'It's me,' Arkadian said, tapping '*Religion*' and '*Scars*' into the search box and hitting return.

'Heeeey,' she said, drawing out the middle of the word in a way that still got him twelve years after he'd first heard it. 'You coming home?'

Arkadian frowned as the results came back, all four hundred and thirty-one thousand of them.

'Not yet,' he said, scrolling through the first page.

'Then what are you calling for, getting a girl's hopes up?'

'Just wanted to hear your voice. How was work?'

'Tiring. You try teaching English to a roomful of nine-year-olds. I must've read *The Hungry Caterpillar* at least a couple of hundred times. Though by the end, there was one kid I swear could read it better than me.'

He could tell from her voice she was smiling. She was always happiest when she'd spent the morning in a room full of kids. The realization also made him feel sad.

'Sounds like a know-all,' he said. 'You should get *him* to read it to the class next time, see how he copes under pressure.'

'It's a girl, actually. Girls are cleverer than boys.'

Arkadian smiled. 'Yes, but you end up marrying us. So you can't be all that bright.'

'But then we divorce you and take all your money.'

'I don't have any money.'

'Oh well . . . then I guess you're pretty safe.'

He clicked on a link and scrolled through pictures of tribesmen with raw wounds slashed red into ebony flesh. None of them matched the scars on the monk.

'So what case are you working?' she asked. 'Anything gruesome?'

'The monk.'

'You find out who he is yet, or can't you say?'

'I can't say because I don't know.' He clicked back to the results page and opened a link dealing with stigmata, the unexplained phenomenon of wounds similar to those Christ suffered during his crucifixion appearing on ordinary people.

'So you going to be late?'

'Too early to tell. They want to get this one squared away.'

'Which means "yes".'

'Which means "probably".'

'Well . . . just be careful.'

'I'm sitting at my desk doing Google searches.'

'Then come home.'

'I always do.'

'Love you.'

'You too,' he whispered.

He looked up at the office, humming with noise and attitude. Most of the people currently occupying it were either divorced or well on their way, but he knew that would never happen to him. He was married to his wife, not the job; and even though that choice had meant he'd never been given the sexy, high-profile cases from which careers and reputations were made, he didn't mind. He wouldn't swap his life with any of them. Besides, there was something about this suicide that made him feel he might just have caught a live one. He clicked randomly on one of the stigmata websites and started to read.

The site was pretty academic and consisted of dense, dry text only occasionally punctuated by a juicy photo of a bleeding hand or foot, though none of them matched the scars he'd found on the monk.

He removed his glasses and rubbed at the indentations they left on the side of his nose when he wore them too long, which was every day of his working life. He knew he should be getting on with his other cases while he waited for word to come down from the Citadel, or until the American woman answered her phone, but the case was already getting under his skin: the apparent public martyrdom, the ritualized scars, the fact that the monk didn't appear to officially exist.

He closed the search window and spent the next twenty minutes typing the few facts he had gathered and his initial thoughts and observations into the case file. When he had finished he reread his notes, then jogged back through the post-mortem photos until he found the one he was looking for.

He looked again at the thin strip of leather laid out on the evidence tray, the harsh light of the camera flash picking out the twelve numbers scratched crudely on its surface. He copied them into his mobile phone then closed the file, grabbed his jacket from the back of his chair and headed for the door. He needed some air and something to eat. He always thought better when he was on the move.

Two floors down, in an office stacked high with old file boxes, a pale hand dusted with freckles tapped a hacked security code into a computer belonging to an admin clerk working a switch shift who wasn't due in for another couple of hours.

After a brief pause the monitor flashed into life, bathing the dark office in its cold light. An arrow slid across the screen, found the server icon, and clicked it open. A finger stroked the wheel on the mouse, jogging down through the file directory until its possessor found what he was looking for. He reached under the desk and plugged a flash memory stick into the front of the processor tower. A new icon appeared on the desktop. He dragged the monk's case file to the icon and watched the contents copy on to it – the post-mortem report, the photos, the audio commentary, Arkadian's notes.

Everything.

32

Liv Adamsen leaned against the rough trunk of the single cypress that sprang from the lawn by the hospital. She tilted her head back and blew long, relieved streams of cigarette smoke towards the overhanging branches. Through the canopy she could see a large illuminated cross fixed to the top of the building, like a twisted moon in the slowly brightening sky. As a defective tube blinked fitfully inside it, something glistened on the bark a few feet above her head. She reached up and touched it tentatively. Her hand came away sticky and smelling of the forest. Sap; quite a lot of it – far too much to be healthy.

She stood on tiptoe to examine the source of the flow. She made out a series of indentations and cracks in the bark. It looked like seiridium canker, a common disease in this type of tree, no doubt brought on by the long, dry, icy winter. She'd noticed the same thing on the leylandii in Bonnie and Myron's garden. The increasingly warm summers were drying out the ground and weakening root systems. Sharp, cold periods were allowing these cankers and other forms of rot to take lethal hold on even the strongest of trees. You could cut out canker if you got it early enough, but by the looks of it this tree was already too far gone.

Liv laid her hand gently on the trunk and inhaled deeply on her cigarette. The smell of the sap on her fingers mingled with the smoke. In her mind she saw the cypress burning where it stood, branches twisting and blackening, hungry flames licking at the red sap as it boiled and hissed. She looked at the silent car park, checking she was still alone, spooked by what her imagination had just conjured up. She put it down to her own fragile emotional state, coupled with the exhaustion of witnessing a 'natural' labour that had ended with white-coated men whisking Bonnie to a waiting ventouse. At least both babies, a boy and a girl, were healthy and well. It wasn't quite the story Liv had set out to write, but she guessed it would do. It certainly had plenty of drama. She remembered the moment when she had pulled the emergency cord.

Then she remembered the call.

She'd had the cell for years. It was so old she could barely send a text, let alone take a picture or surf the net with it. Not many people even knew she had it. Fewer still possessed its ex-directory number. She ran through the very short list of those who did while she waited for it to get up to speed.

Liv had adopted what she called her 'home and away' system shortly after starting work on the crime desk. The very first story she'd covered had required her to chase down and interview a particularly slippery attorney representing an even more slippery local property developer being sued by the State on several counts of bribery to obtain building licences. She'd left a number for the lawyer to get back to her. Unfortunately the man who'd called her back was his client. She'd been half-way up a cherry tree with a pruning saw in her hand when she'd taken the call. The force of the abuse he'd hurled at her had almost made her fall out of it, but she'd walked into the kitchen, grabbed a pen and paper and jotted down everything he said, word for word. The entire incident, and the direct quotes arising from it, became the cornerstone of the damning article she subsequently wrote.

She learned two valuable lessons from the incident. The first was never to be afraid to put herself in the story, if that was the best way to tell it; the second was to be more selective about who she handed out her number to. She bought herself a new cell and began to use it exclusively for work. Her old one, with a new SIM card and number, had subsequently been reserved exclusively for friends and family. It now shuddered in her hand as it ended its start-up sequence. She peered down at the screen. She'd missed only one call. There were no waiting messages.

She pressed the menu button and scrolled through to the missed-call log. Whoever had called her had done so from a withheld number. Liv frowned. As far as she could remember, everyone who had this number was also in her address book, so should automatically be recognized. She took a final drag on her cigarette, ground it into the damp pine needles and headed back towards the hospital to say goodbye to the human part of her human interest story.

33

The church that filled one side of the great square in the old town was always busiest in the afternoon. It seemed to scoop up the crowds who had spent the morning wandering around the narrow cobbled streets, staring up at the Citadel. The weary visitor would enter the cool, monolithic interior and be immediately confronted with the answer to their unspoken prayers: row upon row of polished oak pews offering, for no charge, a welcome place to sit and contemplate life, the universe and how unwise their choice of footwear may have been. It was a fully working church, holding services once a day and twice on Sunday, offering communion for those who wanted it and confession for those who needed it.

It was into this throng that a man now entered, slowing momentarily to remove his baseball cap in a half-remembered gesture of deference and let his eyes adjust to the gloom after the sun-bleached brightness of the streets. He hated churches – they gave him the creeps – but business was business.

He threaded his way through the knots of tourists staring up at the soaring columns, stained-glass windows and arching stonework of the clerestory – all eyes to heaven, as the architects had intended. Nobody gave him so much as a glance.

He reached the far corner of the church and his mood immediately soured. A line of people sat on a bench by a row of drawn curtains. He briefly considered jumping the queue, but didn't want to risk drawing attention to himself, so sat down next to the last sinner in line until an apologetic-looking foreigner tapped him on the shoulder and pointed to a vacant booth.

'It's all right,' he stammered, avoiding eye contact and gesturing towards the corner. 'I want the one on the end.'

The tourist looked perplexed.

'Go ahead. I'm funny about where I do my confessing.'

The man hunkered down on the bench. Normally his freelance business took him to the shadowy recesses of a bar or a car park. It felt weird, doing it in a church. He watched two more sinners emerge before the stall he needed finally became available. He was out of his seat and into the booth almost before the previous incumbent had emerged. He yanked the curtain shut behind him and sat down.

It was cramped and dark, and smelt of incense, sweat and fear. To his right a small, square grille was set into a wooden panel slightly lower than head height.

'Do you have something to confess?' prompted a muffled voice.

'I might,' he replied. 'Are you Brother Peacock?'

'No,' the voice replied. 'Please wait.'

Whoever was on the other side of the grille got up and left.

The man waited, listening to the whispers of tourists and the clicking of cameras. They sounded to him like the rasping legs of scuttling insects. He heard movement on the other side of the grille.

'I am the emissary of Brother Peacock,' a low voice announced.

The man leaned forward. 'Please forgive me, for I have sinned.'

'And what have you to confess?'

'I have taken something from my place of work, something which does not belong to me, something I believe concerns a fellow Brother of your church.'

'Do you have this thing with you?'

A pale hand dusted with freckles took a small white envelope from an inner pocket.

'I do,' he said.

108

'Good. You understand that the purpose of confession is to enable sinners who enter the house of God burdened with their sins to leave again free of those burdens?'

The man smiled. 'I understand,' he said.

'Your sin is not grave. If you bow your head before God I believe you will find the forgiveness you seek.'

A hatch slid open beneath the grille. He passed through the envelope, feeling a slight tug as it was taken from him. There was a brief pause. He heard it being opened and inspected.

'This is everything you took?'

'It's everything there was to take as of about an hour ago.'

'Good. As I said, your sin is not grave. I bless you in the name of the Father, of the Son and of the Holy Spirit. You may now consider your sins absolved – provided you remain a friend to the Church. Bow your head before God once more and he will reward his faithful servant.'

The man saw another envelope poking through the hatch. He reached down and took it. The door slid shut and whoever had been on the other side departed as quickly as he had arrived. Inside the envelope was a thick wad of unsigned hundred-dollar traveller's cheques. They always paid him this way, and he smiled at the neatness of it. If he had been followed, which he knew he hadn't, he could plausibly claim they'd been mislaid by a tourist. They were also untraceable, probably purchased by someone using a fake ID at any one of the Bureaux de Change that lined the old streets.

He pocketed the envelope and slipped out of the booth, past the patient queue, his eyes making contact with nobody until he'd left the church well behind him.

34

Five minutes after Brother Peacock's emissary had absolved the man with the freckled hands, the envelope was placed in a basket alongside twelve dead chickens and eight pounds of ham at the foot of the tribute wall on the shadowy northern side of the mountain, then winched up on a swaying rope until it disappeared from sight.

Athanasius wiped a sheen of sweat from his skull as he watched the refectory monks haul in the basket. He retrieved the envelope before it joined the rest of its contents in the large copper stockpot. He had walked down nearly half a mile of corridors and stairwells to get to the tribute cavern. Now he had the envelope he turned wearily on his heels and walked right back up them again, heading to the ornate splendour of the Abbot's private chambers.

Athanasius was breathing heavily by the time the gilded door closed behind him. The Abbot snatched the envelope and ripped it apart, hungry for the knowledge it contained. He stalked over to a writing desk set against the wall by the stained-glass window and folded down the front to reveal a sleek modern laptop.

A few mouse clicks later, the Abbot opened the case file Inspector Arkadian had closed less than an hour before. The face of Brother Samuel returned to haunt him, pale and ghastly under the stark lighting of the autopsy room. 'I'm afraid the body appears remarkably undamaged by the fall,' he said, scrolling rapidly through the first few images.

Athanasius winced as he caught sight of ribs poking through

the shattered body of his former friend. The Abbot opened a text document, mercifully obscuring the ghastly images, and started to read. When he got to the final comments his teeth clenched.

Whoever this man was, he chose to fall. He waited until he had witnesses then ensured that he would land in city jurisdiction. Was his pre-death vigil some kind of signal? If so, who was he signalling to – and what message was he trying to communicate?

The Abbot followed the Inspector's train of thought as it brought him dangerously close to forbidden territory.

'I want the source who gave us this file to keep us regularly updated.' The Abbot closed the case notes and opened another folder labelled *Ancillary Evidence*. 'Any new discovery, any new development, I want to know about it immediately.'

He clicked on an image file and watched the screen fill with a slide show of close-ups of other evidence relating to the case: the coiled rope, the blood-soaked cassock, rock fragments retrieved from the torn flesh of the monk's hands and feet, a strip of leather lying on an evidence tray . . .

'And send word to the Prelate,' the Abbot said gravely. 'Tell him I need a private audience as soon as his holiness is blessed with sufficient strength to grant one.'

Athanasius could not see what had so unsettled the Abbot, but it was clear from his tone that he had been dismissed.

'As you wish,' he said, bowing his head and backing silently out of the room.

The Abbot continued to stare at the image until he heard the door shutting behind him. He checked he was alone then reached into the front of his cassock and pulled a leather thong from around his neck. Two keys dangled from it – one large, one small. He bent down to the lowest drawer of the desk, fitting the smaller key into the lock. Inside it was a mobile phone.

The Abbot turned it on as he stared once more at the image frozen on his computer screen.

He punched the numbers into the phone, checked they were correct then pressed the call button.

35

Liv was driving slowly back along the I-95 with about ten thousand other people when her cell began to vibrate.

She glanced at the display. The caller's ID was withheld. She dropped it back on the seat and returned her gaze to the slow-moving traffic. It buzzed a few more times then fell silent. Having been awake for what felt like a week, her only priority now was to get home and into bed.

The buzzing started up again almost immediately – too quick to be the answering service calling back. Whoever it was must have hit redial as soon as they'd heard the voicemail message. Liv looked at the river of red brake lights snaking into the distance ahead of her. She clearly wasn't going anywhere in a hurry, so she swung her car over to the verge, slammed it in park, cut the engine and switched on her hazard lights.

She grabbed the cell and hit the answer button.

'Hello?'

'Hello.' The voice on the other end of the line was male, unfamiliar and roughened round the edges by the hint of an accent. 'Who is it I'm speaking with please?'

Liv's antennae bristled. 'Who are you trying to reach?'

There was a brief pause.

'I'm not exactly sure,' he said. 'My name is Arkadian. I'm a police inspector trying to identify a man who was found with this phone number on him.'

Liv ran his response through her journalist's mind, weighing every word. 'What department are you with?'

'Homicide.'

'So I guess you've either got a perp who won't talk or a victim who can't.'

'That's correct.'

'So which is it?'

He paused. 'I have an unidentified body. An apparent suicide.'

Liv's heart lurched. She ran through the list of men who had this number.

There was Michael, her ex-boyfriend, though she didn't really peg him as the suicidal type. Her old college professor, but he was on holiday with a new girlfriend who was about twenty years his junior – he *definitely* wasn't suicidal.

'How old is . . . was this man?'

'Late twenties, possibly early thirties.'

Definitely not her professor.

'The body does have some distinguishing marks.'

'What sort of marks?'

'Well . . .' The voice faltered, as if weighing up whether or not it should divulge anything further.

Liv knew from experience how reluctant cops were to give out information.

'You said this was a suicide, right?'

'Correct.'

'Well then, it's not like a murder where you need to hold back information to weed out false confessions, is it?'

Another pause. 'No.'

'So why don't you just tell me what sort of distinguishing marks you found and I'll tell you if I know who it is?'

'You seem very well informed about how these things work, Miss . . .?'

It was Liv's turn to falter. So far she'd managed to give nothing away while the caller had revealed his name, his profession and the purpose of his call. The crackle of the long-distance line punctuated the silence. 'Where are you calling from, Inspector?'

'I'm calling from the city of Ruin, in southern Turkey.' That explained the crackly line and the accent. 'You're in the United States, aren't you? New Jersey. At least, that's where your number is registered.'

'They clearly didn't make you an inspector for nothing.'

'New Jersey's the Garden State, isn't it?'

'That's the one.'

The crackle returned to the line. Arkadian's attempt to loosen her up with small talk clearly wasn't working. 'OK,' he said, trying a fresh tack. 'I'll do you a deal. You tell me who you are, then I'll tell you what distinguishing marks we found on the body.'

Liv chewed on her bottom lip, weighing her options. She didn't really want to give up her name, but she was intrigued and she really wanted to know who had been walking around with her very private phone number and was now lying on a mortuary slab. A beep sounded in her ear. She glanced at the grey display screen. A triangle with an exclamation mark flashed above the words LOW BATTERY. She normally had about a minute between this and total shut down, sometimes even less.

'My name's Liv Adamsen,' she blurted. 'Tell me about the body.'

She heard a faint and infuriatingly slow tapping as her name was fed into a computer.

'Scars –' the voice said finally.

She was about to ask another question when the floor gave way beneath her.

Late twenties, early thirties . . .

Her left hand moved involuntarily to her side. 'Did the body . . . does he have a scar on his right side, about six inches long . . . like a cross laid on its side?'

'Yes,' the voice replied with the softness of rehearsed condolence. 'Yes, he does.'

Liv stared straight ahead. Gone were the I-95 and the

morning traffic crawling into Newark. Instead she saw the face of a scruffily handsome boy with dirty blonde hair grown long, standing on Bow Bridge in Central Park.

'Sam,' she said softly. 'His name's Sam. Samuel Newton. He's my brother.'

Another image filled her mind: Sam back-lit by a low spring sun casting long shadows across the tarmac of Newark International Airport. He'd stopped at the top of the steps leading up to the plane that would take him to the mountain ranges of Europe. Shifted the bag on his shoulder containing all his worldly goods and turned to wave. It was the last time she had seen him.

'How did he die?' she whispered.

'He fell.'

She nodded to herself as the image of the golden boy faded and was replaced by the shimmering red river of the Interstate. It was what she always thought had happened. Then she remembered something else the Inspector had said.

'You said it was suicide?'

'Yes.'

More memories surfaced. Troubled memories that made her soul feel heavy and brought fresh tears to her eyes. 'How long do you think he's been dead?'

There was a brief pause before Arkadian answered. 'It happened this morning . . . local time.'

This morning? He'd been alive all that time . . .

'If you want, I can call your local police department,' Arkadian said, 'send some photos over and get someone to bring you in to formally identify the body.'

'No!' Liv said sharply.

'I'm afraid we need someone to identify him.'

'I mean it won't be necessary to send photos. I can be there in . . . maybe twelve hours . . .'

'Honestly, you don't need to come here to identify the body.'

'I'm in the car now. I can head straight to the airport.'

'It really isn't necessary.'

'Yes it is,' she said. 'It is necessary. My brother disappeared eight years ago. Now you're telling me that, until a few hours ago, he was still alive. I've *got* to come . . . I *need* to know what the hell he's been doing all these –'

Then her battery ran out.

36

The man with the freckled hands sat at the café pretending to read the sports pages. The place was busy, and he'd only just managed to grab a table right at the edge of the cool shadow cast by the awning that stretched over the pavement. He watched the sun creep slowly across the white linen tablecloth towards him and shuffled back in his chair.

From where he was sitting he could see the Citadel rising up in the middle distance, almost as if it were watching him. The sight of it made him uneasy. His paranoia was not entirely groundless. Almost as soon as he had finished paying the traveller's cheques into an account at the First Bank of Ruin that no one but he knew about, he had received two new messages. The first was from someone he'd occasionally done business with, requesting the same information he had just sold. The second was from his contact in the Citadel, offering to pay handsomely for his ongoing loyalty and regular updates. It was proving to be a very lucrative morning indeed. Nevertheless he did feel slightly uneasy taking money for 'ongoing loyalty' when here he was, in plain view of the Citadel, about to give the same information to somebody else.

He glanced up from his paper and waved at the waiter to bring him his bill. It was odd that this case in particular was proving of such interest to so many. It wasn't a murder or a sex case, both of which were traditionally his best earners. The waiter swept past, leaving a small round plate on the table with the bill trapped beneath a mint at its centre. He'd only had a coffee but he pulled out his wallet, selected a particular credit card and exchanged it for the mint, which he popped in his mouth. He laid his paper on the white linen tablecloth and smoothed it down, feeling the slight lump inside it. He leaned back in his chair and looked away, just another tourist enjoying the weather, as the waiter scooped up the newspaper and the plate without breaking his stride.

The sun continued to creep across the sky and the man pushed his chair further back. It had to be sex. He'd had a peek through the file himself the first time he'd swiped it and there was definitely something kinky going on, judging by all those scars. His guess was something weird that the holy folks were trying to cover up.

He also knew that the other party he was hawking the information to had no love for the Citadel, or the people inside it. The information he'd fed them before proved that. He'd given them the case file relating to the paedophile priest scandal a few years back, and another time he'd provided names and numbers of key witnesses when a bunch of charities affiliated to the Church were being investigated for fraud. He figured this must be the same kind of deal. They were probably trying to find out as much as possible so they could fan the flames of any breaking scandal and embarrass the hell out of the holier-than-thous up on the hill. All of which was good news for him. A nice juicy sex scandal with a religious angle would play out nicely in the tabloids – and they were the best payers of all.

He looked back up at the mountain and smirked. If they wanted to give him a bonus for his loyalty then more fool them. Maybe that kind of thinking worked up there where people believed in the great hereafter, but in the real world the only thing that mattered was the here and now. He wasn't going to give them an update anytime soon either. Getting large files to them was such a pain. He didn't mind forwarding bullet-points via the new text number they'd given him; at least that was a step in the right direction. But he'd already trekked up the holy hill once today with a flash drive in his hand; the update could wait until tomorrow. They still paid him either way.

The waiter drifted past again, placing the dish back on the table with the credit card tucked under the receipt. The man picked it up and put it back in his wallet. He didn't need to sign anything or punch in his PIN number, his coffee was already paid for and his account had just been credited with over a thousand dollars. He buttoned his jacket and with a final nervous glance up at the cloudless sky, he put on his cap and slipped away from the café and back into the crowd.

Kathryn Mann sat four tables behind him in the depths of the awning's shadow. She watched the informant shuffle away through the foot traffic on the great eastern boulevard, his baseball cap and raincoat incongruous in the bright sunlight. The waiter appeared by her side and placed her bill on the table along with the newspaper. She tucked it into her bag, feeling the bulge of the envelope inside it. Then she paid her bill in cash, making sure she left an extravagant tip, and headed off in the opposite direction.

37

Liv sat in the big steel-and-glass box of Newark Liberty Airport – Terminal C – sipping what was practically a bucket of black coffee. She stared up at the departure board. Her flight still wasn't boarding.

As soon as her phone had died she'd raced home as fast as the so-called 'rush-hour' traffic had allowed and booked herself on the next flight to Europe. The first leg of her journey was due to takeoff at ten-twenty, which gave her just enough time to stuff a few things into a holdall, grab her work cell phone and charger and jump into a cab.

She'd switched the SIM card from her private one on the way and discovered that Arkadian had left her a long message trying once again to dissuade her from coming. He'd given his direct line and cell number and asked her to call him back. She saved the message and stared out of the window all the way to the airport. She would call him back. She'd call him when she was staring out of the window of a Turkish taxi and heading to his office.

It was only when she'd finally checked in that the adrenalin ran out and exhaustion took over. She knew she'd be able to sleep as soon as she got on the flight, or at least grab as many z's as premium economy would allow, but first she had to stay awake long enough to get on the plane, hence the industrial-sized coffee.

Her phone vibrated in her pocket. She pulled it from her jacket and checked the caller ID. The number was withheld. She should have turned it off. Now she was going to have the

Inspector asking more questions or trying to persuade her to stay away. She exhaled wearily, suddenly craving a cigarette, and pressed the green answer button to stop the infernal buzzing.

'Hello,' she said.

'Hello,' a deep voice replied.

It was not the Inspector.

'Who is this please?'

There was the slightest pause, one that even in her sleep-starved, coffee-frazzled state put her immediately on her guard. In her experience the only people who hesitated when you asked their name were people who didn't want to tell you.

'I'm a colleague of Inspector Arkadian,' the voice rumbled. The English was accented like Arkadian's, but he sounded older, more authoritative.

'Are you his boss?' she asked.

'I'm a colleague. Has he contacted you?'

Liv frowned. Why was one cop checking up on another via a witness? That wasn't the way things worked. They talked to each other, not to outsiders.

'Why don't you ask him?' she said.

'He hasn't been in the office for a few hours,' the voice replied. 'So I thought I'd give you a try. I assume you have spoken with him.'

'We spoke.'

'Of what did you speak?'

Her antennae continued to bristle. This new guy just didn't sound like a cop, at least not any she knew. Maybe they bred them differently over there.

A loud announcement echoed through the terminal, calling her flight. She squinted up at the departures board. Her flight was now boarding at gate 78, about as far away as it was possible to get without leaving the state.

'Listen,' she said, heaving herself wearily to her feet and grabbing her holdall, 'I've had virtually no sleep, I've drunk about a gallon of coffee, and I've just had some really bad news, so I'm really not in the most sociable of moods. If you want to be briefed on my earlier conversation, ask Arkadian. I'm sure his memory is every bit as good as mine, probably a damn sight better right at this moment.'

She hung up and hit the 'off' button before it had a chance to ring again.

38

As soon as Liv hung up, the Abbot ordered Athanasius to fetch Brother Samuel's personal file from the library. He'd also asked him to bring the files of each current member of the Carmina as a plan formed in his mind.

Bad news, she had told him. *Some really bad news . . .* And Arkadian had taken the trouble to call her . . .

It wasn't possible. No one could enter the Citadel if they had any living relatives. The absence of family ties meant there would be no emotional pull away from their work inside the holy mountain and no desire to communicate with the outside world. The security of the Citadel and the preservation of its secrets were absolutely reliant on this rule never being broken, and the background checks for any new applicant were exacting, rigorously carried out and always erred on the side of caution. If someone's family records had been destroyed in a fire, they were rejected. If they had one distant cousin, whom they'd never met and believed to be dead but couldn't trace, they were rejected.

The files arrived within five minutes. Athanasius placed them wordlessly on the Abbot's desk then vanished from the room.

Like all inhabitants of the Citadel, Brother Samuel's file was thorough and detailed and comprised copies, and even some originals, of every significant document tracing the story of his life: school reports, work history from his social security number, even police arrest sheets – everything.

The Abbot scanned the documents for all references to

family. He found death certificates; his mother had died when he was just a few days old, and his father perished in a car accident when Samuel was eighteen. Both sets of grandparents had long since passed on. His father had been an only child, and his mother's only brother had died of leukaemia aged eleven. There were no uncles, no aunts, no cousins, no brothers, no sisters. All was as it should be.

A gentle tap dragged his attention from the file. He looked up as the door opened far enough to allow Athanasius to slip back into the room.

'Forgive the intrusion, Brother Abbot,' he said, 'but the Prelate has just sent word that he is feeling well enough to see you. You are to go to his quarters half an hour before Vespers.'

The Abbot glanced at the clock. Vespers was two hours hence. The delay was probably to give the vampires who kept the Prelate alive enough time to pump some fresh blood into him. He had hoped to have more comforting news to impart by the time he had his audience. He glanced across at the large stack of red files containing the personal details of the Carmina. Maybe he would.

'Very well,' he said, closing Brother Samuel's file and placing it to one side. 'But I need you to do something for me beforehand. I want you to contact the source that provided us with the police file. I believe the inspector on the case has since spoken with a woman. I want to know who she is, I want to know what was said, and most of all – I want to know *where* she is.'

'Of course,' Athanasius said. 'I will find out all I can and brief you before your meeting.'

The Abbot nodded and watched him bow and back out of the room before returning his attention to the tower of files before him.

There were sixty-two in total, each containing the detailed history of a Carmina, the red cloaks, the guild of guards who protected the passageways to the forbidden sections of the mountain; men who had proved themselves fit for these martial tasks both in their previous lives and in their subsequent devotion to the Citadel. As members of the Carmina they were also possible future Sancti, though as yet they knew nothing of the true nature of the Sacrament, so could, if necessary, be sent back into the world without compromising its security.

He slid the first folder from the top of the pile and opened it, shuffling aside the usual collection of medical records and school admission reports in search of other documents – military service histories, arrest reports, prison records – that would tell him if this man was the one he was looking for.

39

Kathryn Mann sat in the privacy of her apartment, studying the contents of the stolen file on her laptop. Because she'd received it more than an hour after the Citadel got their copy, hers was slightly more up to date and contained a rough transcript of Arkadian's conversation with Liv. It also had a link to her profile page at the American newspaper she worked at. She speed-read the case notes then grabbed her phone and pressed the redial button.

'I've got it,' she said as soon as her father answered.

'And?'

'Definitely a Sanctus,' she said, reviewing the stark images from the post-mortem showing the familiar latticework of ceremonial scars on the monk's body.

'Interesting,' Oscar said. 'And there still appears to be no official word from the Citadel claiming him. They're frightened of something.'

'Maybe, but there's something else in the file, something . . . unbelievable.' She looked at the photograph of the pretty young journalist staring out at her from the browser window. 'He has a sister.'

She heard her father catch his breath.

'That can't be,' he said. 'If he had a sister, he can't have been a Sanctus. He can't even have come from inside the Citadel.'

'But he has the scars,' she said. 'He was definitely fully ordained. He's been branded with the Tau. So he must have come from inside the Citadel and he *must* have seen the Sacrament.'

'Then find the sister,' Oscar said. 'Find her and protect her with everything we have. And I mean *everything*.'

The line went quiet. Both of them knew what he meant.

'I understand,' Kathryn said finally.

'I know it's dangerous,' Oscar said, 'but this girl will have no idea what's coming at her. We have to protect her. It's our duty.'

'I know.'

'And one other thing . . .'

'Yes?'

'Make up the spare room and get some good scotch in,' he said, the warmth returning to his voice. 'I think it's time I came home.'

40

The Abbot swept through the dark stone corridors of the mountain on his way to the Prelate, troubled by the lack of comforting news he carried with him. It was bad enough that for the first time in nearly ninety years someone had almost escaped from the Citadel. That he had perished in the process was the only bright spot on the horizon. The fact that he now appeared to have a living relative made it possibly the worst breach of Citadel security in the last two hundred years – perhaps even longer. There was also no getting away from the fact that it was ultimately his responsibility.

Nothing short of rapid and successful containment of the situation would be expected, and in order for that to happen he needed to be given a free hand to act as decisively as he saw fit – not only inside the Citadel, but outside as well – and for that he would need the Prelate's blessing.

He nodded to the guard permanently stationed by the Prelate's private quarters. Traditionally the Citadel guards would have been skilled with crossbow, sword and dagger, but times had changed. Now a wrist holster containing a Beretta 92 double-action pistol with a full clip loaded with parabellums nestled within the loose sleeves of their russet red cassocks. The guard heaved open the door to let him pass. He wasn't one of the men he'd picked from the stack of files.

The door banged shut behind him, echoing briefly in the cavernous hallway. The Abbot strode towards the elegant stairway leading up to the Prelate's stateroom. He heard the hiss of a ventilator somewhere in the darkness ahead, rhythmically forcing oxygen into its occupant's ancient lungs.

The chamber was even darker than the hallway and the Abbot had to slow as he entered it, unsure of what lay in his path. A meagre fire crackled in the grate, sucking air from the room in exchange for a little illumination and a dry, smothering heat. The only other light came from the bank of electronic machines that worked round the clock, oxygenating the Prelate's blood, removing his waste, keeping him alive.

The Abbot moved tentatively towards the huge four-poster bed dominating the space and began to make out the gaunt shape, white and insubstantial, lying in the middle of it. In the dim glow it looked as though the Prelate was trapped in the centre of a web of tubes and wires like a cave-dwelling spider. Only his eyes appeared to have any substance. They were dark and alert and watched his visitor make his approach.

The Abbot reached across the acres of linen to take the Prelate's claw-like hand. Despite the stifling heat in the room, it was as cold as the mountain. He lowered his head and kissed the ring hanging loosely on the third finger which bore the seal of his exalted office.

'Leave us,' the Prelate said, in a voice both dry and laboured.

Two Apothecaria in white cassocks rose from their seats like phantoms. The Abbot had not even noticed them in the shadows. Each checked and adjusted something on one of the many machines, turning up the alarm volumes so they could hear them from the stairs, then silently glided from the room. The Abbot turned back to his master and found the bright eyes burning into him.

'Tell me . . . everything . . .' the Prelate whispered.

The Abbot outlined the sequence of the morning's events, leaving nothing out, while the Prelate continued to skewer him with his needle eyes. Everything sounded worse spoken out loud than it had when rehearsed in his head on the way over. He also knew from experience that the Prelate was not a man given to leniency. He had been Abbot himself the last time a novice had betrayed them, during the time of the First Great War, and his ruthlessness in clearing up that potential mess had ultimately provided his ticket to the Prelature. The Abbot secretly hoped that a successful containment operation now might do the same for him.

The Abbot finished his report and the old man's eyes released him and fixed instead on a spot somewhere in the darkness above the bed. His long hair and beard were wispy and whiter even than the sheets that covered him like a shroud. His only movements were the rhythmic rise and fall of his chest and the quiver of arteries pulsing weakly beneath the paper-thin skin.

'A sister?' the Prelate said finally.

'Not yet confirmed, your holiness, but nevertheless a source of grave and immediate concern.'

'Grave and immediate concern . . . for her, perhaps . . .'

The Prelate's speech was fractured into small clusters of words, each sentence broken every few seconds by the respirator as it pushed air into his tired lungs.

'I'm glad your holiness agrees,' the Abbot replied.

The sharp eyes turned on him once more.

'I have agreed nothing,' the Prelate replied. 'I assume by this visit . . . where you bring me nothing . . . but bad news . . . and question marks . . . that you wish for me . . . to grant you permission . . . to silence the girl.'

'It would seem prudent.'

The Prelate sighed and returned his gaze to the canopy of darkness above his bed.

'More death,' he said, almost to himself. 'So much blood.'

He took several deep breaths and the hiss of the respirator rose to fill the silence.

'For thousands of years now,' he continued in the same halting manner 'we have been keepers . . . of the Sacrament . . . a secret that has been handed down . . . in an unbroken line . . . from the original founders . . . of our church. Dutifully . . . we

131

have kept the secret . . . but it has also kept us . . . It keeps us still . . . locked away from the world . . . demanding so much sacrifice . . . so much blood . . . just to keep it hidden. Do you ever ask yourself . . . Brother Abbot . . . what is our purpose here?'

'No,' he replied, unsure of where the question was heading. 'Our work here is self evident. It is God's work.'

'Do not patronize me with seminary platitudes,' the Prelate said with surprising energy. 'I am not a fresh-faced novice. I mean our *specific* purpose. Do you really believe it is God's pure work we do here?'

'Of course.' The Abbot frowned. 'Our calling is righteous. We shoulder the burden of mankind's past for the sake of its future.'

The Prelate smiled. 'How blessed you are, to have such confidence in your answer.' His eyes drifted upwards once more. 'As death creeps nearer . . . I must confess . . . things look very different to me . . . Life shines . . . in strange ways . . . once lit by death's dark light . . . But I will be cured of life . . . soon enough . . .'

The Abbot began to remonstrate, but the Prelate raised his almost transparent hand to silence him.

'I am old, Brother Abbot . . . too old . . . As I approach my second . . . century, I feel . . . the burden of my years . . . I used to think . . . the long life, and staunch . . . health one enjoyed . . . as a result of living . . . inside this mountain . . . was a blessing . . . I believed it was proof . . . that God smiled upon us . . . and upon our work . . . Now I am not . . . so sure . . . In every culture . . . and in all of literature . . . long life is ever portrayed . . . as nothing more . . . than a terrible curse . . . visited upon the damned . . .'

'Or the divine,' the Abbot said.

'I hope you are right . . . Brother Abbot . . . I have given it . . . much thought of late . . . I wonder . . . when my time finally comes . . . will the Lord be pleased . . . with the work I have done . . . in His holy name . . .? Or will He be ashamed . . .? Will all my life's efforts . . . prove to be nothing . . . more than a bloody exercise . . . in protecting the reputations . . . of men who have long since . . . turned to dust . . .?'

His voice trailed away with a dry rattle and the dark eyes flitted across to a pitcher of water by his bed.

The Abbot poured a glass and lifted the Prelate's head to it, helping him take tiny sips between the relentless insinuations of the ventilator. Despite the oppressive heat, the Prelate's head felt inhumanly cold. He laid it carefully back down on the pillow and returned the glass to the table. When he looked back, the Prelate's eyes were focused once more on the patch of nothingness above his bed.

'I stare death in the face . . . every day . . .' he said, studying the darkness. 'I watch him . . . and he watches me . . . I wonder why . . . he keeps his distance . . . Then you come here . . . talking soft words . . . that do little to hide your . . . hard desire for blood . . . and I think to myself . . . perhaps Death is cunning . . . Maybe he keeps me alive . . . so I can grant you . . . the powers you request . . . Then your actions will provide him . . . with far fresher souls . . . than mine to sport with . . .'

'I do not desire blood,' the Abbot said. 'But sometimes our duties require it. The dead keep secrets better than the living.'

The Prelate turned once more and fixed the Abbot with his unwavering gaze.

'Brother Samuel . . . may disagree . . .'

The Abbot said nothing.

'I am not going to . . . grant your wish . . .' the Prelate said suddenly, his eyes crawling over the Abbot's face, feeding on his reaction. 'Locate and monitor her . . . by all means . . . but do not harm her . . . I expressly forbid it . . .'

The Abbot was stunned.

'But, Your Holiness, how can we let her live if there is even the smallest chance she knows the identity of the Sacrament?'

'I doubt . . . she knows anything . . .' the Prelate replied. 'Having a telephone number . . . is one thing . . . Having a telephone . . . another thing entirely . . . Do you really think Brother

Samuel . . . would have had time . . . to make a call . . . between learning our great secret . . . and his unfortunate death . . .? Are you really so eager . . . to take a life . . . on the basis of such . . . a slender possibility . . .?'

'I do not think we should take even the smallest chance, when our order is at risk. The Church is weak. People don't believe in anything any more. Any revelations now about the origins of their faith may destroy everything. You have seen within these walls how some react when the Sacrament is revealed to them, even after they have been carefully screened and prepared. Imagine if it were revealed to the world? There would be chaos. With respect, Your Holiness, we need to protect the Sacrament now more than we ever have. The future of our faith may depend on it. This girl is too dangerous to live.'

'All things must end . . .' the Prelate said. 'Nothing lasts forever . . . If the Church is weak . . . then maybe all this . . . has come about for a reason . . . Maybe it is time . . . for us to put ourselves . . . in the hands of fate . . . Let the dice fall . . . how they may . . . I have made my decision . . . Tell my attendants . . . I wish to rest . . . And close the door . . . as you leave . . .'

The Abbot stood for a few moments, not quite believing either that the interview was over, or that his petition had been denied. He watched the Prelate staring upwards like the carving upon a tomb.

Would that you were already in one, he thought as he bowed his head and backed slowly away from the bed before slipping from the stifling room.

Outside, the Apothecaria hovered in the gloomy hallway.

'Leave him,' the Abbot said as he stormed past. 'He wishes to be alone with thoughts of his legacy.'

The white cassocks exchanged puzzled looks, not sure what the Abbot meant. By the time they turned to ask him, he was already at the bottom of the stairway.

Old fool, the Abbot thought as he threw open the door and

surged past the guard. *No wonder our beloved church has become so weakened, with such a man at the head.*

He welcomed the chill of the mountain and mopped sweat from his brow with his sleeve as he made for the great cathedral cave, where the denizens of the mountain would soon be heading for Vespers.

Locate her and monitor her.

The Prelate's words echoed in the Abbot's mind, taunting him. But there was one piece of information he had kept back. When he'd spoken to the girl he'd heard a Tannoy in the background. She had been at an airport. She was coming to Ruin.

He'd locate her all right, and put her somewhere she could be monitored very closely. And the moment Death finally finished toying with his master, he would deal with her in his own way.

41

Robbery and Homicide was calmer now. It was just after six o'clock in the evening. Quiet time, except for the steady clatter of keyboards being pecked by one-fingered typists. People didn't tend to commit robberies or murder in the afternoon, so it was a good time to catch up on paperwork. Arkadian sat at his desk and frowned at his computer. His phone had hardly stopped. Somehow the press had got hold of his direct line and it rang every two or three minutes with someone new asking about the case whose file currently filled his screen. The chief of police had also called him personally. He wanted to know when they could issue an official statement. Arkadian assured him he'd have one as soon as the witness checks came back. And that was why he was frowning.

Following his conversation with the girl he'd run the name she'd given him through the various personnel databases and managed to build up the beginnings of a dossier on Samuel Newton. He'd found his birth certificate at least, though even that seemed incomplete. It confirmed that he'd been born in a place called Paradise, West Virginia, to an organic horticulturalist father and a botanist mother, but the name of the infant was recorded simply as 'Sam', not 'Samuel'. Several other parts of the form were blank, including the column recording the child's sex, but his search had also thrown up an associated death certificate – recording the sad fact that his mother had died eight days later.

His first few years were sketchy and a lot of the usual documents Arkadian expected to find were missing. A collection of assorted newspaper clippings picked up his story aged nine and charted the development of his precocious mountaineering abilities. One included a black-and-white photo of the young Sam clinging to a precipitous rock he had obviously just conquered. Arkadian compared the image of the skinny, grinning boy with the head shots he had taken during the post-mortem. There was definitely a resemblance.

According to the last of the newspaper clippings, dated nine years later, it seemed that young Sam's climbing skills had led indirectly to the death of his father. One spring, as they were driving back from a competition in the Italian Alps, their car had spun out of control during a freak blizzard and slid into a ravine. Both father and son initially survived the crash, though they had suffered some pretty significant injuries. Sam had woken up with snow coming in through a broken side window, not really remembering where he was or how he'd got there. His arm hurt like hell; other than that he felt cold, but OK. He discovered that his father, though awake and fairly alert, was bleeding from a large gash in his head. He was also trapped under the twisted wreckage of the dashboard and complaining that he couldn't feel anything from the waist down.

Sam had wrapped his father as warmly as he could with whatever he could find in and around the car, then made his way up the wall of the ravine in search of help. It had taken him quite a while to scale the icy rock face because he was fighting a raging blizzard and the arm he'd described as 'hurting like hell' was actually fractured in two places. He eventually managed to climb back up to the road and flag down a passing truck.

By the time the Medivac team arrived, his father had lost too much blood, been in the cold too long and slipped into a coma from which he never recovered. He died three days later. Sam was just eighteen. He flew back to the US with his climbing trophy in his hand and his father in a box in the hold.

Arkadian had also managed to track down a passport application made when Sam had first started travelling the world on climbing expeditions. In a section headed 'Distinguishing Marks' the bearer was described as having a lateral scar at the base of the ribs on the right-hand side of his body; a scar in the shape of a cross. Arkadian felt that he'd found his man; yet there was still a lot that didn't add up.

Standard procedure for victim identification required that checks be carried out on any person stepping forward to identify a body, a necessary precaution to prevent false witness. When Arkadian had run the checks on Liv Adamsen of Newark, New Jersey, he'd discovered all the usual stuff: where she lived, her credit history and so on, none of which was particularly noteworthy. But the deeper he'd looked, the more puzzled he'd become.

Two things in particular rang alarm bells in his naturally suspicious mind. The first was her occupation. Liv Adamsen was an investigative reporter working on the crime desk of a large New Jersey paper. This was bad news, particularly on a case as public and newsworthy as this one. The second was less of a problem and more of a mystery. Despite the fact that Liv had correctly identified the dead man and reacted as a sister would, there was not one single record, in all of the checks he'd carried out, of any kinship. As far as Arkadian could establish from the complex paper trail weaving its way back through Samuel Newton's life, there was absolutely no evidence at all that he had a sister.

42

The Lockheed Tri-Star shuddered as the Cypress Turkish Airlines flight took off from London Stansted en route to the furthest edge of Europe. The moment the wheels left the tarmac the wind took over and the aircraft lurched as if unseen hands were trying to tear it apart and fling it back down to the ground.

It was a large plane, which was comforting; but it was also old, which was not. It still had aluminium flip-top ashtrays in the armrests that rattled as the plane wrestled its way upwards. Liv eyed them now, imagining a time when she could have calmed her nerves the old-fashioned way. Instead she tore the top off a packet of pickled ginger, the remains of an over-priced sushi takeaway she'd grabbed during her stop-over, and popped a sliver under her tongue. Ginger was good for stress and helped reduce travel sickness. She folded the top of the packet and squirrelled it away for the journey. She had a feeling this flight would test its reputation to the hilt.

She chewed the ginger slowly and glanced around at her fellow passengers. The cabin was only half-full; it was a particularly unsociable time of night. The old Lockheed lurched again as a fresh gust shoved it sideways. She could see the port wing from her window. It appeared to be flapping, albeit stiffly. She forced herself to look away.

She had hoped to get some sleep during this final leg of her journey, but there was absolutely no chance of that while crash anxiety continued to light up her nerve endings. She pulled out the other purchase she'd made during her stop-over – a travel guide to Turkey.

She flipped to the index. There was a whole chapter devoted to Ruin and a map reference. She turned to the map first. Like most people, she only had the vaguest idea where Ruin was. The ancient city, and the Citadel in particular, were like the pyramids in Egypt: everyone knew what they looked like, but few could pinpoint them in an atlas.

A triple-page fold-out showed Turkey, stretching like a bridge between mainland Europe and Arabia, hemmed in top and bottom by the Black Sea and Mediterranean respectively. The grid reference drew her to the right-hand side of the map, close to the border where Europe rubbed shoulders with the biblical lands of the Middle East.

She spotted two airport symbols to the north and south of the city of Gaziantep – where she was due to land in around four hours – but she couldn't see Ruin. She checked the reference and looked again. It was only after a few minutes' close scrutiny in the gloom of the cabin that she found it – west of the uppermost airport, where the Eastern Taurus mountains started to rise, right in the fold of the page and almost totally obscured by the straight black line of the grid. It struck Liv as bitterly apt that her brother should choose to hide away in such a place; somewhere so well known yet so obscure, nestling enigmatically in the crease of a map.

She flicked through the book until she found the chapter on Ruin and started to read, sucking up facts about the place she was heading to, logging and arranging them in her journalist's mind until they started to form a picture of the city where her brother had lived and died. It was a major religious centre; that made sense, given what Samuel had said to her the last time she'd seen him. It was also the world's oldest place of pilgrimage, owing to the health-giving properties of the waters that bubbled plentifully from the ground, ice melt from the mountains that surrounded it. That made sense also. She could imagine him working as a mountain-guide, hiding under a borrowed name somewhere well off the beaten track while he sought the peace he'd set out to find.

I want to be closer to God. That's what he'd said.

She'd often wondered at these words in the silence that followed his disappearance, torturing herself with the darkest possibilities of their meaning. But somehow she'd known, even as that silence stretched into years, that he was alive. She'd still believed it even when the letter from the US Bureau of Vital Records had told her otherwise. And now she was following the path he had trodden, to find out about the life he had led there. She was hoping the Inspector would be able to point her to where he'd lived and maybe some of the people who'd known him. Maybe they could give her some answers, and fill in the blanks that echoed in her mind.

She turned the page and stared at a photograph of the old town clustered at the base of the soaring mountain. The caption beneath identified it as *The most visited place of antiquity in the world and supposed repository of a powerful, ancient relic known as The Sacrament.*

On the page opposite was a brief chronicle of the Citadel, expanding on its incredible age and outlining its constant presence throughout human history. Liv had assumed the Citadel was a Christian shrine, but the text revealed that it had only aligned itself with Christianity in the fourth century following the Roman emperor Constantine's conversion. Prior to that it had been independent of any organized religion, though it had exerted a huge influence in almost every ancient belief system: the Babylonians had considered it the first and greatest Ziggurat; the Ancient Greeks worshipped it as the home of the gods and renamed it Olympus; even the Egyptians held it as sacred, the Pharoahs journeying across the sea to the Hittite empire to visit the mountain. It was even believed by some that the great pyramids of Giza were attempts to recreate the mountain in the hope that the magical properties of the Citadel could be reproduced in Egypt.

Once the Citadel had made its political move to endorse Christianity, the operational centre of the Church moved to

Rome to enjoy the full protection of the newly created Holy Roman Empire. The Citadel, however, remained the power behind the throne, issuing its edicts and dogma through Rome now, as well as a new version of everything through the publication of an authorized bible. Any dissent from this official view was seen as heresy and was crushed, first by the might of the Roman army and subsequently by any king and emperor trying to curry favour with the Church and, by extension, with God.

Liv scanned the blood-soaked details, disturbed as much by the riot of exclamation marks and adverbs as anything they described. She didn't care about the brutal history of the place, or what secrets it was meant to contain; she only cared about her brother, and what in this ancient city had driven him to his death.

The plane shuddered and a soft *bong* caused Liv to look up. The fasten seat belt sign had been turned on again. The no smoking sign stayed resolutely on. It taunted her through the rest of the flight as the night got darker and the storm grew steadily worse.

43

The devotional day within the Citadel was divided into twelve different offices, the most important being the four nocturnes. They took place each night when it was believed the absence of God's light allowed the forces of evil to prosper. It was a theory any police officer, in any major city in the world, would agree with: dark deeds are almost always done under cover of night.

The first of the nocturnes was Vespers, a formal service held in the one place large enough for the entire population of the Citadel to witness the dying of another day – the great cathedral cave in the eastern section of the mountain. The first eight rows were filled with the black cassocks of the spiritual guilds – the priests and librarians who spent their lives in the darkness of the great library. Behind them sat a thin white line of Apothecaria, then twenty rows of brown cassocks, the material guilds – masons, carpenters, and other skilled technicians whose job it was to constantly monitor and maintain the physical wellbeing of the Citadel.

The russet cassocks of the guards slashed across the body of the congregation, separating the higher guilds at the front from the numerous grey cloaks at the back; the administrative monks who did everything from cooking and cleaning to providing manual labour for the other guilds.

Above the multi-coloured congregation, in their own elevated gallery, sat the green-clad brethren of the Sancti – thirteen in all, including the Abbot, though today there were only eleven. The Abbot was not among them, and neither was Brother Gruber.

When the sun had dipped past the three great casements behind the altar, the large rose window flanked by two triangles representing God's all-seeing eye, everybody filed out for their last meal in the refectory before retiring to the dormitories.

All, that is, but three men dressed in the red cassocks of the Carmina.

A sandy-haired monk with a flat, impassive face and the build of a middleweight boxer headed across the echoing space towards a door directly below the Sanctus balcony. The other two followed. No one said a word.

Cornelius's record as an officer in the British Army had singled him out to the Abbot as the group's natural leader, so he had passed a note to him on the way into Vespers, containing the two other names, instructions and a map. Cornelius glanced at the map as he passed out of the cathedral cave, turning left as instructed and proceeding down the narrow, less trodden tunnels towards the abandoned section of the mountain.

Dusk deepened in the tangled sprawl of the old city. The last of the tourists were ushered from the old town by polite stewards and portcullises clanked emphatically into place, sealing it for the night. To the west, in the section known as the Lost Quarter, the shadows began to take human form as the nightly traffic in flesh resumed its furtive trade.

To the east, Kathryn Mann sat in her living room waiting for her printer to complete its task. She now regretted having programmed it for the highest quality image as she watched it appear line by steady line. The TV news reported large groups of people having gathered in silent tribute to the man they did not yet know as Brother Samuel in America, Europe, Africa, Australia, even China, where public demonstrations, particularly of a religious nature, were not undertaken lightly. A woman interviewed outside the Cathedral of St John the Divine in New York City was asked why she felt so strongly about the monk's death.

'Because we need faith, you know?' Her voice was taut with emotion. 'Because we need to know the Church cares for us – and is lookin' out for us. If one of their own is driven to this, and the Church don't even say nuthin' about it . . . well, where does that leave us . . .?'

People on every continent were saying more or less the same. The monk's lonely death had clearly touched them. His mountain-top vigil seemed to symbolize their own sense of isolation, and the silence that followed, evidence of a Church that did not care; a Church that had lost its compassion.

Maybe change is happening, she thought as she finally removed the sheet of paper from the printer and stared at the photograph of Liv Adamsen lifted from the police file.

Perhaps the prophecy is coming true after all.

She turned off the TV and grabbed a couple of apples on her way out. The airport was a thirty-minute drive away. She had no idea how long she'd have to wait there.

44

A heavy door shrieked open on rusty hinges. Cornelius stepped through it and reached for the burning torch that had been left for them. He held it in front of him as they made their way into the forgotten depths of the Citadel. Brother Johann at his shoulder, his dark matinee-idol looks belying a Scandinavian ancestry, his blue eyes full of the ice of his homeland. Brother Rodriguez brought up the rear, towering a foot above them both, his slender height at odds with his urban Hispanic roots, his golden eyes watchful and blank as he loped through the low tunnels.

The crunch of their footfalls and the crackle of the burning flambeaux echoed around them as the mountain's history rose out of the dark to greet them. Doorways yawned here and there like mouths frozen in mourning. Beyond them they glimpsed remnants of the lives once lived here: beds sagging under the weight of water-logged straw and splintered benches that could hardly bear the weight of the ghosts who now sat upon them. From time to time crumbled stone littered the pathway and streaks of limescale flared white in the darkness like the passing phantoms of those who had once walked there.

Ten minutes later they saw a faint orange light ahead, flickering from a doorway that dribbled smoke across a ceiling carved in a time when people were smaller. They smelt burning wood as they got nearer and felt the cold air give way to a little warmth. Cornelius pushed through into a cave that might once have been a kitchen. On the far side of the chamber a figure squatted by an old-fashioned range, poking with a stick at a struggling fire.

'Greetings, Brothers,' the Abbot said, like an innkeeper welcoming travellers in from a blizzard. 'My apologies; this is a poor excuse for a fire. I'm afraid I seem to have lost the art of it. Please . . .' He gestured towards a table set with two large loaves and some fruit. 'Sit. Eat.'

The Abbot joined them at the table, watched them break bread in silence, taking none for himself. He scrutinized them as they ate, putting names to faces he had last seen in their personnel files. The tall one: Guillermo Rodriguez. Twenty-two years old. Originally from the Bronx. Former street rat and gang member. His records showed a string of arrests for arson, with stiffer sentences handed down each time. Spent half his life with a drug-addicted mother and the rest in a succession of juvenile detention centres. Found God after AIDS made him an orphan.

Opposite him sat Johann Larsson. Twenty-four. Dark haired, blue eyed and strikingly handsome. Born in the Abisko forests of northern Sweden into a separatist, pseudo-military religious commune he had been raised in the belief that the end was close, when the sinful millions would become devils and turn on the righteous. In order to protect himself and his extended 'family' from these imagined hordes he had learned how to use a gun at the same time as his A-B-C's. The end, when it did come, took a more tragic form. A lorry driver first raised the alarm when he spotted a timber wolf dragging a human leg across the road in front of him. The police unit that was dispatched discovered that the commune had been wiped out by a suicide pact. Johann was the only survivor. They found him curled up on a bed next to the corpse of his younger brother. He told the police his father had given him some pills to 'let him see God', but he'd been angry with him because he'd shouted at his brother, so had thrown them away. A succession of foster families failed to touch this beautiful, troubled boy. He was withdrawn, violently distrustful of strangers and clearly on the path to self-destruction. Then the church stepped in, sent him to one of their rehabilitation seminaries in America, and took him on as a lost son.

Then there was Cornelius Webster. Thirty-four. Grew up in an orphanage and went straight into the British Army as soon as he was old enough. Invalided out after watching his platoon burn alive in front of him when their armoured vehicle was hit by a rocket-propelled grenade. The scars on his face, like drops of pale wax that made his beard grow in patches, were the badges of this tragedy. The day he left the army he'd swapped the institutionalized life of a soldier for the institutionalized life of a monk. The Citadel was his family now, as it was to all of them.

The Abbot also matched their various skills to the mission he was about to give them: Cornelius with his age and authority; Johann with his distracting looks and perfect English, bait to catch a female fish; Rodriguez with his US passport and knowledge of the streets. Each had violence in their past and a sharp and zealous desire to prove themselves to God. He waited until they'd finished eating before speaking again.

'Please forgive the unorthodox nature of this meeting,' he said, the fire now framing him in a hazy red glow. 'But when I explain the reason, you will understand the need for such caution and secrecy.'

He tapped a finger against his pursed lips.

'This section of the mountain once housed a garrison of warrior monks, the Carmina, the red knights of the Citadel, the illustrious forebears of the guild you serve. They rode forth to root out false religions, crush false gods, destroy heretical churches, and purge misguided worshippers of their sins in the purifying fires of the Inquisition. These crusades were known as the *Tabula Rasa* – the Clean Slate – for no trace of heresy was ever left in their wake.'

He lowered his voice and leaned forward against the table, making it creak like the timbers of an ancient ship.

'The Carmina were not bound by the ordinary laws of man.' He regarded each of them individually. 'Nor by the laws of whatever land they found themselves in; for those were but the laws of kings and emperors, and the Carmina answered only to God. I bring you here now to resume their sacred mantle. We may no longer find ourselves besieged by armies, but we still have enemies. And we still have need of soldiers.'

He slid an envelope across the table to Cornelius.

'Here are details of what you must do and instructions as to how you can leave the mountain. I have chosen you because you each have within you the character and past experience to do God's work. Be guided by Him and not by earthly laws. Like your predecessors you must be single-minded in the performance of your duty. The threat is real. You must eliminate it.'

He pointed to the far side of the room where three identical canvas bags were propped against the wall.

'Inside those you will find currency, identification documents and civilian clothing. You will be met outside the walls of the old town two hours after midnight by two men who will provide transport, weapons and whatever else you need. Just as your forebears used mercenaries to assist them in their missions, you must use these men to help you in yours. But never forget that what you are doing for the love of God, *they* are doing for the love of money. So use them – but do not trust them.'

He paused.

'It is not lightly that I send you on this mission. Should you fall in your duty, as some of you might, then know you will be embraced by God as a blessed warrior, as those who fell before you. Those who do return will be welcomed back, not as members of the guild of guards you currently serve, but as the highest of our kind – a green cloak, a Sanctus. You may be aware,' he added, 'that there are already two vacancies. But I would expand our number to accommodate all of you who prove so worthy. And in rising to the highest level of our brotherhood you would, of course, be blessed with the sacred knowledge of that which I now ask you to protect.'

He rose from his seat and removed his Crux from his rope belt. 'You have a few hours in which to change and prepare for your return to the world. I will bless you now in the tradition of the order we revive here tonight.'

He raised the Tau above his head and began uttering the ancient blessing of war, in words as ancient as the mountain they now prayed in, and behind him the fire crackled and hissed, and threw his huge shadow across the ceiling of the cave.

Some hours later, a light tremor shook the ground by the old city wall, an echo of the storm flickering its way over the mountain peaks to the north. At the end of an alley between two multi-storey car parks, a heavy steel shutter rumbled upwards to reveal a gap just wide enough for a man to pass through. Three shadows peeled themselves away from the darkness, pieces of night dispersed by the wind. They headed down the alley towards a parked van with its rear doors unlocked.

The first fat spots of rain pinged down on the thin steel roof of the van and cracked against the bone-coloured flagstones as the three figures slipped inside. The doors clanged shut and the engine growled into life. The headlights flicked on, sweeping the dusty road as rain erupted across it like a contagion.

The van moved off, heading for the inner ring-road and the great eastern boulevard that would take them all the way to the airport. The rain intensified as they circled the old town, black tears weeping for all that had happened and all that might, running down the sides of the Citadel, down to the chalky earth where a moat once flowed and a man once swam, down narrow cobbled streets where red knights had ridden, to wash away the flowers and cards marking the spot where the monk had so recently fallen.

45

The Lockheed Tri-Star yawed and rolled as it slipped through the storm clouds guarding the descent into Gaziantep Airport. Lightning flared in the dimmed interior and the engines moaned as they struggled to grab hold of the slippery air. Liv clutched her guidebook as if it was a bible and looked around at the forty-or-so other passengers. None of them were sleeping either. Some appeared to be praying.

God damn you, Sam, she thought as the plane lurched again. *Eight years without a word and now you put me through this.*

She looked out of her rain-lashed window in time to see another bolt of lightning actually strike the wing. The engines roared in pain. She hoped to God the two incidents weren't connected and glanced yet again at the ashtray in her armrest, wondering what the penalty was for smoking on a commercial airliner. She was seriously considering it, whatever it was.

She peered once more into the turbulent night, hoping for some respite. As if by divine instruction, the clouds parted to reveal a dark, jagged landscape that twitched restlessly with the near constant flashes of lightning. In the distance she could make out the glow of a large town held in the natural cup of the mountain range like a shallow pool of gold. The rain running off the window made it shimmer like it wasn't quite solid. In its centre was a spot of darkness with four straight lines of light radiating out from it. It was Ruin, and the darkness at its centre, the Citadel. From her lofty vantage point it looked like a black gemstone set in the centre of a bright cross. Liv fixed on it, remembering everything she'd read about the place and all the blood that had been shed for the sake of the secret it contained.

Then the Lockheed banked unsteadily away, continuing its descent into Gaziantep Airport, and the Citadel slipped back into the night.

Kathryn Mann stood watching the flood of people pour through into the arrivals hall. Following the revelations in the stolen police file she'd figured the girl would come to Ruin as soon as possible to take possession of her brother's body. She'd felt the same way twelve years ago when her husband had been killed. She still remembered the urgent need to be with him, even though she knew he was dead.

Given the time of the phone interview recorded in the file, a travel agent's website had indicated that this was the first connecting flight the girl could have caught.

Freed from the customs hall, passengers raced for taxis or waiting relatives, or to be first in the queue to pay for their parking. Two flights had arrived at once, making it difficult to see anyone clearly as they emerged. Kathryn had memorized the girl's face from the printout but also had a name card as back up. She was about to hold it up when she spotted a man behind the opposite rail, holding up an identical sign. LIV ADAMSEN was printed on it in magic marker.

Kathryn felt her scalp prickle.

She slipped her hand into her coat pocket and curled it round the grip of her pistol, watching him out of the corner of her eye. He could be police. It was possible there had been further contact that she did not yet know about.

He was fairly tall and bulky. A sandy beard covered what looked like scarring on his cheeks. There was something unsettling about the way he surveyed the crowd, like a bear eyeing salmon in a stream. He had an air of authority, and it was this above all that made Kathryn fearful. They wouldn't send a ranking officer just to pick up a witness, especially not this late at night. He wasn't police.

A woman emerged from the customs hall and was moving with the crush of people. She had dirty blonde hair that fell forward over her face. She was looking down at a holdall, searching for something. She looked the right height, the right age.

Kathryn glanced across at the man with the sign. He'd seen her too. The girl fished a mobile phone out of her bag and looked up. It wasn't her. Kathryn's fingers relaxed and emerged from her pocket. The man continued to stare intently at the girl, watching her drift closer. When she was just a few feet from him he held up his sign, his face breaking into a quizzical grin. She just looked straight through him and carried on past.

The grin vanished and he returned to his surveillance. Kathryn did the same. By the time the last passenger drifted out into the concourse it was clear the girl had not been on this particular flight and Kathryn had learned two other things. Her instincts had been correct; the Sancti had indeed sent people to intercept the girl. And for whatever reason, they had no idea what she looked like.

46

It was not yet two in the morning when Liv cleared customs and emerged into the high-ceilinged and airy arrivals hall. Expressionist murals and hanging sculptures filled its cavernous space. She recognized some of the more dramatic moments of Ruin's long and bloody past from her in-flight reading.

The energetic historical figures contrasted starkly with the real people shuffling about below them. There were a few sharp-suited business types, scrutinizing their laptops and BlackBerrys, but not many. Small herds of dead-eyed visitors trundled aimlessly across the marble floors while a couple of bored cops looked on, each with an automatic weapon slung over their shoulder.

Most of the tourist traffic heading to Ruin flew into the larger airport north of Gaziantep as it was closer to the ancient stronghold. Liv hadn't considered any of this when booking her ticket; she'd just bought the first flight she thought she could catch. According to the guidebook there were still plenty of buses to the ancient city from the old airport, but at this time of the morning she figured she'd probably have to splash out on a cab just as soon as she'd got hold of some local cash.

As she scanned the place for a *bureau de change* she saw the tall, good-looking guy staring straight at her. She glanced past him at first, flustered by his direct gaze, then looked back. He was smiling at her now. She smiled back. Then he held up a card with her name written across it in magic marker.

'Miss Adamsen?' he asked, drifting closer.

She nodded, not quite sure what to make of him.

154

'Arkadian sent me,' he explained. His voice was deep. It sounded like it belonged to someone older. There was no trace of an accent in it.

'American?' Liv asked.

'I studied there,' he said, the smile remaining cool and steady. 'But don't be impressed. This is a tourist town, everyone speaks English here.'

She nodded as one mystery was solved, then frowned again as another presented itself.

'How did you know which plane –?'

'I didn't,' he cut in. 'I've met the last few international flights on the off chance you'd be on one of them.' He sounded pretty cheerful for a guy who'd been up half the night staking out an airport.

'First one I could get . . .' she said, feeling bad he'd been landed such a crappy detail.

'It's not a problem.' He pointed at the crumpled holdall dangling from her hand. 'That your luggage?'

'Yeah; but don't worry, I got it.' She hoisted it on to her shoulder and began following him across the shiny marble floor.

You sure don't get this kind of service in Jersey City, Liv thought as she fixed her eyes on the broad back cutting a swathe through the bovine knots of tourists. His long black trench coat billowed out behind him as he breezed along, giving him an air of dashing chivalry very much in keeping with the murals.

She slipped into a slowly moving revolving door. In the confined space she found herself standing close enough to be enveloped by his scent. Clean, astringent, with hints of leather and citrus and something ancient and comforting – incense maybe. Most of the cops she knew generally considered Old Spice the height of sophistication. She glanced up. He was taller than she'd thought, and handsome in a traditional, tall, dark kind of way – his eyes blue and icy, though his hair wasn't black, as she had first thought, but very dark brown. He was exactly the sort of man mothers warned their daughters about and fortune-tellers found lurking in crystal balls if you paid them enough.

The revolving door spun them gently into the night and the smell of rain on concrete rinsed through her travel-numbed senses. It was the freshest thing she'd encountered in more than twelve hours, but in the twisted world of the nicotine addict all it did was remind her how much she needed a cigarette. She stopped just outside and opened her bag. 'Where're you parked?'

The man turned and watched her fishing through the jumbled contents of her holdall. 'Right there.' He nodded towards the short-stay car park across the road.

Liv glanced out into the rain-whipped night. 'I packed in kind of a hurry,' she said. 'Don't . . . think . . . I've got a coat in here.'

The man held up his umbrella but Liv ignored it. She only had eyes for the crumpled pack of Luckies she'd finally managed to find. She tapped one out and plucked it from the packet with her mouth.

'Bit windy,' she said, hunching up her shoulders against the cold. 'Don't want you to bust your umbrella on my account. Tell you what . . . why don't you go get the car? I'll stay here and have one of these, then I won't get drenched and you won't have to sue me for passive smoking.'

The man hesitated, looked out at the sheets of rain gusting across the drop-off zone. 'OK. Don't move. I'll be right back.'

She watched him stride away, the wind grabbing the tails of his coat. She cupped her hand around the end of her cigarette, lit up and pulled nicotine and night air deep into her lungs. She breathed out, feeling the tension of the flight begin to melt and float away with the smoke. She stuffed the pack back into her bag, dug around until she found her cell phone and powered it up.

A van swished by in the rain, passing a bus shelter across the way where a security guard appeared to be rousting three young people who'd tried to bed down for the night. They looked like students who'd been partying too hard, or just regular vagrants who spent their life being moved on from one place to the next.

Welcome to Ruin . . .

The phone buzzed in Liv's hand as it caught a signal. There were three missed calls and two new messages. She was shifting her thumb across the keypad to dial her voicemail when a non-descript Renault saloon pulled up in front of her. The window slid down and the well-dressed cop smiled at her from behind the wheel. He leaned across and popped open the back door.

Liv took a final hungry drag on her cigarette, buried it in the sand-filled ashtray by the revolving door, then grabbed her bag and dashed across the wet sidewalk into the warm, dry comfort of the car.

'What's your name?' she said, pulling the door closed and reaching for the safety belt.

He put the car in gear and fell in line behind the cars and taxis pressing slowly towards the exit signs. 'Gabriel,' he said.

'Like the angel?'

She saw his eyes crinkle in the rear-view mirror. 'Like the angel.'

She leaned against the door and felt the weariness settle on her like a blanket. She was about to close her eyes when she remembered her messages. She dialled her voicemail and lifted the cell to her ear.

'Who are you calling?' the driver asked.

'Just getting my messages.' She stifled a yawn. 'Where we headed exactly?'

'Ruin,' he said, steering away from the traffic and down a service road. 'Where else?'

Then, through the crackle of storm static, her first message started to play.

47

'Hello ... er ... Miss Adamsen. This is Inspector Arkadian. I just wanted to say again how sorry ... for your loss ... e-mailed some photos to a Detective Berringer ... Newark PD ...'

Liv pressed the phone hard against her ear as the static rose, swamping parts of the message.

'He'll call you in the ... formally ID the ... He can deal with everything his end ... don't hesitate ... call me if you have an ...'

The message ended and her eyes jerked to the man sitting behind the wheel. If Arkadian had sent pictures for her to ID, it meant he didn't think she was coming. So why would he send someone to collect her? The second message started to play.

'Hi, my name is Detective Berringer with the Newark City Police Department ...'

She didn't wait to hear the rest.

He'd said his name was Gabriel. He'd said he was a cop.

No.

He'd never said he was a cop. He hadn't shown her his badge when he'd introduced himself. He just said Arkadian sent him and she had assumed the rest. *Stupid.* She'd been suckered by her own exhaustion and by the fact that he was nice-looking and polite. So who the hell was he?

'Everything OK?'

She looked up and met his eyes in the mirror.

'Yeah,' she said, suddenly aware that her face must look a picture of concern. 'Just work. I hopped the flight here in a bit of a hurry. Didn't have time to finish off a few things before I left. My boss is real pissed at me.'

His eyes flicked back to the road as a van hissed past in a cloud of spray. A squeal of tyres and the interior flooded with red. The van in front had braked hard. Too hard.

Gabriel followed suit. The Renault's wheels squealed across the greasy surface of the road. There was a violent jolt as its front bumper smashed into the back of the van. Liv was thrown forward hard against her belt. There was a sharp crack and for the briefest of moments, before the airbags deployed, she thought she'd been shot.

Then everything went into slow motion.

48

Before the driver's airbag even started to deflate Gabriel was beating it down, unclasping his seat belt and reaching for the door. He kicked it open as hard as he could, rolling into the rain before it had time to swing shut again. It happened so fast that Liv was still looking at the empty driver's seat when her own door opened.

She turned, and came face to face with the muzzle of a gun.

'Out!' a voice shouted from somewhere behind it.

She looked past the black hole of the barrel at the young man holding it. He wasn't much more than a boy. Acne scars showed through the fuzz of a sparse blonde beard and rain poured from the peak of a baseball cap pulled low over pale blue eyes.

'Out!' he shouted again.

He leaned forward and grabbed her with his free hand just as the glass behind her exploded, showering the interior with tiny, glittering shards. The boy jerked backwards, pirouetting as if someone had yanked hard on a rope attached to his left shoulder. Liv glanced back to see Gabriel framed in the jagged remains of the window.

'Run!' he shouted, then in a flash of movement he was swept from view.

Liv whipped her head back and stared through the open door at the pale-eyed boy lying where he had fallen, staring up at the stinging rain. A shower of glass jewels fell to the floor as she fumbled for the release button and her seat belt slid across her body. She splashed past the corpse towards the shadows

160

on the far side of the street. She expected to hear the crack of a gunshot behind her at any moment and feel the thump of a bullet punching her in the back and spinning her to the ground.

She made it to the sidewalk and skidded across it to a verge of low bushes and grass. Given two years' growth and kind winters the wiry shrubs might have offered some sort of cover, but in their current state they served as little more than obstacles. She zigzagged between them, slithering over ground so saturated it was like running on ice. She shortened her stride. Risked a glance behind her.

Visibility was practically zero through the thick curtain of rain. She could just make out the outline of the car and the van in front of it, but nothing else. Something whacked into her, throwing her violently backwards. She lay there for a few moments, blinking up into the rain as the coldness of the earth seeped into her body. For the second time in as many minutes she thought she'd been shot, then she became aware of a shape in front of her, stretched across the darkness like a huge spider web. She followed its faint outline until she saw something thin and sturdy jutting up from the ground. A post. She'd run smack into a chain-link fence.

She risked another glance in the direction of the two cars and saw her cell glowing on the ground near her head, thrown from her grasp when she'd fallen. She grabbed it, terrified that its meagre light might act as a beacon for whoever might be stalking her. She smothered the display with her hand, pressed hard on the off button. From her new position she could no longer see the car or the van. It made her feel better – but only for a second.

A shot rang out, followed by the sound of an engine starting up and the tortured shriek of tyres on tarmac. She heard the whine of bullets against metal from somewhere down the street and a window blowing out. The fleeing vehicle powered round a bend and was gone.

She looked back up towards the road. Saw nothing but the yellow haze of the streetlights. She imagined someone standing beyond the shallow ridge, gun in hand, scanning the darkness. Looking for her. But who was it? One of the guys who'd ambushed them, or Gabriel? All she wanted was to lie perfectly still, not run, not draw attention to herself. But when she had bolted from the car she'd headed straight to the first bit of cover she'd seen. She hadn't even run at an angle. She was lying in the first place whoever was up there would look. She had to move.

She looked to her right, in the direction they'd been driving. A row of service buildings marked a junction. Storage units, most likely. Full of luggage or freight, and maybe even people working night shifts – just a few hundred yards away from her. In the other direction the glow of the airport terminal highlighted the underside of the low cloud. She had no idea how far away it was, but it was a lot further than the service buildings. She listened out for someone approaching. Heard the hiss of the rain. Her own rapid breathing. Nothing else.

She took three quick breaths, scrambled to her feet, and ran. The logical thing was to head for the nearest units and try and raise the alarm, so she went the other way. Back to the warm, brightly lit concourse, and the crowds of tourists staring blankly up at the departure boards, and the two cops with the semi-automatic weapons slung from their shoulders.

She crouched low, keeping the fence to her right, hoping to God that whoever was up there was looking in the opposite direction. A sudden flash of lightning split the night, burning an image on Liv's retina of everything that lay in her path: the gate in the chain link fence about sixty feet in front of her, row upon row of parked cars beyond it. If she could just make it amongst the serried ranks of bullet-stopping family saloons and weekend runabouts, she might be safe.

Thunder rumbled overhead. The gate was now just forty feet away and the verge to her left started to flatten out as it dropped level with the entrance road. She was losing what little cover she had on that side, but there was nothing she could do about it.

The black-and-yellow stripes of an automatic barrier stretched across the opening in the fence. She forced herself to focus on it rather than on whoever was behind her.

Twelve feet now.

Ten.

Five.

Her right foot connected with the firm asphalt of the road and she launched herself towards the box containing the barrier's mechanism, ducked behind it, fell gratefully back against the cold, wet metal and for the briefest of moments felt safe.

Then the rain stopped.

It was so abrupt it seemed almost unnatural. One minute she was enveloped in an almost tropical deluge, the next, the curtain lifted. She heard the gurgle of the gutters along the main road and the gentle sucking of the saturated earth. In the sudden silence her every breath sounded like the rasp of a chainsaw. She strained her ears for other sounds. In her fevered imagination the silence spoke of an enemy nearby, listening for her slightest movement, a gun pointing at the cold earth until a warmer target could be found.

The terminal building was still too far away, but she could pick out every detail of it now – which meant whoever was looking for her could too. She felt an overwhelming urge to sprint back to the cover of the parked cars, but fought it back.

Fifteen feet of tarmac was all that separated her from them. And now she noticed that the section where she crouched was lit more brightly than the rest. Elsewhere she could see comforting corridors of shadow where the pools of light didn't quite overlap. She'd be much harder to spot if she ran along one of those. The nearest was about twenty feet away. Plus fifteen more to the cars. Or she could chance it and run from where she was.

She closed her eyes and rested her head against the steel upright. Then she launched herself across the narrow stretch of road, keeping her head level with the black-and-yellow barrier.

Gabriel heard her distant footfalls on the wet tarmac and watched her bolt across the entrance road, change direction as she came to a stretch of shadow, then disappear into the ocean of metal.

He turned back and scanned the scene of the ambush, checking to see if they were compromised. A few security cameras were sited at the edge of the car park, but all of them were pointing inwards at the vehicles. The same story with the service buildings. No cameras trained on the road. It was safe to assume that none of what had happened in the last few minutes had been recorded.

He picked up the brass shell casings from the seven rounds he'd fired at the retreating vehicle. Most of them had been on target, but none had stopped the driver from escaping. He dropped the casings into his pocket with a muffled clink and turned his attention to the body.

49

Liv nearly wept with relief as she stumbled through the revolving door into the merciful brightness of the terminal building. She limped on, trailing mud and rainwater in her wake, as fearful groups of tourists backed away from her. One of the cops by passport control looked up, alerted by the disturbance. She saw him nudge his partner and nod in her direction. The second recoiled as he locked eyes on the half-mud, half-mad creature heading towards him. He pressed a button on his walkie-talkie and started speaking into it. Both of them dropped their hands to hover near the trigger guards of their automatics.

Great . . .

I make it all this way and now I'm going to be gunned down by these two bozos.

She dug deep into her scant reserves of strength and raised her trembling hands in the internationally recognized sign for surrender. 'Please,' she breathed, sinking to her knees in front of them. 'Call Inspector Arkadian. Ruin City Homicide. I really need to talk to him.'

Rodriguez stood at the baggage check and watched the security guard empty the contents of his holdall on to the steel table and start going through it. An alert crackled through the walkie-talkie clipped to his belt, but he took no notice of it. The message called for back-up to deal with a woman in need of assistance. Rodriguez turned and looked back over the queue on the other side of the walk-through metal detector.

His height gave him a clear view to the main concourse, but he couldn't see the source of the disturbance.

'Thank you, sir, have a nice flight.' The guard pushed his canvas holdall to one side and reached for the next bag rattling down the rollers from the X-ray machine.

Rodriguez stepped aside and quickly repacked the passport he never thought he'd need again, the Bible his mother had died holding, the clothes that hung a little baggy on his slender, six-foot-five-inch frame. The last item he folded carefully, as if it were a flag to lay on a soldier's coffin. It was a red nylon windcheater with a hood, meaningless to most but symbolically important to him.

He pulled the drawstring tight and picked up a small leather-bound volume, given to him by the Abbot, chronicling the history of the rides of the *Tabula Rasa*. He'd written a woman's name and two addresses inside the cover. The first belonged to the offices of a newspaper in New Jersey. The second was residential.

He swung the bag over his shoulder and headed for the boarding gate. He didn't look back. Whatever was going on in the terminal building wasn't his concern. His mission lay elsewhere.

III

For there is nothing hid, except to be made manifest, nor is anything secret, except to come to light.

Mark 4:22

50

Liv stared at the blank, soundproofed walls and the small mirror she knew from experience concealed an observation room. She wondered if anyone was in there now – watching her. She studied her reflection in the toughened glass, her clothes grimy, her hair plastered to her skull. She raised her hand to smooth down her fringe then gave it up as a waste of time.

To begin with she thought they'd brought her here because interview rooms were the one place in any police station you were still allowed to smoke, but looking at herself now, she wasn't so sure. Maybe they were just keeping her out of the way because she looked like a crazy woman. She'd felt a little mad as she'd given her statement, describing the sequence of events from her arrival in the terminal building to the moment she'd staggered back after the attempted kidnapping.

It was as if it had all happened to someone else. Her sense of disconnection had increased when the officer taking her statement had gone outside to fetch her another smoke and returned with a subtly different attitude. His quiet sympathy had been replaced by a cool distance. He'd completed the ritual in near silence, got her to read and sign the document then disappeared without a word, the blinds on the outside of the window preventing her from seeing where.

There was no handle on the inside of the door. His change of tack and the silent wait in this stark room, with its table and chairs bolted to the floor, conspired to make Liv feel like she had been arrested.

She picked up the cigarette burning slowly away to nothing

in the ashtray and breathed it in. It tasted foreign and unpleasant, but she persevered. Her own crumpled Luckies were still in her holdall in the back of Gabriel's car, along with her passport, her credit cards, everything except her cell phone. Arkadian was on his way in, apparently. Hopefully he'd be more sympathetic than his colleague. She thought back to her own journey, driving up through the winding road between the dark shapes of mountains, then along bright streets through a city that managed to appear both incredibly old and very modern. She remembered the sights sliding past her exhausted eyes as she stared out of the back of the police car: the familiar logo of Starbucks, and the chrome and glass storefronts of modern banks standing right next to open-fronted shops, carved out of stone, that sold copper goods, and carpets, and souvenirs, as they had done since biblical times.

She took another drag on the foul-tasting cigarette, screwed up her nose and crushed it out in the ashtray with a picture of the Citadel printed on the bottom. She pushed it to one side and laid her head on her arms. The sound of the air-con hummed at the periphery of her senses. She closed her tired eyes against the glare of the strip lights and, despite everything she had just been through, was asleep within seconds.

51

The Cat, Pet and Canine Clinic sat on the corner of Grace and Absolution in the heart of the Lost Quarter. A vet's presence in such a sleazy and down-at-heel section of the city was surprising enough, but the fact that a light now burned behind its frosted-glass frontage was even stranger.

In the circles in which Kutlar moved it was generally referred to as the Bitch Clinic – testimony to the work that went on here during the hours of darkness. Most of these procedures, where medical records weren't required and the bills were paid in cash, were performed on women. There wasn't a pimp in the city who hadn't used the clinic at one time or another for anything from a hastily arranged backstreet abortion, to a cut-price sterilization job done under the guise of fitting a contraceptive device. IUDs and slow-release hormone pills were relatively expensive, so it was more economical to sterilize them. Most of the girls didn't even know about it until years later.

The clinic also offered other, more specialist services; ones that commanded a much higher premium due to the steeper prison sentences that resulted from discovery.

Kutlar had never used the place before. He owned no pets and until recently had been fortunate enough, considering his line of work, not to require any of its under-the-counter arrangements either. This had all changed on the rain-lashed airport service road when the nine millimetre round had flattened on its way through the van door and split in two as it entered his right leg. Part of the slug now lay in a stainless-steel tray. Kutlar looked at it now, felt his stomach lurch and turned away. He caught his reflection in the door of a medicine cabinet. His close-shaved head was varnished with sweat and shone in the overhead lights that made hollow shadows of his deep-set eyes. He realized he looked like a death's-head, shuddered, and looked away.

He lay on his left side, propped against a raised part of the examination table while a fat man with a white coat and grey skin continued his delicate search for the second half of the round. Occasionally he felt a tugging sensation or heard a wet, tearing sound that made his stomach roll, but he fought back the nausea, forcing himself to breathe steadily – in through the nose, and out through the mouth – while focusing on a picture of a black Labrador slobbering happily from a large poster pinned to the opposite wall.

Kutlar had heard about the clinic from an acquaintance who specialized in the import and export of various items not generally advertised in the classifieds. He'd told him the doctor was generous with the painkillers, provided he hadn't fallen off the wagon and snarfed them all himself. The clink of metal on metal announced the reunion of the second piece of the slug with its twin.

'That appears to be most of the hardware accounted for,' the fat man said in a voice that would not have sounded out of place coming from the mouth of a consultant. 'I need to irrigate the wound now, flush out any smaller fragments that may still be there. Then I can seal the veins and start closing you up.'

Kutlar nodded and gritted his teeth. The doc picked up a clear plastic bottle with a thin spout and squeezed it with a doughy hand, carefully directing a stream of cold saline into the red chasm of his upper thigh. Kutlar shivered. He was still wet from the rain. His damp clothes, coupled with the blood loss, had started to shake him up a bit, probably with a little post-traumatic stress thrown in as a chaser. He looked back at the poster of the happy dog, realized it was recommending some kind of worm treatment, and felt the nausea rise again.

He thought about the ambush on the road, trying to work out where it had gone wrong. He'd dropped the first two guys at the car-hire place outside the main airport, then headed off to the other airport with his cousin Serko to drop off the skinny Hispanic so he could catch his red-eye to the States.

They'd spotted the dark-haired player in the trench coat just after they'd dropped him off – by the arrivals gate, holding up a sign with the girl's name on it. He looked like police, but was alone. They'd held back, watching until the girl suddenly appeared on some half-full flight out of London. Kutlar had weighed it up and figured there'd be a nice bonus if he and Serko could jump the guy and come back from the drop-off with the girl in tow, so they'd followed them outside. They almost had a chance to grab her straight off when the chaperone headed for the car while she'd held back for a smoke. Only there'd been some security guys across the road, rousting vagrants from the bus stop. So they'd waited. Followed them in the van. And decided to spring the ambush on the service road.

The plan had been simple. He was to take care of the babysitter while Serko transferred the girl to the van. Nice and easy. Except the driver had come flying out so fast he'd been knocked backwards and dropped his gun. By the time he'd recovered, a shot had been fired. He'd thrown himself at the man, kicked his gun from his hand, then scrambled back to the van and taken off. Except the girl hadn't been there. Neither had Serko. As he sped away he'd looked in the rear-view mirror and seen something lying in the road. He'd nearly spun round and gone back until bullets started chewing up his side panels and punched out his window. He only realized he'd been hit when he tried to apply the brakes and his leg wouldn't move. Going back would have been suicide. He'd had no choice. Dead men couldn't settle scores. Cousin or no cousin.

A phone started ringing in the waiting room. Kutlar knew who it was. Wondered how much time he had before they caught up with him. He'd done odd jobs for the Church in the past, mostly low-level acts of intimidation and delivering messages with menaces. Never anything like this. Never kidnapping. Never anything that required a gun. But the money had been too good to turn down. Even so, as soon as the doctor was done he was out of there, pay-off or no. He didn't want to go down for this. He listened to the phone ringing and wished he hadn't told them about the clinic. Not that he'd had much choice. The older guy had specifically asked where they should go if there were any casualties. That was the word he'd used – *casualties*. They should have walked away then. Too late now. Too late for Serko, at least.

'I'll give you some antibiotics for the fever,' the fat man said in the voice he'd salvaged from a previous lifetime. 'It'll also act as a prophylactic against infection.'

Kutlar nodded again, felt sweat prickling his scalp and running down his neck and back. Rumour had it that the good doctor had practised proper medicine at one time in his past, before lack of willpower and unfettered access to morphine had been his undoing. 'You need to go somewhere and rest,' the doc said. 'Take it easy until this heals.'

'How long?' Kutlar croaked, his mouth dry and woolly from the Novocaine or whatever it was he'd had pumped into him.

The doctor dropped his eyes back to the ragged red hole and examined it like it was some kind of rare orchid. 'A month, maybe. Couple of weeks at least before you should even try walking on it.'

The voice from the doorway made them both start.

'He needs to be good to go when we leave.'

Kutlar watched Cornelius walk into the room, the waxy patches on his face glistening under the surgical lights. Johann followed close behind. Their red windcheaters were slick with rain. They looked like they'd been dipped in blood.

'OK,' the fat man said. He knew better than to argue with his clients. 'I'll strap it up tight and give him some heavy-duty painkillers.'

Cornelius stopped by the table and leaned in to examine

the wound with a connoisseur's eye before the doctor started bandaging it up. He looked up at Kutlar and winked, a smile creasing the corners of his eyes and pulling at the pale patches of skin on his cheek. Somewhere within the cold numbness of his leg, Kutlar felt something stir. His friend had been right, the doc had been generous with the meds; but the walls of Novocaine were beginning to crumble and an army of pain was starting to invade.

The doctor finished dressing the wound and reached for a syringe. 'I'll give you some morphine now and some tablets to take with you.'

A blur of red flashed across the room as Johann grabbed the doctor and covered his mouth. Bloodshot eyes went wide and frantic behind greasy spectacles and snot bubbled from his nose as he started to hyperventilate. Cornelius plucked the syringe from his pudgy fingers and jabbed it through the white sleeve and into his arm. He depressed the plunger and the magnified eyes passed from panic to glassy resignation as the opiates flooded his system. Johann dragged him to a chair and dropped him into it while Cornelius found another ampoule and re-filled the syringe. He stuck it in the same area as the first jab, pushing the plunger until it was empty.

'Tabula Rasa,' he whispered, glancing over at Kutlar. 'No witnesses.'

He withdrew the syringe from the fat man's arm and stepped closer.

Kutlar would have run if his leg had been up to it, but he knew it was futile. He wouldn't even make it out of the room. He thought of Serko lying on the wet road. Hoped these ruthless bastards, whoever they were, would at least catch up with the guy who'd killed him and return the favour. He watched the syringe coming nearer, dangling loosely between Cornelius's thick fingers, the tip stained pink with the doctor's blood.

I hope he's going to use a different needle, Kutlar thought, before realizing that it didn't really matter.

'We need to get out of here,' Cornelius said. He reached over and took a paper towel from a box on the side table and wrapped the syringe in it. 'You good to go?'

Kutlar nodded. Breathed again. Cornelius dropped the syringe in the pocket of his windcheater then grabbed him under the shoulder and helped him to his feet. Kutlar felt the swollen flesh of his leg expanding against the tight bindings. The room began to swim. He tried to take a step but his legs wouldn't obey him. The last thing he saw before passing out was the image of the dog on the poster, bright-eyed, healthy and ecstatically worm free.

52

Dawn was beginning to filter through the canopy as Gabriel slid the car to a stop twenty feet short of the quarry edge and killed the engine. The old stoneworks were cut into the rim of mountains to the north of the city, at the end of what had been a major thoroughfare linking up with Ruin's great northern boulevard. More than a hundred ox carts a day had once rumbled along it, laden with stone for the city.

Most of the masonry for the public chapel in the centre of Ruin had come from here, so had large portions of the north and west walls. Nowadays the road lay buried beneath thick, scrubby trees and hundreds of years of accumulated leaf mulch, the occasional broken slab jutting like a shattered bone, the only reminder that it was there at all. It was two and a half kilometres off any kind of beaten track and no longer marked on modern maps; almost impossible to find, even in full daylight, unless you knew it was there.

Gabriel walked to the edge, breathing in the thick primordial smells unlocked by the previous night's deluge, and looked over. Eighty feet down was a carpet of green algae slicking the surface of a pool whose depth it was impossible to gauge. It was undoubtedly pretty deep. Stone quarries collected water like giant rain butts. He listened for the sound of engines, or dogs, or chainsaws, or anything that would indicate the presence of other people in the area. All he heard was the plop of a few stones falling into the green water far below.

Satisfied that he was alone, he headed to the back of the car and popped the boot. Staring up at him were the pale, unseeing eyes of the dead man. On his chest a large pink bloom surrounded a small dark hole. He picked up the dead man's gun; a Glock 22 – weapon of choice for drug dealers, gang-bangers and half the police forces of the Western world. It held fifteen rounds in the clip and another in the chamber. Gabriel racked the breach and ejected a soft-nosed .40 S&W with a light charge. The S and W stood for Smith and Wesson, although its detractors claimed it stood for 'Short and Wimpy' as the light gunpowder load meant the slug travelled relatively slowly. But there was also no sonic boom, so much less noise – not necessarily a bad thing if you didn't want to draw too much attention to yourself. But the dead man had not managed to get off a single shot, and now he never would.

Gabriel reached over the body and hauled two black canvas bags from the back of the boot. He laid them on the ground and unzipped the first. Inside were two large plastic bottles of bleach. He tipped the entire contents of one over the body, making sure to douse all the areas he had touched to destroy any trace of his own DNA. The second bottle was destined for the car's interior. He wrenched open the rear passenger door.

Lying in the footwell, partially buried under the driver's seat, was the bag Liv had been carrying when he'd picked her up. He lifted it out and dropped it on the ground before pouring bleach over anything she might have touched. Then he turned the key in the ignition and hit the window buttons. Three slid down all the way. One was already blown out. He poured the remainder of the bottle over the steering wheel, the gear stick and the driver's seat, then dropped the empty bottle back into the boot. He took his silenced SIG P228 from his shoulder holster and put a 9mm round through the floor of the boot, then closed the lid and put another round through that.

He scanned the forest floor for a branch, snapped it in half and brought it over to the Renault. He depressed the clutch and slipped it into first gear, then pushed the stick against the throttle pedal until the engine was revving gently. He jammed the other end against the seat, making sure the steering wheel was centred and pointing straight ahead, then released the handbrake in a single fluid motion and stepped away.

His weight shifted from the clutch, the car dropped into gear. The front wheels started spinning on the soft ground. For a moment the car remained stationary, until each tyre caught hold of the stone beneath the mat of rotten mulch and it lurched forward. Gabriel watched it pick up speed. The wheels found air and the Renault tipped from view. He heard it strike the quarry wall then there was a slap as it hit the water, silencing the whining engine for ever.

Gabriel walked over to the edge and looked down. The car was on its back, drifting towards the centre of the pool and sinking as air escaped from the open windows and perforated boot. He watched until it disappeared beneath the surface of the water, leaving nothing behind but a weakening stream of bubbles and a small patch of oil. He cocked his head to one side like a bird of prey.

In the silence he could hear ripples slapping against the walls below him, getting softer as the memory of what caused them began to fade. It was finally so quiet that the phone ringing in his back pocket sounded like a siren. He snatched it out and flipped it open before it could do so a second time, glancing at the caller ID.

'Hello, Mother,' he said.

'Gabriel,' said Kathryn Mann. 'I was beginning to wonder where you were.'

'There was a problem at the airport.' He glanced down again at the green water. 'After the girl arrived, someone else showed up. I've had to do a bit of housekeeping.'

There was a pause as she took in the information.

'Is she with you?'

'No. But she's not with them either.'

'So where is she?'

'Safe. She'll be with the police by now. I'll be back in Ruin in about twenty minutes. I'll find her again.'

'Are you OK?' she asked.

'I'm fine,' he said. 'Don't worry about me.'

He hung up and slipped the phone back in his pocket.

He kicked the mulchy ground flat again where the wheels had churned it up, then walked over to the second canvas bag. He unzipped it and took out two wheels, several black tubular components and the engine of the portable trail bike he had been using for most of the summer on the Sudan project. Both the frame and the 100cc engine block were aluminium, which made the machine very light, and it folded away so neatly you could strap four of them to a pack horse and take them into some of the most inaccessible regions of the world. It took Gabriel a little less than five minutes to snap it all together.

He took a black crash helmet from the bag and replaced it with Liv's holdall and the other empty bag. He zipped it shut, slung it over his shoulder and hopped on to the saddle, bouncing the springs to loosen them. It took a couple of kick starts to work fuel into the engine then it roared into life. Anyone listening would have mistaken it for the sound of a small chainsaw. He swung the bike round, dropped it into gear and headed back down the tyre ruts the Renault had made on the way in.

53

Liv woke with a start, her heart beating wildly in her chest as if someone was trying to kick their way out of it. She'd just had one of those falling dreams, where you tip forward and jolt yourself awake before you hit the floor. Someone once told her that if you ever fell the whole way it meant you were dead. She'd always wondered how they knew this.

She raised her head from her arms, squinting against the brightness of the interview room.

A man was sitting in the chair opposite.

She jerked back instinctively. The chair creaked against the bolts in the floor that kept it firmly in place.

'Morning,' the man said. 'Sleep well?'

She recognized the voice. 'Arkadian?'

'That's me.' His eyes dropped to a folder lying on the table between them, then back up again. 'Question is, who are you?'

Liv looked down at the folder, feeling as though she'd just woken up on Planet Kafka. Next to it was a bag of bread rolls, a full mug of black coffee and what looked like a pack of wet-wipes.

'Closest thing to a shower and breakfast I could rustle up at short notice,' Arkadian said. 'Help yourself.'

Liv reached for the bread, saw the state of her hands, and grabbed the wipes instead.

'Now, I'm a fairly trusting man,' Arkadian said, watching Liv scrub away at the dried mud and grime between her fingers, 'so if someone tells me something, I'm inclined to believe them, until something else comes along to persuade me otherwise.

Now you gave me a man's name when I called you up, and that name checked out.' He glanced down at the folder again.

Liv felt her throat tighten as she realized what it must contain.

'But you also said that man was your brother – and that's what I'm having a problem with.' His brow creased, like a patient and indulgent father who'd been badly let down. 'You also turn up at the airport in the middle of the night talking about people being ambushed and people being shot, and this also tests my faith, Miss Adamsen.' He looked at her with sad eyes. 'There have been no reports of any car shunts near the airport. No reports of gunfire. And, so far, no one has found any bodies lying on any roads. In fact, as of this moment, the only person claiming any of this happened is –'

Liv dropped her head and scratched violently at her mud-caked hair, going at it with both hands like a frenzied dog rousting a flea until a shower of what looked like tiny diamonds began to patter down on the tabletop. The frenzied scratching stopped as suddenly as it had begun and her green eyes blazed from her grime-streaked face. 'You think I always carry bits of shot-out car window around in my hair, just in case I need to back up a story?'

Arkadian looked at the tiny crystals sparkling across the scarred surface.

Liv rubbed her eyes with cleanish hands that now smelt of baby lotion. 'If you don't believe I was nearly kidnapped, fine. I don't care. All I want is to go see my brother, have a good cry, then make all the no-doubt tedious arrangements to take him back home.'

'And I'd be more than happy to let you. But I'm not yet convinced that he is actually your brother and you're not just some journalist looking for an exclusive on the big story.'

A look of confusion clouded Liv's face. 'What big story?'

Arkadian blinked, as if something had just clicked into place in his mind. 'Answer me one question,' he said. 'Since I first spoke to you, have you seen a paper or caught any news reports?'

Liv shook her head.

'Wait right there.' Arkadian rapped on the window. The door opened and he disappeared.

Liv grabbed a bread roll from the bag. It was still warm. She devoured it while she looked out at the scruffy open-plan office through the crack in the door, heard the hum of phone calls and conversation, saw the edges of desks piled high with paper-work. It made her feel strangely at home.

Arkadian returned just as she was washing the first roll down with the coffee and reaching for a second. He slid yester-day's evening edition of the newspaper across the table.

Liv saw the picture on the front page. Felt something inside her break, like it had on the lakeshore in Central Park. Her vision started to swim. She reached out to stroke the grainy image of the bearded man standing on top of the Citadel. A sob wrenched itself from somewhere deep inside her and tears finally began to fall.

54

Dawn drew everyone back into the great cathedral hall for Matins, the last of the four nocturnes, to bear witness to the death of night and the birth of a new day. Because it carried with it so many powerful symbolic overtones of redemption, rebirth, deliverance from evil, and the triumph of light over darkness it was compulsory for everyone in the Citadel to attend.

Only today, something was different.

Athanasius noticed it when Father Malachi was in the middle of one of his rhetorical flights of fancy from the pulpit, and he glanced absently across the lines of red-cassocked guards standing in front of him. Despite the strictness of the rule that all should attend Matins, one of them was missing. At six foot five, Guillermo Rodriguez usually stood out, quite literally, from the others. But today he wasn't there.

He remembered the sixty-two personnel files he'd delivered to the Abbot's chamber the previous day. Sixty-two red files for sixty-two Carmina. He turned his body slightly as if listening intently to the sermon and conducted a silent head count.

The trapped air of the cathedral cave shook with the deep sound of every voice in the Citadel chanting the final doxology in the original language of their church. 'Every day will I bless thee; and I will praise thy name forever and ever. Blessed art thou, O LORD: teach me thy statutes.'

Athanasius just managed to finish as the lines of the congregation started to disperse. There were fifty-nine guards. Three were missing.

As the sun rose, the great windows lit up above the altar; God had opened his great eye and was gazing down upon his loyal congregation. Light had, once again, defeated darkness; the new day had begun.

Athanasius filed out of the cathedral in the crush of brown cassocks, his mind filled with the possibilities of his discovery. He knew a little of Brother Guillermo's past and guessed now at the reason the Abbot might have singled him out. It was a thought that troubled him greatly. He had always prided himself on his ability to curb the Abbot's impulsiveness. The fact that three of the guards were now missing made him anxious – not just because he feared the Abbot's response to Brother Samuel's death, but because he'd had to discover it for himself.

By revealing the prophecy to him in the forbidden vault the day before, which seemed to foretell the end of the Sacrament and a new beginning, he thought the Abbot had demonstrated a thawing of the crippling secrecy that he believed kept the Church frozen in the past. Now his suspicions suggested quite the opposite. Far from looking forward toward an enlightened future, he feared the Abbot might be returning to the medieval behaviour of their dark and violent past.

55

Liv sat in silence in the harshly lit interview room.

She continued to stare at the picture on the newspaper while Arkadian gently filled her in on the details. When he finished he laid his hand on the blue folder by his side. 'I'd like to show you some more photographs,' he said. 'We took them prior to the post-mortem. I realize this may be difficult and I'd fully understand if you don't want to, but it may help us understand more about Samuel's death.'

Liv nodded, wiping tears from her cheeks with her hand.

'But I need to clear something up first.'

She looked up at him.

'I need you to convince me that you're really his sister.'

Liv felt exhaustion settling upon her. She didn't want to get into her entire life story right now, not the way she was feeling, but she also wanted to know what had happened to her brother. 'I only found out the truth myself after my father died.' The things she had discovered eight years ago began to surface, things she usually kept locked away. 'I had some pretty fierce identity issues on the boil. I'd never really been sure where I fitted. I know most kids go through a stage of thinking that they aren't really part of their family, but I had a completely different name from my dad and my brother. I never knew my mother. I asked Dad about it one time, but it just made him go quiet and withdrawn. Later that night I heard him crying. In my over-imaginative teenage state I assumed it was because I'd picked the scab off some shameful family secret. I never asked him again.

'When he died, my grief, or sense of loss, or whatever you want to call it, seemed to settle on this one unanswered question. I fixated on it. I felt like I'd not only lost my father but any chance of finding out who I really was.'

'But you did find out,' Arkadian said.

'Yes,' Liv replied. 'Yes, I did.'

She took a deep breath and sank back into her past.

'I'd just started my freshman year at Columbia. I was a journalism major. My first big assignment was a three-thousand-word investigative piece on a subject of my choice. I decided to kill two birds with one stone. Dig into the big family secret. I caught a Greyhound to West Virginia, to the place where my brother and I were born. It was one of those towns that could be listed under 'Americana' in the dictionary. One long main street. Stores with awnings stretching out over the sidewalk – most of them closed. It was called Paradise. Paradise, West Virginia. The Founding Fathers clearly had high hopes.

'The summer we were born my mom and dad had been travelling all over, chasing work where they could find it. They were organic horticulturalists, ahead of their time in many ways. Mostly they ended up working regular gardening jobs, a few municipal positions here, some farm labouring there, anything to earn enough money to tide them over for when the babies came. They checked in whenever they were passing some local medical facility, but I think taking blood pressure and listening in to check on two little heartbeats was about as far as it went in those days. They didn't have ultrasound scans. Mom and Dad had no idea there was anything wrong – until it was too late.

'The "hospital" I was born in was a medical centre at the edge of town. When I went back it was standing in the shadow of a huge WalMart, which was no doubt responsible for all the empty stores on Main Street. It was one of those rural facilities whose main function is either to patch people up and ship 'em back out with a jar full of aspirin, or refer them on to proper hospitals. It was rudimentary enough when I found it, so God knows what it was like when Mom and Dad fetched up there.

'I got chatting to the nurse at reception, explained what I was doing and what I was looking for. She showed me a store-room stacked high with boxes of old medical records. It was a mess. Took me an hour just to find a box from the right year. Inside, the documents were all mixed up. I went through it and dug out the birth records and read through them. Mine wasn't there, so I wrote down the names of all the staff who'd been around back then and convinced the receptionist to put me in touch with one of them, a nurse who'd worked at the centre in the eighties – Mrs Kintner. She'd been retired a few years but still lived locally. I went to see her. We sat on her porch drinking lemonade. She remembered my mother. Said she was beautiful. Said she'd fought for two days to give birth to us. They couldn't see what the problem was until they took us out "the sunroof" as she described it – emergency C-section.'

She rose slowly from her chair.

'I was born Sam Newton,' she said, in a voice barely louder than a whisper. 'My brother's name was Sam Newton. We were born at the same time, on the same day, to the same parents. We're twins.' She turned to her right and pulled her shirt from the waistband of her jeans. 'But not ordinary twins.'

She lifted her shirt.

Arkadian saw a scar, white against her pale skin. A crucifix lying on its side. Identical to the one he'd found on the monk's body.

'Lots of brothers and sisters are described as being joined at the hip,' Liv said. 'We really were. Or joined at the side, at least. Our three lower ribs were fused. It's what the supermar-ket tabloids luridly describe as Siamese twins. More accurately, we were what's known as omphalopagus twins, where two infants are joined at the chest. Sometimes they also share major organs, like the liver. We just shared bone.'

Liv lowered her shirt and sank back on to her seat.

'Nurse Kintner said it caused quite a stir. There'd never been a case of fused twins being different genders before, so the doctors got quite excited. Then, when my mother worsened, and so did we, they started to panic. She'd lost so much blood trying to give birth to us, suffered so much internal damage delivering an awkward-shaped double baby, that she never regained consciousness. I suppose they realized that they, or the hospital at least, were responsible, so they hushed everything up. She died eight days after we were born – the same day Samuel and I were surgically separated. It was only then that they discovered only one birth certificate had been issued. They quickly issued a new one for me, giving the date of our separation as my birth date. I suppose, technically, it was the day I became an individual. It was my father's idea to name me in Mother's memory. Liv Adamsen was her maiden name, the name of the girl he'd fallen in love with and married. That's why he never wanted to talk about it.'

Arkadian took in the new information. Held it up against what he already knew, searching for any questions it still hadn't answered. 'How come your grandmother's name was different from your mother's?'

'Very old Norwegian tradition. Granny always preferred the old ways. All children used to adopt their father's name. Granny's father was Hans, so she was called Hansen, which weirdly means "son of Hans". My mother's father was Adam, so she was Adamsen. Tracing family trees is a bitch if you're Scandinavian.' She looked down at the newspaper. Samuel's face stared back at her. 'You said you wanted to show me something that might help explain my brother's death,' she said. 'What is it?'

She watched Arkadian's hand tap uncertainly on the blue folder. He had softened towards her, but was still guarded.

'Listen,' she said. 'I'm just as keen to find out what happened to him as you are. So you can either trust me or not, it's up to you. But if you're still worried about what I do for a living, then I'll sign any gagging order you care to throw at me.'

Arkadian's hand stopped drumming the file. He got up and left the room, leaving the folder behind.

Liv stared at it, fighting the urge to grab it and look inside while the Inspector was out of the room. He returned moments later with a pen and the Homicide unit's standard non-disclosure agreement. She signed it and he checked the signature against a faxed copy of her passport. Then he opened the folder and slid a six-by-four glossy across the table.

The photo showed Samuel's washed body lying on the examination table, the bright lights making the dark network of scars upon it stand out clear and grotesque on his pale skin.

Liv stared at it, dumbfounded. 'Who did this to him?'

'We don't know.'

'But you must've spoken to the people who knew him. Didn't they know anything? Didn't they say if he'd been acting strangely – or seemed depressed about something?'

Arkadian shook his head. 'The only person we've managed to speak to is you. Your brother fell from the top of the Citadel. We assume he had been living inside it for some years, seeing as there's no evidence of him living elsewhere in the city. How long did you say he was missing?'

'Eight years.'

'And in all that time there was no contact from him?'

'None.'

'So if he was there the whole time, the last people to see him alive would've been others inside the Citadel, and I'm afraid we're not going to be able to talk to any of them. I've sent a request, but that's just procedure. No one will speak to me.'

'Can't you make them?'

'The Citadel is, quite literally, a law unto itself. It's a state within a state with its own rules and system of justice. I can't make them do anything.'

'So they can choose to say zilch, even though someone has died, and there's nothing anyone can do about it?'

'Pretty much,' Arkadian said. 'Though I'm sure they'll say something eventually. They're as aware of positive PR as anyone. In the meantime, there are other avenues of enquiry we can explore.' He removed three more photographs from the folder and slid the first across the table towards her.

Liv saw her phone number scratched on to a thin piece of leather.

'We found that in your brother's stomach. That's how we managed to contact you so quickly.' He slid the second photo towards her. 'But that wasn't all we found.'

56

The roads in the Lost Quarter had first been haphazardly scratched into the earth by handcarts and horses in the early part of the sixth century and were now utterly unequal to the volume, speed and width of modern traffic. As road-widening required demolition, which wasn't an option here, the town planners had implemented a one-way system so complex it ensnared cars like flies in its unfathomable web.

Driving his ambulance through these medieval streets was something Erdem had nightmares about. His paramedic's operating manual required him to respond to any callout in the greater metropolitan area within fifteen minutes. It also required him to bring his vehicle back in the same state it went out. Which meant that a trip into this stony warren of paint-scraped walls at anything like the necessary speed to fulfil the first obligation inevitably resulted in a drastic failure to comply with the second.

He watched the cross on the side of the ambulance emerge slowly from the shadow of a stone archway, revealing the rod of Asclepius at its centre entwined with a serpent. He eased up the power and switched his eyes back to the road, trying to make up a little time until the next obstacle forced him back to a timid crawl.

'How we doing?' he asked.

'We're at fourteen already,' Kemil replied, checking the watch. 'Don't think we're going to be breaking any records on this one.'

The subject they were heading to was a white male who'd been found unconscious on one of the side streets at the edge of the Lost Quarter. Given the time of day and the man's location, Erdem figured he was either an OD, or had suffered a gunshot or knife wound. Whoever had called it in hadn't given much information, just enough to warrant an ambulance callout; all in all the perfect start to a perfect day.

'Any news from the police?' Erdem asked.

Kemil checked the radio scanner's readout for a squad-car number. 'Nope,' he said. 'Probably still finishing off their coffee and breakfast rolls.'

The squad car was obviously not treating it as an emergency. Unlike the paramedics, they were under no pressure to respond within fifteen minutes – especially at breakfast time.

'Here we go.' Erdem eased round a corner and spotted a crumpled pile of clothes on the far side of the shadowy street. There was no sign of a police car. There was no sign of anyone.

'Seventeen minutes,' Kemil said, punching a button on the radio that would register their arrival time back at base. 'Not too bad.'

'And not a scratch on her,' Erdem said, bringing the ambulance to a standstill, taking the keys from the ignition and slipping from the driver's seat in a single practised move.

The man on the pavement was deathly pale and the moment Erdem rolled him into the recovery position he discovered why. His entire upper right leg was wet with blood. He lifted a flap of material in the torn trousers to see how bad the trauma was – and stopped. Instead of a gaping wound he was staring down at the blood-stained gauze of a tightly wrapped and fairly fresh dressing. He was about to turn and holler for Kemil when he felt the cold hard barrel of a gun against the back of his neck.

Kemil hadn't even managed to get out of his seat before the bearded man appeared by his open window and pointed the pistol in his face.

'Call it in,' he said with an accented voice that sounded English. 'No assistance required. Tell them the man you found was just drunk.'

Kemil reached blindly for the radio handset, his eyes flicking between the black hole of the muzzle and the steady blue eyes of the man holding it. This was only the second time he'd been ambushed in nearly six years. He knew the thing to do was stay calm and stay helpful, but this guy was *really* unsettling. The last time he'd been 'jacked, the gang wore ski masks and had been so strung out and jittery they were as likely to drop their guns as fire them. This guy was calm, and he wore no mask. All that disguised his appearance were a thick beard growing in patches round ridges of old burn tissue and the red hood of a windcheater pulled low over his long sandy hair.

Kemil's hand found the radio handset. He picked it up and did as he was told.

57

Liv stared down at the new photograph.

Another stainless-steel tray lined with a white paper towel, on top of which lay five small brown seeds, each with something scratched on to its shiny surface.

Arkadian slid a third photo across the table.

'The symbols were scratched on both sides,' he said. 'Five seeds, ten symbols – mostly letters, a mixture of upper and lower case.'

He arranged the photographs so one overlapped the other. The letters were now lined up in pairs.

$$\underline{T} \quad a \quad M \quad + \quad k$$
$$\underline{?} \quad s \quad A \quad a \quad l$$

'They're arranged in the same order in both photographs so you can see which marks were scratched on to each seed in case the pairings were deliberate. I can't see anything in them myself, but perhaps that's the point. Maybe it's not supposed to be obvious to anyone. Maybe it was just meant for you.'

Liv looked at the jumble of letters.

'Mean anything?'

'Not immediately,' she said. 'Can I have that pen back?'

Arkadian reached into his pocket and handed it over.

She took the newspaper, smoothed it flat and copied the symbols into the blank sections of sky surrounding the image of her brother. She saw her own name emerge from the letters and spelled it out, adding the rest of the symbols underneath to maintain the original pairings.

$$\begin{array}{ccccc} \text{s} & \text{a} & \text{M} & \text{l} & \text{?} \\ \text{a} & + & \text{A} & \text{k} & \underline{\text{T}} \end{array}$$

Was it shorthand telling her SAMUEL had been ATTACKED? It seemed a bit of a stretch. Besides, the seeds had been discovered during his post-mortem, which surely made the warning somewhat redundant.

'Haven't you got expert code breakers for this kind of thing?'

'There's a cryptology professor at the big university in Gaziantep who helps us from time to time, but I haven't called him. It seems to me your brother went to extraordinary lengths to make sure this message wasn't found by the wrong people, so the least I could do was respect that. I honestly think it was intended for you and you're the only one who'll be able to make any sense of it.' Arkadian lowered his voice. 'No one else knows about these seeds. Just the pathologist who found them, me – and now you. I kept the photographs out of the file. If news of this got out, I'd have every Ruinologist and Sacramental conspiracy theorist offering their take on its meaning. I'm trying to solve this case, not the identity of the Sacrament – although . . .' He scrutinized the seeds once more.

'Although what?' Liv prompted.

'Although I rather suspect they may well turn out to be the same thing.'

58

Two floors down, a freckled hand tapped out the user name and password that would grant access to the police database. The screen flashed and a mail account launched, telling him he had seven new messages. Six were departmental memos no one would ever read, the seventh was from someone called GARGOYLE. There was nothing in the subject line. The man glanced nervously over the top of his monitor then clicked it open. It contained just one word. *Green.*

He deep deleted the message, removing all trace of it from the network, then opened up a command module. A black box appeared on the screen asking for another user name and password. He entered them both, worming his way deeper into the network and scanning the recently updated files.

GARGOYLE was a relatively simple piece of software he had written himself, which made the job of monitoring the status of any case he wasn't supposed to be looking at much, much easier. Rather than go through the tedious process of hacking into the central database and manually checking for new updates, he could simply attach the program to the architecture of any file, and whenever it was updated GARGOYLE automatically let him know via email.

He found the file on the dead monk, opened it, and started scrolling through. On page twenty-three he spotted a small block of text the program had highlighted in lime green. It detailed the taking into custody of one Liv Adamsen following her uncorroborated report of an attempted abduction at the airport. She was upstairs in an interview room on the fourth floor. That was Robbery and Homicide. He frowned, not quite sure what all that had to do with the dead monk.

Still . . .

Not his problem.

Both parties had requested that any new additions to the case file be reported to them directly. Who was he to play gatekeeper?

He plugged a flash drive into the USB port on the front of his computer, copied and pasted the details then closed the case file and carefully retraced his steps through the maze of the database, re-locking all his invisible doors as he retreated.

When he was back at the default desktop he opened an innocuous spreadsheet for the benefit of anyone curious enough to glance at his screen, grabbed his coat and phone and headed for the door. He never sent anything from his own terminal, even encrypted. It was too risky and he was too careful. Besides, there was an Internet café around the corner where the baristas were hot and the coffee was better.

59

Liv spent the next few minutes looking for words in the jumble of letters and writing them down in a list. She got words like SALT, LAST, TASK, MASK – nothing earth-shattering, nothing like 'GRAIL' or 'CROSS' or any of the other things the Sacrament was rumoured to be; certainly nothing worth dying for.

She tried making a single word from the capitalized letters – MAT – and studied what was left – s a l a k. She looked up at Arkadian. 'What language do they speak in the Citadel?'

He shrugged. 'Greek, Latin, Aramaic, English, Hebrew – all the modern languages and lots of the dead ones. There's supposed to be a massive library in there, full of ancient texts. If your brother had anything to do with that side of things, I suppose the message could be written in any language.'

'Great.'

'But I don't think he'd do that. Why would he send you a message you wouldn't understand?'

Liv let out a long breath and picked up the photograph of her brother's body. Her eyes traced the neat lines encircling his shoulders, upper thighs and neck, the T-shaped cross burned deep into the flesh of his left shoulder.

'Maybe there's something in these scars,' she said. 'Like a map, maybe.'

'I agree they're significant, but I think these symbols are more important. He took pains to scratch them on to five tiny seeds, then swallowed them, along with your phone number, and jumped into our jurisdiction so that they would be found during a post-mortem.'

Liv turned her attention back to the newspaper, the picture of Samuel now surrounded by the letters he'd taken such trouble to hide.

'I want to see him,' she said.

'I don't think that's wise,' Arkadian said softly. 'Your brother fell from a very great height. His injuries were extensive, and we've conducted a thorough post-mortem. It would be better for you to wait.'

'Wait until what? Until he's been tidied up?'

'Miss Adamsen, I don't think you realize what happens to a body during a post-mortem.'

Liv took a deep breath and fixed him with her bright green eyes. 'After a thorough external examination the coroner makes a Y-shaped incision on the torso, cracks the sternum and removes the heart, the lungs and the liver for further examination. The top of the skull is then detached with a saw and the face is peeled forward to gain access to the brain, which is also removed for examination. Ever been to New Jersey, Inspector?'

Arkadian blinked. 'No,' he replied.

'Last year in Newark we had one hundred and seven homicides – more than two a week. In the last four years I've written stories on every aspect of crime, and researched every element of police procedure, including autopsies. I have personally attended more post-mortems than most rookie cops. So I know it's not going to be pretty, and I know it's my brother, but I also know I haven't flown all this way on a maxed-out credit card – which has since been stolen, by the way – just to look at a bunch of photographs. So please,' she said, turning the photo round and sliding it back across the table, 'take me to see my brother.'

Arkadian's eyes flicked between Liv's face and the image in the photograph. They had the same colouring, the same high cheekbones and widely set eyes. Samuel's eyes were shut but he knew they were the same intense green.

The buzz of his phone cut through the silence.

''Scuse me,' he said, standing up and walking to the far side of the room.

'You're not going to believe this,' an excitable voice babbled in his ear the moment he pressed the answer button. 'Just when you think a case cannot get any stranger,' Reis said, 'the lab results come back!'

'What you got?'

'The monk's cells; they're –'

A high-pitched siren caused Arkadian to jerk the phone away from his head.

'*WHAT THE HELL IS THAT*?' he shouted, holding it as close as he could without bursting an eardrum.

'*FIRE ALARM!*' Reis shouted back through the banshee wail. '*I THINK WE'RE BEING EVACUATED. NOT SURE IF IT'S A DRILL. I'LL CALL YOU WHEN IT'S OVER.*'

Arkadian glanced at Liv. Locked eyes. Made a decision.

'*DON'T WORRY,*' he yelled into the phone, '*I'LL COME TO YOU.*' He smiled and added, as much for Liv's benefit as for Reis's, '*AND I'LL BE BRINGING A VISITOR.*'

60

The deafening noise of the propellers increased as a couple of thousand horse power fed into the Double Wasp engine on the right wing, slewing it round until the rear cargo hatch came to rest in line with the warehouse door.

Kathryn watched men in red overalls scamper forward and jam wooden chocks beneath the oversized wheels of the C-123 light cargo plane which they'd picked up for the princely sum of one dollar from the Brazilian Air Force on the understanding that the charity had to make it airworthy and ship it off the military airbase within thirty days or it would be used for target practice. It had been in such a bad state they only just made it, but it had clocked up over twenty thousand flying hours since.

The pitch of the engines fell and the watery mist whipped up by them began to clear as the rear hatch lowered. Kathryn marched across the wet tarmac, followed by Becky the intern and a customs officer who held his cap in place with one hand and a clipboard in the other. Kathryn had brought Becky so she could check everything in the tightly packed cargo hold against the manifest, and so that her eager prettiness would distract the customs officer and the rest of the ground crew while the most precious and unregistered part of the load was discreetly removed.

Kathryn had seen her father many times over the past few years but never in Ruin. It was too dangerous, even after all this time. Instead she always flew to him in Rio or they met somewhere else to spend a bit of time together, discuss the charity's latest projects, fulminate on whatever injustices were currently being visited upon the planet, and drink good whisky.

She reached the top of the ramp and peered at the large corporate logo stencilled on the thin aluminium skin of the first master pallet. The majority of this particular shipment was high-nitrate fertilizer, a gift from a large petrochemical company to salve its conscience for all the bad it did to the world. Kathryn was always conflicted by accepting such donations, but figured the people who were ultimately going to benefit from them didn't care about the moral high ground; the only ground that mattered to them was the sort they could grow food on.

In a couple of days this fertilizer would be mingling with the sterile dust surrounding a village in the Sudan – *if* the Sudanese government gave them permission to fly it in, and *if* Gabriel managed to persuade the local warlords not to steal it all and turn it into bombs. He'd been making good progress before she'd called him back home. Now he'd have to start all over again.

Kathryn glanced to her side.

Becky and the customs officer were already checking the serial numbers on the crates. Beyond them she saw two of the three-man crew walk round the wing and head towards the rear of the plane. It required an effort of will not to look directly at them. Instead she waited for them to clear her peripheral vision before turning to make her way back down the loading ramp. 'I'll go tell the forklift driver he can come and make a start,' she called over her shoulder.

'Thanks,' the customs officer said, without looking round.

Kathryn headed to the warehouse. It was almost three-quarters full of packing cases and master pallets arranged in evenly spaced lines. Ilker was rearranging some crates containing water-filtration kits. She pointed in the direction of the plane and he flicked her a thumbs-up, spun the forklift and headed for the open door. Kathryn continued down one of the passageways between the crates and into the office at the back of the warehouse.

One of the crewmen was helping himself to coffee from a jug that sat beneath the TV on the far wall. He turned and looked at her, his deeply tanned face already wrinkling into a huge smile. 'Flight officer Miguel Ramirez at your service,' he said, tapping the ID badge on his flight suit.

Kathryn leapt across the room, nearly knocking him over in her desperation to give him a hug. Despite her tiredness, her concerns about the present, the traumas of the day just gone, and the weight of history that hung over the ones to follow, she forgot everything for a moment and just held him.

After ninety years in exile, Oscar de la Cruz had come home.

They held each other tightly until Kathryn's phone chimed in her pocket, breaking the spell. She pulled back, kissed her father on both cheeks then took it from her pocket. Oscar watched her face clench into a frown as she read the email that had been routed to it.

'Gabriel?'

Kathryn shook her head. 'The girl. She's at the police station.'

'Who's the source?'

'Someone inside the Central District building.'

'Reliable?'

'Accurate.'

Oscar shook his head. 'Not the same thing.'

Kathryn shrugged. 'He delivers when required and the information is always good.'

'And what information has this source given us in the past?'

'Police files covering every Church-related investigation in the past three years. We heard about him through a press contact.'

'So I assume he does not give us this information for the love of our cause?'

'No. He gives us this information for money.'

She looked down at her phone, re-reading the message,

registering the time it had arrived, feeling angry with herself that she hadn't seen it before. She cleared the screen and pressed a button to speed-dial a number. She wondered if the source had sent her the information before or after the Citadel. It didn't really matter. By now the people who'd tried to abduct the girl at the airport would undoubtedly have the same information she did and would already be re-grouping.

The dialling sequence ended.

Somewhere in Ruin another phone started to ring.

61

The Basilica Ferrumvia was the largest building in Ruin not belonging to the Church. It had risen piece by piece in the mid-nineteenth century like a red beacon of hope and modern progress from the medieval slums to the south of the Lost Quarter. Despite its ecclesiastical-sounding name, however, the only thing worshipped inside it was commerce. The 'Church of the Iron Road' was Ruin's main train station.

By the time Gabriel pulled up outside the gothic façade, rush hour was well underway. He brought the lightweight trail bike to a stop under the vast glass and wrought-iron awning that stretched from the front of the building and eased it into a space next to a line of scooters. He kicked out the foot-rest, killed the engine and headed briskly into the station like any other commuter with a train to catch.

He walked quickly through the cacophonous central hall and descended into the muted silence of the left-luggage office dug deep into the bedrock beneath Platform 16.

Locker 68 stood in the furthest corner of the room, directly below one of the six closed-circuit cameras that watched the room. The position of the camera meant that, although Gabriel's face was visible to anyone monitoring the feeds, the contents of the locker were not. He punched in a five-digit code and opened the door.

Inside was another black canvas bag, identical in size and make to the one over his shoulder. He unzipped it and pulled out a black quilted jacket and two fully loaded ammunition clips. He laid the clips on the floor of the locker, pulled out his SIG, carefully unscrewed the silencer and dropped it into the open bag. Silence was for night time. Any shooting during the day needed to be loud enough to scare away anyone who shouldn't be there. He didn't want innocent bystanders getting hurt. In the army it was called collateral damage. In the city it was called murder.

He looked round, slipped the bag from his shoulder and shrugged off his jacket, replacing it with the quilted one. The loaded clips went into the pocket. The SIG went back into the pancake shoulder holster, less bulky without the silencer. He picked up the bag, stashed it in the locker then unzipped it and pulled out Liv's holdall. He hesitated, his innate courtesy preventing him from prying into a woman's personal property, then opened it anyway.

He found clothes, toiletries, a phone charger, all the things you'd stuff in a bag if you were heading someplace in a hurry. There was also a small laptop in a case, a wallet, credit cards, a press ID card and a Starbucks loyalty card that was nearly full. A side pocket produced a passport, a set of house keys and a paper 1-Hour Foto wallet. Inside were a dozen or so glossy prints of Liv and a young man on a daytrip to New York. She was a few years younger in the photos than the girl he had met at the airport – early twenties maybe. The young man was clearly her brother. He had the same dark blonde hair, the same softly rounded, attractive face – handsome in him, pretty in her – the same bright green eyes shone with the joy of shared laughter from both faces.

The last image dated the trip to pre-2001. The young man stood alone between the twin towers of the World Trade Centre, his arms pushing outward, his face twisted in a caricature of extreme effort. With his long hair and hint of a beard he looked like Samson in the temple of the Philistines. It was an ominous image, laden with tragedy, not only because of what happened to the towers, but because the image of the happy young man with his arms outstretched aped the pose he would ultimately take in the final hours before he fell.

Gabriel slid the photos back into the wallet. His practical instinct was to leave the bag in the locker, but he slung it over his shoulder, slammed the door and headed to the exit. Keeping it close would act as a talisman for him, a good luck charm, a lens through which to focus his determination and purpose so that when he found the girl and got her to safety he could give it back to her.

In his mind her security had become his personal mission. He couldn't say exactly why or when he had decided that this was so. Maybe when he'd watched her scampering across the rain-slicked car park, fuelled by a fear partly caused by him. Maybe even earlier – when he'd first seen her startling green eyes searching for the truth in his own. He could take the fear away from her at least, if he got the chance.

He emerged from the gloom of the left-luggage office back into the bright glare of the main concourse. The arched glass ceiling, a hundred feet high at its apex, seemed to gather every sound and reflect it back. It was so loud that he felt rather than heard his phone ringing in his pocket.

'The girl's been taken to the Central District,' Kathryn said. 'She's in an interview room on the fourth floor giving a statement about what happened last night.'

'How old's the information?'

'Just got it. But we think the person who gave it to us is also feeding the Sancti.'

It made sense. It also meant the people who'd tried to snatch Liv the previous night would be close by, biding their time until they got another chance.

'I'll call you back,' he said, and hung up.

He slipped on his helmet as he arrived at the bike and contemplated his next move. He figured she was safe so long as she was in the interview room – but she wouldn't stay there forever and the Central District building was vast. Finding her inside it without drawing attention to himself would be almost impossible. He kick-started the engine and glanced across at a newsstand selling the morning edition of the local paper. A new picture of the monk filled the front page, closer this time, obviously taken on a very long lens. The headline above it read THE FALL OF MAN.

He dropped the bike in gear and eased it into the slow-moving morning traffic.

He knew exactly where she'd be going next.

62

Arkadian pushed through the large glass door of the Central District building and held it open. Liv emerged, squinting in the bright morning sun. A small group of uniformed cops and white-collar admin workers congregated around an ashtray rising from the pavement, a shrine to their shared addiction. Liv headed over to join the service.

'Don't suppose I could steal one of those?' she asked someone in a white shirt and blue tie. The admin guys were usually a softer touch than the uniforms. He looked up and recoiled slightly at her bedraggled appearance.

'It's OK, she's with me,' Arkadian said.

He produced a soft pack of Marlboro Lights.

'Thanks,' Liv said, plucking one and tapping it on the back of her hand. ''Preciate it.'

The admin guy held out a light and Liv dipped her head to meet it. She sucked in the dry smoke, hungry for the nicotine hit. It tasted just as bad as the ones she'd had in the interview room. She shot the admin guy a smile anyway and turned to follow Arkadian down the street.

'So when was the last time you saw your brother?' Arkadian asked as she caught up.

Liv took another drag of the cigarette, hoping the familiar bliss would descend upon her soon.

'Eight years ago,' she said, blowing out the acrid smoke. 'Right before he vanished.'

'Any idea why he took off?'

Liv screwed up her face at the aftertaste. What was it with these foreign smokes? They all tasted like burnt tyres. 'Long story.'

'Well then, let's walk slowly. The morgue's only a couple of streets away.'

Liv took one more cautious drag on the cigarette then dropped it down a storm drain as discreetly as she could manage, hoping the nice man who'd given it to her wasn't watching. 'I suppose it started back when Dad died. I don't know how much you know about it . . .'

Arkadian thought back to the file he'd compiled on the dead monk's past and the article outlining the tragic car accident in the frozen ravine. 'I know the details.'

'Did you know my brother held himself totally responsible? "Survivor Syndrome", that's what the doctors called it. He couldn't shake the feeling that he'd been the cause of everything and so didn't deserve to be still living. He spent a long time in therapy, trying to come to terms with it. In the end he turned to religion instead. I suppose it happens a lot. You start looking for answers. If you can't find them in the here and now, you look elsewhere.'

She replayed the events of eight years ago in her mind: her trip to West Virginia; the sound of the crickets on Nurse Kintner's porch as she told Liv what she knew; the clarity and sense it had all made to her; then the darkness that quickly clouded it again when she shared her discoveries with Samuel. 'I should never have told him.'

'Don't be so hard on yourself,' Arkadian said. 'When Samuel blamed himself for your father's death, did you feel the same way?'

'No.'

'And did you tell him it wasn't his fault?'

'Of course.'

'Well, I'm telling you now: Samuel's death wasn't your fault.

Whatever you said to him, whatever you think you did to drive him away, he was already on his own path. There was nothing you could have done, one way or another, to change it.'

'How can you be so sure?'

'Because if he'd harboured some lasting grudge against you, or held you responsible for any of it, why would he go to such great lengths to make sure we found you?'

Liv shrugged. 'Maybe to punish me.'

Arkadian shook his head. 'But that's not the way it works. You must have reported on kidnapping cases, abductions, missing persons.'

'Some.'

'And what's the worst thing about them? For the relatives, I mean.'

Liv thought of the people she'd interviewed: the haunted looks; the constant speculation on all the things that may have happened; the never-ending worry and uncertainty. She thought of the demons that she'd lived with ever since Samuel had vanished. 'The worst thing is not knowing.'

'Exactly. But you *know* what happened to Samuel because he made sure of it. He wasn't punishing you by doing that. He was setting you free.'

The whoop of a siren startled them both as a large fire truck barged through the traffic and turned into the next street. Arkadian watched it disappear then broke into a sprint. Liv watched in surprise for a moment then hurried after him. She caught up as he rounded the corner.

63

Groups of people in lab coats and shirtsleeves filled the street, their hands shoved into trouser pockets, their shoulders hunched against the cold. The truck that had driven past them pulled up next to another already parked in front of what looked like a huge mausoleum. Fire marshals in high-visibility jackets checked names on a piece of paper.

Arkadian strode towards the nearest of them, scanning the faces in the crowd and punching a number into his phone. 'Have you seen Dr Reis?'

The marshal checked his list. 'Nope,' he said. 'Not yet.'

In his ear, Reis's recorded voice asked him to leave a message. Arkadian snapped the phone shut and walked over to two fire-fighters emerging from the entrance. 'What's up?' He flashed his badge. He could smell smoke coming off them.

'Nothing,' the larger man said, pulling off his helmet and wiping sweat from his eyebrows. 'Alarm tripped in a hallway; a fire in a bin in one of the toilets.'

'Deliberate?'

'Oh yeah.'

Arkadian frowned. 'Can I go in?'

The fire-fighter turned his head and spoke into a microphone on his lapel. 'Charlie Four, you found anything else?'

A burst of static was followed by a metallic voice. 'Negative. We're on our way out.'

'Be my guest,' he said.

Arkadian moved across the pavement and up the steps. Liv followed, sticking close behind, looking resolutely ahead and frowning slightly in the hope that it would lend her a sense of professional seriousness and make the fireman think she was Arkadian's partner. The fireman watched her pass, looking instead at her grimy clothes and hair. He opened his mouth to say something but a squawk on his radio distracted him long enough for Liv to bound up the steps and disappear into the building.

She found herself in a large atrium with several doors leading off it, a deserted reception area in front of her and a pair of lift doors to the left. Arkadian punched the buttons and stood waiting for a moment, then turned abruptly through a set of double doors. Liv followed him into a stairwell which echoed with the sound of his footsteps. She matched hers with his, all the way to the sub-basement, so he wouldn't hear her and tell her to go back outside.

Arkadian emerged from the stairwell and into the corridor. He was immediately struck by how quiet it was. A lab coat lay discarded on the floor, knocked from its hook by someone in the rush to get out. Further down the hallway he could see the door to Reis's office. It was open. He punched the redial button on his phone and stalked down the hallway towards it.

He glanced inside and saw Reis's mobile skittering across the abandoned desk. It clinked against a black mug, half-full of milky coffee, steam still rising from its pale surface. Arkadian snapped his phone shut. Heard the silence flooding back. Heard a noise in the corridor behind him. Spun round, his hand reaching for the gun in his shoulder holster.

Liv saw Arkadian's hand dart into his jacket then annoyance flash across his face as he realized it was her. She glanced past his shoulder into the empty office, desperately wanting to know what was going on, but also knowing this was not the time to ask questions.

Arkadian used the sleeve of his jacket to pull the door closed and the sound of her heartbeat quickened in her ears. She'd been around enough investigations to recognize the significance of this move. He was treating the place as a crime scene.

The door clicked shut and Arkadian turned to look at her again.

'Stay here,' he said, heading towards another set of doors at the far end of the corridor. 'Don't touch anything.'

He shoulder-barged his way through. Liv scampered after him, slipping through the gap before they had time to swing shut, and found herself in a narrow, featureless room.

It was just a few degrees above freezing, and the smell of disinfectant and something sweet and faintly nauseating hung in the air. One wall was filled with a grid of large filing drawers – about thirty in all. Liv shuddered in the sudden chill and the knowledge of what they contained.

A trolley had been abandoned in the centre of the room. A plastic sheet was draped across the lower half of it, bunched up like bedclothes. It looked as though the occupant had got up when the fire alarm sounded and left the building along with everyone else. Arkadian swerved round it and came to a halt by a drawer at the far end of the room, three rows in and two up, which had a number eight stencilled above a window containing a handwritten note trapped behind a sheet of clear plastic. Liv couldn't quite read it from where she stood, but she knew what it said.

Arkadian grabbed the handle with the sleeve of his jacket. As it slid open Liv heard a sound behind her. She spun round. A pale, skinny man hovered on the threshold. He held a half-eaten bagel in one hand and pushed a curtain of black hair from his face with the other.

'Where the hell have you been?' Arkadian yelled.

Reis leaned to one side and looked past Liv. 'Missed break-fast,' he said, indicating the bagel. Then his eyes dropped and registered confusion.

Liv followed his gaze, bracing herself. But the body of her dead brother was nowhere to be seen. The drawer was empty.

64

Liv, Arkadian and Reis stood motionless.

Then Arkadian broke the spell. He glanced up into the corner of the room. 'Out!' he said, shepherding them into the relative warmth of the hallway before heading back towards the stairs. 'Don't let anyone go in there,' he called back at Reis. 'Check your office to see if anything's missing – and don't touch anything.'

Reis and Liv exchanged glances. A flicker of recognition showed in his eyes, then a look of uneasiness as he realized who she must be. Liv looked back up the corridor before it turned into pity. She saw Arkadian disappear through the doors leading to the stairwell and started after him, partly to find out what was going on and partly so she wouldn't have to hear the pathologist telling her how sorry he was for her loss.

Arkadian took the stairs two at a time and burst back through the doors leading to reception. It was already full of people making their way back into the building. He pushed his way towards the security office.

'Call central dispatch,' he said to the forbidding-looking matriarch behind the desk. 'Tell them there's been a break-in at the morgue. Tell them to send a forensics team and stand by for a description of the suspects.'

The woman glared at him sternly over a pair of half-moon glasses, her face a picture of indignation.

'Now!' he bellowed, snapping everyone to attention. 'And no one's to go down to the sub-basement.'

The nerve centre of the morgue's security operation was just about big enough to house a chair, a desk and several towers of computer memory recording the feeds from eighteen CCTVs. A couple of flat-screen monitors sat on the desktop, each split into three grids with an image from a different camera in every square. A uniformed man in his fifties looked up as Arkadian entered, the glow of the twin screens glinting on the Reactolite lenses of glasses still dark from the outside daylight.

Arkadian flashed his badge. 'Can you punch up the feed covering the cold-storage chamber in the lower basement?'

Light flooded into the darkened room as the door beside him opened again. Arkadian turned and saw Liv squeeze in behind him. She stared resolutely at the monitors to avoid making eye contact. He thought about asking her to leave, but decided he'd prefer to keep her close.

He dug out his phone and scrolled through the caller log until he found the call Reis had made when the fire alarm had gone off. Nine-fourteen. One of the screens was now filled with the feed from the camera he'd spotted in the corner of the cold store. 'Can you wind it back to o-nine-fourteen, and play it from there?'

The guard pulled down the menu and tapped in the time. The picture jumped and a man appeared in the middle of the previously empty room, manoeuvring an empty trolley towards one of the lockers.

'Who's that?' Arkadian asked.

The security guard peered at the screen. The man stopped and looked around, registering the shrill sound of the alarm.

'Don't know his name, but he works here,' the security guard said. 'I think he's one of the lab techs.'

The recording continued in three-second jerks until the man vanished, moving like a badly animated marionette.

'Look at the sheet.' Liv pointed at the screen. 'Neatly folded on top of the trolley. When we got there it was all bunched up.'

'Can you speed it up a little?' Arkadian asked.

The guard hit a key a couple of times and the numbers jumped forward in five second units, then ten. When the clock flipped to o-nine-seventeen another figure stepped into the frame.

'Hold it,' Arkadian said.

The guard resumed its three-second default.

The newcomer was tall, black hair, black clothes. They couldn't see his face. He kept his back to the camera the whole time. He moved past the trolley and stopped in front of the drawer Arkadian had opened. He reached for the handle with a gloved hand and pulled. Liv felt her heart pound against her ribcage. She saw the outline of a body-bag.

The man unzipped it. Despite the poor quality of the image, Liv recognized the bearded face immediately and felt tears pricking her eyes. A moment later the interloper shifted his position and obscured Samuel's face with his body. He seemed to be searching for something in his jacket pocket. He struggled against the material for a few moments then removed the glove from his right hand and recommenced his search, quickly finding whatever it was he was looking for. He leaned across the open drawer with whatever he had retrieved from the pocket, then whipped his head round towards the door, clearly disturbed by something. He had kept his face tilted down, wary of the camera, but Liv still saw enough to recognize him.

'Gabriel . . .' she breathed. 'He picked me up at the airport last night.'

Arkadian grabbed the desk phone, his eyes never leaving the screen as the man zipped up the body-bag, slid the drawer back into place, climbed on to the trolley and pulled up the plastic sheet.

'This is Inspector Davud Arkadian. We've just had a break-in at the morgue; I want all units on the lookout for a suspect.

A white male. Slender build. Maybe six-one, six-two. Black clothes –'

Two new figures dressed as paramedics appeared, pushing a trolley between them. The taller one glanced up at the camera but it was impossible to see his face. Both wore surgical masks, caps, lab coats and Nitrile gloves. Arkadian watched them move straight to Sam's locker. They checked inside the body-bag, hoisted it on to the trolley, closed the drawer and wheeled the earthly remains of Samuel Newton out of frame. The whole operation had taken less than fifteen seconds.

Gabriel rose like something out of a horror film and followed them, leaving the plastic sheet how they had discovered it.

Arkadian covered the mouthpiece with his hand. 'Is there a camera in the delivery bay?'

The cold-storage chamber was replaced by a raised concrete platform with an ambulance on one side and a set of overlapping plastic doors on the other. Liv thought it looked like the entrance to a meat-processing factory.

After a few seconds the doors buckled and a trolley crashed through them. The two paramedics practically threw it into the back of the ambulance.

Arkadian removed his hand from the mouthpiece. 'We have a new priority. I want an urgent BOLO for an ambulance outbound from the city morgue, heading towards Hallelujah Crescent. Licence plate unknown. Suspects are two Caucasian males, medium-heavy build, one maybe six-three, the other around five-ten, both dressed as paramedics. Be advised the suspects are wanted for break-in and unlawful seizure and are fleeing the crime scene. A photo of the secondary suspect will be circulated immediately.'

He slammed down the phone. 'Can you lift images of the suspects from the footage and email it to central dispatch?' It wasn't a request.

Arkadian didn't wait for the guard's reply. He needed to talk to Reis.

65

Gabriel slipped into the deserted dispatch room and ducked under the central counter, still covered with the morning's post and packages, abandoned as soon as the alarm had sounded. He retrieved his bag and bike helmet from where he'd stashed them and grabbed a medium-sized padded envelope as he heard voices in the hallway.

'You OK there?' A middle-aged woman had appeared at the door, regarding him with flinty suspicion from behind thick designer frames.

'Yeah . . . got a package here for . . .' Gabriel glanced at the label. 'A Dr . . . Makin?' He treated her to a 500-watt smile.

After about a second in its beam her hand fluttered up to her chest and her eyes softened. 'You mean Dr *Meachin*,' she said. 'Need me to sign for it?'

'No, that's OK,' Gabriel said. 'Guy who pointed me here already signed for it.'

He slipped back into the hallway. The place was filled with people. He heard someone shouting in the reception area behind him. He pressed on to the delivery bay. The back of the building was deserted. At the far end of the alley he saw an ambulance easing into the morning traffic on Hallelujah Crescent.

He jumped down from the concrete platform and sprinted to where he'd left his bike behind a large refuse bin. With two hard kicks on the starter pedal he gunned it up the alley then braked hard. Hallelujah Crescent was a one-way street, always crammed at this time of the morning. Gabriel looked left. He couldn't see the ambulance. He began threading his way in and out of the cars, scanning the traffic ahead. The road uncoiled before him, bit by frustrating bit, until it reached the junction with the southern boulevard and split in two – right towards the outskirts and left towards the Citadel. His money was on left, but he eased the bike into the central line for the time being, ready to turn in either direction the moment he spotted his target.

He stamped his heel on the brake, locking the back wheel. A horn blared and a van steered around him, its driver shouting angrily from the safety of his cab. Gabriel didn't even notice. He was looking up the boulevard, checking both ways, confirming that somewhere between the alley and this junction the ambulance had simply vanished.

66

Reis was scanning a sheet of paper when Arkadian walked into his office.

'Anything missing?'

'Nope.' Reis remained at his desk. 'I thought they may have taken this – the lab report I told you about – but I guess they didn't know what it was. It's . . . extraordinary.'

He glanced over the Inspector's shoulder and his face registered surprise. Liv stood in the doorway behind him.

Arkadian sighed. 'Reis, this is Liv Adamsen. She's related to . . . She's the monk's sister.'

'Yeah, I . . . er . . . Hi . . .' A nervous smile tweaked the edges of Reis's mouth. 'Sorry about the, er . . .' He trailed off as his mind tottered through a minefield of inappropriate responses to what had just happened.

'Sorry about losing my brother's body?' Liv suggested.

'Yeah . . . I guess . . .' he said. 'First time it's ever happened.'

'Well, that's reassuring.'

Reis blushed, ruining his well-cultivated pallor, and dropped his gaze. 'No, I suppose . . . er . . . no . . .' He shut up before he could dig himself deeper.

Arkadian pinched the bridge of his nose. 'Miss Adamsen . . .' He fixed her with what he hoped was a look of suitable authority. 'I know you're angry, and you have a right to be, but I've got every uniform out there looking for that ambulance. We'll get your brother back. I shouldn't have let you down here in the first place, and now it's a crime scene you can't be here. I need you to go back up to reception and wait until we've secured this area.'

Liv held his gaze. 'No.'

'It wasn't a request.'

Very deliberately, Liv stepped into the office and sat down opposite Reis. 'Let me explain why I'm staying. In the last twenty-four hours I've discovered that my brother, who I thought was already dead, *has* died, for real. I've flown thousands of miles on uncomfortable planes to come and identify him. I've been kidnapped, shot at, and then – just when I thought I would finally be re-united with him – *you* lost him.'

She let the words sink in.

'I know how to behave at a crime scene. I can't contaminate this one further because I've already been in it. So you might as well keep me here and keep me happy. Because,' she held up the crumpled newspaper, 'if you try and pack me off, the first thing I'll do is call my editor. Think he might hold the front page?'

Reis flicked between Arkadian and the girl as they stared each other out, until Arkadian finally blinked.

'OK,' he said. 'Stay. But if anything does leak to the press, anything at all, I'm going to assume it came from you and charge you with obstruction of an ongoing investigation. Are we clear?'

'Perfectly.' She turned, the ice in her green eyes instantly thawing. 'So – Reis, isn't it . . .?'

The pathologist nodded. Feisty women frightened him at the best of times. He also found them incredibly attractive. This one was off the scale.

'You were saying something about a lab report?'

Reis glanced at Arkadian, who just shrugged.

'OK. Er . . . lab reports are a normal part of the clinical procedure . . . as you probably know. Here we always run a standard batch of tissue tests and tox routines to establish certain things and rule out others, such as whether the subject may have taken, or been given, something that could have contributed to their death. One of these measures the extent of necrosis in the liver, which often helps establish time of death. We didn't really need to in this case because of all the witnesses, but procedure is procedure. These are the results –' He gestured at a red note stapled to the top sheet.

'It came back with a contamination query. They think the sample must have been incorrectly labelled. There was no sign of any necrosis; in fact, quite the opposite. The cells appear to be . . . regenerating. Liver cells do regenerate, of course, but only if the host is alive . . .'

Arkadian wondered – too late – if it had been the smartest move to let Liv hear this.

'I checked it out thoroughly. The sample they got was definitely from the monk. So going purely on these results, and ignoring the fact that I performed the post-mortem myself . . .' He hesitated. 'I'd say he was on the mend . . .'

67

A third of the way along Hallelujah Crescent, in a tall, elegant building that had been hollowed out, reinforced and turned into an extortionately expensive car park, a metal screen rolled up and a plain white transit van edged its way into the traffic.

Gabriel watched from across the street, his face obscured by his visor. He glanced down at a handheld PDA device, like a motorcycle courier checking the details of a delivery. Towards the top of the screen a small white dot pulsed gently while a street map scrolled up around it. The movement of the dot corresponded exactly with that of the van, or, more precisely, the movement of Samuel's body as the transponder he'd inserted in his throat transmitted his location.

He slipped the PDA into his jacket pocket and kick-started the bike. The van reached the end of the crescent and turned left towards the heart of the old town. Gabriel followed a few cars back.

Just short of the northern boulevard the van peeled off down a slip road past a large sign welcoming visitors to the Umbrasian Quarter.

For as long as Ruin had existed, the Umbrasian or Shadow Quarter had been the least popular and therefore least populated part of the city. Tucked below the northern side of the Citadel, the streets here remained permanently shrouded in the shadow of the mountain, even at the height of summer. In the modern era its cheap land prices made it the perfect location for the vast car parks needed to cater for the armies of tourists swarming to the city. It was into this valley of cold, grey concrete that the van now drove.

Once they left the anonymity of the ring road, Gabriel dropped further back and slid in behind a shuttle bus. The van turned sharp right, down a narrow alleyway between two huge multi-storey monstrosities.

Gabriel continued on past, pulled a fast U-turn, mounted the pavement, killed the engine and tilted the bike against its foot-rest. He slid off the detachable side-mirror and sprinted to the corner of the building, flipping up his visor as he went. He squatted against the wall, held the mirror low to the ground, angled down the alley, which ended at a sheer rock face that rose to the old town wall. He watched as the van came to a standstill. A man with long dark hair and a beard leaned out of the driver's window and swiped a card through an entry machine then glanced back in his direction.

Gabriel froze.

With no sunlight to reflect off the mirror the only thing that would give him away was movement.

He studied the driver. The man looked more like a rock star or a movie actor than a hired thug. After a few moments the van eased forward and disappeared into the side of the building.

Gabriel pulled the PDA from his pocket. The pulsing white dot moved across the top of the screen, where the rear of the garage met the side of the mountain. He stuffed the mirror in his pocket and stood up. Hundreds of pairs of headlights peeped over a low wall that stretched away to his left, like convicts contemplating freedom. Gabriel vaulted the wall and hurried inside.

The place was cold and damp and smelt of oil and petrol fumes and urine. Aware that he was probably on CCTV he moved towards a distant Audi, made like he was about to get in it, then knelt as if for a fumbled key and stole another long look at the PDA.

The white dot was no longer within the confines of the car

park, but passing through the bedrock beyond. He watched it cut across the streets and buildings of the old city, aiming straight for the Citadel. When it was two-thirds of the way there, it froze, blinked and disappeared.

Gabriel moved over to the cold concrete of the back wall and held the PDA directly against it to boost the signal. The dot flashed on again, closer still to the Citadel.

Almost at the boundary of the old moat, it flickered out completely.

68

Kutlar sat up front, staring into the jagged darkness of the tunnel. The rumble of tyres across the uneven floor and the hammering of the diesel engine combined to produce a singularly mournful sound. The vibrations rattled the plastic dashboard and plucked at the stitches in Kutlar's leg. He relished the pain – it kept him focused and proved he was still alive.

His head was fuzzy from the pills he'd taken. He realized he'd have to watch that. He'd have to stay sharp if he wanted to think his way out of this one. It had all come clear when Cornelius and Johann helped him out of the clinic and into the van.

'You need to tell us what happened,' Cornelius had said, like he was just offering friendly advice. 'You need to tell us how the girl managed to escape. And, most importantly,' he'd added, so close that the whiskers of his beard brushed against Kutlar's ear, 'you need to tell us what she looks like.'

That was why he was still breathing. They only had her name, but he had seen her face. As long as they were still looking for her, he was more useful to them alive.

The passage rose suddenly and emerged into a cavernous chamber. Johann swung the wheel and the headlights flashed across a steel door before they crunched to a stop. Johann killed the engine and he and Cornelius slipped out of the cab. Kutlar didn't move. He watched them in the side mirrors. The chassis shifted slightly as the back doors opened and Kutlar heard the ripple of heavy plastic as the first of the stiffs was lifted out.

He'd been shocked when they popped the two paramedics. The doc's death had been more acceptable somehow; no one would be that surprised when his body was eventually found slumped in the chair where they'd left him. He'd stepped across the line long ago when he got hooked on junk and started treating gunshot wounds. The medics, though – they were just civilians.

Glowing red in the brake lights, the monks reappeared from behind the van with the first body-bag and laid it by the steel door. When they'd twice repeated the process, Johann took out his swipe card and the door sprung inwards. Seconds later it clicked back into place, sealing the bodies inside.

Cornelius and Johann climbed back into the van.

'I can help you find her,' Kutlar said.

Cornelius turned to him, lip curled. 'How?'

'Get us out of here and I'll show you.' Kutlar tried to conjure up a smile but only managed a grimace. 'I need to make a call.' He shrugged theatrically. 'But there's no signal down here.'

Cornelius said nothing for a moment, just looked at the thin film of sweat bathing Kutlar's skin despite the chill of their surroundings. 'Sure,' he said finally.

Johann twisted the ignition key.

The engine throbbed into life, the sound suddenly overwhelming in the confined space. Kutlar glanced at the wing mirror and watched the red glow fade from the cave as they drove away.

The three body-bags lay in the black silence of the mountain while torches were being lit in the maze of tunnels above by those coming to collect them. A little over twenty-four hours after escaping from the Citadel, Brother Samuel had returned.

IV

In the beginning was the World,
    And the World was God, and the World
was good.

Fragment from the Heretic Bible

69

As crime scenes go, the cold-storage chamber of the city morgue was about as good as it got. Highly restricted access had prevented the usual build up of partial prints, hair follicles and other assorted trace evidence that clouded most investigations. All the surfaces were clinically clean. And there was a complete CCTV record showing where the suspects had been and what they had touched.

'There,' Arkadian said, pointing at the edge of the bunched-up green plastic sheet on the trolley. 'The first suspect touched it as he pulled it over himself.'

Petersen smiled. The only thing easier to lift prints off was glass.

'He also touched that drawer.' Arkadian pointed to locker number eight. 'Let me know as soon as you find anything.' He left Petersen laying out his brushes and unscrewing a tub of fine aluminium powder.

A uniformed officer was stationed by the door, ensuring no one else came in or out. Reis paced the corridor outside his office. He held up a specimen jar as Arkadian approached.

Arkadian took it without breaking his stride. 'Where is she?'

'First-floor staff room,' Reis called after him.

The statement detailed everything that had happened to her from walking into the morgue to identifying the mystery man on the CCTV footage. Liv was preparing to sign it when Arkadian appeared. She still wondered what Gabriel's game was and why he was playing it. She hadn't described him as 'the man who tried to kidnap me'. The most he had done was to impersonate an officer and offer her a lift into the city. He wasn't the one who'd stuck a gun in her face. He hadn't snatched her brother's body either, although she still wasn't sure what he'd been doing in the cold-storage room. In the end she'd settled for 'the man who met me at the airport and claimed he was my police escort'. It wasn't elegant, but it was accurate. She scribbled the date next to her name.

The uniformed officer checked her signature then scraped his chair back from the narrow table. Arkadian closed the door behind him.

Liv dragged a depressed-looking geranium across the table towards her and started deadheading it, pinching the shrivelled flowers from the choked stems and crumbling them into the pot. 'Found him yet?'

Arkadian looked down into the street. It would have been the perfect moment for a police van to screech to a halt in front of the building with all three suspects cuffed in the back, but it didn't happen.

'Not yet,' he said. A diesel rainbow was smeared across the wet road where the fire-trucks had parked. 'We're working on it.' He turned back to the crumpled newspaper on the table between them, the front page now a kaleidoscope of letters and crossings out. 'Had any luck with that?'

'Haven't had much time to focus on it, to be honest. Been kind of distracted.'

Arkadian said nothing, hoping the silence would soften her.

'Do you really believe this is why they took him?' She examined the scrawled symbols and letters once more.

'Maybe. As soon as we catch them, we'll ask. Until then, I'd like to ask you something.' He laid the package Reis had given him down on the table-top.

Liv's eyes narrowed. 'That's a buccal swabbing kit.'

Arkadian nodded. 'Given what Reis got back from the lab,

it would be very helpful for us to compare your DNA with your brother's. It would also establish your biological kinship beyond any doubt.' He slid the kit towards her.

Liv picked the last dead flower from the geranium and mulched it with the others. She rubbed her hands together then opened the specimen jar and wiped the cotton swab inside her cheek. She screwed down the lid and handed it back to him. The Citadel rose up behind the buildings across the street, stark and impassive against the sky. The sight of it made her shudder.

Arkadian followed her gaze. Saw a flash of movement from the street below. 'Jesus,' he said, springing from his chair. A TV news van had pulled up in front of the building.

'I didn't call them,' she said. 'I'm strictly print. We hate those guys.'

There was a knock on the door.

'Sorry, chief,' Petersen said, 'but I've lifted practically a whole set of latents from the sheet. You want me to send them for routine processing or fast track?'

'Hang on a minute, I'll come with you.' He turned back to Liv. 'I know you didn't call that news crew, so don't misread what I'm about to say . . . I think we need to get you out of the building.'

Liv's expression darkened.

'This isn't an attempt to get rid of you; I just think you'd be safer away from here. If the press know what's happened, they'll lay siege to the place. I don't want the people who took your brother finding out on the six o'clock news that you're here. But I think it's best you stay under our protection. I'm going to arrange for someone to drive you back to Central so you can get a shower and a change of clothes. I'll catch up with you later, OK?'

Liv looked down at her mud-encrusted outfit.

'OK,' she said. 'But if you're using this as an excuse to side-line me, then I'm going to walk straight back out and call a press conference.'

'Be my guest,' he said. 'Just stay away from the windows. I don't want to see your face on the news.'

Neither do I, Liv thought as she inspected her grimy blouse. She pulled a dirt-roughened lock of hair down from her fringe and glanced over at the window, trying to catch her own faint reflection in the glass. Instead her eyes were drawn back to the thin, dark mountain soaring into the clear blue sky.

70

Athanasius had been summoned into his master's office shortly after Matins and asked to accompany him on a task – 'for the sake of the brotherhood,' the Abbot had said. '*A task that you must not discuss with anyone.*'

So here they were, picking their way down a narrow, rubble-strewn stairway, the way ahead lit only by the burning torch in his hand. Occasionally they passed other narrow and mysterious passageways.

They had been walking steadily downwards for almost five minutes when Athanasius saw a dim glow up ahead. It came from inside an arched doorway that looked newer and more sculpted than its forgotten surroundings. He followed the Abbot into a small cave where two monks stood silently, each carrying a torch of their own. Both wore the green robes of the Sancti.

Athanasius averted his eyes and noticed another door sunk into the wall, this one made of heavy steel. A thin slot sat to one side of it, similar to the hi-tech locks that guarded the entrance to the great library. The Abbot nodded a silent greeting to the Sancti, reached into his sleeve and removed a magnetic card. There was a muffled clunk. The Abbot pushed the door wide and the three of them passed through. Athanasius stood alone for a moment, then followed.

The chamber was slightly smaller than the one they had just come from and the air inside seemed warmer, thickened by a fine dust that caught the orange glow of the flambeau.

It had an identical steel door built into the far wall, in front of which lay three cocoons of heavy-duty plastic. Athanasius knew immediately what they must contain.

One of the Sancti unzipped the closest far enough for a head to emerge. A thin trickle of blood ran from a small hole in his temple to his hairline. Athanasius didn't recognize him, nor the second body. But he knew the third. He looked upon the face of his dead friend and had to reach for the wall to steady himself.

'The cross has returned to the Citadel,' the Abbot said softly as he too looked down upon the battered face of Brother Samuel.

For a moment all four stared at him, then, as if on a pre-arranged command, he was zipped back into the bag and the Sancti carried him away. He waited for them to return for the other two bodies. But they did not.

'These unfortunates must be disposed of,' the Abbot said. 'I am sorry to have to leave this task to you – I know you will find it distasteful – but I have matters of great importance to attend to, your brothers may not walk in the lower section of the Citadel, and you are the only person I can trust . . .'

He made no move to explain who the men were, or why they were now lying dead on the floor of this forgotten cave.

'Take them to the deserted section in the eastern chambers,' he said. 'Drop them in one of the old oubliettes. Their bodies will be forgotten, but their souls will be at peace.' He paused at the entrance and rubbed his hands together, as if washing them. 'The door will close automatically in five minutes,' he said. 'Make sure you are clear of this room by then.'

Athanasius listened to his footsteps recede into the darkness. *The cross has returned to the Citadel . . .*
Athanasius recalled the words of the Heretic Bible:

> *The cross will fall*
> *The cross will rise*

He wondered what they had in mind for the defiled remains of his friend. He'd be taken to the chapel of the Sacrament, no doubt; why else would Sancti have come to fetch him?

But to think he might rise again . . .

It was the logic of a madman.

He glanced down at the remaining bags, two anonymous corpses in a silent crypt, and wondered what lives they had woken up to that morning and who might now be wondering anxiously at their silence. A wife? A lover? A child?

He dropped to his haunches and said a silent prayer over each as he zipped them gently back into their plastic shrouds. Then he dragged each of them into the antechamber, fearful that the door might click shut at any moment, and turn the dusty chamber into his own tomb.

71

Liv sat in the staff room of the city morgue, looking at the picture of her brother and conjuring images from her past. Relating her family history to Arkadian had been like shining a light into it. She remembered now how she had sat Samuel down in her dorm-room and excitedly told him all the things she'd found out on her trip to Paradise, West Virginia.

She pictured him perching on the edge of the narrow bed, his face, already clouded with pain and sadness, paling to ash as she told him the details of how they had both come into the world. For her it had explained all the unanswered questions about identity that had tormented her throughout her childhood and teens. She had hoped that sharing it would bring him peace also. But her attempt to cool his smouldering self-hatred had only thrown fuel on to it. He already blamed himself for the death of their father. Now she had handed him a reason to blame himself for their mother's too.

He had shambled away like a ghost.

He didn't speak to her for months afterwards. All her calls went unanswered. She even left messages at his therapist's office, until she discovered he'd stopped going and started fervent visits to church instead.

The last time she had seen him was in New York. He had called up out of the blue, sounding happy and vital, just like his old self. He told her he was going on a journey and wanted to see her before he left.

They met at Grand Central Station and spent the day hanging out and doing tourist stuff. He told her he'd realized some things that had given him a new focus. He said that when someone dies so someone else can live, then that someone has been spared for a reason. They had a higher purpose; the journey he was about to begin was his way of divining what that purpose was.

She'd assumed the journey would entail climbing a bunch of scary-assed mountains, but he told her that wasn't the way to get closer to God. He didn't elaborate and she didn't ask him to. She'd just been glad he seemed to have found an exciting new direction. She didn't for one moment think, as she waved him off at the airport, that she would never see him alive again.

Liv blinked back the tears and looked up at the Citadel, standing like a sliver of night against the spring sky. She felt now the pain her brother must have felt back then. She had never blamed herself for her father's death or her mother's, but she blamed herself for Samuel's. No matter what Arkadian thought, it was her desire for self-knowledge that had led to her discovering the truth about their birth, and it was her thoughtless revelation of it to Samuel that led to his fall from the top of that bloody mountain.

The sound of the door clicking open snapped her back to the present. She rubbed at the wetness around her eyes and turned to see a bulky plainclothes cop with a round, pasty face and thinning hair the colour of brick. His eyes peered at her from the softness of his face and his hands rested on his hips, opening his jacket slightly to reveal a hint of shoulder holster, and a set of handcuffs clipped to his belt. His shirt strained to contain his belly and a badge rested on it, suspended from a cord around his neck.

She'd seen a million like him; the insecure kind, who had to let you know they were police, even though they wore no uniform. They were the sort she always cosied up to when working a story, because they liked to talk.

His brow creased. 'You OK?'

241

'Yeah. Just . . . having a moment . . .'

He nodded uncertainly. Tried a smile. Gave up and pointed over his shoulder with his thumb. 'Only, I got a squad car out back when you're ready. I'm going to sneak you out and take you over to Central. We got a gym over there where you can grab a hot shower and a change of clothes.'

Liv blotted her eyes with the sleeve of her blouse. 'Sure,' she said, shooting him a smile that was even weaker than his. 'What's your name . . .?'

'I'm Sulleiman,' he said, lifting his photo ID. 'Sulley, if you want to be friendly.' She caught a glint of what looked like a chrome-plated .38 sticking out of his pancake holster as she looked at the picture. The flash of the camera had bleached out his face a little and he looked more serious in the picture than in real life, but it was definitely him: Sub-Inspector Sulleiman Mantus, RPF.

'OK,' she said, satisfied that she wasn't about to be kidnapped again. 'Let's go, Sulley.' She swept the newspaper from the table and followed him out.

The reception area was humming as they made their way through it. Two uniformed officers were standing guard by the entrance, checking everyone in and out. Beyond them, Liv saw a news crew, lights on, camera rolling, the reporter standing with her back to the building as she taped her report; or maybe it was live. Liv drifted behind the Sub-Inspector into a hushed hallway leading to the rear of the building. Another uniformed officer stood by a pair of overlapping plastic doors. He nodded as they approached.

'After you . . .' Sulley stood aside.

The plastic buckled slightly before delivering Liv into what she momentarily mistook for the blinding sunshine.

Then a woman shouted: 'Are you connected with the disappearance of the monk?'

Liv spun round to head back into the safety of the building but the Sub-Inspector grabbed her arm and hustled her towards an unmarked police car a little way down the alley. She dropped her head so her hair fell over her face.

'Are you under arrest?' the reporter yelled.

A flashgun exploded to her right and a man's voice joined the questioning.

'What is your connection with the missing man?'

'Was the theft an inside job?'

The Sub-Inspector pulled open the rear door of the car, pushed Liv firmly into the back seat and slammed it behind her.

Liv glanced up just as the interior flooded with light from a camera pressed against the window. She wrenched her head away.

The car bounced on its springs as Sulley dropped into the driver's seat.

'Sorry about that.' He caught her eye in the rear-view mirror as he fired up the engine. 'It's amazing how quickly the press catch on to these things.'

He popped the handbrake and eased away from the pack. The last thing Liv saw as she glanced out of the rear window was the dead-eyed stare of a camera lens looking right back at her.

72

Kathryn Mann pointed to a spot on the dusty concrete floor of the warehouse and the forklift pirouetted gracefully and lowered one of the master pallets from the C-123 right on to it. She was trying to arrange things so that the next shipment due out, an agricultural supplies drop to one of their projects in Uganda, didn't end up buried somewhere in the stack. Each master pallet had a thin aluminium skin round it and was the size of two large refrigerators. It was like a massive three-dimensional puzzle, but it beat sitting in the office watching the news with Oscar and waiting for Gabriel to call.

The truck eased its forks from beneath the pallet and peeled back out to the transport plane. Most of the fertilizer would be flying straight back out again in a few days, with a bit of luck.

A loud rapping caused Kathryn to look up. Through the narrow avenue of crates she could see Oscar standing at the window, gesturing for her to come over. His expression was grim.

Kathryn handed Becky her list. 'Could you make sure these ones stay at the front?'

'Look,' Oscar said, the moment she walked into the office. He pointed the remote at the TV on the wall and edged up the volume.

'The investigation into the death of the monk,' the newsreader announced in a tone usually reserved for massacres and declarations of war, 'has taken a turn for the macabre this morning. Sources close to the investigation believe that his body has disappeared from the city morgue . . .'

244

The picture cut to an unsteady image of a bedraggled woman being led to a car.

'Are you connected with the disappearance of the monk?' the reporter's voice shouted. 'Are you under arrest?'

The woman looked up briefly, staring directly into the lens before dropping her head and disappearing behind a curtain of dirty-looking hair.

'That must be the girl,' Oscar said.

But Kathryn didn't hear him. She was transfixed by the sight of the plainclothes police officer at Liv's side. She watched him bundle her roughly into the back seat. Saw the camera tilt up towards his face. Saw him hold up his freckled hand to push it away.

Then he got in the car and drove her away.

73

Athanasius was in a daze as he walked to the private chapel for prayers. He was still sweating from the exertion of dragging each inert body through the complex series of tunnels leading to the medieval caverns in the eastern section. He was back in the main part of the Citadel now, but the ordeal still clung to him, along with the faint chemical tang of the body-bags. No matter how hard he had scrubbed his hands in the rainwater sinks of the laundry, he couldn't seem to get rid of that smell.

The old dungeons held potent reminders of the church's violent past: rusted shackles and fearsome-looking pincers the colour of dried blood. He'd known the Citadel's history, of course, the crusades and persecutions of more brutal times when a strong belief in God and the teachings of the Church had been forged through fear; but he'd thought those times were gone. Now the spectre of that violent past was clawing at the present, like the smell of ancient death that had risen from the oubliette as he'd tipped the bodies into it, one by one. When he heard the brittle crack of them landing on a bed of forgotten bones, he felt something break inside him, too, as if his actions and his beliefs had been pulled so far apart they had finally snapped. As he shivered alone in the cold mountain, the two phrases he'd glimpsed in the Heretic Bible shone in his mind like fresh truths through the darkness.

He paused outside the private chapel, afraid to enter because of the shame he carried with him. He rubbed his hand distractedly over his scalp and smelt again the antiseptic taint of the body-bag on his sleeve.

He needed to pray. What other hope did he have? He took a deep breath and ducked through the entrance.

The chapel was lit by small votive candles flickering around the T-shaped cross on the far wall. There were no seats, only mats and thin cushions to protect bony old knees from the stone floor. He hadn't noticed a candle burning outside the chapel, but as he entered now he saw it already contained a worshipper. He nearly wept in relief when he saw who it was.

'Dear brother ...' Father Thomas stood and put an arm around the trembling figure of his friend. 'What troubles you so?'

Athanasius took deep breaths, fighting to regain control of himself. It took a few minutes before his heart rate and breathing steadied. He glanced back at the doorway, then into the concerned face of his friend. In his mind, Athanasius debated whether to confide in him or tell him nothing, for his own safety. It was like standing at the edge of a precipice, knowing that if he stepped forward he could never step back.

He looked deeply into his friend's eyes, clouded with curiosity and concern, and started to talk. He told him about the visit to the forbidden vault, about the Heretic Bible and the chilling phrases he had glimpsed as the Abbot leafed through it. He told him about the Prophecy the book contained, and then confessed to the terrible task he had just performed. He told him everything.

When he finished, the two men sat in silence for a long time. Athanasius knew that what he had just shared had endangered them both. Father Thomas looked up. Glanced quickly at the door. Leaned in closer. 'What were the phrases you saw in the forbidden book?' His voice barely rose above a whisper.

Athanasius felt a wave of relief sweep through him. 'The first was "The light of God, sealed up in darkness",' he whispered. 'The second: "Not a mountain sanctified, but a prison cursed."'

He leaned back as Thomas's intelligent eyes flitted back and forth across the darkened room in time with the fevered workings of his mind.

'I have, increasingly of late, felt there was something . . . wrong . . . about this place . . .' He picked his words carefully. 'All this accumulated learning, the product of mankind's finest minds, hidden away in the darkness of the library, illuminating nobody. I undertook my work here for the protection of knowledge, for its preservation, not for its imprisonment.

'When I'd finished my improvements to the library, and seen how well they worked, I petitioned the Prelate to publish the blueprints so that other great libraries could benefit from the systems we now use here. He refused. He said books, and the knowledge they contain, are dangerous weapons in the hands of the unenlightened. He said if they faded and crumbled to dust in the libraries beyond these walls, so much the better.' He looked up at Athanasius, his face registering the private pain and disappointment he had kept buried until now. 'It appears I have built a system that benefits no one but those who seek to imprison that most divine of gifts – knowledge.'

'"The light of God, sealed up in darkness,"' Athanasius quoted softly.

'"Not a mountain sanctified, but a prison cursed,"' Father Thomas replied.

They lapsed into silence again.

'It is both frustrating and ironic,' Athanasius said at length, 'that your ingenious security system prevents us from discovering what else that forbidden book contains.' He dropped his gaze to the flickering flame of a votive candle.

Father Thomas watched him for a moment then drew breath. 'There may be a way,' he said, his eyes now shining with conviction. 'We must wait until after Vespers, when most of the brethren are dining or retiring to the dormitories; when the library is at its quietest.'

74

Gabriel felt the phone vibrate in his pocket and checked the caller ID.

'Mother.'

'Where are you?' Kathryn said.

'Following the body snatchers. They took the monk back to the Citadel. Now two of them are in some kind of dive on the edge of the Lost Quarter. The other one's minding their van.'

'What are they doing?'

'No idea, but I thought I should stick with them. I figure the girl's safe enough – so long as she's with Arkadian.'

'That's just it,' Kathryn said. 'She's not safe. She's not safe at all.'

Kutlar sat in the backroom of the junk-filled shop. Cornelius was to his left. Another man sat opposite, behind a desk cluttered with the guts of computers and mobile phones. Zilli was the 'go to' guy for under-the-counter technology. His chair squeaked every time he fed a bundle of money from a red plastic box into his counting machine. Long black hair spilled from a baseball cap advertising a tractor firm that no longer existed. Kutlar knew it hid a bald spot that no one was supposed to notice.

Zilli's Hawaiian shirt was the brightest thing in what looked like any junk-and-repair joint in any down-at-heel neighbourhood, but also served as a front for everything from fencing stolen property to running guns, drugs and sometimes even people. It was Zilli who had recommended the Bitch Clinic to Kutlar as a good place for gunshot wounds.

Zilli watched the last of the notes clatter through the counter with the same gimlet gaze as an addict cooking up a shot. Then he reached under the desk, his eyes never leaving Cornelius. A small fan whirred in the silence, cooling the motherboard of an eviscerated computer.

Kutlar felt pain lance through his leg as Zilli pulled something dull and metallic into view and pointed it at Cornelius. Cornelius didn't flinch.

'Pleasure doing business,' Zilli said, his face cracking into a lopsided smile that revealed surprisingly perfect teeth. 'Any friend of Kutlar . . .'

He pushed the stacks of cash to one side, placed what looked like an electronic notebook in the centre of the desk and folded it open. The screen flashed into life, showing a map of the world with a blank column to its right beneath two search windows.

'Chinese technology,' Zilli said, as though he was selling them a watch. 'Hacks seamlessly into any telecom network in the world. Just tap in a number and it'll give you chapter and verse on all calls in and out: time, duration, even billing details and registered addresses.'

Cornelius regarded Zilli impassively for a moment then took out a piece of paper that had been tucked inside the Abbot's envelope. There were two names and numbers on it. Liv's was the first. He copied it into the search box and hit return. An hourglass icon appeared on the screen and the app started trawling for a match. After a few seconds a new number appeared in the column below the search window.

'It's found the network,' Zilli said. 'That's the only call logged in or out in the last twelve hours. Twelve is the default setting. You can change it in the preference menu, if you want, but I wouldn't recommend it. You just wind up with every pizza delivery outfit on the planet and all sorts of other shit. But here – watch this . . .'

He parked the cursor over the new number. A dialog box popped up next to it listing a voicemail service. It also gave a postal address in Palo Alto, California.

'That'll be the service provider. If the number had belonged to a person, you'd now know where they live.'

Cornelius continued to watch it chattering through the mobile phone networks trying to lock on to Liv's phone. Kutlar glanced at Zilli, willing him to look in his direction. But he didn't. He just kept looking at the screen. A new dialog box finally appeared: NUMBER NOT DETECTED.

Cornelius looked at Zilli.

'OK . . . now the thing is . . .' Zilli's chair screeched as he sat back. 'It only works when the device you're looking for is switched on. Mobiles send a signal every few minutes to check in with the nearest phone mast. No power, no signal, no trace. Type in a number you know is active. You'll see what I mean.'

The pain in Kutlar's leg flared again as the fan moved up a gear.

Cornelius typed his own number into the second search window and hit return. Zilli folded his hands behind his head, tilting the brim of his cap low over his eyes. His face was a mask.

It took about ten seconds. The map which filled the main window was becoming more detailed, zooming in like a camera freefalling from space directly to the centre of Ruin. It slowed as the outline of buildings began to appear then stopped abruptly over a latticework of streets. An arrow pointed halfway along one called Trinity.

'See!' Zilli said, confident enough of the technology not to check the screen. 'It has sat-nav capabilities too; it can triangulate an active signal to within five feet. It can also trace two numbers at a time and show you how far apart they are. Means you can track someone else's phone relative to your own and the software will plot you a route straight to it. You just need them to switch their mobile on.'

Cornelius snapped the notebook shut. 'Thank you for your help.'

'Any time.'

Cornelius glanced at Kutlar, who got up and limped gratefully out of the door. Cornelius turned and followed him.

'You need to take your lunchbox?' Zilli called after him, nodding at the red plastic container on the desk.

'Keep it,' Cornelius said, without looking back.

75

Liv stood under the fierce jet of the shower and turned it up as hot as she could bear. The pain was good. It felt cleansing. She watched the water turn from grey to clear as it sluiced off her body and spiralled down the drain, carrying away the grime of the night.

She ran her hand down her side, finding her cruciform scar, tracing its outline with the tips of her fingers, favouring the part of her that had once been physically connected to her brother. Her hand continued up her side and down her arm to where a cross-hatch of smaller scars corrugated her skin, scores of thin lines scratched during a childhood troubled by the lack of a mother and a sense she was a stranger in her own family.

The pain she felt now under the scalding water brought back the hot bite of the razor, which had focused her teenage mind somewhere other than the numbing chaos of her emotions. If only her father had told her back then what she had discovered for herself on that shady porch in Paradise, West Virginia. She understood now that when he had looked at her with sadness in his eyes it was not through disappointment in her. It was because he saw the woman whose name she carried. He saw the love he had lost.

The hot water continued to beat down and her thoughts drifted now to her own losses: her mother, then her father, now her brother. She turned the tap all the way over until scalding rods of water drilled into her flesh and carried away the tears that leaked from her eyes. Feeling pain was better than feeling nothing at all.

Sub-Inspector Sulleiman Mantus paced the hallway. He had too much nervous energy to sit. But it was a good feeling: the sort an athlete feels in the middle of a game; the sort a hunter enjoys when he's closing on his quarry.

Tipping the press off about the theft from the morgue was just the tip of the iceberg. He knew how these things worked. The division would try and play it down, because whichever way you looked at it they came out of it stinking worse than a jailhouse toilet; and the more they tried to lock it down, the more desperate the press would be for information. No one paid better than journos, and this story was front-page international and syndicated, so he was now pulling down big payments from a major news network as well as both original parties, neither of whose interest in the case appeared to be waning.

He glanced up the hallway. A couple of uniforms were standing by the doors, bitching about something or other. He could hear the murmur of their conversation but couldn't make out what they were saying. He took out his phone, scrolled through the menu and dialled a number. 'I have something you might be interested in,' he said.

76

Cornelius stood by the van watching Kutlar move painfully down the street towards him. If he got much worse they might have to reconsider his usefulness. Johann sat in the driver's seat talking to the informant on the phone. He wrote down an address then hung up.

'The girl's here,' he said.

Cornelius took the slip of paper and looked back down the street. Kutlar was the only one among them who had seen her, but he had his own image in his mind, and had done ever since the Abbot had outlined their mission. He stroked the puckered skin on his cheek where his beard wouldn't grow, remembering a street on the outskirts of Kabul and the plaintive figure in the blue burkha holding out the bundle of rags that could have been a child, slowing their vehicle just long enough for the rocket propelled grenade to lock on to it.

It was good to picture your enemy.

It helped you focus.

So to him the girl was the woman who had helped wipe out his whole platoon, the destroyer of the only family he had ever known – until the Church embraced him. He imagined her threatening this new family and it gave him strength and purpose. This time he would stop her.

Johann slipped from behind the wheel and went to the rear of the van as Kutlar finally limped to a standstill beside them.

'Get in,' Cornelius said.

Kutlar did as he was told, like a dog blindly obeying the master who beat him.

Johann reappeared in his red windcheater and walked past without a word, heading in the direction Kutlar had just come from.

Cornelius climbed into the driver's seat and handed the address to Kutlar. 'Take us there,' he said.

Kutlar felt the vibrations tear through his ruined leg as the van bumped over cheap municipal tarmac poured straight on to the ancient cobbles. He considered the pills in his pocket, but knew he couldn't afford to take one. They killed the pain sure enough, but they also made him feel like everything was fine, and he couldn't afford to feel that way.

Not if he wanted to live.

Johann didn't look up as the van drove past. He continued round the corner and down towards Zilli's place. As he drew closer he took out his mobile phone with his right hand and dropped his left into the windcheater and closed it around the stock of his Glock.

Zilli was standing on a chair behind the counter, slotting a red plastic box on to a high shelf between an empty disk spindle and an old Sega Megadrive.

'D'you unlock these things?' Johann held up his phone.

Zilli turned and squinted at it.

'Sure.' He stepped down. 'What you got there – BlackBerry?'

Johann nodded.

'Nice piece.' He tapped the keyboard of a PC that despite its ancient appearance could hack into any phone known to man.

He pressed the menu button and realized too late that it was already unlocked.

77

The roasted aromas of the coffee maker in the corner of the office did little to mask the odour of the morgue. Arkadian sat behind Reis's hopelessly cluttered desk as a large PDF file downloaded on the computer screen. Outside, the clink and buzz of the path labs signalled a return to something approaching normality.

The file was being sent from the records department of US Homeland Security in response to the fingerprint they had lifted from the plastic sheet. They'd got a positive hit in less than a minute. Arkadian couldn't quite believe it. Sure, all they had to do in any TV cop drama was run some prints through the computer and within seconds they had a name, address and recent photo of the perp looking like a whack-job; it was a standing joke in any precinct. But in the real world fingerprints were hardly ever used to identify suspects; they were part of the detailed chain of evidence that bound a suspect to a crime *after* they had been caught by other, more time-consuming means. Most prints were simply not on record for comparison.

The file finished downloading and Arkadian clicked on the icon. As the first page filled the screen he realized why they'd caught a match so quickly. It was a military service file. Men and women in the armed forces were routinely fingerprinted. It helped identify them in the event of their death in the line of duty. Until recently, most nations had been very protective indeed of their ex-service personnel files – but that was before 9/11. Now it seemed they were available to any friendly nation who came asking.

Arkadian scrolled past the cover page and started to read.

The file detailed the complete military service history of Sergeant Gabriel de la Cruz Mann (retired), formerly of the 5th US Special Forces Group. A photograph showed a uniformed man with a severe white-walled buzz cut and penetrating pale blue eyes. Arkadian checked it against a printout from the CCTV footage. The hair had grown out, but it was the same man.

Arkadian scrolled through it all – background, psych reports, security checks, everything. He was thirty-two, American father, half-Brazilian, half-Turkish mother. Father an archaeologist, mother worked for and later ran Ortus, an international aid charity – so early years spent travelling the world.

Education a patchwork of interrupted study at a series of international schools then a Harvard scholarship majoring in modern languages and economics. Spoke five languages fluently including English, Turkish and Portuguese, and could get by in Pashto and Dari following his tours of duty in Afghanistan.

Something in the file caught Arkadian's eye and he stopped skimming and started reading. At the beginning of his final year at Harvard, something happened that clearly had a seismic effect on young Gabriel. Whilst cataloguing a major new find of ancient texts unearthed in the Iraqi desert near a place called Al-Hillah, Dr John Mann had been killed, along with several colleagues. It caused a major international stir. Saddam Hussein, still dictator in residence at the time, blamed Kurdish rebels. The worldwide community suspected Saddam might have done it and pinned the blame on the Kurds while he looted the priceless treasures for himself. None of the texts were ever seen again.

It was not clear from the file who Gabriel blamed for his father's death, but the fact that he dropped out of college and enlisted in the US Army in advance of the impending war in Iraq suggested he may have harboured certain suspicions. He enlisted as a private – though his academic record would have guaranteed him a commission – and passed out of basic training with such high grades he was immediately accepted for Special Airborne training.

He spent nine months at Fort Campbell on the Kentucky–Tennessee border, learning to fly planes, jump out of them and kill people in an assortment of ways and with a variety of weapons. The file became more opaque as the specifics of his duties became more classified, but he served as a platoon sergeant in Afghanistan during Operation Enduring Freedom, and was decorated twice, once for courage under fire and once for his part in a covert hostage rescue operation; he and his platoon had rescued a group of kidnapped aid workers from a Taliban stronghold. He'd left the service four years ago. It didn't say why.

There was an additional page tagged to the end of the file detailing his known movements since his discharge. He worked as a security advisor for Ortus, and had travelled extensively to South America, Europe and Africa.

Arkadian Googled Ortus. Its website homepage displayed an eerily familiar image: the stone monument of a bearded man, arms outstretched – the statue of Christ the Redeemer overlooking Rio de Janeiro. Ortus claimed to be the oldest charitable organization on earth, formed in the eleventh century by the dissolution of an ancient order of monks – the Brotherhood of the Mala – whose lineage stretched back into prehistory. They had been forced to renounce their spiritual vows after the church denounced them as heretical. Many had been burned at the stake for their belief that the world was a goddess and the Sun was a god and all life came from their union. Others escaped, regrouped and re-emerged as a secular organization dedicated to continuing the works they had previously undertaken as holy men.

He scrolled down to their ongoing projects, the ones Gabriel de la Cruz Mann would have been involved with. There was a major project in Brazil protecting large tracts of rainforest from illegal loggers and gold prospectors, another in the Sudan replanting fields laid waste by the civil war, and another in Iraq restoring natural marshlands drained by systematic industrial land grabs and years of war.

Arkadian could only imagine what being a security advisor in these places entailed. Protecting unarmed volunteers from guerrillas and bandits while they tried to bring food and water to the world's poorest regions; trying to bring law to places where there was none. Whoever this guy was, he was clearly a saint – which made his presence in the morgue that morning all the more baffling.

He clicked back to the home page and selected the 'Contact Us' link. The first address on the list was in Rio de Janeiro. That explained the statue. There were others in New York, Rome, Jakarta and one in Ruin – Exegesis Street in the Garden District, just east of the police building.

He wrote it on the back of the grainy printout of Gabriel's face from the CCTV footage, folded it in half and slipped it into his jacket pocket.

78

Alone in the white-tiled changing room, Liv blotted her reddened skin with the thin, scratchy towel. She could hear someone doing laps in the pool beyond the shower block.

The small pile of white and blue gym clothes the Sub-Inspector had given her positively sparkled next to her old blouse and jeans. She slipped into the tracksuit bottoms and pulled the white T-shirt over her head. 'POLIS' was printed on the front and back in large black letters. She went through her pockets, transferred the few dollars and change and wiped the mud-caked phone clean. She jogged the on button and the screen flashed on. It shivered gently in her hand; a new text message. She didn't recognize the number.

She opened it and felt the chill return.

DO NOT TRUST THE POLICE

The capitals couldn't have been more emphatic.

CALL ME AND I'LL EXPLAIN

She thought of the warning she had received last night, before the crash and the gunfire.

Liv stood stock still. She could hear the trickle of shower water, the splash of whoever was in the pool and the hum of air conditioning overhead, but nothing else. No approaching footsteps. No muffled conversations in the corridor. But she suddenly had the feeling that someone was in the room with her, standing behind the wall that divided the changing area from the main door, listening to her movements.

She slipped the phone in her pocket and pulled on a pair of white gym socks.

I think it's best that you stay under our protection . . .

Arkadian had said that before packing her off with her chaperone.

Police protection. Her brother hadn't benefited too well from it, had he?

She laced her grubby trainers over the pristine socks. The dark blue sweat-top swamped her slender frame. It too had POLICE emblazoned across it. She glanced once more towards the door then scooped up her ink-stained newspaper and headed in the other direction, past the still-dripping showers towards the pool.

The air in the pool enclosure was warm and damp and scraped the back of Liv's throat with chlorine fingers as she made her way around its edge towards the fire exit. A slash of morning sunlight had somehow found its way through the crush of surrounding buildings and sparkled on the surface of the pale blue water.

Liv pushed down on the horizontal locking bar. A high-pitched siren echoed through the building. She pushed it closed behind her, killing the alarm as suddenly as it had started. The swimmer didn't look up, just carried on doing steady lengths, sending glittering reflections across the white painted walls.

Sulley was on the phone to a news producer. The warning only sounded for a few seconds but it snapped him to attention.

'Listen,' he whispered, 'I'll have to call you back.'

He approached the entrance to the ladies' locker room, the soles of his shoes squeaking against the shiny vinyl floor. *Women. Jesus.* She'd been in there for a lifetime. He listened for the sound of the shower. Heard nothing. Knocked gently.

'Miss Adamsen?' He pushed the door open far enough to poke his head through.

No reply. There was a partition just inside, so he couldn't see a thing.

'Miss Adamsen?' A little louder this time. 'You OK in there?'

Still nothing.

He peered around the corner. Apart from a small pile of dirty clothes and a wet towel, the place was empty. Sulley felt a hot flush rising under his shirt, turning his pale flesh pink. *Miss Adamsen?*

He looked left. All four toilet cubicle doors were wide open. He whipped back round to the showers.

Empty.

Moving on through, he found himself in the brightly lit chemical fug of the pool area. He squinted at the swimmer, hoping it was her; saw the short black hair and police issue swimsuit he hadn't given her, knew it was not. He spotted the fire exit and felt his throat go dry. He jogged towards it. The moment he pushed it open and the alarm sounded he realized what had happened.

Outside, the street was teeming in both directions; people in suits, tourists in casual leisurewear. He searched amongst them for a dark blue, police-issue sweat-top. He saw nothing. The door swung shut behind him and the alarm stopped shrieking. His phone started vibrating in his hand and he glanced down at it, anxious in case it was Arkadian calling for an update. The number was withheld.

'Hello?'

A white transit pulled up beside him.

'Hello,' the driver replied.

79

Liv threaded her way through the crowds. She had no idea where she was heading but knew she had to stay out of sight and put as much distance between herself and the district building as possible while she got her head together. She pulled the hood of her new sweat-top over her wet hair and fell in step with a group of women, staying close enough for it to look like she was with them. At this time of day most people on the streets were tourists. Her clothes would have stood out a mile bobbing along in a river of suits and she hadn't seen many blonde locals.

Street sellers energetically offered their wares to the passing trade, mostly ethnic copper trinkets and rolled-up rugs, and ahead of her a newsstand rose up in the middle of the pavement, parting the flow of people like an island in a stream. Liv glanced at the front pages as she drifted past; every one carried a picture of her brother. She felt the emotion rise up inside her again, but not grief now – more anger. There were too many question marks surrounding his death to waste any more time trying to solve word puzzles. She felt partly responsible for setting her brother on his tragic course, but something else had driven him to take his own life, and she owed it to him to find out what.

She looked up and saw the Citadel soaring above the bobbing heads of the tourists, everyone moving slowly towards it, pulled by its gravity like leaves towards a whirlpool. She felt drawn too, for entirely different reasons, but for now it would have to wait. It cost twenty lira to enter the old town, she'd read it in the guidebook, and at the moment all she had was a few dollars to her name.

She took her cell phone from her pocket, opened her last text message and punched call-back.

The van eased its way down the street. Sulley sat by the door, next to the guy who was sweating like it was mid-summer. The big guy with the patchy beard drove. All three watched the street in silence.

Sulley hadn't wanted to get in with them. Selling information was one thing, being directly involved in what was obviously going to be a kidnapping was way off the scale. He couldn't be doing this. It was criminal, for God's sake. It was jeopardizing everything. But the big man with the melted face had been insistent. And because Sulley didn't want to stand outside the district building having a lengthy conversation, he'd got in.

He looked out of the window scanning the crowds for a flash of the girl's blonde hair or the white lettering on the dark blue sweat-top, hoping he wouldn't see either. Back at the station he'd catch heat for losing her, but that kind of heat he could handle. It would be a whole lot better than finding her with these guys.

'Got her!' The sweaty guy in the middle of the bench seat angled the screen of the finder towards the driver. He studied it for a beat then looked ahead to where the road curved left and a wide paved area stretched beyond a barrier of concrete bollards; a no-car zone where the antiquated buildings had been hollowed out and turned into chain stores. It was packed with people. 'She's in there,' he said.

Sulley scanned the area as the van drew nearer. Saw a group of tourists walking away from them. One was wearing a dark blue sweat-top. The crowd parted slightly just before they disappeared behind a newsstand and he glimpsed POLICE printed on the back of it.

The driver saw it too. 'We'll drive round to the other end, where it rejoins the road.' He stopped by the kerb. 'Go get her.'

Sulley felt a cold panic rise up inside him.

'You lost her in the first place,' the driver said. 'She's less likely to run from you.'

Sulley opened and closed his mouth like a fish as his eyes flicked between the driver's cold blue gaze and the puckered burn scar on his cheek. He wasn't the kind of guy you could argue with, so he didn't try. He opened the door, slipped out on to the pavement, and headed to where he'd last seen the girl.

80

The phone clicked in Liv's ear.

'Hello?'

'You sent me a warning,' Liv said. 'Who are you?'

There was the briefest of pauses. Ordinarily she wouldn't have noticed it; now it made her instantly suspicious.

'A friend,' the woman replied. 'Where are you now?'

Liv continued to drift with the tourist tide, felt the comforting press of other ordinary, straightforward human beings around her. 'Why would I tell you that?'

'Because we can protect you. Because there are people looking for you right now. People who want to silence you. Liv, there's no easy way of saying this. These people want to kill you . . .'

Liv hesitated, somehow more unsettled by the sudden intimacy of the woman using her name than by the announcement that someone wanted her dead.

'Who wants to kill me?'

'Ruthless, formidable people. They want to silence you because they think your brother shared knowledge with you; knowledge that no one is supposed to have.'

Liv glanced down at the letters scrawled across the newspaper in her hand. 'I don't know anything,' she said.

'It doesn't matter to them. If they think you know something, that's enough. They risked taking you at the airport. They also stole your brother's body because of it and they'll keep looking for you until they find you. They don't take chances.' The woman let the statement hang in the air for a beat before continuing in a softer tone. 'If you tell me where you are, I can send someone to bring you to a safe place. The same man I sent to protect you last night.'

'Gabriel?'

'Yes,' Kathryn replied. 'He's with us. He was sent to look out for you. He did look out for you. Tell me where you are and I'll send him to you.'

Liv wanted to trust her, but she needed time to think before she could allow herself to trust anyone else right now. Apart from the borrowed clothes on her back, all she had was her few dollars in change, a phone that was about to run out of battery, and yesterday's copy of a local newspaper. She looked at it now. Saw her brother's face staring out at her from a halo of scrawled letters and symbols. Realized something. Twisted the paper round and read the small print on the back page.

'I'll call you back,' she said.

Sulley moved past the newsstand.

The girl was less than fifty feet in front of him. He jostled through the slow-moving crowd, gradually closing the gap between them, still not quite sure what he was going to do when he got to her. He thought about simply turning round and making his way back to the district building. But if he did, the guy in the van could rat him out; an anonymous tip giving the name of the person who'd been leaking information with copies of the files as proof. He'd been careful to cover his tracks – but even so. If they could link the monk's disappearance with him, he'd be looking at some heavy shit: compromising an ongoing investigation, perverting the course of justice, selling privileged information. He could go to prison – every police officer's worst nightmare.

So he kept on walking, keeping the crowd between him and the girl in case she looked round and saw him. Standard surveillance procedure. As he closed in on her he thought about just telling her to run, then disappear himself until all this blew over.

He fixed his eyes on the dark blue hood and walked a little faster. Just ten feet away now.

Five.

He was almost upon her when he saw the white van pull to a stop at the far end of the pedestrian street, trapping her like a rat in a drainpipe. There was no way she could get away now. No way either of them could. He had to go through with it.

He slowed, allowing the distance between them to lengthen again as the flow of people took her closer to the van. He didn't want to drag her further than was absolutely necessary. Up ahead he saw the big man with the beard step out of the van and move round to open the rear doors. They were only ten feet away now. He stepped forward. Reached out to grab her. Noticed the other guy inside the van frowning at the notebook then looking up and shaking his head.

Too late.

His freckled hand landed on the girl's shoulder and he spun her round.

'Hey!' She twisted out of his grip.

Sulley looked at the shocked face framed in the blue hood. It wasn't the girl.

'Sorry,' Sulley said, jerking his hand away like he'd touched a live cable. 'I thought you were ...'

He pointed at the POLICE sweatshirt. 'Where did you get this?'

The girl glared at him. He dug out his badge and watched the defiance vanish.

She pointed back in the direction they'd come. 'I swapped it with some girl.'

Sulley followed her outstretched arm. Saw nothing but a mass of strangers. 'How long ago?'

She shrugged. 'Couple of minutes.'

'What did you swap it for?'

'Just another sweatshirt.'

'Could you describe it?'

The girl raised her palms. 'White. Kind of . . . washed out. Bit worn at the sleeves.'

In the midday warmth most of those filling the street had now dispensed with their coats and jackets; more than half were wearing something white. With his back still turned to the van, Sulley allowed himself a smile.

Nice work, missy, he thought to himself. *Nice work indeed.*

81

Liv walked out of the tourist information office and headed against the flow of people, which bothered her slightly, back in the direction of the police building, which bothered her more.

She checked the free map she'd been given, tracing different routes to the street circled in black felt pen. She could have chosen a more circuitous route, but it would take longer and she was already on borrowed time. She'd just have to risk it. She pulled her phone from her pocket and checked the screen. The battery icon was empty. She pressed the speed-dial key anyway, praying there'd still be enough power to make one call.

'It wasn't her,' Kutlar said, before the policeman had a chance to speak. He wanted to remind Cornelius of his usefulness.

'No, it wasn't,' the officer said, leaning in through the open window. 'She switched to a plain white top. The girl she swapped with couldn't say which direction she was headed.'

Cornelius started up the engine. 'Get in,' he said.

The policeman shuffled uncertainly, pointed over his shoulder with his thumb. 'You know I should probably –'

'Get in,' Cornelius repeated.

He got in.

Kutlar glanced at the screen and started to relax a little. Knowing what the girl looked like was the only thing keeping him alive right now. Having the policeman tag along made him nervous because he knew what she looked like too. The sooner he split the better.

The van moved off, jarring Kutlar's leg again on the uneven road.

He hit return and the hourglass icon appeared as the system reached out for the girl's signal.

82

The ringing tone kicked in as Liv passed a street stall selling freshly made flat breads. The thick, hot smell of roasted spices and onions reminded her how long it had been since she'd had anything substantial to eat. The sun beat down on the bone-coloured flagstones and buildings that all looked like churches.

'Where the hell have you been?' the familiar voice yelled. Rawls Baker, owner and editor of the *New Jersey Inquirer*, was not one of life's whisperers. 'You'd better be calling to file copy on that birth story; I got a hole in the lifestyle section you could drive a truck through.'

'Listen Rawls, I –'

'Don't give me excuses. Just give me that story.'

'Rawls, I haven't written it.'

There was a moment's pause. 'Well, you'd better start writing it right this –'

'What's the story on the front page of the *Inquirer* this morning?' she asked, before he could launch into a full-blown roasting.

'What the hell's that got to do with anything?'

'Just answer the question.'

'The monk. Same as every other paper.'

'He was my brother.'

The phone went silent.

'You're shitting me!'

'I'm in Ruin now; I flew in this morning. There's something strange going on here. I don't know what it is, but it's something big. I'm in the middle of it and I need your help.'

The silence flooded back. She could picture him in his office, staring out at the river, calculating how much an exclusive might be worth. Her phone beeped loudly in her ear and for a moment she thought she'd been disconnected. Then Rawls's voice rumbled back through the ether. 'What do you need?'

'I'm heading towards the offices of a local newspaper called *Itaat Eden Kimse*. I want you to call ahead and get them to kit me out with some petty cash, a notebook and some pens. Maybe the loan of a desk for a few hours.'

'No problem.' She heard the scratch of Rawls's pen. 'Just don't go sharing anything valuable with them. Remember who's signing your paycheque. Tell them you're writing a travel piece or something.'

'OK,' she said. The low-battery signal beeped in her ear again. 'My cell's about to die. Can you see if they can hook me up with a charger as well?' She gave him the make and model, but there was only silence at his end of the line.

The screen was blank. She slipped it back into her pocket. Looked back up the road. Saw a vehicle approaching.

83

'Over there . . .' Kutlar pointed at a group of people eating stuffed flatbreads from a food stall but kept his eyes on the screen. Cornelius turned towards them. Sulley's door was open almost before they came to a stop. 'I'll look around,' he said, and slammed it back shut with a pungent cloud of spices and onions. Kutlar glanced up from the screen. He watched the policeman hitching up his trousers and scanning the crowd.

'You see her?' Cornelius said.

Kutlar scrutinized the mass of faces on both sides of the street. 'No,' he said finally. The smell of the food made him feel nauseous.

Cornelius took the notebook from him. The street map was frozen, the arrow at the centre pointing at the place they were now parked. The side column showed the last number she had called and an hourglass icon spun slowly next to it as the system searched through the networks, hunting it down.

Kutlar glanced in the side mirror. The policeman was now talking to the stallholder and helping himself to some food. His stomach lurched and he looked away. Thanks to the brutal one-way system it had taken them nearly five minutes to get here. He could have done it in half the time, but the sat-nav had sent them along busy main roads and he'd had no desire to challenge it. The longer they kept looking for her, the more chance he'd have of working his way out of this situation.

He also had another agenda, not quite as strong as his instinct for survival, but strong nonetheless. It involved the man who had put the bullet in his leg and forced him to leave his cousin lying dead in the road. He'd never been particularly close to Serko, but he was family. He figured if these guys found the girl then maybe they'd find the guy who killed him as well. He really hoped he'd try and get in their way.

The hourglass icon had disappeared from the screen and in its place was a dialogue box listing a name and address. He watched Cornelius copy the information into a text message.

'The guy says he saw someone about five minutes ago sounds like our girl.' The policeman leaned in through the open window, chewing his last mouthful of bread. Kutlar recoiled at the garlic on his breath. 'Says he thinks maybe she hopped in a cab.'

Cornelius pressed *send*. Waited for it to go.

'Listen,' Sulleiman said, 'if she's mobile she could be anywhere by now. I mean, you'll pick her up again as soon as she switches her phone back on. But I really need to be getting back to the station. I took a big risk to give you guys a head start . . . and if I don't get back and call the girl in missing, it's going to get ugly.'

Cornelius waited until *message sent* flashed up then squinted at the traffic. Every other car was a cab. 'Sure,' he said finally. 'Hop in, we'll give you a ride.'

Sulleiman hesitated for a beat then climbed in.

Kutlar edged away from him as far as he could. The smell of garlic and sweat coming off the policeman almost made him gag.

84

It was cold in New York, colder than Rodriguez remembered it, and he'd put on the red windcheater as soon as he shuffled off the plane with the other passengers. He was walking through the international arrivals hall when his cell phone vibrated in its pocket. He glanced at the new name and address: somewhere in Newark; residential, by the look of it.

He looked around for a newsstand or a bookstore. The old TWA Flight Centre was all curved edges and scooped, elegant lines; it looked like it had been built by giant bugs rather than bureaucrats and Teamsters. He spotted a Barnes and Noble.

The last time he had been here was six years ago. Back then he thought he was leaving his country and his old life for ever. Now here he was, back in town and back to something close to his old ways. He cleared the message and dialled a number from memory. He had no idea if it was still valid, nor even if the person he was trying to contact was dead or in jail. The phone started ringing as he walked into the bookstore, past displays of cookbooks by celebrity chefs and paperbacks with one-word titles.

'Hello?'

The voice sounded like the rustle of dry paper. He could hear a TV turned up loud in the background; angry people shouting, other people yelling and applauding.

'Mrs Barrow?' He'd arrived at the shelf where they usually kept the city guides.

'Who dat?' The tone was guarded.

'Name's Guillermo,' he said, upping his old street accent, which now tasted strange on his tongue. 'Guillermo Rodriguez. Used to go by the name Gil. I'm an old friend of JJ's, Mrs B. Been outta town fo' while. Be nice to hook up with him – if'n he's around.'

There was a pause filled with more TV applause and whoops of encouragement. It sounded like *Springer*, or *Ricki Lake*. The type of show he'd forgotten existed.

'Loretta's kid!' the woman said suddenly. 'Used to live in that two-room walk up over on Tooley Street.'

'Sure am, Mrs B. Loretta's kid.'

'Ain't seen nothin' o' her in a while.'

An image flashed into his mind. Skin stretched tight over brittle bones. Tubes feeding medicine into spots on her arms where the junk used to go.

'She died, Mrs Barrow,' he said. ''Bout seven years back.'

'Aw yeah? I'm real sorry, son. She was a nice lady, far as she went.'

'Thanks,' he said, knowing what she meant but letting it go all the same.

The strident voices from the TV stretched into the silence again until he began to wonder if she'd forgotten he was there.

'Say, son, give me your number,' she said suddenly. 'I'll pass it on to Jason. If'n he wants to talk with ya, he'll talk.'

Rodriguez smiled. 'Thanks, Mrs Barrow,' he said. 'Really 'preciate it.'

He gave her his number and she hung up while he was in the middle of thanking her again. He grabbed an ADC street map of Newark and headed over to the till. His phone rang again as he collected his change. He thanked the cashier and went back into the concourse.

'Gil? That you, mon?'

'Yeah, JJ my man, it's me.'

'Goddamn. Gilly Rodriguez.' A big smile lit up his voice. 'I heard you got took by the God Squad.'

'Nah, man. Just been outta town fo' while . . .'

He let the silence hang. In his old life being 'outta town' generally meant being in the pen.

'So where you at now, man?'

'Queens. Got a few things lined up, you know how it is. Just need to get hooked up again.'

'Yeah?' JJ's tone narrowed in the same way his grandma's had. 'What y'all need?'

He thought of what he'd read on the flight over; first-hand accounts of heretics being purified in the flames of the *Tabula Rasa*. 'You think you can line me up with something a little . . . specialized?'

'I can get you whatever you want, long as you got the money.'

Rodriguez smiled. 'Yeah,' he said, pushing through the exit door and into the chill of a New York morning. 'I got money.'

85

The brass plaque on the wall announced that the building housed the offices of *Itaat Eden Kimse*, translated underneath as the *Ruin Observer*. The cab driver turned on his hazards and Liv handed him her phone. 'I'll send someone right out,' she said.

She was directed by the world's oldest receptionist to the international desk on the first floor. As soon as she walked into the open-plan office she instantly felt at home. Every press room she'd ever been in looked exactly like this one: low suspended ceilings; nests of desks separated by half-height partitions; strip lights that kept the place lit in the same non-descript fashion, day and night. It never ceased to amaze her that all the great works of modern journalism, all the government-baiting, Pulitzer prize-winning, life-enriching material that poured on to newsstands on a daily basis was conceived in surroundings so deeply uninspiring they could just as easily be used to sell life insurance.

She scanned the bland magnificence of the office, and clocked the eager woman with dark 1940s hair marching towards her, smiling most of the way through perfect lipstick. She looked so full of bristling energy that if she'd suddenly burst into song or a tightly choreographed dance routine, Liv wouldn't have been at all surprised.

'Miss Adamsen?' The woman thrust out a manicured hand like a low-flying Nazi salute.

Mesmerized, Liv nodded and held out her own hand.

'I'm Ahla,' the vision said, taking it, shaking it, then handing it back like a punched ticket. 'I'm office manager.' Her voice was surprisingly deep and guttural, quite at odds with her china-doll looks. 'I'm just getting OK for your cash float,' she added, turning and leading the way across the office.

'Oh,' Liv said, the mention of money snapping her to attention. 'There's a taxi downstairs holding my phone to ransom. Could someone rescue it for me? I have absolutely no cash.'

The perfect lips pursed. 'Not a problem,' she said, in a way that left Liv in no doubt that it was. 'For today, you use this,' she flourished a manicured hand in the direction of an unoccupied desk. 'But if you need any longer, you'll have to share. Everyone's in town for the Citadel story. You also?'

'Er, no,' Liv said. 'I'm writing a . . . travel piece.'

'Oh! OK, well here's what you asked for. I bring cash as soon as I get someone to sign. I'll . . . go and pay taxi.' She swivelled on an elegant heel. 'Oh, and your boss asked you to call him,' she said over her shoulder. 'Dial nine for outside line.'

Liv watched her march away, all energy and purpose. In a movie she would be played by a youngish Katharine Hepburn.

She gave the borrowed desk the once-over. Took in the standard-issue beige computer and multi-line desk-phone, a cactus that was being tortured to death by over watering, and a framed photo of a man in his mid-thirties leaning over a woman who hugged a squirming three-year-old boy on her knee. The kid was a miniature version of the man. Liv wondered which of them the desk belonged to: the man, probably. He looked kind of anal. Whoever usually lived here was suspiciously tidy for a journalist.

But maybe she was just jealous.

She looked at the frozen tableau of joyous family life. Saw the blaze of emotions that shone from the photograph, binding the three people together with invisible but unbreakable bonds. It felt like flicking through the brochure of an amazing holiday destination she would probably never visit.

She pulled her eyes away from the photograph and grabbed a notebook, one of the old-fashioned pads with a big spring on the top. She flipped it open and wrote the date and her location at the top of the first page. In the normal course of things she went through so many of these things it was vital to be able to match their contents to a time and a place.

Next she drew the outline of a human body and traced from memory the pattern of scars she'd seen in the post-mortem photos. When she'd finished, she gazed at the image, each stroke a record of her brother's suffering.

She turned the page and copied the original pairings of seed letters and symbols from her newspaper as well as every word she'd so far managed to extract from them. Studying the results, she found herself honing in repeatedly on two in particular: 'Sam', for obvious reasons; and 'Ask', because it stood out. It was one of the few verbs and it read like a command.

Her college professor had told her that all journalism boiled down to this one word. He'd said the difference between a good reporter and a bad one was simply the ability to pose the right question. He'd also told her if she ever got bogged down in a story, to ask the five 'W' questions and focus on the gaps.

Liv flipped to a new page and wrote down:

Who – Samuel
What – Committed suicide
When – Yesterday morning at about 8.30 local time
Where – At the Citadel, in the city of Ruin
Why –

The empty line stretched away from the final question. Why had he done it? Ordinarily she would seek out and interview anyone who had spoken to the victim in the run-up to their death, but Arkadian had said that was impossible. The Citadel spoke to no one. It was the silence at the centre of everything.

'There,' the office manager said, suddenly reappearing with Liv's phone and a bulging envelope. 'I took twenty lira to pay taxi. Receipt is inside. Sign please . . .' She held out a receipt ledger with blue carbon paper separating the pages.

Liv signed and plugged the phone charger into the wall. The screen lit up and the charging symbol appeared. 'Say, who should I talk to round here to get some background on the Citadel?'

'Dr Anata. But she very busy with monk story. Maybe too busy to talk about – travel piece . . .'

Liv took a deep breath and forced a smile. 'Well, why don't you give me her number anyway?' she said, wishing she'd picked a cover story with a bit more kudos. 'The least I can do is give her a try.'

86

Rodriguez watched his old life sliding past the cab window. Freshly scrubbed new builds on patches of former wasteland and sandblasted brownstone tenements for people who couldn't afford Manhattan, or even Brooklyn, so had to settle for the South Bronx. The closer they got to the 16th District, it all started looking more familiar. New money still hadn't reached these parts yet, leastways not the sort that showed up on tax returns, and by the time the cab reached Hunts Point, it was like he'd never been away.

The driver pulled over on Garrison Avenue and twisted in his seat. 'Far as I go, my friend,' he said from behind his pitted Perspex cage. They were still three blocks from the address JJ had given him. Rodriguez said nothing, just paid the guy, got out and started to walk.

The 'hood may have stayed the same, but in the years he'd been away Rodriguez had become something else. Last time he'd been here his life had been shadowed by fear and suspicion. Now he stood in the warmth of God's light. He could feel it on his back as he strode down the polluted streets. Others sensed it too; he saw it in the way they looked at him. Even the dealers on the corners and the crack-whores didn't hassle him. He'd become like the guys he used to cross the street to avoid. A man with a purpose. Confident. Fearless. Dangerous.

He passed a stripped-out car parked on cinder blocks and a store with scorch marks blackening the fringes of its steel-shuttered windows. He remembered torching the place himself when he'd lived here. It had been a pizza joint back then. He'd stuffed rags through a cracked window, set light to them and watched from the shadows until a group of guys showed up and doused it. He'd always loved to see stuff burn. Now he'd found a flame that never went out. He could feel its purity inside him, lighting his way in this place of permanent darkness.

The house looked empty, so did the whole street, but he could feel eyes upon him as he walked up the steps. The door opened before he reached it. A kid in a G Star hoodie ducked outside, scoped the street and checked him out. He made no move to let him in. From somewhere behind him, Rodriguez could hear the sound of gunfire.

'JJ in?' he said.

'Let the man pass,' a voice hollered through the explosions. The kid blinked slowly then stood aside.

Inside it was a different house. The short hallway opened into a room stuffed with brand-new furniture and electronics. A huge aquarium filled one wall and a flat-screen TV the size of a double bed dominated the other. A high-def surround-sound combat game was in full flow. Two guys were welded to the screen, thumbs jabbing away at handsets, triggering CG weapons while their real guns rested alongside an ashtray and a crack pipe. One of them glanced up fleetingly then returned his attention to the virtual warzone.

'Gilly Rodriguez!' he shouted through the carnage. 'Look at you, mon, all beardy. Look like Jesus in a parka.' He laughed at his own joke.

Rodriguez just smiled, sizing up his old friend and seeing a shadow of what he might have become. JJ had lost about thirty pounds since he'd last seen him and his skin had the same greyness his momma's had when she was too deep in the life and too far gone to care. He had all the trappings of street success, with his clothes and his crew, but street years weighed heavy. His youth was almost gone and his light was dimming. Rodriguez gave him two years maybe. Perhaps less. 'Good to see you,' he said. 'You looking good, man.'

JJ shook his head ruefully. 'Nah, I need t'lay off a little. Maybe grow a beard, git you to introduce me to your tailor.' He hit pause on his controller and held it out to the kid by Rodriguez's shoulder. 'You take over,' he said. 'Shoot me some white folks.'

He levered himself out of the soft leather sofa and stood in front of Rodriguez. 'Man,' he said, looking up at him. 'You get taller?'

Rodriguez shook his head. 'I always been this big. You just ain't seen me in a while.'

They embraced, bumping shoulders and slapping each other on the back like it was old times, then stood back and regarded each other awkwardly, because it wasn't.

'You got something for me?' Rodriguez said.

JJ dipped into the fish tank and pulled a dripping plastic bag from behind a tower of coral. 'Some exotic tastes you got, my friend.'

Rodriguez took it and examined the contents: a Glock 34, a spare clip, an Evolution-9 silencer and a small plastic lunch box containing a pistol with a fat barrel and twelve stubby, shotgun-style cartridges.

'What you need that for?' JJ asked. 'Scared of the dark?'

Rodriguez snapped the lid down tight and slipped his bag from his shoulder. 'I ain't afraid of nothing,' he said, and tossed across a thick wad of cash.

He watched JJ count the money, his jittery fingers rubbing his nose every few bills like he had an itch that wouldn't quit. His momma used to do that. Rubbed it until it was raw. He glanced over at the other two, blazing away at each other with fake guns while real ones lay on the table. JJ definitely wouldn't last another two years, not unless he saw the light that led to salvation. He'd be lucky if he made it to Christmas.

87

Dr Miriam Anata was standing by a drinks machine in the hall-way of a local news station when the tinny strains of 'Ode to Joy' sounded inside her jacket – charcoal grey today, but still a pinstripe; she liked to think of it as her trademark.

She was supposed to have turned off her phone, but too many people were ringing her for interviews and she was damned if she'd give them the excuse to call someone else. She reached in to answer it, but accidentally disconnected the call in the process. She looked around to see if anyone had noticed.

Turning her attention back to the drinks machine, she fed in enough coins to bail out a bottle of iced tea and send it thumping down into the tray. She popped the lid and drank thirstily. She'd been under hot studio lights almost constantly since the monk had fallen to his death the previous day. Not that she minded. It was a heaven-sent opportunity to boost her book sales. The key, she'd learned early on, was to frame all her answers in reference to one of her titles. That way the producer couldn't edit them out.

'Ode to Joy' piped up again and she pounced on the answer button before it had finished the opening bar.

'Hi, Dr Anata?' The voice belonged to a woman. American, she thought, or possibly Canadian – she could never really tell the difference; either way it was a big market for books.

'This is she.'

'Great,' the woman continued. 'Listen, I know you're busy, but I could really use your help right now on some background information.'

'Is this an interview request?'

'Erm . . . I suppose it is, yes.'

'And what channel did you say you were with?'

The line went silent for a moment.

'Dr Anata, I'm not calling from a news channel . . . I'm part of the story,' Liv said, before she had a chance to cut her off. 'I'm . . . I'm the monk's sister.'

Miriam paused, not sure if she'd heard right – not sure if she believed her.

'I've seen his body,' Liv continued, 'or photos at least. He disappeared before I got to see him in person. There were some markings on him, some kind of ritual scars. I wonder if you could take a look at them and give me your expert opinion on what you think they might mean.'

Miriam felt light-headed at the mention of scars. 'You have these photos?' she whispered.

'No,' Liv said. 'But I can show you what they look like. And there's some other stuff as well. Stuff that might have something to do with the Sacrament.'

Miriam leaned heavily against the vending machine. 'What stuff?' she asked.

'It's probably easier if I show you.'

'Of course.'

'When are you free?'

'I'm free right now. I'm in a TV studio, close to the city centre. Where are you?'

Liv paused, cautious of revealing her location to anyone. A cop friend had once told her the best place to hide was in a crowd. She needed somewhere public and busy and close by. She looked at the newspaper with the picture of Samuel standing on top of the most visited ancient attraction in the world. 'I'll meet you at the Citadel,' she said.

88

Kutlar could still smell the garlic and sweat coming off the empty seat beside him. He blinked as the van emerged from the tunnel. A silhouetted figure walked down the alley between the car parks towards them.

Kutlar opened the notebook. He stared intently at the hourglass icon, watching the tiny black pixels tumbling inside it, virtual sand showing him how quickly his own time was running out.

Johann reached the van and swapped places with Cornelius as the street map on the screen reconfigured itself. An arrow pointed to the location of Liv's phone. The hourglass reappeared momentarily then the map widened to show a second arrow, above and to the left of the first – their own position, traced through Cornelius's signal.

They were close.

Cornelius watched the arrow at the centre of the screen jump a little further up the street. 'She's moving.'

Johann turned towards the ring-road.

The next time the screen refreshed itself the second arrow was moving too, circling the first one now, like a buzzard homing in on its prey.

Brother Samuel's body had been stripped to the waist and arranged with his arms outstretched, echoing the shape that loomed from the altar at the far end of the chapel of the Sacrament. The Abbot cast his eyes across the ruined flesh, glowing bright and waxy against the stone floor, pierced repeatedly by broken bones, held together by rough sutures where the coroner had sliced it apart.

Could these remnants of a man really rise up and fulfil the prophecy?

The Abbot noticed the thin tendril of a blood vine curl around the altar. He followed it into the darkness until he found its root twisting up from one of the wet channels cut into the floor. He wrapped it around his hand and tugged hard until it tore free then stepped over to one of the large hemp-and-tallow torches and held the sinewy plant over the flame. It hissed in the heat, shrivelling away to nothing but blackened fibre and a smear of red sap on the Abbot's hand.

The torch flame guttered as the door opened behind him. The Abbot turned, rubbing his hand against the rough wool of his cassock where the sap was starting to irritate his skin. Brother Septus, one of the monks who had helped bring Samuel up the mountain, hovered on the threshold.

'We are ready for you, Brother Abbot,' he said.

The Abbot nodded and followed him to another room in the upper chambers of the Citadel, one that had lain mostly silent since the time of the Great Inquisitions.

The door closed behind them, sealing Brother Samuel inside with the Sacrament. The candles flickered once again in the displaced air, and their light shimmered gently across his body.

For a moment it seemed as if he was moving.

89

Rodriguez was also looking at Samuel, standing on the famous bridge in Central Park, his arm draped over the shoulder of a girl who looked just like him. The photo was in a cheap clip frame that matched several others dotted across the wall of the apartment.

Breaking in had been easy enough. The girl lived on the ground floor of a purpose-built block close enough to the city centre to attract young professionals, and by the time he'd got there, everyone was out at work. He'd just had to hop into her tiny garden, with dense enough foliage to give plenty of cover, hold up his windcheater to deaden the noise and punch out a window. His brothers in Ruin would deal with the girl. He had to make sure she'd left no loose ends.

He hadn't known Samuel that well inside the Citadel so seeing fragments of his previous life frozen on his sister's wall was a strange experience. There was another shot of him looking much younger, sitting in a rowing boat with an equally fresh-faced version of the girl, both squinting against the sunlight. He'd spotted the photos by the phone, partially hidden by the tendrils of one of the many plants that covered practically every horizontal surface.

Rodriguez pressed the flashing message button and listened to the playback while he piled all the paper he could find in the middle of the living-room floor. There were two calls, both from what sounded like her boss, bawling her out for skipping town without filing copy.

He dragged her duvet off the unmade bed and added it to the heap, remembering a film he'd seen as a kid about some guy who was obsessed with aliens and filled his house with a mountain of junk like this.

He felt like an alien now.

When he'd gathered enough flammable material in the living room he went through the rest of the apartment splashing gasoline over the bed, the carpets, the couch. He didn't have time to check the place thoroughly so he needed to make sure everything would be destroyed.

He went back out the way he'd come in, then tossed a lit match through the broken pane, heard the other windows crack with the pressure wave as the gas fumes caught. He didn't stop to watch it burn, though he'd have liked that a lot. He had two more stops to make before he could fly away from here for ever.

He was doing God's work. There was no time for pleasure.

90

Liv didn't need the map to find the Citadel. All she'd had to do was head in its general direction until the main flow of tourist traffic picked her up and swept her along, all the way past the ticket stands, through the gates and up the narrow streets towards the most famous mountain in the world.

She had never really appreciated how ancient the place was until she entered this, the oldest part of it. The streets here were cobbled, but it was the buildings on either side that really brought it home. They were all tiny, with miniature windows and low doors, built for people with bad diets and hard lives who seldom lived beyond thirty. They were also constructed and repaired from various bits of material salvaged from throughout the city's long history. Roman pillars emerged from medieval walls with the gaps between filled with oak beams and wattle and daub. She passed a partially opened door with an iron hand of Fatima curling downwards from its centre, a reminder of the long Moorish occupation of the city during the time of the Crusades. Beyond it lay a small courtyard surrounded by scalloped arches and bursting with assorted greenery, lemon trees in blossom, and banana plants unfurling their long scrolled leaves, all spilling out over elaborately mosaiced walls and floor. The next house along looked like an eighteenth-century Italian townhouse; the one next to that half Ancient Greek villa, half Napoleonic fort. Occasionally a gap would open up between the mis-matched houses and she would see modern buildings on the plains below, stretching away in the distance, clear to the red-rocked, serrated edge of the mountains that enclosed the city on all sides.

A breeze tumbled down the narrow street bringing warm air and a smell of food, which reminded her how hungry she was. She drifted upwards, drawn to the stall from which the tempting aromas had come. It sold flat breads and dips, another reminder of how the city had sucked up different influences over the centuries. For all the bloody history that had swirled around the Citadel, and all the religious wars that had been waged in its shadow, all that now remained of those lost empires were the solid staples of architecture and good food.

Liv fished a banknote out of the petty cash envelope and exchanged it for a triangular piece of bread, studded with seeds, and a tub of baba ghanoush. She scooped up the thick paste and shovelled it into her mouth. It was smoky and garlicky, a mixture of toasted sesame oil, roasted aubergine, and cumin with some other spices dancing around in the background. It was the most delicious thing she had ever eaten. She dipped the bread back in the pot, and had just loaded it up again when her phone rang in her pocket. She stuffed the bread in her mouth and reached for it.

'Hello,' she said through a mouthful of food.

'Where the hell have you been?' Rawls yelled down the phone. Liv groaned inwardly. She'd turned her phone on when she'd left the newspaper offices so the Ruinologist could contact her; she'd forgotten all about Rawls.

'I'm worried sick over here,' he hollered. 'I just saw you on CNN getting bundled into the back of a police cruiser. What the hell's going on over there?'

'Don't worry,' Liv replied through a mouthful of food. 'I'm fine.'

'You sure?'

'Yeah.'

'So why didn't you call me? I told the girl at the office to get you to call me.'

'Must've slipped her mind. She seemed a little ditzy.'

'So tell me what's going on.'

This was exactly the conversation she'd hoped to avoid. 'I'm just trying to find out what happened to my brother,' she said. 'I'm fine. Don't worry about me.'

'You sound out of breath.'

'I am out of breath. I'm walking quickly up a really steep hill.'

'Oh right. Well you still shouldn't be wheezing that way. You need to look after yourself. You should quit smoking.'

Liv realized that, despite the high-stress situation she found herself in, she hadn't craved a cigarette in hours. 'I think I have,' she said.

'Good. That's good. Listen, I need you to do one thing for me.' Here it was. She'd known he couldn't be calling out of overwhelming concern for her wellbeing. 'Write down this number,' he said.

'Hold on.' She grabbed her pen and scribbled the number on her hand.

'Who's this?' she asked.

'It's that traffic cop you watched give birth to twins the other night.'

'Bonnie?'

'Yeah, Bonnie. Listen I know this is a real bad time, but I need that story to run this weekend. I still got a hole in the Lifestyle section, so I need you to call her up and smooth the way for someone else to pick up the story, OK?'

'I'll call her right now. Anything else?'

'No, that's it. Just you be careful – and take lots of notes.' Liv smiled.

'I'm always careful,' she said. Then she hung up.

Rawls snapped his phone shut and closed his front door. He was late for a fundraiser over at City Hall and wanted to meet the guy everyone was tipping as the next mayor. It always paid to get close to the incoming king.

He slid behind the wheel of his Mustang, absolutely nothing to do with his midlife crisis, and was about to turn the key in the ignition when he heard the tap on the window. He turned and saw the wide muzzle of a gun pointing at him. The man who held it motioned for him to wind the window down. He was wearing some kind of red windcheater and had a beard that looked wrong on his young, thin face.

Rawls held his hands up and did as he was told. When the window was halfway down a large bottle of mineral water was pushed through the gap. 'Hold this,' the gunman said. Rawls took it. 'What do you want?' He noticed the fumy smell clinging to the plastic bottle and realized it didn't contain water at all.

'I want your silence,' the man replied, and fired a piece of burning magnesium from the flare gun, through the bottle of turpentine and into Rawls Baker's chest.

91

Bonnie's answer-phone kicked in just as Liv passed through the large stone arch leading to the square by the public church. Listening to the small-town voice politely asking her to leave a message whilst being confronted with the massive Gothic splendour of the church was a surreal experience.

'Hey, Bonnie,' she said, drifting across the square along with the hordes of tourists. 'This is Liv Adamsen – from the *New Jersey Inquirer*. Listen, I hope everything's going great with you and Myron and the twins, and I'm really, really sorry to spring this on you, but I've had to leave town for a few days. We love your story, though, so someone else will be calling you real soon to pick right up where I left off. I know they still want to get you into the weekend edition, if that's OK. Listen, I'll call you when I'm back in town. Take care.' She hung up and passed through the second archway.

She emerged from the shadow, squinted up into the brightness – and stopped. There in front of her, rising up like a wall of darkness, was the Citadel. Seeing it this close was both terrifying and awe inspiring. Liv's eyes lifted to the summit then dropped slowly down, following the path of her brother's fall. As her gaze reached the bottom she saw a large crowd of people gathered next to a low stone wall. One of them, a woman with long blonde hair and a long dress, was holding her arms out by her sides. The sight sent ice spiders scuttling across Liv's skin. For one awful moment she thought the ghost of her brother was standing there. The crowds of tourists bumped her as they pushed past, nudging her closer to the group, until she began to see a blaze of colour at the centre of the crowd. It was a sea of flowers, laid there by strangers and looking now as if they had seeped up through the broken flagstones and bloomed in silent tribute to the man who had cracked them. Liv's eyes moved across them, reading hidden meanings in their colours and forms: yellow daffodils for respect, dark crimson roses for mourning, rosemary for remembrance, and snowdrops for hope. Cards stuck out here and there like the sails of boats half-sunk in a shallow sea. Liv picked one up and felt a cold finger run down her spine when she saw what was on it. There were two words 'Mala Martyr', and above them, filling the uppermost part of the card, was a large 'T'.

'Miss Adamsen?'

Liv whipped her head round, instinctively leaning away from the voice as her eyes sought the source of it.

Standing over her was a stylish woman in her fifties wearing a charcoal grey pinstripe suit a few shades darker than her precisely cut hair. She switched her gaze from Liv to the flowers stretching out on the ground behind her, then back again.

'Dr Anata?' Liv asked, rising up to greet her. The woman smiled and held out her hand. Liv shook it. 'But how did you know it was me?'

'I've just come from a television news studio,' the woman said, leaning in conspiratorially. 'And you, my dear, are very much breaking news.'

Liv glanced nervously across at the crowd. Their attention was currently split between the mountain and the spectacle of the silent woman holding her arms out. No one was looking at her.

'Shall we go somewhere a little quieter?' Dr Anata suggested, gesturing further along the embankment to where a small army of plastic tables spilled out from several cafés.

Liv looked back at the shrine marking the place where her brother had died, then nodded, and followed Miriam as she led her away.

*   *   *

The van pulled up by the wall of the old town close to the southern gate. Cornelius glanced at the screen. The arrow remained steady, pointing to a spot by the dry moat on the old embankment. The girl hadn't moved for the last few minutes.

He slipped out of the passenger seat and held the door open. Kutlar closed the electronic notebook, handed it to Cornelius and slid stiffly across the seat to join him on the pavement. The drop down to the ground was not high but the moment his foot connected with the street it felt as if someone had shot him in the leg again. He gritted his teeth against the pain, determined not to appear weak; felt the sweat beading up beneath his shirt. He held on to the door to steady himself, his head drooping forward as he forced his leg to straighten. In his peripheral vision he could see Cornelius's boots pointing in his direction. Waiting. There was no way he could do this on his own.

Kutlar reached into his pocket and pulled out the bottle of pills he had been denying himself for the last few hours, unscrewed the top and tipped a few gel capsules into his damp palm. The label said he was supposed to take one every four hours. He threw two into his mouth, nearly gagging as he dry swallowed them down.

He looked up and past Cornelius towards the Southern gate. She was somewhere in the old town. And as he was the only one who knew what she looked like, and bikes were the only things allowed up the steep, ancient streets, they were going to have to walk. He stuffed the pills back in his pocket, let go of the van and started limping towards the ticket booths by the entrance. His leg was already numb by the time he was halfway there.

92

The café was heaving, even though it was set back from the embankment and away from the main drag. It was slightly less popular than the other cafés as it had no clear view of the Citadel, but Liv could still feel its presence all the way through the stone building that blocked it out. It was like a shadow made solid, or a storm coming. She sat opposite the Ruinologist, away from the crowds and facing the wall, while a brisk young waiter in a white apron and black waistcoat took their orders. He tore off the order chit and trapped it beneath the ashtray.

'So,' Miriam said as soon as he was out of earshot, 'how can I help?'

Liv placed her notebook on the table. The card she'd picked up was still in her hand. She turned it over and re-read the words:

T

MALA
MARTYR

'How about telling me what this means,' she said, sliding it across the table.

'All right,' Miriam said. 'But first you must tell me something.' She pointed at the T. 'You said you'd seen marks on your brother's body. Was this one of them?'

Liv flipped to the first page of her notebook and turned the pad round to reveal the rough drawing she'd made of Samuel's body. 'It was branded on his arm,' she said.

Miriam stared down at the network of scars, transfixed by their savage beauty. She quickly closed the notebook as the waiter reappeared and placed their drinks on the paper table-cloth. 'It's called the Tau,' she said, the moment he scurried off again. 'It's a very powerful and ancient symbol, as old as this land which took its name.'

Liv frowned, not following how the word 'Tau' could become 'Turkey'.

'I'm talking about the land upon which the Citadel stands,' Dr Anata said, sensing her confusion. She nodded towards the distant peaks, just visible between the buildings, their jagged outlines like teeth against the sky. 'The kingdom of the Tau.'

Liv followed her gaze, remembering the map in her guide-book and the mountain range that curled around the city and stretched across the country like a spine. 'The Taurus moun-tains,' she said, the first syllable now heavy with new meaning.

Dr Anata nodded. 'In order for you to properly understand the importance of the Tau, and what it means to this place, you need to know a little history.' She leaned forward, steepling her long, silver-ringed fingers above the pristine white of the paper tablecloth. 'The first records of human life in this region describe a struggle between two warring tribes, each seeking dominance over the land. One was called the Yahweh. They lived in caves halfway up a mountain, and were believed to protect a sacred relic that gave them great power. Even in those prehistoric times other tribes revered, or at least feared them so much that they made pilgrimages to the mountain, bring-ing offerings of food and livestock to the gods they believed lived here.

'In time a town grew up, prospering from the pilgrims who came to the mountain to give offerings and partake of the miraculous waters that flowed from the ground and was said to bestow good health and long life on all who drank them. A public church emerged to look after the temporal interests of the Citadel, and to preach the word of God passed down from the mountain in written form. In these scriptures the name of God was written as YHWH, which translates as Jehovah or Yahweh – the same name as their tribe. It described how the world was made and how men came to populate it. Anyone who questioned this official version was branded a heretic and hunted down by ruthless warrior-priests riding under a banner bearing the symbol of the Citadel's divine authority.' She pointed at the sign of the T. 'The Tau. The one true cross. The symbol of the relic that had first given them power over others. The symbol of the Sacrament.'

Cornelius stopped just short of the great stone archway leading into the public square and flipped open the notebook to check the signal. His arrow had moved closer, but the girl's pointed to the same spot.

He glanced back down the steep street towards Kutlar. He was about twenty feet behind, struggling stiff-legged up the hill, the front of his shirt wet with sweat, each halting step the same rhythmical cousin of the one that preceded it: the bad leg slowly swinging forward, landing gently on the ground, the good leg hopping quickly forward to put as little weight on it as possible.

Cornelius planned to shoot him with the silenced gun in his pocket once he'd identified the girl, then prop him on one of the benches lining the embankment. It would hopefully shock the girl into obedience so she would walk down the hill on her own, though he also had a syringe full of Haldol in his pocket if necessary. He watched Kutlar's metronomic progression towards him. Waited until he had almost caught up, then glanced back down at the screen. The girl still hadn't moved. He closed the notebook, tucked it into his pocket and headed into the shadow of the arch.

93

Liv looked at the T-symbol – the Tau. She'd read a lot about the Sacrament on the flight over, never dreaming it would somehow be connected to her brother's death.

'The fact your brother had this mark on his arm means he had knowledge of the Sacrament,' the Ruinologist continued. 'He may have been trying to share it.'

Liv remembered what Arkadian had said: Solve the mystery of the Sacrament, solve the mystery of Samuel's death. She looked up at Dr Anata. 'You must have come to your own conclusions about what the Sacrament might be,' she said.

The Ruinologist shook her head. 'Whenever I feel I'm about to grasp it, it always eludes me. I can tell you what it isn't. It's not the cross of Christ, as some people believe. Compared to the religious order inside that mountain, Christ is a relative newcomer. So it isn't His crown of thorns either, or the spear that pierced His side, or the Holy Grail He drank from. These are all myths perpetuated by the Citadel over the years as diversions to obscure the Sacrament's true identity.'

'Then how do we know there's anything there at all?' Liv said. 'If no one's ever seen it.'

'You can't build the world's biggest religion on just a rumour.'

'Can't you? Think about it. You've got these two prehistoric tribes fighting it out. To get the upper hand, one holes up in this mountain and claims it's got some divine weapon. Maybe there's a drought or an eclipse and they claim they did it. People start believing they have power and treat the tribe like gods. They like it, so they keep up the bluff. So long as no

303

one finds out there's nothing there, the bluff still works. Wind forward thousands of years and people still believe it, only now a massive religion has been built on it.' She thought of Samuel walking away from her. Telling her he wanted to get closer to God. 'And if my brother found that out, discovered after everything he'd been through that the one thing keeping him going, his faith, was actually built on – nothing . . .'

Miriam saw the tears in Liv's eyes. 'But there is something there,' she said. 'Something with power.' She picked up her bottle of water and looked at the picture on the label. 'Let me ask you this . . .' She poured water into her glass and her silver rings clinked against the bottle. 'What do you want from life? What do we all want? We want health, happiness, a long life, right? Same now as it ever was. The most ancient of our ancestors, the ones who first made fire and sharpened sticks to protect themselves against the wild beasts, they wanted exactly the same things: and the mountain existed even then, and so did the holy men within it. And those simple tribesfolk, who just wanted to live a little bit longer and not get sick, they worshipped those people, not because of some clever rumour, but because the people in the mountain lived a long, long time, and disease did not touch them. Tell me, when you think of God, what image comes to mind?'

Liv shrugged. 'A man with a long white beard.'

'Where do you think that image comes from?' She turned the bottle round and pointed to the picture of the Citadel on the label. 'The earliest man looked up at this mountain and saw occasional glimpses of the gods who lived there; men with long hair and long white beards. Old, old men in a time when you were lucky to live past thirty.

'This water is exported all over the world, has been since Roman times when the emperors first found out about it. You think they shipped it all the way back to Rome 'cause it tasted nice? They wanted what every man has always wanted, and kings more than most: they wanted more life. Even today a person can expect to live on average seven years longer in Ruin than in any other major capital city and people still come here in their thousands and get cured of all sorts of things. These things are not rumour. These things are fact. Still think there's nothing there?'

Liv dropped her eyes down to the ashtray. Her ten-year nicotine addiction did seem to have vanished since arriving in Ruin. Miriam was right, there had to be something there. Samuel would not have dragged her into all this if there was no point to it; and he wouldn't have scratched those letters on the seeds unless they pointed to something. The question was, *what*?

She turned to the page in her notebook where she'd copied the letters. Looked at them again. And like the sun breaking through clouds, she recognized something new in them.

94

Cornelius stood in the glare of the afternoon sun surveying the heaving throngs of coach parties and other tourists that flooded the wide embankment: people posing for pictures; people congregating around tour guides; people just staring up at the Citadel, lost in their own thoughts. There were plenty of young women; any one of them could be the girl. He stroked the puckered skin on his cheek, picturing his enemy. As he'd laid in the hospital, recovering from the skin grafts in a blur of morphine, he'd thought about her often. He kept seeing her stepping out from nowhere, holding out the bundle of rags, her body shrouded in a burkha that hid all but her eyes and her hands. Sometimes it was a parcel of newspaper she held, like the parcel his mother had wrapped him in before leaving him by the orphanage door and walking in front of an express train to Liverpool. He'd never known her face either. But he didn't need to know their faces to know what they were. Betrayers all.

Behind him, Kutlar's ragged breathing and halting footsteps announced his arrival like a leper shuffling from a cave. Cornelius slipped his hand into his pocket and curled it round the grip of his Glock.

'Which one is she?' he said.

Liv stared at the letters she had copied from the seeds in their original pairings:

$$\begin{array}{cccccc} \underline{T} & a & M & + & k \\ \underline{?} & s & A & a & l \end{array}$$

Then compared them to the card she had found in amongst the flowers:

T

MALA
MARTYR

She took her pen and wrote the word 'Mala' in her notebook, crossing out the letters to see what she was left with.

Assuming the 'T' was the Tau, it left just three letters – s, k and A, and two symbols – '+' and '?'. She stared at them, wrote down one final word and the last two symbols, then read what she had written.

T + ?
Ask Mala

The positioning of the underlined symbols made it look right. So did the capital letters at the beginning of each word. Was this the message her brother had sent her? It made some sense. The T was the Tau, the symbol of the Sacrament, and the plus sign could be a cross. The question mark symbolized the mystery of its identity, leaving the remaining two words reading like an instruction – 'Ask Mala'. She looked up at the Ruinologist.

'Who are the Mala?' she asked.

Miriam looked up from the notebook where she had read the words as Liv had written them. 'I told you that, in the beginning, there were two tribes of men,' she said. 'One of them was the Yahweh, the men of the mountain. The other was the outcast tribe who believed the Yahweh had stolen the Sacrament and, by imprisoning it, had usurped the natural order of things. They believed the Sacrament should be discovered and set free – this tribe were called the Mala. They were persecuted by the Yahweh, their people hunted and killed for the beliefs they held. But they kept their faith alive and a secret church grew, even in the shadow of the mountain's ascendancy. By the time the Yahweh did their deal with the Romans to 'rebrand' state religion, they had bled their poisonous hate of the tribe into the language – in Latin 'mala' means 'evils'. But even though the Citadel demonized these people, and burned their chapels and confiscated and destroyed their sacred texts, they could not destroy their spirit.'

Liv felt her skin tighten. 'Do they still exist?' she asked.

Miriam opened her mouth to answer but her eyes shifted suddenly upwards. Liv twisted round, saw a large man appear behind her, silhouetted against the bright sky. Her eyes adjusted to the glare and his features began to take form within the darkness of his outline, eyes first – pale, and blue, and staring straight into Liv's. A nervous tremor fluttered in her chest as she realized who it was.

'Yes,' Gabriel said. 'Yes, we do.'

95

From where Kutlar stood he could see the whole of the embankment curling around the base of the mountain to a row of stone buildings in the distance promising all kinds of spa treatments to heal and revive.

'She's not here,' he said.

Cornelius let go of the gun in his pocket. Kutlar was stalling, he was sure of it. He opened the notebook and looked at the wire-frame map of the embankment. The two arrows almost overlapped at the centre, pointing directly to where they now stood. 'She *is* here,' he said, removing his phone from his pocket and quickly copying in Liv's number from the search box.

He stepped forward and pressed the call button, dropping the phone down so he could listen for the sound of a phone ringing. He walked closer to the shrine, filtering out the murmur of the crowd, and heard something in front of him.

He cocked his head to one side and his eyes caught a tiny movement as the sound came again. It was down on the ground, in amongst the flowers, buzzing like a large trapped bee. Cornelius squatted down and shoved his hand into the soft petals. His hand closed around the hard plastic case of a phone. It vibrated once more as he pulled it out, leaving a crater in the surface of the flowers. From his own phone he heard a robotic voice asking him to leave a message. He cut the call and scrolled through the menu of Liv's phone, checking the call logs, the address book, the text messages. They were all empty.

Someone had reset the phone and abandoned it.

*   *   *

Miriam watched the bearded man walk quickly away from the shrine. She saw him stop by the far wall, talk to another man, and look down at something that appeared to be a small laptop. Gabriel was right. They had been tracking the girl's phone signal.

She reached into her pocket and pulled out her own phone. She headed off, towards the row of health spas and away from the men with the laptop. She switched her phone off, thought about dropping it into one of the bins that lined the moat wall, but slipped it back into her pocket and decided to leave town for a few days instead. She could always get rid of it later – depending on how things panned out. At least the girl was safe now. That was the main thing.

The motorbike rumbled down the narrow cobbled streets weaving between the tourists and the food stalls. Liv wore no helmet and the wind whipped her hair across her face as she clung to Gabriel. She could feel the hardness of his body beneath his clothes, and her legs clamped involuntarily against him each time the bike bucked and slipped on the uneven street. The scent she had noticed so powerfully when they'd met less than twenty-four hours previously now wrapped itself round her again, washing over her in a slipstream of warm afternoon air. She realized now, as her head hovered level with his broad shoulders, and she resisted the urge to rest it there, that it wasn't cologne as she had first thought, it was the smell of him, and it was delicious.

She had no idea where they were headed, nor how she could contact anyone now she had no phone, nor anything about the man she now clung to. Nevertheless she felt strangely secure for the first time in days. There was something about his urgency that had compelled her to go with him. He made her feel as if everything he was asking her to do was for her, not for him. Like *her* safety was his only concern. And he belonged to the

Mala. And if what she'd just discovered with the Ruinologist was true, the least she could do was take a leap of faith and go in the direction her brother had pointed her.

Besides, she thought as the bike passed through the western gate and filtered into the traffic creeping round the inner ring road and heading out of the city, *what else would I do?*

96

Arkadian was sitting in the passenger seat of an unmarked patrol car, staring at a line of stationary traffic when the switchboard picked up.

'Ruin Police Division.'

'Yeah, could you put me through to Sub-Inspector Sulley Mantus,' he said.

'Who's calling, please?'

'Inspector Arkadian.'

The line cut out and a tinny version of Vivaldi's *Four Seasons* counted away the seconds. The traffic had managed to move forward a whole car length by the time the operator returned.

'Sorry, that line isn't answering.'

'OK, could you patch me through to his mobile?'

The line cut out again. This time it went straight to answerphone. *Where the hell had he got to?* 'This is Arkadian,' he said, his voice flat and annoyed. 'Call me back immediately.'

He hung up and stared out at the traffic-choked street. He'd called Sulley the moment he found out about the news-crew ambush at the morgue. He'd watched it on TV, Sulley practically dragging Liv past the cameras then shoving her into a police car like she was a suspect. He was going to tear him a new asshole when he got hold of him. Maybe Sulley suspected as much and that's why he wasn't returning his calls. The phone chirruped in his hand and he snapped it open. 'Sulley?'

'No, it's Reis. I've got some news for you.'

Arkadian blew out his frustration at the windscreen in a long stream of air. 'Is it good news?'

'It's . . . intriguing. I just sneaked into the lab and had a peek at the DNA fingerprint to see how things were shaping up. I've lined up the girl's buccal sample with one from the monk. It's about halfway through the electrophoresis, but I fluorized it anyway to see how the strands were separating.'

'I don't know what any of that means. Just tell me: do they match?'

'They've still got a way to go before they're fully extruded, but the way it's looking now I'd say they're more than just a match, they're identical. Which is odd.'

'Why? It backs up her story.'

'Yeah, it does. But I was kind of expecting the results to prove the girl *wasn't* the monk's sister.'

'How come?'

'Because in the entire recorded history of conjoined twins there has never been a single case where they were different sexes. Genetically they have to be the same gender because they're effectively one person.'

'So it's not possible?'

Reis paused. 'Medically speaking, it's extremely unlikely.'

'But not impossible?'

'No. There're plenty of recorded cases of dual sex character-istics in individuals – hermaphrodites and such; and consider-ing the religious slant on this whole case, I guess if you believe in a virgin birth it leaves the door wide open for the possibility of all sorts of . . .'

'Miracle?'

'I was going to say "unexplained phenomena".'

'Isn't that the same thing?'

Reis said nothing.

'So, based on the evidence, you think the girl's telling the truth?'

Reis paused again, weighed down with the natural scepticism of the scientist. 'Yes,' he said finally, 'I think she is. I didn't until I saw the results of the DNA match, but you can't fake that.'

Arkadian smiled, pleased that the trust he'd put in the girl had not been misplaced. He was now convinced more than ever that she was the key to the whole thing. 'Do me a favour, would you?' he asked. 'Could you add all this to the case file and I'll go through it when I get back to the office.'

'Sure. No sweat. Where are you now?'

Arkadian glanced up at the static traffic jammed into the narrow streets leading to the Garden District. 'Still looking for the dead monk,' he said. 'Though a dead man could move faster than me at the moment. How're things back there? The press got bored yet?'

'Are you kidding, there's hundreds of them out there now. Bet you can't wait for the six o'clock news.'

'Oh, sure,' Arkadian replied, thinking of the inevitable MONK'S BODY SNATCHED FROM UNDER COPS' NOSES headlines. 'Goodbye, Reis,' he said, and hung up before he could say anything more. He turned to the plain-clothes officer sitting silently next to him. 'Think I might take a stroll,' he said, slipping off his safety belt. 'You've got the address, I'll meet you there.'

He twisted out of the passenger seat before the driver had time to answer and started walking up the street, weaving between slow-moving cars, earning himself an extended lean on someone's horn and the finger from a van driver. Walking felt good. It shook loose some of his frustration. But Sulley's continued silence bothered him. He scrolled through his calls received menu until he found Liv's number, hit the call button and looked up. In the distance he could see Exegesis Street written on a street sign that wavered through the heat haze and rising fumes.

He walked towards it, listening to a robotic voice telling him the person he was trying to reach was unavailable. He frowned. The last time he'd called it had been Liv's own voice telling him to leave a message. He redialled. Got the same robot operator. It was definitely her number – it just wasn't her. He disconnected without leaving a message.

Exegesis Street was much wider than the street he had come from and was lined with once-grand houses that were now just a shabby collection of office buildings turned black by traffic and time. He walked down the shady side, counting down the houses until he found the number 38 carved deep into a stone pillar by a wide door. Beneath it a square of brass shone against the stone, spelling out the word *Ortus* above a logo of a four-petalled flower with the earth at its centre. He slipped the phone into his pocket and hopped up the three steps leading to the heavy glass doors, incongruously modern in the carved stone entrance. He pushed against them and went inside.

97

Sulley came round slowly.

He felt as if he was rising gently from the depths of a dark, oily pool. He knew something was wrong even before he opened his eyes. Wherever he was smelt of damp and smoke and – darkness. He tried to open his eyes but they just rolled behind heavy lids that refused to budge. His head throbbed as if he'd been on a weekend bender, but he knew he hadn't – not for a while. He took a deep breath, flooding his nose with more of the dank, dark smell then, grunting like a weight lifter, he put all his concentrated energy into opening his left eye. In the brief glimpse he got before his eyelid banged shut again he saw where he was. He was in some sort of cave.

He rested for a moment, exhausted from the effort, trying to clear his head and make sense of what he'd seen. He listened out for any sounds that might give him a clue. All he heard was the hiss of blood in his ears. It sounded like heavy waves breaking on a shingly beach. Its steady rhythm soothed him until his breathing deepened and he sank back down into the deep, drugged pool of his unconsciousness, his fogged mind still trying to work out how the hell he had ended up in a cave by the sea.

There was nothing gentle about the next time he rose from the black depths of sleep. This time it felt as though he was being yanked up by a spike hooked into the base of his skull. He tried to cry out but all that emerged was a strangled mew. He tried shifting his head away from the pain but it wouldn't move. His heavy eyes struggled open, rolling sluggishly in their sockets as he sought the source of his agony. He caught glimpses of uneven stone walls illuminated by dancing firelight. Saw the outline of sinister-looking contraptions sketched against the darkness. He could not see the cause of his pain, and this, more than anything, lit up a fear inside him that brought him round quicker than iced water.

At last the pain began to subside, and a memory rose up from the fog. He remembered getting into the van, turning to grab his seat belt and feeling a sharp pain in his right leg. He recalled the shocking sight of the syringe, and how he'd reached for it with arms that would not respond. There was nothing else.

He looked down now at the spot where the needle had been, tried to touch it with his hand but his arms wouldn't move. He tried to look down but his head wouldn't move either. Instead his eyes rolled down as far as the sockets would allow. He could see his forearms strapped tightly to the arms of some kind of chair. He also saw something else, something utterly surprising and incongruous in the dank setting of the cave. By his right hand was a small table and sitting on it was a laptop with a mobile phone attached by a short cable. He thought for a moment he must be having a surreal dream, but the pain in his head and the trickle of something warm and wet down the back of his neck made it real enough. He tried to move his feet, but they too were bound tight to the chair he sat on. He struggled against his restraints, testing their strength until the sharp point of pain reappeared suddenly in the back of his neck, pressing forward with a terrible insinuation. He tried to arch away from it but the straps across his forehead and throat held him fast. He couldn't move. He couldn't breathe. It pressed on until the torture was so exquisite he thought his spine would snap. He was held there for a few moments, at the pinnacle of his pain, before it gently eased back bringing a tiny but welcome relief.

He heard the scuff of a foot on the floor behind him through the hiss of blood rushing in his head. 'Who's there?' he croaked, failing to keep the crack of fear from his voice.

He felt something tug at his right hand and found it had been loosened. He tried to lift it to rub the back of his neck but a solid *clunk* jarred it to an almost immediate stop. A thick leather manacle encircled his wrist, connecting it to the arm of the chair by a short chain. He dropped it back down with a clinking of metal, listening out for further movement.

'I'm a police officer,' he called into the darkness, wielding the words like a talisman.

The sudden closeness of the voice by his left ear made him whimper with surprise.

'You have the colouring of a betrayer,' it said. 'For was not Judas a redhead?'

Sulley swivelled his eyes left. He could see nothing but dark walls and flickering light.

'You are in a garrotting chair,' the voice continued, deep and steady, rumbling out of the darkness close by. 'One of the chief weapons used to stamp out the cancer of heresy during the Inquisition. It has a purity to it I'm sure you'll appreciate. There is a broad metal screw positioned in the headrest just below your skull. If I twist it one way . . .' Sulley felt the spike drill back into his neck and gasped in agony ' . . . the screw tightens and you will feel pain. If I turn it the other way . . .' the skewering pressure subsided once more ' . . . you will feel relief. So,' the voice said, moving in closer. 'Which is it to be?'

'What do you want?' Sulley asked the darkness. 'I can give you money. Is that what you want?'

'All I want is your loyalty,' mumbled the reply. 'And some information. Please know that bringing you here is not a pleasure but a necessity, brought about by your own actions. We asked for your loyalty. You chose not to give it. You betrayed the Church – and that is a sin.' The voice moved closer until he could feel the air that carried it whisper across his ear. 'Would you like to confess your sins now?'

Sulley's mind hummed with a mixture of pain and indecision. Should he admit he had sold information to others or deny it? If he denied it, he might be hurt until he admitted it anyway. He didn't want the pain to come back.

'I'm sorry,' he said, quickly. 'I made a mistake. If that's a sin ... then – please, forgive me.'

'Raise your right hand,' the voice commanded.

He lifted it as high as he could before the restraint snapped it to a halt.

'That chain is called the *mea culpa*,' the dark voice said. 'It enabled the heretic to sign his confession at the end of his inquisition. *Mea culpa* means "my fault". Admitting fault is the first step toward forgiveness. Do you know what the second step is?'

'No,' he squeaked, his voice stretched tight between peaks of fear and pain.

'Atonement. You must perform a righteous act to make amends for your sin.'

Sulley took a few shallow breaths, trying to calm the panic that threatened to overwhelm him, but he understood a deal when it was being offered.

'OK,' he said. 'What do you want me to do?'

98

Arkadian flipped his badge as he reached the reception desk.

'I'm looking for Gabriel Mann,' he said with a reassuring smile. 'Does he work here?'

'Oh,' the receptionist gasped, glancing at the badge then back at him with the flustered, guilty reaction of the truly innocent. 'Yes. Well . . . not usually, no. I mean, he's usually away somewhere or other, but he does work for the charity. Let me find out for you.'

She tapped an extension number into the desk phone and spoke in a low voice. Behind her an elegant wooden staircase curled upwards and brought down sounds of the upstairs offices. The receptionist punched a key and looked over at him.

'He's in the Sudan,' she said. 'He's not expected back for a month at least.' Arkadian nodded, thinking about the fingerprint that had placed him in the city morgue not two hours previously. 'I can try and get a number for him, if you like,' she suggested. 'There's probably a line into the base camp, or maybe a satellite phone. I was trying to get hold of his mother to see if she'd spoken to him. She runs the charity,' she explained.

'Do you have *her* number?' Arkadian asked. 'Or any idea when she might be back?'

'Of course,' the woman said, taking a pen and copying a number on to a notepad from a directory sheet in front of her. 'Here's her mobile number. I expected her back from the air-port by now. I can get her to call you . . .'

'No, it's OK,' he said, taking the piece of paper and looking at the name and number written on it. 'I'll give her a call. Which airport will she be coming in from?'

'City. It's where all our air freight comes in.'

Arkadian nodded and smiled. 'Thanks for your help,' he said. Then he turned and headed out through the heavy glass doors and into the street where the police car was parked and waiting for him.

99

The Abbot watched the Informer's trembling hand drift across the laptop, the short chain clinking as he typed in a sequence of remote access codes. The Internet connection through the phone was slow and it took a long few minutes before he finally managed to open the monk's case file.

'I'm in,' he announced to the darkness, sweat dripping from the end of his nose despite the stony chill of the cave.

'Has anything been added?' the Abbot replied, leaning closer to the screen.

The chain stretched and coiled again as the freckled hand tapped in a few more codes to open up an email account, then scrolled through an in-box and opened a message sent by GARGOYLE that comprised of just one word: 'Red'.

'Look out for anything highlighted in red,' the Informer explained in a wavering voice. 'That's the new stuff.'

He deleted the mail message, opened the monk's case file and started scrolling through it. The Abbot watched pages flash across the screen, each filled with details of things no one outside the Citadel should ever have seen. It made him sick to think of all the eager eyes that had crawled over these pages, greedily picking at the morsels they contained like ants on a bone. A band of red splashed across the page throwing a crimson light over the faces turned toward it. The freckled hand went still. The Abbot started to read. It was a brief transcription of Liv's conversation with Arkadian relating the strange account of her birth and why she had a different name and birth date to her brother. The Abbot read through it, nodding to himself. It solved the mystery of why no sister had been discovered in the background checks when Samuel had first entered the Citadel.

'Continue,' he said.

The red text rolled away and for long minutes only white pages flitted across the screen as the Informer scrolled through the entire file. It was only at the very end, in the pathology section, that the red text returned and cast its bloody glow back into the cave.

The new section was in two parts. The first was a note recording how a sample of the monk's liver cells had been flagged as contaminated on the grounds that the cells appeared to be regenerating. The Abbot wondered if this was evidence that Brother Samuel was re-animating, as the prophecy had predicted, or just the latent effects of his close exposure to the Sacrament. As he read the second red section, however, he was seized with a new interpretation and his blood quickened. It was a brief note from a Dr Reis detailing the results of comparative DNA samples taken from the fallen monk and the girl.

The Abbot stared at the red screen, his mind singing with the pathologist's findings and deductions. They were the same. Not only did Brother Samuel have a sister, she was his *identical* twin.

This one piece of information made sense of everything. The prophecy was right. Samuel had indeed been the cross. But he had fallen, and now the girl had risen in his place: flesh of his flesh, bone of his bone. The same.

She was the cross now.

She was the instrument that would kill the Sacrament and rid the world of its heresy. *She* was the key to everything.

'Destroy the file,' he said. 'Copy it to the laptop then wipe it from the police database.'

The Informer paused, clearly reluctant to perform such an obvious act of vandalism. The Abbot laid a hand lightly on the tightening screw sending a tremor through the spike and into his spine. It was enough to send the chain ratcheting back across the arm of the chair as he frantically obeyed, attaching a virus to the original file in the police database that would destroy the contents, the directory, then itself.

The Abbot glanced at the mobile phone connected to the laptop, his mind shining with the light of the new information. He needed to alert Cornelius to ensure the girl was brought back quickly and unharmed; then he could use her to fulfil the prophecy and deliver on a millennia-old promise to God. This was his destiny, he realized that now; it was what he'd been born to do. He thought of the Prelate, lying in the darkness, worrying about God's opinion of his own life's work, and pitied him. He would not end his days fretting over missed opportunities. While the Prelate had advised he do nothing he'd had the courage to listen to his heart, and take the action necessary. And now here they were.

He pictured the Prelate turning from him the last time they'd spoken, his skeletal hand waving away his request to act. He was weak, but he was stubborn, and that stubbornness had almost cost them this chance of deliverance.

But he was still in charge.

The Abbot considered this point. The Prelate's weakness and unwillingness to act could still prevent him from fulfilling his destiny. Going against the Prelate's word outside the mountain was one thing, but inside his influence was much stronger: people had allegiances to the office if not the man. The Prelate could stop him. Worse still, he could take over. He could rise from his bed and carry out the prophetic sequence, the last act of a man desperate to crown his long, empty life with true meaning. And with the prophecy fulfilled, what then? Would they assume the Sacrament's power, as many theologians believed? Would they achieve permanent immortality rather than the hint of it? If so, then the Prelate would never die and the Abbot would forever be his lieutenant.

The Abbot looked up, suddenly aware of the silence. On the laptop a progress bar edged its way to one hundred per cent then vanished. 'Has it all been wiped away?'

'Yes,' the Informer said. 'It's gone.'

'Good,' the Abbot said, laying both hands on the tightening screw. The Prelate was an issue. He could still ruin everything. 'Tabula Rasa,' he whispered. Then he started to turn.

V

Thou shalt not suffer a witch to live

Exodus 22:18

100

An early spring dusk was already starting to bruise the fringes of the afternoon sky when the bike pulled away from the guard-house and headed past the row of silent warehouses towards the squat-looking cargo plane by hangar 12.

Gabriel raised his hand and waved back at the guard who'd just let them through. Liv couldn't believe he'd let her in without any ID. Airport security was no way that relaxed back home – at least, she hoped it wasn't. Gabriel had told the guard he needed to drop something off at the hangar and introduced her as his girlfriend. She hadn't contradicted him. In fact she'd kind of liked it.

They coasted under the wing of the plane and in through the open door of the hangar, the sound of the bike's engine suddenly deafening in the enclosed space. It was stacked high with silver packing cases, the tunnels between them just wide enough for the bike to pass through. They headed down one, towards the back of the building where warm lights burned behind the windows of an office. Gabriel swung the bike to a stop in front of them and killed the engine. 'End of the line,' he said.

Liv let go of his waist and slid from the seat. She was just smoothing her wind-whipped hair when the door of the office opened and a beautifully elegant woman stepped out, followed by a sprightly old man in flight overalls. The woman hardly looked at her. Instead she moved to where Gabriel was pull-ing the bike back on its kickstand. She embraced him, her eyes closed, her silky dark hair bunched against his chest by the tightness of her grip. Liv experienced a sudden tug of confusion and surprising jealousy. She looked away and found herself staring into the attentive face of the old man.

'My name is Oscar de la Cruz,' he said, stepping back through the open door of the office, his caramel voice welcoming her. 'Please, come inside.'

She glanced over once more at the extended hug still binding Gabriel to the elegant woman, then followed him inside. The office was warm after the chilled bike journey and the smell of coffee and comforting low murmur of a TV set made the place feel almost homely.

'Would you like coffee?' Oscar asked, his dark eyes twinkling within his deeply tanned face. 'Or . . . maybe something a little stronger.' He shot a look towards the door. 'Between you and me, I've got a flask of whisky in my jacket.'

'Coffee's fine,' Liv said, sitting on a chair next to a desk containing a stack of paperwork and a computer.

She turned slightly as Gabriel came in. He had his arm round the beautiful woman and his head dipped low. He spoke softly but rapidly, a look of earnest concentration on his face. The woman closed the door as Gabriel finished speaking, then looked up at Liv and moved round the desk to sit down opposite her, a smile softening her face. 'I'm glad you're safe here with us,' she said. 'I'm Kathryn. I left you the warnings. My son's just been filling me in on what's happened.'

Liv's eyes flicked between her and Gabriel.

Her son?!

Gabriel pulled two chairs over from the far desk and sat on one of them, slipping the black canvas bag to the floor as he settled and opening it up. Seeing them side by side Liv could now see a strong physical similarity between them – though the woman hardly looked old enough to be his mother. Gabriel pulled something from inside the bag and handed it to her. It was her holdall. She smiled, feeling such gratitude for his simple yet thoughtful act. It was like being reunited with a piece of normality. She found the paper envelope in the outside pocket, lifted the flap and looked at the top photo of her and Samuel.

'I'm very sorry for your loss,' Kathryn continued. 'And for the trials you've endured since you learnt of your brother's death. I would not have chosen for you to be caught up in our ancient struggle, but fate had other plans.'

Oscar appeared by her side and placed a mug of black coffee on the desk by Liv before sitting in the last remaining chair. As his face lined up with theirs Liv noticed he too resembled them.

'Your brother was a member of an ancient brotherhood of monks,' he said, leaning forward in his chair. 'Their sole purpose, to guard and protect the Sacrament. We think his death was an act of supreme self-sacrifice to send a message revealing its identity.' He fixed Liv with his bright eyes, the deep wrinkles surrounding them suggesting a lifetime of laughter. 'We think he sent that message to you.'

Liv stared at him for a moment then slowly lifted up her notebook and laid it on the desk between them. She looked down and turned to the second page where she had copied the symbols from the seeds.

'This is what he sent to me,' she said, sliding the notebook across the desk towards them. 'I've re-arranged them every which way to try and make sense of it. Then I met Dr Anata, and found this on the spot where my brother fell.' She slipped the card from between the pages and showed them the cryptic message:

T

MALA
MARTYR

'From that I managed to re-arrange the letters into this –' She pointed at the last thing she had written:

T + ?
Ask Mala

'That's when you arrived,' she said, glancing up at Gabriel and discovering he was already looking at her. He smiled a small smile that travelled all the way to his eyes. She looked away, feeling the heat of a blush rising beneath her skin. 'So,' she said, looking instead at the old man. 'You're the Mala. I guess I'm asking you – what is the "T"?'

Oscar looked at her, his eyes suddenly tired and sad. 'It was ours once,' he said, 'and is sometimes referred to as the Mala T. But as to what it is – I'm afraid we don't know.'

Liv stared at him for a beat, not trusting what she'd heard. 'But you must,' she said, 'my brother staked his life on it. Why would he send me to find you if he didn't think you'd be able to help?'

Oscar shook his head. 'Maybe this isn't the message.'

Liv stared down at the phrase at the bottom of the page. She'd pulled every combination of words she could from the letters. This was the only thing that had made any sense. She reached out for her notebook and flicked to the first page. 'Look,' she said, pointing at the rough drawing of her brother's body where the T was burnt on to his arm. 'He had the same thing branded on to his body as well as these other scars. Maybe the message is in them!'

A sudden ripping sound made her look up. 'The scars are not the message,' Oscar said, pulling open another Velcro fastening on his flight suit, 'they are merely a badge of office. They are part of the ritual associated with the Sacrament, but they do not reveal what it is.'

He shrugged his arms out of the green one-piece and rolled it down over the white turtleneck sweater he wore underneath, then pulled his shirt up over his head. Liv stared at his body beneath. It was the colour of mahogany and covered with the dark, puckered lines of old scar tissue. Her eyes traced the familiar shapes they made. All of them precise. All deliberate. All of them identical to the scars she had seen on the body of her dead brother.

101

The Angelus bell was still echoing softly through the dark corridors of the Citadel as Father Thomas passed through the airlock into the great library. The bell marked the end of Vespers and the start of supper. Most of the mountain's inhabitants would be heading to the refectories now for their evening meal. He didn't expect to find many in the library.

The second door slid open, disgorging him into the entrance hall, and he glanced round at the few circles of light bobbing in the darkness with the dark form of a monk at the centre of each, like a tadpole ready to hatch. They were black cloaks mostly, librarians come to tidy up after a day of messy scholarship. He spotted Brother Malachi, the head librarian, seated by the entrance to the main chambers. He looked up as Thomas entered and immediately rose from his chair. Thomas had expected him to be here. Nevertheless, seeing him now, walking towards him with his sharp, serious face set wings of fear fluttering against the walls of his chest. Thomas was not used to keeping secrets. It did not suit him.

'Father Thomas,' Malachi said, leaning in close and conspiratorial, 'I have removed those scrolls and tablets from the prehistoric section as requested.'

'Ah good,' Thomas replied, aware of the strain in his voice.

'Might I ask what purpose their removal serves?'

'Yes, of course,' Thomas said, fighting to keep his voice low and under control. 'The sensors have registered some anomalous moisture peaks in that section of the cave. I've isolated it to a specific area and need free access to the shelves there to check the tanking and run some diagnostics on the climate-control systems. It's just a precaution.'

He saw Malachi's eyes glaze over. The introduction of the printing press was the height of technological sophistication as far as he was concerned. Anything more recent baffled him. 'I see,' the librarian said. 'Let me know when your work is complete and I will arrange for the texts to be re-sited.'

'Of course,' Thomas said. 'Shouldn't be long. I'm just going to run the diagnostics now.' He performed a shallow bow then turned and headed, as casually as his racing heart would allow, over to a small door opposite the entrance which he opened and slipped gratefully inside.

Beyond the door was a small room containing a desk, a computer terminal and a man wearing the burnt-earth-coloured cassock of a guard. He looked up.

'Evening, Brother,' Thomas said cheerfully, continuing past him towards another door set in the far wall. 'Any problems?' The guard shook his head slowly. He was chewing on a piece of bread someone had brought him. 'Good,' Thomas said as he arrived at the door and tapped a code into the security lock next to it. 'I'm just running some checks on the lighting matrix. There's been a delay in some of the follow lights. Your terminal might go offline briefly,' he said, pointing at the computer on the monk's desk. 'Shouldn't take long.' He twisted the door handle and disappeared into the next room before the guard had a chance to reply.

Inside, the air was cool and hummed with the insectile noise of busy electronics. Every wall was filled with racking shelves containing the hardwired brain of the library's lighting, air-con and security systems. Thomas headed down the corridor of wires and air-cooled circuitry towards the user station set in the middle of the right-hand wall.

He logged on, tapped in an administrator password and a wire-frame floor plan of the library appeared on the flat-screen monitor. Small dots quivered on the screen, floating within the black like bright specks of pollen. Each one represented someone currently inside the library. He moved the mouse arrow over one of the dots, and a window opened next to it identifying it as Brother Barabbas, one of the librarians. He repeated the process, parking the arrow over each quivering dot in turn, until he finally found who he was looking for drifting erratically across the centre of the cave of Roman texts. He glanced nervously at the door, though he knew the guard did not have the code to access the room. Satisfied he was alone, he pressed three keys simultaneously to open a command window and started to run a small program he'd written earlier on a remote terminal. The screen froze briefly as the program initialized, then all the tiny dots jumped back to life, drifting and quivering across the black screen as before.

It was done.

Thomas felt the prickle of sweat on his scalp despite the cooled air inside the machine room. He took a few calming breaths then closed the command module and exited the room.

'Everything still online?' he asked, emerging through the door and squinting past the guard at his screen. The guard nodded, his mouth too full of bread and cheese to allow speech. 'Good,' Thomas said, turning sharply on his heel and skittering quickly through the room and out to the main entrance hall to avoid further discussion or questions.

He spotted Athanasius standing by the corridor leading to the older texts as he emerged. He was consulting a floor plan fixed to the wall, his finger tracing the maze of chambers, his smooth forehead knitted in concentration. Father Thomas walked up beside him and made a show of consulting the map. 'He's in the Roman section,' he said softly, then turned and drifted away.

Athanasius waited a few seconds then followed him, his eyes fixed on his friend's circle of light bobbing ahead of him, receding into the vast darkness of the great library of Ruin.

102

Liv stared at the network of scars criss-crossing the old man's dark skin. She looked into his eyes, her brows knitting into a question.

'I lived in the Citadel for four years,' Oscar explained. 'I was scheduled to be ordained as a full Sancti when I was . . . discovered.'

Liv shook her head, recalling the background reading she'd done on the plane. 'But I thought no one had ever come out of the Citadel.'

'Oh, they have. But never for very long. They are always ruthlessly hunted down and silenced. What you see before you,' he said, a smile crinkling his face as he carefully folded his shirt in half, 'is a dead man.' He laid it gently in his lap and smoothed it down with his hand. 'You know the story of the Trojan Horse?' he asked, looking up.

Liv nodded. 'The classic example of how to break a siege.'

'Exactly. Just like the frustrated Greeks at the gates of Troy, our people eventually decided to use guile instead of might to try and penetrate the impenetrable and reclaim the divine mandate of the Sacrament. They devised their own Trojan Horse.'

'You!'

'Yes. They found me in an orphanage at the turn of the twentieth century. No parents. No siblings. No relatives of any kind; the perfect background to be considered for the brotherhood. I entered the Citadel when I was fourteen on a secret, open-ended mission to discover the identity of the Sacrament and escape the mountain with the knowledge of it.

'It took me three years to get even close. Most of that time I spent working amongst the vast collection of books they hoard in their library, sorting through the boxes of new acquisitions. One day, a couple of years into my time there, a crate arrived full of relics from an archaeological dig in ancient Nineveh. The documentation with it referred to the contents being part of a forbidden book possibly relating to the Sacrament. Inside were hundreds of slate fragments. I stole one of the larger pieces before the head librarian noticed what the case contained and moved me on to something else. In private I examined the piece, but it was written in a language I had never seen, so I began to learn. I would assist the older monks in the library, picking up the skills and knowledge I hoped would help me decipher it while continuing to scour each new acquisition for anything that might help unlock the secret of the Sacrament. In the end fate guided me along a more direct route. My enthusiasm for learning was noticed by the senior monks and I was singled out to join the novitiate of the highest order within the Citadel – the *Sanctus Custodis Deus Specialis*, the Keepers of God's Holy Secret, the only ones who know the identity of the Sacrament.'

Liv looked at his scars, the same ones her brother bore. 'What caused those marks?' she asked.

'Part of the preparation is a ceremony, held every month in an ante-chamber in the restricted upper part of the mountain. Each novice is given a wooden Tau with a sacrificial dagger concealed within it. We were expected to cut deep,' he said, his eyes looking inward, his finger drawing along the circular line at the top of his left arm as he remembered what had caused it. 'Deep cuts. Signifying deep commitment. A regular act of faith – always rewarded by a miracle.' His finger drifted across to the other side of his chest, continuing its slow sweep of remembrance along the lines of his former suffering. 'For no matter how deeply we sliced our flesh,' he said, 'our wounds healed, almost immediately.' He looked back up. 'Closeness to the Sacrament was rewarded with great health and great age. I am nearly one hundred and six years old,' he said, 'yet I remain as fit as a man forty years my junior. Had your brother lived, he too would have enjoyed long life, for he was being groomed, as I had been groomed before him.'

He tapped the keyboard on the desk and a familiar image faded up to replace the screensaver. It was one of the photos from the post-mortem showing the raised brand on Samuel's left arm – the sign of the Tau. 'Your brother got further than I,' Oscar said, pointing at the screen. 'He bears the symbol of the Sacrament. And as you can see,' he said, turning to reveal his own bare arm, 'I do not. Only those who were fully ordained received that mark. He knew the secret.'

Liv's vision started to swim as her eyes filled with tears. 'So what happened?' she said. 'How come you didn't discover it?'

'We were not the only ones who had read our history,' he said, pulling the cotton turtleneck back over his head. 'The Sancti had placed someone within our organization too and they discovered my existence, though fortunately not my identity.' He smoothed the shirt down over his arms and adjusted the collar round his neck until all the scars were hidden. 'There was a witch hunt inside the Citadel to try and find me. Fellow monks began accusing each other, often just to settle old scores. It was unbearable. I knew my time was short so I took risks. Became careless. A fellow novice called Tiberius saw me pocket a fragment of slate. When he turned to leave the library I knew he was out to betray me, even though he was my friend. So I started a fire in the library and used the smoke and chaos to cloak my escape. I ran to the lower section of the mountain, threw a bench through one of the windows and followed it out into the night. I fell more than a hundred feet into the moat and swam for my life. The world was at war back then. It was July 1918. A false trail of my flight was laid all the way to the trenches of Belgium and my identity swapped with some poor unfortunate who'd been torn beyond all recognition by a shell.

The knights of the Sacrament – the Carmina – followed the trail, found the broken man and returned, satisfied that I had succeeded only in running from the Citadel and into the arms of death. Meanwhile I was transported to Brazil. I have lived there in secret ever since.'

'So why return now?' Liv asked. 'What is so significant about my brother's death that brings you out of hiding and makes others want to kill me?'

'Because when I escaped I carried that stolen slate fragment in my hand and the knowledge in my head to translate it. It revealed the first few lines of a prophecy foretelling a time when the Sacrament would be revealed and proper order would be restored. *The cross will fall / The cross will rise / To unlock the Sacrament / And bring forth a new age.*

'It gave us hope. Then twenty years ago another piece of the prophecy was found. The man who discovered it was called John Mann.' He looked across at Kathryn, whose bright eyes seemed to dim at the mention of his name. 'My daughter's husband. Gabriel's father. It was in a collection of fragments forming part of a book. From the few pieces he found, John worked out that it described an alternative creation story to the book of Genesis. But news of his discovery reached the Citadel. They have informers everywhere. The dig site was remote. There was a brutal attack, by whom we do not know for sure, but we can guess. We never found his body, or the material he had discovered.' Oscar blinked and looked down, his silence saying far more than any words. The room went quiet as each of them became lost in their own remembrance, the flickering screen of the forgotten TV the only thing that moved.

'My father died seeking the truth,' Gabriel said. 'And not all of the fragments he found were lost. He had taken precautions. The most important one stayed safe. We put it together with the piece my grandfather had taken and found a fuller reading of the prophecy.

The one true cross will appear on earth
All will see it in a single moment – all will wonder
The cross will fall
The cross will rise
To unlock the Sacrament
And bring forth a new age

Liv listened to the words and saw the image of her brother standing on the summit of the mountain making the sign of the Tau with his body. He started to topple.

The cross will fall.

She looked down at the drawing in her notebook and her eyes lit on another fallen cross, the one on her brother's side marking the place where she had once been joined to him. Her hand rose up to the site of her own scar.

The cross will rise.

She looked up at Oscar.

'There's something you should know about me and my brother,' she said. Then she stood up, and in an echo of Oscar's earlier gesture, started pulling up her shirt.

103

Athanasius and Father Thomas entered the Roman section of the library and stood for a moment, searching the darkness and the deadened silence for any signs of occupation.

The Roman section was one of the largest of the older vaults and contained, amongst other treasures, all the apostolic documents that had been collated into the first Bible. Consequently the individual auras of light that accompanied them through the vast darkness had now dimmed to a burnished copper. The only other light in the chamber came from the thin filament of guide lamps embedded in the stone floor. Apart from that, the chamber appeared to be empty.

Athanasius glanced at Father Thomas, then turned and headed away down the first row of shelves. As he hurried down the dark passageway his breathing became more rapid, the desiccated air sucking moisture from his mouth until it was as dry as the scrolls in honeycombed stacks all around him. He reached the end of the passage and came to a junction where another corridor jutted away to the right and continued along the length of the wall, parallel to the central corridor. He stopped and looked back along the path he had just come down. At the end he could see the orangey circle of Father Thomas's light, wavering like a distant candle in the darkness. He kept his eyes fixed on it and started slowly walking up the new corridor. He passed the edge of the bookcase and saw it reappear in the distance as Thomas matched his pace. By this method, Thomas had suggested as they'd plotted in the chapel earlier, they should be able to see anything in the passageway between them silhouetted against each other's light. With luck it would speed up the search.

They continued their steady pace, each row of scrolls, parchments and carved tablets revealing itself then passing quickly into darkness as Thomas's light blinked on and off like a distant lighthouse. With each rhythmic flash the glow dimmed a little more until Athanasius had to squint to make out the distant blob of light. The fading light also created the illusion that Thomas was getting further away, and gave Athanasius a mild feeling of panic. He hated the library at the best of times – and this was very far from being that. It was as this concern rose up, threatening to cloud his mind with irrational fear, that he rounded the edge of another bookcase and saw it – a ragged human form, silhouetted in Thomas's distant light, about halfway down the row.

Athanasius stopped. Peered at it. Tried to discern whether or not it was moving. Thomas must have seen it also for his light remained steady at the far end of the row. Athanasius took a few shallow breaths to steady his nerves then stepped forward, moving silently, narrowing the gap between himself and the apparition. He saw Thomas's orange blob of light wobble and start to grow as he did the same. Thomas reached the shadow first. 'Brother Ponti,' he exclaimed, loud enough for Athanasius to hear, 'it's you.'

Athanasius watched the stooped form of the blind caretaker appear out of the darkness a few feet in front of him, illuminated by the spill from Thomas's light.

'Who else,' Ponti rasped in a voice dried by dust and darkness.

Even in the sudden warmth of the shared light everything about Ponti seemed white and bloodless, like the spiders and other pale creatures that somehow managed to live in the permanent darkness of the mountain.

'I wasn't sure,' Thomas continued amiably. 'I was just running a routine test and a query came up against your trace. The system didn't seem to recognize you. Did you log in properly?'

'Same way as always,' Ponti said, holding up a thin hand in front of milky eyes.

Athanasius edged closer, saying nothing, carefully placing his footfalls so he made no sound. He watched the edge of his own light creep towards the spectral form of the caretaker until it passed over him and he was almost close enough to touch.

At that moment, back in the control room, the program Father Thomas had installed activated. Anyone looking at the main screen showing the floor plan may have noticed the three dots converging in the Roman vault, but they would not have noticed anything out of the ordinary about them. In fact Father Thomas's program had just switched the identity of two of the dots, so the main security system was now tracking Athanasius as if he were Ponti – and vice versa.

In the vault Athanasius stood stock still and held his breath. He'd said nothing and made no noise, yet Ponti, sensing something, turned and stared straight through him with pale, sightless eyes. He raised his head like a rat sniffing the air and made to step forward when Father Thomas caught his arm.

'Could you do me a favour,' he asked, pulling him gently away down the tunnel of books. 'If you'll just step back through the entrance sensor I'm sure the system will re-acquire you and correct itself.' Ponti continued to stare blindly at Athanasius as he was eased away, then turned and obediently shuffled off.

Athanasius felt relief flood through him as he watched them walking away, but it was short lived. He watched the warm orange bubble bob away down the narrow tunnel, with Thomas and Ponti at its centre, carrying the comforting sound of their voices with it until that too was smothered by the strange acoustics. The light got smaller until finally it slipped away on to the main corridor, leaving him suddenly alone in the silent darkness of the library.

104

For the second time that day Liv finished relating the strange circumstances of her birth and waited for the reaction. She examined the three faces opposite her staring at the cruciform scar on her side.

'The cross will rise,' Oscar whispered, 'to unlock the Sacrament.' His eyes flicked up and met hers. There was something close to wonder in them. 'It's you,' he said.

Liv pulled her shirt back down, feeling suddenly exposed and shy. 'Possibly,' she said. 'Only, I have no idea what the Sacrament is so I'm not sure how I'm supposed to "*unlock*" it.'

She sat down and turned to the page in her notebook where she'd copied the letters and re-read the message she'd found in them. When she'd written it down she thought she was on to something. But it had proved to be just another dead end. The Mala had no more idea what the Sacrament was than she did. She suddenly felt unbearably tired, like someone had opened a sluice gate and flooded her with weariness.

'Were the letters scratched on to leather, like the phone number?' Gabriel asked.

'No,' she said, rubbing her eyes with the heels of her hands. 'They were scratched on seeds.' She stopped rubbing and looked up to discover everyone staring straight at her.

'Seeds?' Oscar repeated.

She nodded. The old man's body seemed to contract in a moment of deep concentration, then he breathed out and reached across the desk to pull the computer keyboard towards him. 'During my time in the Citadel,' he said, opening a browser window, 'I did learn some of their secrets.' He typed something into the search box and hit return. An image started downloading on the screen. It was a patchwork of greens, greys and large areas of blue. As it sharpened it manifested itself as a satellite photo of Eastern Europe. Oscar clicked on an area of the picture. The image zoomed into a section of southern Turkey until the screen showed a dense network of streets radiating out from something large and dark at its centre.

'This is a satellite image of Ruin,' Oscar explained, 'taken in the 1980s. Before then all aircraft were forbidden from flying over the city.' The image continued to sharpen. Liv leaned in closer to the screen as the picture stopped downloading. The Citadel sat at the centre. It was oval in shape and completely black except for a large area of dark green close to the centre. 'After NASA published this photograph they lifted the ban,' Oscar explained. 'Even the Citadel's jurisdiction does not yet extend into space.'

Liv focused on the patch of green.

'What is it,' she asked. 'A lake?'

'No,' Oscar replied, zooming the image as close as it would go. 'It's a garden.'

105

Athanasius picked his way through the silent library, his hands reaching out for unseen obstacles, his eyes fixed on the thin line of lights set in the stone floor. Like all who lived in the mountain he was used to the dark, but not like this. A soft white noise seemed to dance at the edge of it, like swarms of silent bees that dispersed the moment he tried to look at them.

He stole a glance behind him, checking nervously for the glow of someone who might have ventured this deep into the library. He saw nothing – just the quivering movement at the edge of his vision and the thin thread of lights stretching away like a crack in the blackness. He turned back, his heart beating so loud in his ears he could hear nothing else, not even the muffled tread of his own feet as they stole across the stone floor. Up ahead he could see the floor lights curve away to the right then disappear. It was where the pathway turned into the final corridor that ended at the forbidden vault. He walked towards it, stepping only on the faint scratch of light in the floor like a wirewalker who knew a step either side would plunge him into the abyss. He followed the curve into the corridor. Stopped.

Ahead of him the thin lights continued to stretch out in a wavering line until, after roughly thirty feet, there was nothing. Athanasius moved forwards, counting his paces as he went, drawn to the awful darkness at the end of the light trail. He counted twenty-eight paces, reached the end of the line, then turned and walked back, twenty-eight paces to the entrance to the corridor. As he counted he recalled Father Thomas's earnest face explaining how he could get round his own security system, but there was nothing he could do once Athanasius was inside the forbidden vault. Once he stepped over the threshold the silent alarm would sound and he would have a maximum of two minutes before the guard arrived.

Athanasius walked back and forth along the corridor, counting the paces to and from the vault, his arms stretched out by his sides as he walked, keeping his balance in the dark. When he was satisfied his escape route was clear he stood once more at the point in the floor where the lights ended and the darkness began, feeling like a man standing on a cliff's edge, preparing to jump.

He pictured the room that lay in front of him: the stone lectern in the middle of the floor; the twelve recesses cut into the cave wall behind it, each one filled with a black box containing the jealously guarded secrets of their order. He figured it would take him a minute to put everything in the vault back the way it was and escape up the corridor. This gave him sixty seconds to find the book. He pictured the Abbot taking it down the day before – three across, two down. In his mind he ran through the actions he had to perform once inside the room. Sixty seconds wasn't long enough – but it was all he had.

He stared ahead into the darkness, aware of the white swarms closing in from the edge of his vision. He took a deep breath. Blew it out slowly. Started counting down from sixty in his head.

And stepped forward.

The guard looked up as the high-pitched alarm sounded. He was off his chair and unlocking the desk before Athanasius had even managed to feel his way to the far wall of the forbidden vault.

Inside the guard's cabinet was a Beretta, a couple of spare clips and a headset with a single telescopic eyepiece protruding from the front. The guard grabbed everything and smacked the first clip into place as he pushed through the door into the main entrance hall.

Father Malachi rose from his chair, his face a mask of concern as he saw the guard moving towards him with the gun in one hand and the night-vision goggles in the other.

'Give me one minute,' the guard said, slipping the gun into his sleeve and heading through the archway and into the main library.

Athanasius felt his way across the wall, counting the recesses as he went. Three across. Two down. His hands reached inside the cold niche. Closed around the smooth box.

He lifted it out and placed it on the floor. His fingers fumbling at the sides for the catches on each edge.

He found them.

Opened the box.

Felt the cold smooth rectangle of slate inside. His fingers fluttered over it. Traced the carved outline of the Tau, then moved on to the edge and opened the book.

No alarm sounded within the library but everyone knew what it meant when they saw the russet gown of a guard swooping down the corridors with his hand hidden in his sleeve.

Standard procedure was to make your way directly to the entrance and wait until someone gave the all-clear. Scholars looked up now, closing their books automatically and watching the guard's halo of light dim as he surged deeper into the vast darkness of the library. Father Thomas was one of these observers. He stood by Ponti, his own circle of light disguising the fact that the blind caretaker now had one of his own, and watched in silence as the guard cleared the medieval section and entered the hall of venerated texts leading to pre-history.

'Trouble?' Ponti asked, sensing the tension the way a dog senses ghosts.

'Possibly,' Father Thomas replied. In the distance he saw the guard raise his arm and pull the night-vision goggles over his head. He took two more strides, then, as he entered the hall of the apostles, his aura of light winked out.

106

Liv peered at the pixellated circle of green on the monitor. The resolution was too low to make out any detail but she imagined the outline of trees and bushes in the slight variations between the blocks of colour.

'One of the great historical mysteries of the Citadel,' Oscar said, his voice rumbling through the silent room, 'was how it miraculously managed to survive years of siege with no food.

'I spent my first year apprenticed to the gardeners: clearing weeds, planting new beds, helping to bring in the fruit harvests. One of my jobs was watering the grounds. We did this from large cisterns that collected rain and waste water from inside the mountain. Sometimes it picked up mineral deposits as it flowed through the stone channels turning it red, so it seemed you were watering the earth with blood.

'Whatever was in it made the soil incredibly fertile. Anything grew in it, even though the garden lay in a crater and was in almost permanent shadow. Once, whilst clearing away some long grass, I found an old rake part-buried in the soil. Green shoots were beginning to spring from its wooden handle.' He looked up and reached for the computer keyboard. 'This garden has nourished the Citadel throughout history,' he said, opening a browser window and typing. 'The green cassocks of the Sancti reflect this – as does the name they used to be known by – The Edenites.' He finished typing and hit return. The satellite photo disappeared and another page started to open. 'Some think this name refers to the age of their order, dating back to the dawn of man. Others, however, believe it has a more literal meaning, and that the Tau is not a cross at all.'

The page stopped downloading. Liv stared at it, the image now filling the screen mingling powerfully with the implication of Oscar's words.

It was a stylized drawing of a tree, its thin trunk rising straight up to where two branches, heavy with fruit, spread out on either side, forming the familiar shape of the 'T'. Winding its way up the trunk was a serpent, and standing either side of it, a man and a woman. She looked across at Oscar, not quite believing what he was suggesting.

'You said the letters were scratched on seeds,' he said. 'Do you know what sort of seeds?'

Liv gazed into his deep black eyes and thought of all the pictures she'd seen in her life depicting Adam and Eve standing in front of the tree of knowledge, one of them always holding the heavy fruit of temptation in their hand.

'Apple,' she said. 'They were scratched on apple seeds.'

107

The vast caves of the library glowed bright and green in the guard's night vision, making all the details of the room visible. He upped his pace now he could see the way ahead and pulled the Beretta from his sleeve. His head scanned left to right, looking for the hotspots of light that would indicate someone's presence. He saw none. The only thing that flared in the green was the thin guide lights, stretching ahead like a phosphorescent vapour trail, leading all the way to the forbidden vault.

It took him less than a minute to get there.

As he approached the entrance to the final corridor he slowed his pace, dropped to a crouch then stopped. He leaned back against the upright of the carved archway. Ducked his head round the edge. Glanced towards the vault itself.

The floor lights blazed in his vision, a bright green line pointing towards the end of the corridor. He peered past the glare. Searching for movement in the dark beyond.

Saw nothing.

Silently he crabbed his way round the edge of the arch and moved stealthily down the middle of the corridor directly toward the vault. His gun extended in front of him. His head perfectly still, like a cat stalking a mouse.

Athanasius saw the line of guide lights break barely six feet in front of him. He was tucked into the shelf that had been emptied earlier on Father Thomas's orders. It was low to the ground, opposite the entrance, facing the vault.

He watched the patch of darkness slide away from him, along the filament of light, showing someone was in the corridor with him. The position of the shelf meant anyone walking down the corridor towards the vault would not see him; anyone walking back up it, however, would spot him in an instant. He needed to be gone before the guard looked round.

Slowly he eased his way out, his ears amplifying every tiny sound, his eyes never leaving the small patch of darkness as it continued to slip away from him down the brittle strip of light in the floor.

He pushed himself to his knees. Then to his feet. He took a step, reaching out into the featureless darkness towards the doorway, lifting and replacing his feet on the floor like a ballet dancer, terrified that the merest scrape of sandal on stone would alert the guard to his presence and bring sudden death.

His hands continued to reach out, groping through the formless black, feeling for the edge of the archway that would lead him away from this trapped corridor. His eyes never left the patch of darkness sliding away down the corridor.

He took a second step.

A third.

A fourth.

On the fifth his hand touched the smooth, cold stone of the wall. He nearly gasped with relief when he felt it. Then he froze. The patch of darkness had stopped moving, just short of the end of the lights. Athanasius moved his hand along the cold stone, heard his dry skin rasp across it, unnervingly loud. In his mind he pictured the guard. Standing at the end of the corridor. Gun in hand. Staring into the vault. How long, after seeing no one there, would it take him to turn round? As this question rose in his mind his hand found the edge of the wall. It curled round it, pulled him through the doorway and into the hall of venerated texts.

Every fibre of his being now screamed at him to run but he knew the hall he stood in was still twenty feet long. Any sound he made here would be heard in the corridor he had just escaped from. He had to stay silent. He put one foot in front of the other, as swiftly and stealthily as he could, in the knowledge that somewhere in the blackness behind him stood a man with a gun who could see in the dark.

The pounding of his heart sounded the pace as he moved swiftly through the black hall towards the exit, his eyes fixed to the floor lights, so pre-occupied with what lay behind that he did not notice the glow of approaching light until it was nearly upon him.

He reached the end of the hall and saw it, a faint glow on the floor and in the curve of the archway he was about to duck through. He froze the moment he saw it. Someone was coming. He watched it grow brighter.

No time to hide.

No place to hide in.

All he could do was stand there and watch as the owner of the light rounded the corner, bursting like a supernova into the chamber not ten feet from where he stood. It was Father Malachi, no doubt on his way to check the contents of the forbidden vault.

Athanasius began to raise his hands in surrender, expecting any moment for the librarian to look up, stop in shock, then shout for the guard. But nothing happened. Malachi continued to stare at the ground, his sharp face stern in thought, his aura of light seeming like a comet to Athanasius's darkness-soaked eyes. Malachi continued down the hallway until he disappeared into the corridor Athanasius had just escaped from, never even glancing in his direction.

Athanasius stared after him for a stunned moment, his eyes re-adjusting to the settling darkness that had just saved his life.

Then he turned. And started to run.

108

Liv stared at the stylized drawing of the tree. For long moments the flickering of the TV in the corner was the only movement, the low murmur of the news broadcast the only sound. It was Kathryn who eventually broke the silence.

'We need to get those seeds,' she said. 'We must get them and analyse them.'

Gabriel stood up and stretched, his lithe body preparing once again for action as his mind began calculating logistics. 'They weren't mentioned in the case file, so the Citadel might not know about them yet. Gives us a head start at least.' He stalked over to the window and stared across the low-stacked crates towards the warehouse door. 'They'll either be in the evidence lockers or most probably the labs. That's a bit of a problem. Security is bound to be much tighter following what happened at the morgue.'

'I could get them,' Liv said. 'I could call Arkadian. Tell him I think I've worked out what the letters mean, but that I need to see the seeds they're written on. Then, when I get them, I'll drop them on the floor or distract him somehow and take one, or swap it for another.' She looked up at Gabriel. 'You only need one, don't you?'

Gabriel stared at her for a moment, his face a mixture of concentration and concern. Then it softened into a smile.

'Yes,' Oscar answered for him. 'We only need one. You must become our Eve and grasp the forbidden fruit. And if these seeds prove to be something extraordinary, just imagine what good we could do with them.'

Liv's mind raced with the incredible implications of what he had just said and a worrying thought struck her. 'But if these seeds are really from the fruit of the . . .' she could hardly bring herself to say it ' . . . from the tree of knowledge,' she managed. 'Then surely messing with them will be . . . a really bad idea.'

Oscar continued to look at her, his widening smile refusing to die in the face of her concern. 'Why?'

'Well,' she said. 'Look what happened last time.'

'You mean the fall of man? Original sin? Being cast out of the garden of Eden to live a life of perpetual pain and hardship?'

Liv nodded. 'That kind of thing, yeah.'

Oscar's smile turned into a dry chuckle.

'And where did you read all that?' he asked.

Liv thought it through and realized what he meant. Of course. She'd read it in the Bible, something written by the men of the mountain, a transcription of source material no one else had ever seen. What better way to stop people seeking knowledge of something than to scare them away from it? Give them an official version of divine teachings, starting with the most terrible tale where eating fruit from a forbidden tree leads mankind to damnation.

'We know there is something in the Citadel,' Oscar continued. 'Something – supernatural. Something so strong that even those outside the mountain can feel its healing power. No wonder the monks have guarded it for so long. Being so close must be intoxicating. Must make them feel more like gods than men. But imagine if that pure life force could be freed from the mountain and spread throughout the world. Imagine no longer needing to pour tons of fertilizer into the dry earth,' he said, gesturing through the office window to the stacks of crates filling the warehouse. 'Just one seed, planted and tended, could make whole areas as fertile as the shadowy garden at the centre of the Citadel. Deserts could become gardens. Wastelands might become forests. Our slowly dying earth could be reborn.'

Liv sat stunned in her seat. This *was* something her brother would have staked his life on. He'd told her the last time they'd met how he thought he'd been spared for a reason. Maybe he *had* died just to get those five seeds to her. She owed it to him to find out if they were worth it. She slipped her hand into her pocket, searching for her mobile, then remembered where she'd left it. 'Arkadian's number was on my phone,' she said, looking up at Gabriel and discovering he was still gazing at her.

He smiled a half-shrugged smile, and Liv felt the blush rising again and turned away.

'His details are at the end of the case file,' Kathryn said, leaning over the desk to open up the relevant document. Liv scanned the office, looking for a phone. Her eyes passed over the TV screen and she froze as she saw the picture of a smiling man hovering behind the shoulder of the newsreader. 'Hey,' she said, her voice a mixture of surprise and concern. 'I know that guy.'

Then every eye turned and looked at the smiling face of Rawls Baker.

109

By the time Athanasius reached the Chamber of Philosophy he had stopped running. The moment he entered he saw a dim glow to his left and stopped.

He stared for a moment at the faint light sketching the outline of a bookshelf, then moved quickly and silently toward it. He reached the edge, took a deep breath and peered round.

For a moment he could not make out who stood at the centre of the bright circle of light, so accustomed were his eyes to the dark; then – as his eyes adjusted and penetrated the glare – he saw with relief who it was.

Father Thomas stood halfway down the row next to Ponti, who was hunched over a reading desk deep with abandoned books, his cart parked beside him full of dusters and brushes, carrying on his work, oblivious to the unaccustomed light he was currently bathed in.

Athanasius moved down the row of shelves towards them, clearing his throat as he went. 'Brother Ponti! Father Thomas!' he said in a voice that seemed unnaturally loud after his long enforced silence. 'I thought I heard something.'

Ponti looked up, staring straight through him with his blank, white eyes. Thomas glanced across and smiled, the relief of seeing his friend lighting up his face.

In the control room by the main entrance two dots converged on a computer screen and the program invisibly transposed their identities then deleted itself.

'There's a security drill underway,' Thomas said matter-of-factly. He watched Athanasius quietly withdraw four sheets of folded paper from his sleeve. 'We should probably make our way to the exit, don't you think?'

'You two go ahead,' Ponti replied. 'They don't even spot me half the time. I'll move on if somebody makes me. Elsewise I'll just carry on with my work.'

Athanasius picked up the largest of the open books on the reading desk, placed the folded sheets of paper inside and gently closed it. 'Very well,' he said. 'Then we won't mention we saw you.' They turned to walk away, dragging the light with them as they went.

'Much appreciated, Brother. Much appreciated,' came the caretaker's dry voice as his spectral form melted back into the darkness.

Athanasius glanced down at the cover of the book. It was a copy of *Also Sprach Zarathustra* by Friedrich Nietzsche, printed in the original German and now containing wax rubbings of most of the contents of the Heretic Bible. The temptation to open it and look at the pages now he had his light back was almost too much to resist. But it was too risky. The guard might return with Father Malachi at any moment. It was best to wait until the alarm was over and the library was re-opened. Then he could read it at his leisure.

Thomas walked on ahead as agreed, heading for the entrance alone so they would not be seen emerging from the depths of the library together. Athanasius held back, scanning the shelves, looking for somewhere to hide the book. He daren't risk whoever had been studying Nietszche to return and discover what it now contained. He reached the end of the row and saw a wall of identical books completely filling a low shelf. He lowered his head and looked over the top. There was a gap between them and the back of the shelf. He quickly slid the volume of Nietzsche over them and down into the gap, then leaned back, straightened the volumes on the shelf and read one of the spines. It was the complete works of

Soren Kierkegaard. Nietzsche had been totally obscured by his Danish counterpart.

Satisfied, he stood back up and headed to the exit, cocooned in the darkness by his rapidly brightening circle of light.

110

The vehicle pulled to a stop just short of the barrier and level with the guardhouse window. The guard looked up from his paper and slid the glass panel to one side. His hat lay on the counter in front of him. An official-looking badge on the front said 'Airport Security'.

'Can I help you?' he said, checking out the men inside.

'Has a Gabriel Mann signed in today?' a voice asked from the passenger seat.

'Maybe. Who's asking?'

Arkadian flipped open his leather wallet and leaned across the driver to show him. The guard peered over the edge of the counter and inspected the gold inspector's badge. He pressed a button underneath the counter and the barrier started to rise. 'Came in 'bout a half-hour ago with his girlfriend in tow,' he said.

Arkadian felt the skin on the back of his neck prickle at the mention of a girl. 'What did the girlfriend look like?' he asked, slipping his badge back into his jacket pocket.

The guard shrugged. 'Young. Blonde. Pretty.'

It wasn't exactly a portrait in words but Arkadian had a fairly good idea who it was. He still hadn't heard back from Sulley – or from Liv. 'And where would I find them?'

'Follow the yellow line,' the guard said, leaning forward and pointing at a line of thick paint on the tarmac that curved away, parallel to the fence. 'It'll take you past the warehouses. They'll be in hangar 12, about three hundred yards on the left. It's the one with the old tail-gunner cargo plane parked out front.'

'Thanks,' Arkadian said. 'And please don't tell them we're coming. This is not a social visit.'

The guard nodded uncertainly. 'Sure,' he said.

The car slipped beneath the barrier, the headlights following the bright yellow line round toward the row of grey, oblong warehouses. Most of them were shuttered up and silent. They slipped past the open windows of the car like headstones.

Up ahead a squat plane was parked on the concrete, its truncated rear pointing back towards a hangar. On the front of the building a large sliding door stood slightly open, spilling orange light out into the gathering gloom. 'Kill the lights,' Arkadian said to the driver, his eyes fixed on the gap, trying to see what lay beyond it. 'And pull up short, I want to take a look-see.'

The driver hit a switch and the headlights died, plunging the road ahead into darkness. He slipped the car into neutral and killed the engine. With the headlights gone, Arkadian could see the stars starting to shine out of the inky sky beyond the hangar as they glided forward with a hiss of tyres on cooling tarmac.

When they got within fifty feet Arkadian held up his hand and the driver eased the car to a stop using the handbrake so as not to fire up the brake lights. Arkadian leaned out of his open window listening for voices, or any other noise coming from inside the warehouse. He heard nothing but the distant whine of jet engines and the ticking of the car as it started to cool in the evening chill.

He unclipped his belt, reached inside his jacket and slipped his gun from its pancake holster. The driver looked across. 'You want me to come with?' he asked.

He was a fresh stripe officer, newly minted. The smell of the street patrolman still clung to him despite the plain clothes. 'No, I'll be OK. Let me take a look first. I'll wave you over if I think I need back-up.'

Arkadian reached up, flicking the switch on the car's interior light so it would stay off then popped his door release and slipped into the night.

111

Kathryn swept the remote off the desk, ramping up the volume on the TV as the newsreader filled in the details.

' . . . *fire crews have rushed to the home of internationally renowned newspaper editor Rawls Baker and we are receiving reports that his body has been found burned to death at the wheel of his car.*'

'Oh my God,' Liv said. 'That's my boss.'

The picture cut to an exterior of a residential street crammed with firetrucks and ambulances. Yellow police tape fluttered in the foreground keeping everyone back, while in the distance firemen, cops and paramedics gathered round the smoking skeleton of a car.

'Did you phone him?' Gabriel asked.

Liv nodded.

'When?'

She shook her head and tried to remember. 'Earlier today,' she said.

'Did you call anyone else?'

She thought hard, running back through the events of the morning. She hadn't called anyone until she'd got away from the cops. Then she'd called her boss, and . . .

She looked across at Kathryn. 'I called you,' she said.

Gabriel sprang across the floor towards his mother. 'Give me your phone,' he said.

She took it from her pocket and handed it to him. He checked the call log. Noted the time of Liv's call. Held the power key to turn it off and turned to Liv. 'We need to get out of here,' he said. 'Looks like they were not only tracing your phone, they were also tracing your calls. So anyone you've spoken to will be in danger.'

Liv looked back at the TV as another photo of Rawls cut on to the screen. It showed him standing in front of the offices of the *Inquirer*, beaming from ear to ear. She couldn't believe he was now dead, just because she'd spoken to him. She couldn't even remember what they'd talked about. Then she looked down, saw the smudged phone number on her hand, and remembered who else she'd called.

112

Bonnie was upstairs in the nursery bedding the twins down when she heard the knock on the front door. She made no move to answer it. Myron was downstairs fixing lunch. He'd let her know if it was for her.

She smiled down at the two tiny faces, peeping out from their soft white blankets and cotton caps, and pressed a button on the plastic box fixed to the side of the double crib they shared. Above them a mobile started to twirl, black-and-white shapes waltzing along to the sounds of seagulls and the shore. One of the babies' tiny mouths curled into a smile and Bonnie lit up at the sight of it – the hell with anyone who suggested it was only wind.

Her mobile phone rang in the bedroom next door, puncturing the moment. It had been going nearly constantly since Myron sent the group text announcing the arrival of Ella – six pounds four ounces – and brother Nathan, two ounces heavier and one minute younger. She took one last look at her babies then padded from the room, dimming the lights as she went.

Bonnie entered the bedroom, moving gingerly toward her phone, which stood charging on the nightstand. She still felt sore from the long labour and traumatic childbirth. She picked it up and glanced at the caller ID. Number withheld. She was about to put it down and let the voicemail deal with it when she remembered Liv's earlier message. It might be the new reporter calling about the story. She'd told just about everyone she knew that her babies were going to be in the paper and she was damned if she was going to be proved a liar. She pressed the button to answer. 'Hello?'

'Bonnie!' The voice was urgent and tight.

'Who's this?'

'It's Liv – Liv Adamsen. The reporter from the *Inquirer*. Listen, you need to take Myron and the kids and get out of there right now.'

'What are you telling me, honey?' she asked, her professional calm automatically kicking in. Then she heard a sound downstairs. Like something soft and heavy falling on the hallway floor. 'Hold on a second,' she said, and started to lower the phone.

'No,' Liv screamed. 'Don't go. Have you got a gun?'

The question was so unexpected that Bonnie froze. Downstairs she heard more sounds. The click of the door gently closing. The *shush* of something sliding along the hallway floor. No sounds of conversation. No footsteps leading back to the kitchen to finish fixing lunch. She felt dread creeping over her as she listened to the silence.

Then there was another sound. Much closer, just along the hallway. The high-pitched wail of a baby crying.

'Gotta go,' she said tonelessly into the phone.

Then she hung up.

Liv heard the dialling tone purr in her ear and frantically searched the display for a redial option. When she couldn't see one she held up her shaking hand and started dialling the number written there.

'Put the phone down please.' The voice was familiar, but totally unexpected.

Liv looked up. Saw Arkadian standing in the doorway. His badge in one hand, his gun in the other. It was pointing at Gabriel.

She heard the rapid beeps of the number sequence starting to connect. 'No,' she said, punching in the last two numbers. 'You're just going to have to shoot me.'

She held the phone to her ear, and stared at him as it started to ring.

113

Bonnie stood in her bedroom. Listening.

From down the hall the crying of her baby pulled at her like an invisible cord, but she forced herself to ignore it and listen instead to the other noises in the house. She searched the silence. Heard nothing. Nothing at all.

She stepped over to the closet, her slippered feet silent on the thick cream carpet, and carefully opened the door, revealing rows of clothes on hangers. Then she heard it. The slow squeak of the kitchen door swinging on hinges that had never been set quite right. Someone was down there. Maybe it was Myron, heading back to fix lunch. But then why was he ignoring the baby?

She glanced across at the closet. Pushed her hand through the curtain of clothes to the small wallet safe fixed high on the back wall. She'd made Myron put it in the moment she discovered she was pregnant. The plastic covering on her patrolwoman's uniform crinkled as her arm pushed past it towards the keypad set in the small steel door of the safe. She tapped her birth date into it and opened the door. Inside was her police badge, a box of 9mm cartridges, two fully loaded clips, and her service weapon.

She picked up the gun and a clip and pulled her arm out of the closet, listening to the wailing and the silent house beyond. She slid the clip into the stock of the squat, L-shaped gun until it made a click, like a tiny bone snapping.

From down the hall the crying grew, getting more desperate, and she felt a tingling behind her nipples as nature began to respond. She held her free arm across her front, padded over to the door, hunkered low behind it, and looked through the crack into the hallway.

Nobody there.

The hungry cry continued and she felt patches of wetness start to soak into her bra. Her grip relaxed slightly on her gun. Maybe she was simply hormonal and imagining all of this. She was tired, there was no doubt about that, and her lioness senses were probably working over-time. She listened for a few beats longer, feeling more and more foolish, and was just about to get up when she heard it.

A stealthy creak of a footfall on the third step of the stairs.

Then another on the fifth.

Myron had always joked that you couldn't sneak up on anyone in this house.

Myron!!

Dear God, where was Myron?

She pressed her eye closer to the crack, trying to get an angle on the stairs, hoping to see him appear and amble towards the nursery. Instead the second twin started crying, and a faint smell of burning flooded her nostrils, then a vision of hell stepped into view.

It was a man. Tall. Bearded. He wore a red rain slicker, the hood pulled tight round his face. In his hand he held a gun, made obscenely long by the silencer screwed tight to its barrel. His eyes flicked between the sound of the babies crying and the partially opened door of the bedroom.

Bonnie looked up at him. Felt the warm wetness spreading across her chest, like she'd been shot. She held the snub barrel of her gun low against the crack of the door, angling it up as best she could so it pointed at the man. She'd been through weapons training at the academy. Learned to sweep through buildings checking for hostile targets. She went to the firing range every couple of weeks to stay sharp. None of it had prepared her for this. Her hand tightened round the gun as she watched him, his head cocked to one side, listening through the crying, as she had done.

The phone rang in the bedroom, startling Bonnie and bringing the demon towards her at terrifying speed. Red filled her vision as he leaned in to the crack in the door, his own gun raised as he looked through to the room.

Bonnie looked up. Angled her gun higher. Saw his head tilt down. His eyes meet hers.

She fired three shots in quick succession, eyes closed against the splinters blowing back in her face from the bullets tearing through wood.

She opened her eyes. Saw the landing was empty. Leapt up in panic, terrified he may have retreated to the nursery, her stitches tearing with the effort but her mind oblivious to the pain. She rounded the door, tears of fury and terror streaming down her face, ears still ringing from the gunshots. She glanced right as she rushed on to the landing, gun drawn and ready to fire. And then she saw him, lying on his back, at the bottom of the stairs where two of her bullets had thrown him.

She whipped her gun round and surveyed the scene from behind it, her heart hammering, the twins still screaming.

Blood spattered the walls and the pale stair carpet, marking the man's violent passage down them. Halfway down, his gun lay balanced on the edge of a step like a broken black cross. Bonnie dropped down the few steps to get it, her gun never wavering from the sprawled red form at the bottom of the stairs. She saw a bullet hole in his side and another in his head. His eyes were open and still. The only movement was the creep of dark blood spreading out from beneath him like a hole opening up to drop him back down to hell. She got closer. Crouched low to pick up his gun. Saw something further along the hallway, a sneaker attached to the foot of someone lying motionless on the floor.

She recognized it, realized what had happened. Then her own scream rose, desolate and terrible, drowning out the cries of her fatherless babies.

114

In the deepening night a van pulled to a halt next to one of the silent warehouses, a few buildings short of the one with the cargo plane parked out front. Johann killed the engine. Cornelius looked out of his window towards the unmarked police car and the hangar beyond, its door slightly open, lights burning inside. Kutlar said nothing. He kept his head down, studying the two arrows on the screen of the notebook, one pointing at Cornelius's phone, the other at the last recorded signal from Kathryn Mann's. They were almost overlapping.

A soft buzz sounded in Cornelius's pocket and he drew out his phone. Opened a text message. Frowned. Showed it to Johann, who glanced at Cornelius then nodded. He opened his door and slipped into the night, taking the keys with him. Kutlar felt the van rock gently as the rear door opened and he heard the muffled sounds of things being moved around in the back. The morphine had started to wear off on the drive to the airport and he could now feel the pain steadily bubbling up inside his ruined leg. The walk up the steep cobbled streets of the old town had ripped apart most of his internal stitching and he felt that the dressings and his trouser leg were now the only things holding it together. He'd tried to hide it from the others by folding his jacket on his lap, but he could still smell the blood, tainting the air with its rusty tang.

The van rocked again as the back door closed and a few seconds later Johann reappeared, ambling slowly across the tarmac towards the cargo plane, his red windcheater pulled tight around him, a canvas bag slung loosely over his shoulder.

In the gloom he looked like a member of the ground crew doing the evening rounds.

Liv was still staring at Arkadian when the phone finally picked up. She could hear babies crying in the background.

'Bonnie?' she said.

'He killed Myron,' Bonnie said, her voice ragged and dry. 'He shot him.'

'Who shot him? Where is he now?'

'In the hallway. He ain't gonna hurt my babies now.'

Liv glanced up at Arkadian, his eyes still on her, his gun still pointing at Gabriel.

'Listen, Bonnie,' she said, 'I need you to get the kids and get out of there, OK? I want you to call someone at the station, someone you trust, and get them to put you and your family in a safe house, somewhere no one can find you. Will you do that for me, honey?'

'No one's going to hurt my babies,' the ravaged voice repeated down the line.

'That's right, Bonnie. You call the station right now, OK?' She looked back at Arkadian, wishing she could ring the station herself, knowing she couldn't push her luck.

The muffled sound of the furious babies rose like the howl of the damned through the crackle of the transatlantic line. She thought of them growing up, never knowing their daddy, all because of a phone call – all because of her. 'I'm sorry,' she whispered into the phone. Then she placed the receiver back in its cradle to cut off the sound of the crying.

115

Cornelius watched Johann close in on the squad car. The text message he'd received from the Abbot had changed things. He didn't like changes to a mission midway through. It made him nervous. On one hand the new directive made things simpler. Just seizing the girl and returning to the Citadel was much easier than having to also silence every possible witness. But his training made him reluctant to just give up on his original mission. Maybe he could still complete both.

When Johann had covered half the distance he opened his door and slid out after him. 'Stay here,' he said, then pushed the door closed.

Kutlar watched him move away, making for the perimeter fence that ran behind the buildings. He reached the back of the warehouse and disappeared round the edge, heading towards the same hangar as Johann. Kutlar put the notebook on the seat beside him and lifted the folded jacket from his leg. A black wetness shone in the dim reflected light of the night sky. His leg looked as though it had been dipped in oil. Seeing its ruined state made it hurt even more. He reached into his jacket pocket and found the jar of morphine capsules – instant relief at his fingertips. He pulled it out and looked up at the distant hangar. Warm light spilled on to the tarmac from the open door. The girl was in there. The guard had told them that. And as soon as they had her, or she was dead, they'd kill him. They'd probably do it here and leave him in the warehouse along with whoever else was in there.

His eyes flicked across to Johann ambling up to the side of

the car. He saw him lean down. Saw a muzzle flash briefly illuminate the interior of the car.

In the distance he could see the terminal building glowing brightly like a mirage. It was too far. His best bet would be to try and make it back to the guard's hut. He'd have a gun stashed somewhere, and a walkie-talkie to call help. He remembered the surprised look on the guard's face as he'd looked up from his newspaper straight into the barrel of Johann's silenced gun. He hadn't reached for anything. He just answered Cornelius's questions. He'd told them the girl was inside and someone else was in there too. Someone who sounded like the man Kutlar had fought on the road the previous night. The man who had shot his cousin Serko and planted this pain in his leg.

He looked back at Johann now, running towards the open hangar door in a loping crouch, keeping clear of the light that spilled from it. He reached the edge of the door and another figure appeared from the rear of the building, slipping through the darkness to join him. They squatted on the tarmac, two demons in the dark, checking their weapons; and like a revelation Kutlar realized this was his chance. He edged over to the driver's side, pain jabbing his leg with every movement. He took the jar of pills from his pocket and twisted the cap off, his eyes never leaving the two crouched figures as he popped a single capsule into his mouth – enough to quell the pain, not enough to blunt his sharp desire to survive.

He thought about the man inside, unaware that the man he had shot was sitting outside and oblivious of the two men by the door with guns in their hands. If Kutlar let things ride, that man would probably be dead in a few minutes. But then the killers would come back for him, and though he dearly wanted revenge for Serko, he wanted to live even more. He apologized to the darkness under his breath, hoping Serko would hear it wherever he was. Then he watched Cornelius and Johann, coiled in preparation, counting on surprise. And waited.

116

'We need to get out of here,' Gabriel said, the moment Liv put the phone down.

Arkadian made no move. Kept his gun steady. 'What were you doing at the morgue?' he asked.

Gabriel sighed and shook his head wearily. 'I haven't time to explain,' he said. 'If you're going to arrest me, go ahead and do it – but you need to let these people go. And you need to do it right n—'

The sudden blast of the horn cut him off mid sentence. His head instinctively whipped round in the direction it came from in time to see the shape of a man slipping in through the open door on the far side of the hangar, body tense, gun rising up and pointing straight at them.

'Down!' he shouted, throwing himself forward, taking Oscar and Kathryn down to the floor with him. Then the world all around them started disintegrating.

Arkadian also saw the gunman. He swung his own gun round just as the window next to him exploded, filling the air with tiny crystals. He let off two shots at the distant figure before he felt something punch him hard on the shoulder, knocking his gun from his hand and spinning him to the floor.

He stared across to where Gabriel was crouched next to the woman and the old man, pulling a gun from a black bag on the floor. Beyond him, on the far side of the office, he saw Liv crouched behind a photocopier, covering her head with her hands as the TV exploded above her, cutting off the news report and showering her with sparks.

More gunshots boomed nearby as Gabriel returned fire.

Arkadian tried to crawl away from the open doorway and pain shot up his right arm. He rolled on to his side, his teeth gritted against the agony, then hands grabbed his jacket and tugged him to safety. He kicked out with both legs to help shift his weight and looked up into the straining face of the woman. He slid across the twinkling floor and into cover just as the doorway started spitting splinters.

The woman let go and reached across his body to retrieve his gun from where it had fallen. She expertly checked the breech, making sure it hadn't been damaged in the fall, the snick-snacking of the action moving smoothly back and forth.

Then everything went quiet.

Cornelius had already dropped into position behind a crate when the car-horn had sounded, but Johann was still coming in through the door. When he crashed heavily to the concrete floor, Cornelius knew he'd been hit. He dragged him into cover, rolled him on his back and checked him over.

There was a large wound on the upper part of his firing arm. It was bleeding but not pumping. Then he saw more blood bubbling from a ragged wound in his neck. Johann looked up with confusion in his eyes, lifted his hand and felt the surge of hot liquid against his palm. He brought it away and stared dumbly at the thick wet redness that continued to ooze rhythmically from the ragged neck wound. Cornelius pressed down hard with his hand, trying to stem the flow. Realized it was useless. Johann knew it too. He twisted away from the pressure. Reached into his canvas bag that had fallen to the ground and pulled out two small objects. They were olive green and round and looked like small steel fruits. 'Go,' he said.

Cornelius glanced down at the grenades then back into Johann's eyes. He saw the brightness slowly fading in them. The blast on the horn had ruined the element of surprise. He should have shot Kutlar rather than leave him alone in the van. Johann was now dying because of his mistake. He would kill Kutlar slowly when he got the chance. He reached over and quickly made the sign of the Tau on Johann's forehead, his fingers tracing a bloody mark where they touched the skin.

'Keep them busy, but don't harm the girl,' he said, remembering the Abbot's message. He released the empty clip from his gun and snapped a new one in place. He took one last look at Johann. Nodded once then angled the gun over the top of the crate and started firing rapidly as he moved backwards across the concrete floor, away from the line of crates and towards the open door.

117

Arkadian's ears were ringing from the gunfire and his shoulder hurt like hell, but he still felt sharp. He reached up. Pressed his hand against the wound. Felt the wet hole in his jacket where the bullet had passed through. Took it away and examined it. The blood on his palm was dark, not bright. It wasn't arterial. He wasn't bleeding too badly. He looked across at Gabriel, crouched low by the shot-out window, his eyes scanning the silent warehouse for movement.

'You OK?' the woman's voice asked. He turned to look at her. She was hunkered down next to an open box of cartridges, her black hair tumbling over her face in a silken wave as she dexterously refilled the clip from his gun.

'I'll live,' he said.

She looked up. Nodded towards the corner. 'You should go look after her,' she said. 'This isn't your fight. It's not hers either.'

He followed her gaze to where Liv was still huddled beside the photocopier. From his new angle he saw something else. Underneath the ruined TV set there was a door set into the wall with FIRE EXIT written across it in bold green letters.

'I wouldn't do that,' the old man said, reading his thoughts. 'They'll know there's a back way. Anyone heading through that door will be walking straight into trouble.'

Kathryn snicked the last cartridge into the clip and smacked it back into the stock of Arkadian's gun. 'Just watch the exit and keep your head down,' she said, holding it towards him by the barrel. 'You got a mobile?' Arkadian nodded and instantly regretted it as another sharp pain shot through his shoulder.

'Then call for backup. They'll respond much quicker to an officer in trouble.'

He held her gaze for a second then reached out with his good hand and took the gun, feeling for the safety catch with his thumb and discovering it was already off.

Johann knew the walls of the office would dampen the blast from a grenade. He needed to get closer, or wait for the people in the office to come out. He figured the girl would stay in the office. She might be stunned by the explosions, or suffer shrapnel injuries, but she'd live. He could feel a numb coldness spreading from the ends of his fingers and feet.

At the far end of the warehouse he could hear the tinkle of glass and the scuff and crunch of cautious movement. His eyes dropped down to his gun lying on the painted concrete floor. He reached over and picked it up. It felt ridiculously heavy. Not a good sign. Slowly he unscrewed the silencer to make it lighter. He placed it on the floor beside him and felt the cold reach his knees as the heat continued to pump out from his neck.

Time was up.

He picked up the first of the two grenades.

118

Gabriel rose slightly and scanned the warehouse over the jagged lower edge of the window. There had been no further movement since the last volley of gunfire. This meant one of two things. Either the man had retreated – in which case he would undoubtedly return with more men and more firepower, or he was still in the warehouse and biding his time. Either way they couldn't just wait it out and hope for the best. They would have to force the situation.

A crunching sound drew his attention and he glanced over at the Inspector moving stiffly across the glass-gravelled floor to where Liv was huddled by the photocopier. He gripped a mobile phone in his mouth and held his wounded right arm stiffly across his chest. In the other he held a gun. Gabriel didn't want to wait around while he called in the cavalry. After his visit to the morgue they would arrest him for sure – and being stuck in a cell for the next few days wasn't going to help anyone. The Inspector reached Liv and leaned in close to whisper something. She looked up at Gabriel and smiled. He smiled back then looked away as more glass crunched behind him. Kathryn and Oscar were taking up a position by the door. Gabriel gripped his gun and raised it up as he glanced back out at the silent warehouse, scanning the gaps between the crates for movement.

Still nothing. Just shadows and air.

He looked over at his mother and grandfather, braced against the wall inside the open door, his mother in lead position. In her hand she held the Glock he had liberated from the man who now rested at the bottom of the quarry. She looked over her shoulder at him, her face sharpened with concentration. He held up his left hand so she could see it. Took a breath. Then dropped it.

As his left hand fell his right hand rose bringing his gun up over the lower edge of the broken window. The moment the barrel cleared it he started firing, letting off a tight pattern over the area he'd last seen the man go down. He fired eight shots. Three rapid rounds to put someone down, five slightly slower to keep them there.

He finished firing and scanned the warehouse through the thin cloud of blue smoke. Saw nothing. He glanced down over the edge of the broken window. Kathryn was now outside in the warehouse, her back pressed against one of the crates, in position and ready to go.

Johann heard the bullets rip through the air above his head and ping into the steel door beyond. One round clipped the top of the crate he was slumped against, showering him with wood and shards of aluminium before it ricocheted off to the right, whining as it went. All the while he kept his hand clamped to his neck, keeping the pressure on, staunching the flow of blood to buy himself just a little more time. He counted the shots and noted their frequency – three quick, five slower – classic cover fire. They were changing position. It meant they were coming for him. He smiled and closed his free hand round the two grenades in his lap. He was starting to feel cold and drowsy.

Not long now – he thought.

He started to recite one of the vigil prayers in his head.

He was dying doing God's work, and God always gathered his own.

* * *

Gabriel reached the open office door and took up the position his mother had recently vacated. Three quick shots tore through the silence from outside and he spun away and was out of the door before the first of the slower shots sounded.

Johann counted the three quick shots and shifted his position, leaving bloody handprints on the cold concrete floor.

Every movement was an effort but he couldn't wait any longer.

FOUR

The first of the slower shots rang out and his hand closed around the first grenade.

FIVE

He pulled the pin, pulled his arm back and threw it round the edge of the crate towards the office at the back of the warehouse.

SIX

He rolled over through the slick of his own blood. Pulled the pin on the second grenade. Hurled it down the gap on the other side.

SEVEN

Swept his gun from the floor and pushed himself upwards.

EIGHT

Rose above the top of the crate. Raised his gun. And started firing.

Gabriel saw the red figure rise, the gun rising with him, up towards the spot where his mother stood. He saw flame spit from the end of the barrel and a piece of packing case tear free from a crate halfway between them. The boom of the first shot echoed through the warehouse and the gun jerked up from the recoil, bringing the barrel closer to its intended target.

A second shot boomed out, this time from Gabriel's gun.

A puff of red mist appeared behind the gunman's head and it jerked backwards, like he'd been punched. Then he began to fall. Gabriel watched him crumple as the gunshot echoed through the cavernous hangar. It was only as the sound died away that he heard the metallic, clinking sound of something else, skittering across the concrete towards them. He shifted his aim and tracked the sound drawing closer, bouncing along the narrow channel between the crates. He realized what it was moments before it rolled into view right by the spot where his mother was crouched.

Kathryn turned to look at it but his body was already in motion, his legs pushing against the concrete, hurling his weight towards her as she began to rise. He connected with her like a charging linebacker, driving forwards and through her, using his momentum to carry them both as far from the grenade as possible before it detonated.

It was only as his head passed over her shoulder and his body slammed against hers that he saw the second grenade skip out from behind the crates towards the exact spot they were now heading.

119

From round the edge of the office door Oscar had a clear view down the tunnel created by the rows of stacked crates. The grenade was halfway down when he spotted it, bouncing across the warehouse floor towards him. His reaction was instinctive. He stepped through the door, his hands rising up in warning, his head turning towards Gabriel and Kathryn. When he saw them locked together, unstoppably launched in his direction, he experienced a moment of divine clarity and everything slowed almost to a stop.

His eyes dropped back down to the grenade, turning slowly in the air, barely an inch above the ground. It bounced once, with a sound like a hammer striking stone, and continued moving towards him. He tensed his legs and shifted his centre of gravity towards it.

Ninety years . . . he thought, as his body started to move. *I have dodged the enemy's arrows and spears for ninety years . . .*

The grenade spun closer, struck the outer wall of the office then bounced back, coming to rest right in front of him.

Not bad for a dead man.

He fell forward, flattening himself on the ground, smothering the grenade with his body.

Gabriel saw Oscar crumple and realized what he was doing. He reached out as their momentum brought them closer. Felt his fingertips brush the back of Oscar's flight suit. Started to close his hand around the heavy-duty cotton.

Then the first grenade exploded behind him.

The pressure wave tore the flight suit from his grip, lifting him up and forward, over Oscar's prone body and into the warehouse wall beyond. He hit it head first, with the full force of the explosion behind it, then slid heavily to the floor behind a crate. As he landed he felt consciousness being hammered out of him. He tried to shake his head clear. Tried screaming to shock himself awake. Then Kathryn crashed down on top of him, cracking his head against the concrete floor, finishing the job the wall had started.

The last thing Gabriel was aware of before he passed out was the ground shuddering beneath him and a muffled crump as the second grenade exploded.

120

Arkadian had just raised himself up slightly, holding the phone above him, searching for a signal when the shock wave from the first explosion tore through the office. It slammed him against the horizontal locking bar of the fire door, swinging it open and spilling him out into the night. Pain exploded in his shoulder as he hit a patch of gravel, knocking the phone and gun from his hand. He bit down hard to stifle a howl of agony and rolled on to his side, away from the pain, taking deep breaths to smother it as he frantically scanned the area for signs of danger.

He saw Liv sprawled across the threshold of the open door, half in and half out of the warehouse. His phone lay on the gravel between them, shining a cold blue display light up into the night. He reached for it just as the second explosion shook the ground beneath him. He grabbed the phone and continued to look for his gun. Saw movement. Looked up at the fire door swinging slowly shut. Then he saw the man standing behind it.

Liv felt the second explosion more than heard it. It rumbled through the earth like muffled thunder, shaking her gently out of her daze. She looked up and saw Arkadian sprawled on the ground outside. He reached for his phone and picked it up. Then his eyes twitched up and past her, growing wide in shock at what they saw.

He jerked twice as two holes appeared in the front of his shirt then he flopped backwards on to the gravel revealing a gun on the ground, right where he'd been sitting.

Liv's hands tore at the ground as she scrambled towards it. The square of light from the open door narrowing as it continued to swing shut behind her. She didn't look round. Just focused on the gun. It's grip towards her. The safety-catch off.

Her hand closed round it, a fingernail tearing against the ground as she hooked it through the trigger guard. She twisted round just as something heavy cracked across the back of her head, flooding it with light and blinding pain, then darkness. Then nothing at all.

121

Sweat stung Kutlar's eyes as he limped across the blacktop towards the guardhouse. He could feel the cool night air on his damp skin but it did nothing to quench the heat boiling up inside him. His wound was infected, he was pretty sure of that. He was also in shock from losing so much blood. He needed to get help fast or he might die after all. He couldn't let that happen. Not now. It seemed like hours since he'd leaned on the horn and finally escaped from the van, but it was probably only a few minutes.

He'd heard the muffled exchange of gunfire through the pounding of his heart, then the silence that had followed the two explosions. Maybe everyone was dead. Even the guy who'd killed Serko. With no witnesses he could still talk his way out of this one. Just needed to get to the guardhouse and call for help.

The headlights lit him up from behind when he was just thirty feet away. The blood was pumping so loud in his head he hadn't even heard the engine. Panic rose in his throat. He tried to run. Stumbling forward. Felt what was left of his stitches pulling and popping inside his leg.

The lights got brighter and lit up the side of the guardhouse just twenty feet in front of him. He could see the faint spray of red on the back wall. The guard hadn't reached for a gun, but he must have one somewhere. If he could get to it, he might stand a chance.

He could hear the engine now, rising up through the thump of his heartbeat. The guardhouse pulled closer. Just fifteen feet now.

Ten more agonizing steps.

... Eight more ...
... Seven.

Cornelius drove straight through Kutlar as if he wasn't there. He felt the crump as the police car smashed through both his legs and saw the windscreen cobweb where his head struck it on his way over the top.

He glanced in his rear-view mirror. Saw the body land head first on to the concrete, arms flopping lifelessly, legs twisting at unnatural angles. He slammed on the brakes. Threw the car into reverse. He didn't want to leave anything to chance where Kutlar was concerned and he also didn't want to leave a body in plain view.

The engine screamed as he hit the accelerator and the crumpled pile of flesh and clothes grew bigger in the rear-view mirror. He braked a metre short, popped the boot and slipped from behind the wheel, leading with his gun. He rounded the rear of the car, half hoping to find Kutlar still alive. He liked the idea of him spending the rest of his life as a cripple, drinking through straws and shitting in bags. He was met instead by a fixed, blank stare and was almost disappointed.

He ducked down and quickly scooped the body from the ground. Felt broken bones crunch inside the swollen flesh of Kutlar's legs as he wedged him inside the tight boot space next to the body of the driver. He had to lean his whole weight on the boot lid to get it to click shut then looked around the open ground of the airport as he made his way back to the driver's seat. He saw no movement. Heard no distant sounds of sirens heading his way. He wanted to go back and sweep the warehouse, tie up any loose ends, but he had his orders and his primary objective had been achieved.

He climbed behind the wheel and glanced in the back where the girl lay unconscious. A set of handcuffs fed through a thick D-ring in the floor held her arms out in front.

He watched her chest move as she breathed and figured the crack on the head would keep her out long enough to get where they were going. He locked the doors anyway, just to be safe, then put the car in gear and eased on to the service road leading away from the airport and back to the city of Ruin.

VI

I beseech you, my brothers, remain faithful
to the earth, and do not believe those who
speak to you of otherworldly hopes!

Also Sprach Zarathustra
FRIEDRICH NIETZSCHE

122

'Leave us!' the Abbot said.

The Apothecaria looked up, surprised by a command coming from someone other than their master. They rose uncertainly, their attention switching from the Prelate, to the life-support machines they monitored, to the Abbot standing massively by the door.

'You will find,' the Prelate's dry voice rustled from somewhere in the nest of white linen, 'that I am in charge here. You would do well to remember that.'

'Forgive me, Father,' the Abbot said, 'but I have urgent news . . . regarding the Sacrament.'

The Apothecaria continued to hover, waiting for further instruction. 'Then you may leave,' the Prelate said. The Abbot watched them check their machines then glide from the room, shutting the door behind them.

'Come closer,' the Prelate called out to the dark. 'I want to see your face.'

The Abbot moved towards the bed, stopping by the machines the phantoms had just deserted. 'I'm sorry to call unannounced,' he said, turning down the volume on the life-support monitor. 'But there is something happening with the Sacrament. Something extraordinary.' He arrived at the Prelate's bedside and was immediately skewered by his sharp black eyes.

'And does this, have anything to do, with three Carmina, who cannot be found in the mountain?'

The Abbot smiled. 'Ah, that,' he said.

'Yes, that.' There was surprising energy behind his anger.

'That is what I wish to discuss.' The Abbot looked down at the old man. He had aged even more in the few hours since he had last seen him, his life energy was almost gone, his regenerative powers almost spent. 'I have just received word that they have found Brother Samuel's sister,' he said, watching the Prelate, waiting for his reaction. 'I have instructed them to bring her here, to the Citadel – to me.'

The merest hint of heat coloured the gelid skin of the old man's face. 'It is customary to wait, until one is Prelate, before one starts acting as such.'

'Forgive me,' the Abbot said, reaching over as if to tenderly brush some lank hair away from the Prelate's eyes. 'But sometimes one must act like a leader, in order to become one.'

He grabbed a pillow and pressed it down hard on the Prelate's face, smothering it with one large hand while the other seized his wrists, holding them tightly so the taloned fingers couldn't scratch. Behind him he heard the faint sound of an alarm from one of the machines registering a dangerous change in the old man's vital signs. The Abbot glanced at the door, listening for the arrival of hurrying steps. There were none. He held the Prelate until the fight faded from the struggling sticks of his arms, then removed the pillow. The Prelate's eyes stared up towards the darkness above his head and his mouth hung open, forming a circle. The Abbot moved across to the life-support machine and turned up the volume on the alarm, giving voice to his final, silent howl.

'Help! Come quick,' he yelled, leaping forward to the bed.

Footsteps scurried across the stone landing outside and the door flew open, bringing the Apothecaria into the room. One swept over to the machines, the other came to the Prelate. 'He started choking,' the Abbot said, stepping back. 'Is he all right?'

*　　*　　*

The alarm continued to howl through the room and the Apothecaria by the bed started pounding the old man's chest while the other dragged over a defibrillator.

'Do what you can,' the Abbot said, 'I'll fetch help.'

He slipped through the door and into the empty hallway, heading not for help but to the lower chambers of the mountain. There would be no inquest, for the Abbot was now acting Prelate and he would not request one. Besides, his sad death would be greatly overshadowed by what was still to come.

The Abbot had removed his final obstacle. Now he could fulfil his destiny.

123

Gabriel came round gradually.

At first his eyes refused to open and he lay where he'd fallen, breathing in air that smelt of explosive and scorched wood – and something else. It was a smell he'd last encountered in the Sudan after guerrilla forces ambushed one of their aide trucks. When Gabriel went to inspect the site with government troops the same smell had hung in the air like a greasy cloud. It was only when he saw the blackened body of the driver fused to the steering wheel that he'd realized what it was. His eyes flew open as he made the connection and remembered what had happened.

He looked around. Saw he was lying on the floor against the wall of the warehouse, his mother slumped on top of him. He slapped her face a couple of times. Pressed nervous fingers against the side of her neck and felt her pulse. It was strong and regular.

He grabbed her shoulders and gently rolled her off him and on to her side, his head pounding as he shifted position and put her in the recovery position. He listened through the painful pulse for sounds of movement elsewhere in the building. Heard nothing.

His gun lay on the concrete floor where it had been knocked from his hand. He scooped it up and pulled the slide back, checking the gun was undamaged and the action still smooth, then he slipped from behind the crates. He did not look towards the office. He didn't want to see what he knew was there, not until the area was clear or he was sure the bastard who'd done it was good and dead.

He ducked into the tunnel between the rows of crates, and made his way quickly towards the front of the warehouse, keeping low all the way. He had no idea how long he'd been out, which was a problem. When the firing started, the Inspector had been calling for backup. Airport security also patrolled the perimeter every twenty minutes. If he got trapped in a security clamp-down of any sort he'd be put out of circulation and that just played into the hands of the Citadel. He reached up to the back of his head and felt a lump swelling where his head had struck the wall. The hair around it was wet with blood from a deep, swollen tear on his scalp. He glanced at the blood on his fingers. It was bright red, not dark, not too sticky. It hadn't started to coagulate. He can't have been unconscious for too long, which was good, but he still had to move fast.

He reached the end of the tunnel and squatted low to the floor. Holding his gun out in front, low and close to his body, he glanced round the edge of the crate in a rapid darting movement, *out and in*, his gun following the direction of his eyes, ready to fire if he had to. A man lay sprawled between the open hangar door and the first stack of crates. His eyes were fixed open. The back of his head was missing. Gabriel moved towards then past him, his eyes scanning for movement as he headed for the open door of the warehouse.

Outside, all was quiet – no police cars, no airport security. A white van was parked by one of the neighbouring warehouses. He was pretty sure it was the same one he'd followed earlier. There had been three men inside it then. So far he'd found only one. He grabbed the edge of the door and rolled it shut, dropping a thick metal latch across to keep it shut. With his back now covered he returned to the dead man.

The bullet that killed him had entered at the intersection of a Tau drawn on his forehead in blood. There was no blood around the wound. Death must have been instant. Pity. He blew out a long stream of air to disperse the emotion tightening his throat and pricking the backs of his eyes. He needed to stay focused. Two men were still unaccounted for and cops couldn't be far away.

Gabriel dropped down and searched the dead man, his hand hissing over the dry surface of his red windcheater, avoiding the wet pulpy sections round his neck where the blood had soaked through. At least he'd suffered before he died.

He found a set of van keys and a blank plastic rectangle the size of a credit card. He remembered the van waiting at the end of the alley by the old town wall. The driver had swiped a card then. He slipped it into his pocket with the van keys and picked up the dead man's gun. A silencer lay nearby, next to a canvas bag. Gabriel crabbed over, picked up the tube of black metal and used it to lift the cover flap of the bag.

Inside were four full 9mm clips, two grenades and a plastic box containing preloaded hypodermic syrettes, the same type soldiers carried into combat. There were also a couple of spare ampoules of clear liquid. He glanced at the label. It was Ketamine – a heavy-duty tranquilizer usually used by vets to knock out horses. He dropped the Glock into the bag along with the silencer, swung it over his shoulder and slipped between the stacked crates heading towards the office at the back of the warehouse.

As he approached the end of the passageway he smelt the burnt-air bitterness of explosives and saw the shredded outer wall of the office. On the floor in front of it a sooty circle showed the point of the blast. There was another on the underside of the steel roof above it. The reinforced concrete of the floor had obviously reflected most of the explosion upwards, undoubtedly saving his life. He reached the end of the passageway and took a deep breath to dampen his swelling anger, then moved forward.

What was left of Oscar lay by the office door.

Gabriel had seen battlefield casualties before, flesh torn and shredded by the teeth and claws of modern weaponry – but never someone he was related to. He moved towards his grandfather, choking down his grief, trying not to look at the red mess of his body, focusing instead on the face that had somehow remained remarkably untouched. Oscar was face down, his head tilted to one side, his eyes closed as if resting. He looked almost serene. A bright splash of blood stood out against the dark mahogany of his cheek. Gabriel reached down and gently wiped it away with his thumb. The skin was still warm. He leaned down and kissed him on the forehead, then stood and looked around for something to cover him with before his emotions dragged him further down. He still hadn't secured the area, or found Liv. He dragged a tarpaulin from one of the crates, carefully draped it over Oscar's body, then ducked through the door and into the office.

124

The moment Gabriel saw the open fire door at the back of the room he knew something was wrong. He raised his gun, crunched towards it and looked outside. The Inspector was lying on the ground. Liv had gone.

He stepped out, checking along the perimeter fence for the patrols then grabbed the Inspector under his shoulders, leaned back to drag him inside, and nearly dropped him again when he let out a low, ragged moan.

He hauled him inside, closed the fire door and felt for a neck pulse. He found one, and frowned at the two bullet holes in the front of his shirt. They were ragged and closely grouped. He poked his finger through one of them and touched warm metal. He dragged his finger towards the second hole, tearing the shirt material between them and revealing a black body armour vest beneath with two flattened bullets at the spot where the heart should be. The impact would have been enough to knock him out, crack the ribs maybe, but not kill him.

'Hey,' Gabriel said, slapping him sharply on both cheeks. 'Come on, wake up.'

He slapped him harder until Arkadian's head finally rolled away to one side and his eyes struggled open. He looked at Gabriel. Focused. Tried to get up.

'Take it easy,' Gabriel said, resting a hand on his chest where the bullets had struck. 'You've been shot. If you get up you could pass out again and crack your head. I need to know what car you came in.'

'Unmarked car,' Arkadian rasped in a dry voice he didn't recognize.

'It's gone,' Gabriel said, reaching into his pocket and taking out his mobile phone. 'Whoever took it is probably the same guy who shot you and left you for dead. I want you to call it in as stolen. It'll be on the road somewhere between here and the Citadel. But advise caution. The girl's in the car with him.'

Arkadian looked at the phone and remembered the officer he'd left sitting behind the wheel. 'The driver?' he said.

Gabriel looked at him, his face blank. 'He'll be in the car too.'

Arkadian nodded, his face darkening. He reached out with his good hand and took the phone. He started to dial the number for central dispatch but managed only the first three numbers before both men froze as something moved, outside in the warehouse.

Gabriel surged forward, moving low across the floor towards the open door, keeping below the line of the windows. The sound came again. Like electrical static, or the crinkle of heavy plastic. He realized what it was a split second before he reached the door and a terrible sound tore through the air – the banshee howl of pain and lament.

His mother was standing just outside the door, holding the tarpaulin in her hand, and staring down at what was left of her father's body.

125

Cornelius headed up through the rising mountains keeping a steady few points below the speed limit, wary of his broken windscreen and the two corpses stashed in the boot. The tail end of the rush-hour traffic still leaked out of the city. Very little was heading in his direction. He made it all the way up the Southern Boulevard and on to the inner ring road before Arkadian managed to report the car he was driving as stolen. He was already easing down the slip road and headed into the Umbrasian Quarter by the time the dispatcher called it out on the radio and instigated a search. Following the daily exodus of coaches and cars after the old town closed its portcullises for the night the Quarter was practically deserted. Cornelius turned into the alley, and brought the car to a stop by the steel door. He tapped a message into his phone explaining where he was, and who was in the car with him.

Then he waited.

After a long minute a deep *thunk* sounded inside the steel door and it started to rise, gradually revealing the dark tunnel beyond. The headlights swept across smooth concrete then rough stone walls as he eased the car forward, following the curve of the tunnel away to the right. Behind him the steel door sank back towards the ground. Cornelius listened to the soothing rumble of the tyres on the uneven floor. It occurred to him that this was possibly the last time he'd ever drive a car or set foot outside the Citadel. He found these thoughts soothing. He had no love for the modern world, or the people who inhabited it. He'd seen enough hell on earth during his time in the army.

Salvation lay ahead, away from the world, high in the mountain – closer to God.

The car bounced on its springs at the bottom of the dip then rose up towards the chamber at the end of the tunnel. As the headlights swept down at the top of the rise they lit up two figures standing like phantoms in the centre of the vault. Cornelius pulled the wheel to the right, steering away from the apparitions, before coming to a halt in a cloud of dust and exhaust fumes. He killed the engine but left the headlights burning, the bounced light from the beams illuminating the two figures drifting towards him through the gritty fog. Both wore the green cassocks of the Sancti. Cornelius opened his door, stepped out, and found himself crushed in an embrace.

'Welcome back,' the Abbot said, holding him out again at arm's length and inspecting him like a father greeting a long-lost son. 'Are you hurt?' Cornelius shook his head. 'Then you must change quickly and come with us.'

The Abbot snaked his arm round Cornelius's shoulder and lead him towards the doorway in the back wall. He stepped through into the small ante-chamber and noticed something on the floor. The Abbot smiled and gestured towards it. Cornelius felt tears prick his eyes as he bent down to pick up the wooden Crux lying on top of the dark green robes of a fully ordained Sanctus.

126

The phone went dead in Arkadian's ear. He looked at the display. The signal had vanished. He frowned, partly in frustration, partly because of what the dispatcher had just told him. He looked down at the red mess of his shoulder. He needed to get to a hospital, he needed to call his wife too so she didn't hear about all this second-hand, but all he'd managed to do was report the car stolen. He rose painfully to his feet, holding the phone in front of him as he cast about for a signal. He heard another fit of sobbing echo through the warehouse and realized he was probably not the only one who needed a hospital. He picked his way across the glass-pebbled floor towards the splintered office door and looked out.

The scene that greeted him was a tableau from a renaissance painting of biblical grief. The broken body of the old man lay on the floor shrouded in a thick plastic sheet shining like silk under the soft glow of the overhead lights. Gabriel was kneeling beside him, his arms cradling his mother's head against his chest. She wept and wrung the material of his jacket with her hand. Gabriel looked up.

'The car?' he asked, in a voice stretched thin by grief.

'They know where it is,' Arkadian said. 'All squad cars have a transponder fitted so they can be found quickly if a radio goes down. The dispatcher said this one must be faulty. She said it looked like it was moving in a straight line across the buildings and streets of the old town before it stopped – right in the middle of the Citadel.'

Gabriel closed his eyes. 'Then we're too late,' he said.

'No,' came a ragged voice. Kathryn lifted her head and stared straight at Arkadian. 'The seeds the monk swallowed! You need to make sure they're safe,' she said. Arkadian frowned. No one was supposed to know about them. 'We think they may be the Sacrament,' Kathryn explained, sensing his confusion.

Arkadian shook his head. 'But they're just common apple seeds,' he said. 'We tested them.'

A heavy silence hung in the wake of his words. Nobody moved for long seconds. Arkadian watched Gabriel and Kathryn line up this new information with what they already knew. Then Gabriel leaned forward, tenderly kissed his mother on the top of her head and rose to his feet.

'If it's not the seeds,' he said, moving past Arkadian and into the office. 'Then it's the girl. She is the key to everything. She always has been. And I'm going to get her back.' He crunched across the floor, picked up the black canvas bag from the floor and placed it on the nearest desk.

'Let me handle this,' Arkadian said, glancing back down at the phone which now showed one bar. He pressed redial to get through to central dispatch. 'If she's been kidnapped and taken to the Citadel they can't just deny it. We can get the commissioner involved, bring political pressure to bear. Force them to cooperate with the investigation.'

'They'll deny everything,' Gabriel said, opening the bag and reaching inside. 'And it'll take far too long. The girl will be dead before any politician gets involved. You said the car was still moving when you spoke to the dispatcher. That means she's only about twenty minutes ahead. We need to get there fast and get her out.'

'And how are we going to do that?'

Gabriel spun round in a blur of motion and Arkadian felt a bang on his arm, like a slap. '*We* don't,' Gabriel said.

Arkadian looked down. Saw a syringe sticking out where Gabriel had hit him. He looked up with shock, staggering backwards as he reached up to try and bat the syringe away. His arm already felt heavy. He hit the wall and felt his legs buckle. Gabriel stepped forward and caught him, controlling his fall all the way to the ground. Arkadian tried to speak but his tongue wouldn't work.

'I'm sorry,' Gabriel said in a voice that sounded liquid and distant.

The last thing he remembered was that the gunshot in his arm didn't hurt any more.

127

Cornelius had never been in this part of the mountain before. The stone staircase rising steadily upwards was ancient, and narrow, and dusty from lack of use. The guard led the way, his flambeau sending orange light over the rough walls and the slump of the girl lying over his shoulder, her arms hanging down like the legs of a slaughtered deer. Cornelius could hear no hum of voices, no clatter and echo of distant activity – the usual trapped noise of the mountain. The only thing to disturb the silence was the sound of their own breathing and the steady tramp of their feet pressing onwards and up the relentless staircase.

It took them almost twenty minutes to reach the top and by the time he stepped into the small vaulted cave marking the end of their climb Cornelius was sweating through his new green robes. Candles set into the walls spilled enough light to reveal several tunnels leading away from the cave, each one narrow, and roughly cut. A dim light wavered at the end of the central tunnel and the Sanctus guard headed towards it, his stride still steady despite having carried the girl almost the entire height of the mountain. Cornelius followed, with the Abbot close behind, and had to stoop as he entered, the passage having been cut thousands of years previously by men who rarely grew higher than the wild grass that had once whispered on the great plains surrounding the mountain. He continued forward with his head bowed, fitting reverence for what he knew must lie ahead. It was the *Capelli Deus Specialis*, the Chapel of God's Holy Secret – the place where the Sacrament was kept.

As they got closer, the glow at the end of the tunnel increased, throwing more light across the walls and ceiling. It revealed that, far from being roughly chiselled as Cornelius had first thought, they were covered with hundreds of carved icons. His eyes picked out individual images as they slipped past: a serpent twisting round a tree that was heavy with fruit; another tree, this one in the shape of the Tau, with a man standing in the shade of its outstretched branches. There were also crude figures of what looked like women in various states of agony – one being broken on a rack, another screaming in fire, another being ripped apart by men with swords and axes. Each one looked the same to him. They looked like the woman he had imagined in the burkha and seeing their agony brought him a certain peace. It reminded him of a time, a few days before he lost his platoon, when they had stumbled across an ancient temple in the desert scrub off the main Kabul road. Its crumbling walls had been covered with similar hieroglyphics, simple lines worn down by time and weather, depicting ancient and brutal things long forgotten and rendered to dust.

As he continued down the tunnel the icons on the walls grew fainter, as if thousands of years of passage had worn them thin like ancient memories, until finally they melted back into the rock and the passage widened, opening out into a larger antechamber. Cornelius stood up as he emerged into it, squinting at the sudden brightness that glowed hot and red from a small forge built into the far wall. Arranged in a line in front of it, sketched by the Halloween light, were four round whetstones set on wooden frames, and behind them a large circular stone dominated the back wall. It was perhaps a little shorter than a grown man, and looked like an old-fashioned millstone with four wooden stakes jutting from its surface at even points round the edge. The sign of the Tau was carved into its centre. When Cornelius saw it he thought for a moment that this strange stone was the Sacrament and he wondered at its meaning. Then he noticed the deep, straight channels cut into the rock above and below it and saw how the wall behind was worn smooth.

It was a door.

The true Sacrament must lie beyond it.

Down through the dark tunnels, in the lower part of the mountain, the library began to flicker with the lights of returning scholars. One of them belonged to Athanasius. It had taken the guards nearly an hour of searching and checking before they had declared the incident a false alarm and finally re-opened the doors.

The entrance chamber seemed uncommonly bright as Athanasius passed back into it, illuminated as it was by the combined glow of all the monks who now congregated there to gossip and speculate. He saw Father Thomas emerge from the control room, a look of professional concern on his face, followed closely by Father Malachi pecking at his heels like a stressed goose. He looked away quickly, for fear their eyes might meet and their shared secret arc between them like electricity. Instead he clutched the files he was holding to his chest and stared resolutely ahead towards the darkness beyond the archway that led back into the main library and the forbidden knowledge he'd left hidden there.

128

The scrape of the steel fuel can echoed through the warehouse as Kathryn dragged the last of them across the floor to where the white van was parked with its rear doors open. She was sweating from the strain and urgency of the work, and the muscles in her arms and legs burned with the effort, but she welcomed it. It helped distract her from the deeper pain she felt.

Gabriel jumped down from the van, grabbed the fuel can and hoisted it into the back to join the large pile they'd collected from around the warehouse: sacks of sugar; rolled-up blankets; stacks of polypropylene water pipes and plastic sheeting, anything that was explosive or flammable and would create lots of smoke when it burned. It was all packed neatly around a central stack of white nylon bags with KNO3 stencilled on the side. These contained potassium nitrate, the nitrogen-rich fertilizer that had been on its way to the Sudan. They were now going to serve the cause in a different way.

Gabriel pushed the last fuel can into place near the edge of the pile then looked back through the open doors at the haunted face of his mother. She looked exactly like she had after his father had been killed: grief mixed with anger and fear.

'You don't have to do this,' he said.

She looked up at him. 'Neither do you.'

He looked at her, and realized the pain in her eyes came not only from what had already happened, but from what still might. He jumped down. 'We can't just leave her,' he said. 'If the prophecy is right, and she is the cross, then she could change everything. But if we do nothing – then nothing will change, and all that has happened here will have been for nothing. And we'll spend the rest of our lives looking over our shoulders, because they will torture her. They'll torture her, discover everyone she's spoken to, then they'll kill her and come looking for us. I don't want to spend the rest of my life in hiding. We have to finish this now.'

She looked up at him with liquid black eyes. 'First they took your father,' she said. 'Now they've taken mine.' She reached out and laid her hand on his cheek. 'I can't let them take you.'

'They won't,' he said, wiping a tear from her cheek with his thumb. 'This isn't a suicide mission. I became a soldier after Dad died so I could fight them in other ways. Academic arguments don't change anything, and protests outside cathedrals don't shake the walls.' He glanced at the contents of the van. 'But we will.'

Kathryn looked up at him. Saw his father standing there. Saw his grandfather. Saw herself there too. She knew it was pointless arguing with him. There was no time anyway.

'All right,' she said. 'Let's do it.'

He leaned forward and kissed her gently on the forehead – long enough for it to count, not long enough for her to think it was goodbye. 'OK,' he said, reaching into the back of the van for the black canvas bag. 'This is what you do.'

129

The Sanctus guard let the girl's body slip to the ground next to the forge then reached up and took a thin metal rod from a hook on the wall. He laid it in the heart of the fire and started pumping the bellows, filling the room with the fire's rhythmic roar. The forge glowed brighter, throwing yellow light across the whetstones in front of it. The Abbot moved to the nearest one, shrugging his shoulders out of his cassock and letting it fall to the floor. Cornelius looked at the network of scars on his body.

'Are you ready to receive the knowledge of the Sacrament?' the Abbot asked. Cornelius nodded. 'Then do as I do.'

He unsheathed the ceremonial dagger from his wooden Crux and began working the foot-pedal to set the sharpening stone spinning. He laid the edge of his dagger on the stone and started to work the blade backwards and forwards, his eyes fixed on the sharpening blade. Cornelius shrugged out of his own robes and felt the heat of the fire on his skin. He removed the dagger from his Crux and started his own wheel spinning.

'Before you enter the chapel,' the Abbot said, his voice rumbling under the hiss of the bellows and the grinding stones, 'you must receive the sacred marks of our order. These marks, cut into our own flesh, remind us of our failure to carry out the pledge our ancestors made to God.' He lifted his blade from the stone and held the edge up to the light. 'Tonight, thanks to your great service, that pledge will finally be honoured.'

He turned to Cornelius and raised the point of his dagger until it rested at the top of the thick raised scar running down the centre of his body. 'The first,' he said, pushing the blade into his flesh and dragging it down towards his stomach. 'This blood binds us in pain with the Sacrament. As it suffers, so must we, until all suffering ends.'

Cornelius watched the blade slice through the scar until blood dripped down the Abbot's body and on to the stone floor. He held his own dagger up. Pressed it into his own flesh. Pierced his skin with its point. He dragged it downwards, shutting his mind to the pain, willing his hand to obey him until the first incision was done and blood ran hot from his own mortified flesh. The Abbot raised his dagger again and made the second cut at the point where his left arm met his body. Cornelius did the same, dutifully mirroring this and every cut the Abbot made, until his body bore all the marks of the brotherhood he was now part of.

The Abbot finished the final cut and raised the bloodied tip of his blade to his forehead, wiped it once upward, turned it, then wiped it once across, leaving a smeared red Tau in the centre. Cornelius did the same, remembering Johann as he did so and tears ran down the pale, puckered skin on his cheek. Johann had died a righteous death so that their mission could succeed. Because of that sacrifice, he was about to be blessed with the sacred knowledge of the Sacrament. He watched the Abbot slide his dagger back into the wooden scabbard of his Crux and step over to the forge. He lifted the metal rod from the heart of the flames and carried it across to Cornelius.

'Do not worry, Brother,' the Abbot said, misreading his tears. 'All your wounds will soon heal.'

He raised the glowing tip of the iron and Cornelius felt the dry heat approaching the skin of his upper arm. He looked away and remembered the bloom of the explosion that had burned him once before. Felt the searing agony again as the branding iron pressed against him. He gritted his teeth, clamping down on a scream, willing himself to endure it as the smell of his burning flesh corrupted the air.

The iron was removed, but the pain remained, and Cornelius forced a look at it to convince himself it was over. He sipped shallow breaths, looking down at the charred and blistered patch of flesh that marked him now as one of the chosen. Then he saw the flesh start to harden, knit together and heal.

A grinding sound scraped through the flickering darkness, dragging his eyes away. The guard was heaving against the wooden stakes in the huge circular stone, rolling it along channels worn smooth by millennia to reveal a chamber beyond. At first glance it appeared to be empty. Then, as Cornelius's eyes sank into the blackness, he saw candlelight flickering inside.

'Come,' said the Abbot, taking his arm and leading him towards it. 'See for yourself. You are one of us now.'

130

Athanasius scanned the swirling darkness in the Chamber of Philosophy; looking past the edges of his own contained light for the glow of others.

There were none.

He hurried over to the bookshelf halfway down the room and reached over the collected works of Kierkegaard where his fingers closed round the slim volume of Nietzsche. He withdrew it and slipped it under his sleeve, not daring to look at it as he hurried away from the central corridor towards the reading tables stationed at the quiet and private edges of the chamber. He found one against a wall, buried amongst the most obscure and unsought titles, checked the darkness once more, then laid the book gently down on the desk top.

He stared at it for a moment, as if it was a mousetrap about to spring. It looked suspiciously isolated on the bare desk so he reached across to the nearest shelf, took down a few more volumes and laid them beside it, opening some at random. Satisfied with the makeshift camouflage of study he had created, he sat down, checked the darkness one last time, then opened the volume to where the folded sheets of paper lay. He removed the first one, carefully unfolded it and pressed it flat against the desk.

The page was blank.

He reached into the pocket of his cassock and removed a small stick of charcoal he had rescued earlier from the Abbot's fire. He ground it against the desktop until he had a small pile of fine, black powder then, very gently, he dipped the tip of his finger into it and began to rub it back and forth across the greasy surface of the paper. As the dust found the gaps in the wax, small black symbols began to rise from the creamy blankness, until two dense columns of text filled the page.

Athanasius looked down at what the dust had revealed. He had never seen so much of the forbidden language of Malan collected into one document before. He held his breath as he leaned forward, as if the merest gasp might blow the words from the page, and started to read, translating in his head as he went.

> *In the beginning was the World*
> *And the World was God, and the World was good.*
> *And the World was the wife of the Sun*
> *And the creator of everything.*
> *In the beginning the World was wild,*
> *A garden teeming with life.*
> *And a being appeared, an embodiment of Earth,*
> *One to bring order to the garden.*
> *And where the One walked, the land blossomed,*
> *And plants grew where there had been none,*
> *And creatures nested and prospered,*
> *And each was given a name by the One*
> *And took what it needed from the Earth and no more.*
> *And each gave itself back to the Earth*
> *When its life was done.*
> *And so it was through the time of the great ferns,*
> *And the time of the great lizards,*
> *Even to the dawn of the first age of ice.*
> *Then one day man appeared – the greatest of all animals.*
> *Close to being a god – but not close enough for him.*
> *And he began to see not the great gifts he possessed*
> *But only those he lacked.*
> *He began to covet that which was not his.*
> *And this made an emptiness inside him.*

And the more he yearned for that which he had not,
The greater this emptiness became.
He tried to fill it with things he could possess:
Land, chattels, power over animals, power over others.
He saw his fellow man and desired more than his share,
He wanted more food, more water, more shelter.
But none of these things could fill the vast emptiness.
And above all else he wanted more life.
He did not want his time on Earth
To be measured by the rise and fall of the sun,
But by the rise and fall of mountains.
He wanted his time to be immeasurable.
He wanted to be immortal.
And he saw the One. Walking the Earth.
Never ageing. Never withering.
And he became jealous.

131

Gabriel climbed into the cockpit of the cargo plane and looked through the windshield. In the distance the van's brake lights flared red as it slipped past the guardhouse and pulled out on to the road. He figured it would take his mother about thirty minutes to drive to the Citadel and get into position. Once he was airborne it would take him less than ten.

He sat in the left-hand pilot seat and scanned the controls. He had flown second seat several times, but not for a while, and never solo. The C-123 was not designed for a one-man crew. When fully laden it weighed sixty thousand pounds and needed two strong men hauling on both sticks to shift it through the air. Landing was the hardest part, especially with a full load in a cross-wind: at least that wasn't going to be a problem.

He raced through the pre-flight checks, dredging his memory for the procedures drummed into him during his military training, then heaved on the flaps and rudder to remind himself of their weight. They were heavier than he remembered. He engaged the brake, pumped the fuel and pushed the starter button. The stick shuddered in his hand as the starboard Double-Wasp engine juddered then coughed into life with a spluttering roar. The port engine followed with a belt of black smoke and he felt the braced power of the props straining against the stick, impatient to push the plane forward. He feathered the throttle down a little then slipped on a headset, hit the comms and hailed the tower. He gave his call-sign and heading and requested clearance for immediate takeoff.

Then he waited.

There were only two runways at the airport. Fortunately the cargo flights mainly came and went on runway two, the one closest to the hangar. If the wind was in the wrong place, however, he would have to taxi the long way round to the other strip. The seconds ticked by.

He saw movement, over to his right, two sets of blue lamps spinning lazily above the bouncing beam of oncoming headlights. It was a patrol truck, skimming across the blacktop, parallel to the perimeter fence, heading towards the guardhouse. Gabriel saw it starting to slow.

Time to go.

He pushed the twin throttle levers forward, eased off the brake and felt the plane lurch as the twin props caught the cold night air and pull him forward across the tarmac. Over to his left a big passenger jet was waiting at the end of the main runway. It was pointing in the same direction. This meant the wind was ahead of him, so if he did have to takeoff without proper clearance he'd at least be heading in the same direction as the rest of the traffic.

The C-123 bounced over the ground, picking up speed as it lumbered towards the head of runway two. The patrol truck had parked now and someone in uniform was climbing out of the driver's door.

The scratchy sound of a voice snapped him to attention. 'Romeo – niner – eight – one – zero – Quebec,' it squawked through the static and clattering engine. 'You are cleared to depart, runway two. Taxi into position and hold. Over.'

Gabriel felt his hands relax on the steering column. He confirmed the order and pulled back on the throttle, easing the aircraft further away from the drama unfolding behind him.

To his left he could see the passenger jet picking up speed down the main runway. He would be next. He'd left the Inspector lying just inside the warehouse with his badge lying open on his chest. That way they'd find him quickly and call the medics. He had no idea how much Ketamine he'd pumped into him. Too much, probably. The last thing he wanted was the Inspector's death on his conscience.

The metallic voice crackled loudly in his headset. 'Romeo – niner – eight – one – zero – Quebec,' it said, as over to his left the passenger jet lifted off and pulled up its wheels. 'You are cleared for immediate takeoff. Over.'

'Roger that,' Gabriel responded. He released the wheel brakes and pushed the throttle most of the way forward. The sudden thrust pressed him back into his seat until the nose lifted and the wheels let go of the runway with a loud bump. He reached for the landing gear control then decided to leave the wheels down. Now he was airborne he would get to the Citadel well before his mother and the extra drag would reduce his airspeed.

He cleared the perimeter fence and Gabriel dipped the port wing. Over in the distance he saw the Taurus mountains rising up from the plain. Within them he could see a glow bouncing off the underside of the clouds showing him where Ruin was. He continued to climb, describing a wide circle that took him over the mountains until he was approaching the ancient city from the north. He kept the plane steady, fighting the rising winds from the mountain peaks, until they fell away to reveal the shallow bowl containing the ancient city, with the line of the great northern boulevard pointing straight towards a ragged patch of darkness at its centre. He dialled a heading into the autopilot that would take the plane directly over the Citadel and on to the coast beyond. There was fuel for about forty-five minutes of flight time – enough to carry the plane well out to sea before it came down.

He checked his direction one last time then engaged the autopilot, taking his hands off the steering column as ghostly hands took over, adjusting flaps, throttle and rudder to keep the plane on course. He let the autopilot fly the plane for a few minutes, watching the patch of darkness creep closer until it disappeared below the nose of the plane. Finally satisfied that the autopilot was working and the course was steady, he unclipped his seat belt, slid from the pilot's chair and headed into the hold to prepare.

132

Cornelius stepped through the stone entrance and into the chapel of the Sacrament.

After the roaring brightness of the forge it was dark with an unnatural blackness that clung tightly to whatever secrets it held. A few candles flickered in a cluster by the door barely illuminating the shelf upon which they rested, guttering now as the Sanctus guard stepped past and moved through the darkness towards the far end of the room. Cornelius scanned the darkness and saw something lying on the floor in the centre of the chapel. The guard slowed as he drew near and let the girl slide from his shoulder and on to the ground next to it. It was the body of Brother Samuel, his feet pointing towards the dark end of the room, his arms stretched out on either side to form the sign of the Tau.

The guard reached down, grabbed Samuel's arms and dragged him over to the far wall, where he dumped him without ceremony, before turning his attention back to the girl. He dragged her feet round to point down into the darkness at the far end of the chapel, took her arms and stretched them out until she formed the shape her brother had so recently held.

'Thank you, Septus,' the Abbot said. 'You may leave us now. But stay close by.'

The monk nodded and sent the candles fluttering again as he swept from the chapel.

Cornelius felt the Abbot take his arm and lead him forward. 'Come closer,' he said.

Cornelius drifted along, his eyes fixed on a spot ahead, where the darkness was beginning to take form beyond the figure of the girl. He took another step and felt his wounds start to itch, as if ants were crawling along the sliced edges of his flesh. He looked down and saw the skin closing up, like hot wax running together. Looked up again. Saw the thing in the darkness at the end of the room solidifying into form with every step he took, rising up from the altar, a shape both familiar and strange. Then he saw something else, something so unexpected that he stumbled backwards at the shock of it.

The Abbot gripped his elbow tighter. Steadied him. Leaned in closer. 'Yes,' he whispered. 'Now you see. The Sacrament. The greatest secret of our order, and our greatest shame. And tonight you will witness its end.'

133

Bright headlamps swept across the grey concrete wall of the multi-storey car park as Kathryn turned into the alley. At the far end she could see the medieval wall, marking the boundary of the old town, rising up above the modern buildings.

She pulled to a stop by the heavy steel shutter and reached out through her open window, swiping the electronic key card Gabriel had taken from the dead monk. She waited, listening to the low throb of the van's engine echoing down the night-blackened walls of the alley. Nothing happened.

She glanced up at the thin rectangle of sky framed by the high walls of the multi-storey car parks. Her son was up there, somewhere, heading this way. An image of Oscar's twisted body flashed into her mind and she screwed her eyes shut to push it back. Now was not the time to grieve. She was in shock, she knew that. She also knew it was all going to come crashing down on her at some point – but not now. She had to be strong, for the sake of her son. Her actions now would help him stay alive. He had to live. She couldn't lose him.

She jumped as a loud clang sounded inside the steel door and the shutter started to rise, creeping upwards like the opening mouth of a grave. When it reached the top it clanged to a stop, echoing again against the low rumble of the engine.

She glanced up one last time at the dark patch of sky then slipped the van into gear and entered the tunnel.

134

The empty hold of the C-123 felt like it was shaking itself to pieces as Gabriel pulled himself along the ribs of the plane towards the point in the floor where it angled upwards. He reached it and hooked his right leg and arm into the cargo net lining the fuselage, then braced himself for the suction and hit the red punch button to lower the ramp.

A loud clunk punctuated the thunderous clatter of the engines and a thin horizontal crack appeared at the back of the plane pulling the air from the fuselage as the ramp started to lower. Gabriel held on, felt the howling wind tug at the flaps of his wing-suit until another loud clunk told him the ramp had locked fully open. Outside he could see the reflected glow of the city on the underside of the tail. He pulled the skydiver goggles over his eyes and crawled towards the edge. He peered over the side and through the arctic blast of outside air. Below him, nearly two miles down, was the city of Ruin, the four straight lines of the boulevards converging like crosshairs on the darkness at its centre.

He'd done airdrops from this plane before, but never at night and never at this altitude. It was a useful way of getting round red tape when governments dragged their heels over visas while the people on the ground desperately needed help.

He unhooked his leg from the net and shuffled round until he lay centred on the ramp, his feet pointing back towards the howling night. He did a final pre-flight check on the packs strapped to his front and back then edged backwards towards the lip of the ramp, his hands clinging tightly to the cargo net and straining against the pull of the slipstream.

His feet hit the edge and he slid them over into the freezing air, continuing to work his way backwards until his hands were the only thing still holding on. He was in the air now, his body stretched out horizontally from the back of the plane, held up by the fluid roaring rush of the night. He held on tight, staring straight down at the city, watching the patch of darkness creep closer. He fixed his left eye on it and closed his right, as though sighting down the barrel of a rifle.

Then he let go.

The plane was doing a little over eighty miles an hour when he dropped into the churning, frozen air of its prop wash. The moment he cleared the turbulence he opened his legs and arms, flaring the Parapak membranes stretched between them and inflating the wing. The combination of airspeed and the shape of the suit generated instant lift and he felt himself being pulled upwards. He adjusted his arms, leaning one way then another, his open eye never leaving the dark target below as he flew down towards it.

Wing-suit training had been the last course he'd completed before mustering out of the army. They were the latest development in HALO jumps – the High Altitude Low Opening drops that were the cornerstone of covert ops deployment. The theory went that by jumping at high altitude the delivery aircraft could stay well out of range of surface-to-air missiles and by deploying a chute at very low altitude it minimized the risk of being spotted by forces on the ground. A man in freefall is also too small to be picked up on RADAR. It was the perfect method of inserting highly trained troops quickly and covertly into enemy territory. It was also the perfect way of getting into a mountain fortress no one had ever breached.

Gabriel checked the altimeter on his wrist. He was already below four thousand feet and dropping at eighty feet per second. He leaned over and began to turn in a tight circle, watching the darkness grow as he spiralled down towards it, searching its dark centre for the garden he knew was there.

135

Kathryn spotted light ahead of her in the tunnel and her fingers tightened around the steering wheel. She reached over to the black canvas bag on the passenger seat, slipped her hand inside and pulled out her gun.

She thought about the pause, out in the alley, after she'd swiped the card, before the steel shutter had started to rise. Maybe they were expecting her. Perhaps she was now heading straight into an ambush. If so, there was no point in stopping. The tunnel was too narrow to turn round and reversing would be too difficult. Besides, running wasn't going to help Gabriel. So she kept her foot on the accelerator and her eyes on the patch of light, growing brighter beyond the wash of her own headlights. She brought the gun up over the dashboard just as the van cleared the top of the rise. The headlights cut down through the dark revealing a cavern and a car. Lights on. No one inside. Driver's and passenger doors open.

She jerked down hard on the wheel, bringing the front of the van round just in time to clear the rear bumper of the parked police car. She slammed on the brakes, bringing the van to a crunching halt, brought her gun round, and scanned the cavern for movement. She noticed the closed steel door in the wall in front of her, but apart from that there was nothing.

She reached over and killed the van's engine but left the headlamps burning. The sudden silence was oppressive. She grabbed the black bag from the passenger seat, opened the door and slipped out, taking the long way round the car, gun first, checking there was no one hidden behind it. Still nothing.

She moved to the back of the van and wrenched open the rear doors.

The contents had shifted around a little on the journey but the pile of fertilizer, sugar and smoky combustibles was still pretty much intact.

One giant smoke bomb, Gabriel had said. *With enough explosive power to blow out every door in the lower part of the mountain.*

She carefully placed the black canvas bag down on the metal floor next to a large cardboard box wedged against the rear wheel arch. Inside the box was a hurricane lamp and two of the sheet sleeping bags they used in hotter countries. She lifted out the lamp, set it on the floor and knotted the sheets together to make a long white cotton rope. She dropped one end in the box and fed the other under the door towards the petrol cap.

She noticed the camera as she rounded the end of the van, set high in the back wall, red light burning steady by the lens. She fumbled the key into the petrol cap, twisted it off, and turned her back to the camera while she carefully fed the other end of the rope down into the fuel tank, leaving the middle part looped under the door and trailing on the floor. She ducked round to the back of the van, grabbed the hurricane lamp and unscrewed the reservoir cap at the base. She doused the length of the cotton rope with kerosene splashing a generous puddle where the middle section draped on to the cavern floor.

This is your fuse, Gabriel had explained.

She emptied the last of the kerosene into the box in the back of the van then reached into the bag and took out two grenades, their dark green surfaces now buried beneath multicoloured layers of rubber. It was the sum total of every single elastic band she had managed to find in the warehouse office. She placed them carefully in the centre of the kerosene soaked box.

These are your detonators, Gabriel had said.

Do not arm them until the very last minute.

She took the first grenade, slipped her finger through the ring, then stopped. She was getting ahead of herself. She put it down again and reached over for the last thing Gabriel had hauled into the van before sending her on her way.

The lightweight trail bike slid out of the back of the van and bounced on to the stone floor. The helmet was threaded through the handlebars, but she left it there, mindful of the security camera and the ticking of the clock.

She leaned it against the tailgate and picked up the grenade again. There was a small *snicking* sound as she pulled the pin then she carefully laid it down at the bottom of the kerosene-soaked box.

If the spoon springs open after you pull the pin you have six seconds to get away.

Gabriel had told her.

Her eyes bored into the metal arming spoon as she slowly forced her fingers to let go of it.

The lever didn't move. The rubber bands had held it in place.

She blew out a long stream of air, picked up the second grenade and pulled its pin before her nerve failed her. She placed it in the box next to the first then pushed the whole lot further into the van until it rested against the fuel cans and the sacks of fertilizer. She pulled a large box of matches from the black canvas bag – the last piece of the bomb.

Kathryn slung her leg over the bike, reached into her pocket for the swipe card and jammed it between her teeth. She struck a match, fed it into the open box and dropped the whole lot on to the puddle of kerosene just as the matches flared inside the box. The kerosene *whumped* alight and bright yellow flames scuttled up the soaked cotton rope, one way towards the fuel tank, the other towards the grenades.

From lighting the fuse you'll have about a minute to get out, Gabriel had said.

Maybe less.

Kathryn turned the front wheel of the bike towards the dark

mouth of the tunnel, twisted the throttle and kicked down hard on the starter.

But nothing happened.

Yellow light from the spreading flames brightened around her as she pumped the throttle some more to feed in fuel. She stamped down hard a second time.

Still nothing.

She released the throttle, terrified of flooding the engine, heard the soft roar of fire behind her, pushed hard with her legs, away from the flames and toward the dark of the tunnel. The trapped air whispered past her ears as the bike rolled forward into the dip. She flicked on the headlight and saw the bottom ten feet in front of her. She knew she'd get just one chance at this.

She pulled on the clutch and stamped on the foot pedal twice to put the bike in second gear as the bottom rolled closer. The bike jerked beneath her as she released the clutch. The engine coughed as it dropped into gear and the momentum of the bike turned the engine. It spluttered once then roared into life. She twisted the throttle and grabbed the clutch with her other hand to stop it stalling. The chainsaw buzz rattled down the tunnel as she gunned the engine to clear the fuel lines, then she eased off the clutch and felt the bike jerk forward as the gear engaged and the wheels pulled her across the uneven stone floor and mercifully away from the burning van.

136

The darkness continued to grow in Gabriel's vision, spreading like an ink stain over the brightness of the city as he fell towards the Citadel.

Round the edges he could now see individual lamps on the deserted streets of the old town lighting up store fronts, and shuttered souvenir shops, and swinging signs hanging below the sloping sides of steepled rooftops. He could also see shapes rising up from the dark mountain as he fell towards it. He could see the highest peak, from which Samuel had fallen, sheer on one side and dropping steeply away on the other. It flattened to a ridge and ran round the lower part of the mountain, curling around the impenetrable dark in the middle like a noose. He still could not see the garden.

He spiralled down, aiming at the centre of the blackness to a spot he remembered from the satellite photo of the garden. When it centred in his vision he yanked down hard on the ripcord. He felt the slight tug of the guide chute shooting up from his pack then the wrench of the main chute deploying. The canopy arched over him like a huge curved airbed as he slipped his hands through the handles of the guide ropes and steered himself down through the darkness.

With the roar of the wind gone he could now hear the sounds of the city: the hiss of traffic on the ring road, music from the bars beyond the southern side of the wall mixed with the sound of talking and laughter. Then the sound was cut off, along with most of the light, as he dropped below the high ridge and into the dark crater at the heart of the mountain.

The moment the light went Gabriel switched eyes and the night vision that had been preserved in his right eye instantly made sense of the flat blackness. He could see fissures in the mountain walls and round, fluffy shapes rising in soft-edged clusters from a large area below him that looked lighter than the rest of the mountain. It was the garden. Much closer than he had imagined. Rising fast.

He pulled down hard on both guide ropes. Felt a bounce and a soft yaw in his stomach as the chute pulled him up. He lifted his legs away from the feathery top of a tree rising up from the darkness. His boots clattered noisily through the thin branches as he caught the top. He pulled hard on the right-hand rope to swing away from the tree. Felt his leg get snagged by a thicker branch. Kicked free and looked up just as the next tree rushed out of the darkness towards him.

The monk looked up from the fireplace – listening.

He rose and moved over to the door, his red cassock the only colour in the monochrome lower hallway of the Prelate's private quarters. He put his ear to the door leading out to the garden and heard it again – quieter this time. It was like a huge bird shifting about in the trees, or maybe someone pushing their way through bushes. He frowned. No one was allowed in the garden after dark. He reached into his sleeve for his Beretta, shut off the lights and opened the door.

The moon was still hours from rising and the monk's eyes could see nothing in the deep darkness of the garden. He stepped outside, closing the door quietly behind him, then scanned the darkness, turning his head like an owl, listening for the sound of movement.

A sharp crack split the silence and his head snapped round towards it. He listened harder. Heard a faint whispering, like a branch shaking, then silence flooded back. The sounds had come from the orchard. He stole down the stone steps to the pathway and stepped over the gravel path to the silent grass beyond. It whispered softly against his hurrying feet as he moved towards the copse of trees, gun extended, the darkness taking form as his eyes grew accustomed to the night.

He could see the trees now, and something else near the centre of the orchard, lighter than the prevailing night, moving in the darkness like a ghost. He levelled his gun at it, moved closer, keeping the uprights of the trees between himself and the apparition. As he drew nearer he noticed ropes draping from its edges, then saw an empty harness at the end of them, trailing on the ground. He realized with a jolt what it was just as his vision whipped round and everything flashed white in time to a deafening crack. The monk tried to turn and level his gun at whoever had grabbed him but the lines of communication between his head and the rest of his body had already been severed by his broken neck. He collapsed to the floor, smelt the rich moist fug of the dark soil mixed with the rotten mulch of last year's leaves, was aware of someone loosening his rope belt and his cassock being tugged. Then his eyes fluttered shut, and darkness engulfed him.

137

The bike's headlamp swept across the jagged walls of the tunnel, curving up and away towards the flat steel upright of the entrance.

The solid shutter loomed up and Kathryn stamped hard on the brake, locking the wheels and slithering across the concrete floor until the front wheel clanged against it, bringing her to a sudden, echoing stop. She snatched the key card from her teeth and reached across to swipe it through the lock, dropping the bike to the ground where it stalled into silence. From behind her she thought she could hear the crackle of fire echoing down the tunnel and she dropped to the floor next to the bike, ready to slide outside the moment the shutter started to rise.

But nothing happened.

She looked down at the card, bent slightly from where she'd bitten down on it, flexed it straight and swiped it again.

Still nothing.

She looked round, searching for another lock or way of escape and saw a security camera, squatting like a crow high in the corner, peering down with its large glass eye. The red light on its front winked and she realized with rising panic that the door was not going to open.

She was trapped.

Gabriel's left arm burned with pain as he rolled the stripped body of the monk into the parachute and dragged it across the wet grass to where a tangle of cut branches lay in a pile. He'd knocked it badly when he hit the trees and now the adrenalin of the free-fall was easing off, the pain was flooding in. He could just about move his fingers but could hardly grip anything worth a damn. It felt like it was broken.

He cradled it to his body and pulled some branches over the cocooned shape of the monk with his good right hand then headed back to where he'd stashed his backpack at the base of an apple tree. Above him he could hear the dry whisper of leaves and the distant hum of the city beyond, but no muffled boom shook the ground beneath his feet. Maybe something had gone wrong.

He reached inside the bag and switched on his PDA. He closed his right eye to preserve night vision, ducked his head down to the opening of the pack and peered inside.

The monitor was showing a white dot, expanding and contracting towards the top of the screen. There was no other information. The wire-frame lines sketching the skeletal outlines of streets had gone. He was off the map. Without any points of reference he would have to use it as a simple direction finder, following the signal from the transponder in Samuel's body. He was pretty sure that wherever they'd taken him would be where they'd now take Liv.

He closed the bag and gritted his teeth against the pain as he pulled the hood of the russet-coloured cassock over his arms and head. Through the trees he could see the faint glow of a light behind a window cut high in the wall. He watched it while he reached into the backpack to remove the gun and PDA, listening for the rumble of the explosion. It should have happened by now. He was counting on the shock of the blast and the smoke that followed to cause enough confusion for him to get safely lost in the mountain. But he couldn't wait for ever. Someone might miss the monk he'd just killed and come looking for him, or sound an alarm and put the whole mountain on alert. He couldn't afford to let that happen. Not if he wanted to get Liv out alive. His mind drifted to thoughts of what might have happened to his mother but he quickly shut them down. Speculation wouldn't get the job done.

He waited for a few more seconds, flexing his stiff left hand to test it. It hurt like hell but it would have to do. The light in the window shifted slightly as someone moved behind it and he rose from the ground, his hands buried in the sleeves of the cassock – the good one holding his gun, the other gripping the PDA as best he could. He headed across the grass, following the line of the pathway that would lead to a door and into the Citadel.

Kathryn could feel panic rising inside her like whistling steam.

She had no idea how long she had left before the van exploded. She scanned the passage frantically for a way out, her mind screaming with her desire to survive.

Think dammit!

The tunnel was curved. It was possible the shape of it would protect her from the direct force of the blast. She pictured the shock wave travelling down the narrow space, throwing her against the steel shutter like a hammer on an anvil. She needed to get down, tuck into the wall as tightly as she could, and offer the smallest possible area for the blast to act upon. She hopped over the bike and dropped to the ground, noticed the helmet still hooked over the handlebars, yanked it free and jammed it on to her head as she rolled to the left where the curve of the tunnel might deflect some of the blast. She hit the smooth upright of the wall and tucked herself into the gap where it met the floor, her frantic mind casting about for anything else she should do. In the confines of the helmet her breathing was deafening.

She snatched a quick breath.

Pinched her nose.

Blew hard into her sinuses.

138

The boom echoed through the mountain like thunder shaking free from the ground. In the darkness of the great library it sent books tumbling from shelves and dust drifting down from the vaulted roof. Athanasius looked up in a numbed daze. It was as if the mountain had read the words over his shoulder and shuddered at what it discovered there.

He reached out, folded the waxy pages back inside the volume of Nietzsche and rose from his seat. He needed to know if what he had found buried in the smudged words of the dead language was true. His faith depended on it. Everybody's faith depended on it. He walked down the passageway towards the central corridor, stepping over all the books that had been shaken to the floor, oblivious of the chaos around him and the raised voices puncturing the deadness as he approached the entrance. He felt detached from himself, like he had become pure spirit unfettered by the constraints of his physical self. He passed into the entrance chamber and drifted across the hallway towards the airlock, barely aware of the wailing librarians tearing their hair as they surveyed their ruined library.

The smell of smoke hit him the moment he stepped out of the airlock and into the corridor. It had an acrid, bitter quality – like sulphur – and mingled with the clamour of confusion and fear echoing up from the lower corridors. Two monks wearing the brown cassocks of the guilds hurried past, heading down into the mountain towards the source of the smoke. In his mind Athanasius imagined them scurrying towards a crack in the rock from which the foul smoke now poured: A crack filled with brimstone and fire.

He turned and walked in the opposite direction, heading up the mountain towards his own revelation. He knew this path was forbidden and would probably lead to his death, but somehow this did not frighten him. He could not live in the cold shadow cast by the words he had just read. He would rather die discovering they were not true than live suspecting they were.

He ducked into a stairwell and followed the steps as they curved towards the upper landing of the lower mountain. At the top he turned into a cramped hallway with several other passageways leading off it. At the far end the red-coloured cassock of a guard stood by the doorway that led to the upper part of the mountain. He had no idea how he was going to get past him, but in his heart he felt sure that, somehow, he would.

He realized he still had the book in his hand containing the stolen pages of the Heretic Bible and raised it to his chest now like a talisman. He took a couple of steps towards the guard and saw him look in his direction just as another doorway opened halfway down the landing. Another guard emerged into the narrow hallway, his hood pulled low over his face.

Then the lights went out, plunging the hallway into total and impenetrable darkness.

139

Liv woke thinking of thunder.

She opened her eyes.

Hundreds of pin-points of light quivered before her in the liquid darkness. She focused. Felt the cold hard ground tremble and settle beneath her. Saw candle flames reflected in lines of mirrored blades shivering to stillness against a dark, stone wall. Then she saw something else, lying on the floor. A body, naked from the waist up, familiar lines standing proud and grotesque on the surface of its faintly glowing skin.

She reached out for him, ignoring the pain in her head that came with the movement. Her outstretched hand touched a face as cold as the mountain and rolled it towards her. A low animal moan escaped from her throat. Despite the violence of his death, and the brutal medical enquiries that had followed, Samuel looked serene. She pulled herself across the floor towards him, hot tears scalding her eyes, and rose up to kiss his face. She pressed her lips against his cold skin and felt something shift inside her. Then everything lurched as she was grabbed from behind and pulled violently away from her brother.

Gabriel spotted the guard moments before the lights went out.

He dropped down in the sudden darkness, jarring his arm and sending pain screaming through his body. He choked it down and forced himself to move silently across the black corridor, towards the far wall, reaching out with his good hand but careful to shield the gun so it didn't clatter against the stone when he found it. His left hand remained buried in his sleeve, throbbing with pain but still clutching the PDA. He had stolen a glance at it just before entering the corridor. The signal from the transponder was coming from somewhere beyond the door at the end of the corridor, the one the guard had been standing by.

The back of his hand touched the cold, stone wall and he dropped lower, levelling his gun at a spot ahead of him in the black where he had last seen the guard. Behind him a rising confusion of voices echoed up from the depths of the Citadel: some calling for lamps, some for help, others for hoses to feed water down to where the mountain was burning. He could feel the panic. Nothing unsettled people like the smell of smoke.

He kept the gun steady and with his free hand held the PDA out towards the centre of the corridor and slightly in front of him. His arm screamed as he willed his thumb to search for the button to turn on the display. He found it. Pressed it. And the cold glow of the screen lit up the corridor as the PDA tumbled from his hand to the floor. The guard was not by the door. He was crouched over to the left, his gun pointing down the corridor. He fired twice, aiming above the light source, probably going for a headshot, the sound deafening in the stone confines of the corridor.

Gabriel fired with his own silenced weapon, watched the guard twitch then slump back against the door, his gun clattering to the ground. He sprang forward using the glow from the PDA to light his way and kicked the gun away from the guard's hand. He reached for his neck with his good hand, feeling for a pulse, but keeping a tight grip on his gun in case he found one. He found nothing. His hand skimmed across the rough surface of the cassock, skirting the warm wetness of the chest wound until he found what he was looking for.

He tracked back, picked up the PDA and wedged it in the claw of his left hand, directing the light towards the heavy studded door. The keyhole was in the centre. Gabriel slotted in the key he had taken from the guard, twisted it and leaned against the door, revealing a flight of steps behind it heading up into the dark of the mountain.

140

Samuel's body wrenched from Liv's view as she was yanked to her feet and whirled round to face a grotesque figure standing close by in the darkness. It stared at her, with grey eyes shining above a thick beard, its upper body glistening darkly with blood running from cuts that were both fresh and familiar. 'The marks of our devotion,' the Abbot said, following her gaze. 'Your brother bore them too – but he could not bear our secret.'

He twitched his head towards the darker end of the cavern and Liv was jerked round to face the blackness. She twisted her head to the right, hoping to catch sight of her brother. A hand grabbed her hair and forced her to face forward. 'Search the darkness,' the Abbot commanded. 'See for yourself.'

She looked.

Saw nothing but shadow. Then a breeze seemed to blow through her body as something took form in the gloom.

It was the shape of the Tau, at least as high as she was and just as solid. As her eyes continued to make sense of the darkness, the breeze strengthened and brought with it a whispering sound, like the wind moving through trees. She could feel it flowing through her, gently rinsing away her pain.

'This is the great secret of our order,' the voice behind her said. 'The un-doer of all men.'

The hands pressed her closer and more details emerged. The main upright was about the width of a small tree, though its surface was flatter and made of something darker than wood. At its base was a rough grille from which something seeped into channels cut into the stone floor. It reminded her of the sap she'd seen oozing from the dying tree outside the hospital in Newark. Where this sticky substance flowed, thin vines had somehow taken root, their tendrils snaking up the strange, uneven surface of the Tau. Her eyes drifted up, following the vines past raised joints in the surface where crudely beaten iron plates had been welded together to make the central pillar. The breeze strengthened, carrying with it now the warm, comforting scent of sun-toasted grass. She arrived at the place where the central upright met the thinner arms of the horizontal crosspiece; then saw something else – something inside the shape – and the shock of it drove the breath from her lungs.

'Behold,' the Abbot whispered, sensing her discovery. Liv stared at the narrow slit cut into the dull metal surface of the Tau – and the pale, green eyes that stared back at her. 'The secret of our order. Mankind's greatest criminal; sentenced to death for crimes against man – but unkillable. Until today.' He stepped into view and pointed at the floor where Samuel's body lay crumpled and discarded. '*The cross will fall*,' he said, shifting his finger to point at Liv. '*The cross will rise*,' his hand swept over to the Tau, '*to unlock the Sacrament, and bring forth a new age, through its merciful death*.' A sharp metallic snap echoed through the chapel as he undid a clasp on the side of the cross. 'She who once robbed man of his divinity will now restore it.' More sharp snaps cracked through the air until the front of the structure shifted and swung slowly open, dragging an agonized, animal shriek from the woman it contained.

The Tau was not a cross, it was a metal coffin filled with needles, each one shining darkly with the same wetness Liv had thought was sap. Now she saw the terrible truth. It was not sap but blood, leaking from hundreds of evenly spaced puncture marks on the frail and naked form of the woman inside it. She was young. More like a girl than a woman, yet her long hair shone white in the darkness, sticking in thick coils to a body mired with blood and gouged with ritualized wounds, each one terrible and familiar.

'The scars we bear are reminders of our failure to rid the world of its evil,' the Abbot chanted, as though he was reciting a prayer. 'The rituals we practise keeping it bloodless and weak until justice can finally be done.'

Liv looked into her eyes. Green like a lake, and wide like a child's, yet fathomless and silted with pain. Despite the grotesqueness of the situation Liv experienced a rush of intimacy with her, as if the chapel was just a room, and the girl before her just a lost friend from childhood. Looking at her now was like encountering a version of herself, like catching an unsuspecting reflection staring up from a deep well. It was as if the soft breeze that flowed out of her, carrying with it the scent of grass, connected them somehow. The green eyes stared deep into hers, and she felt laid bare and accepted; seen but not judged. And like a window they let Liv see too. And she saw everything in her, and her in everything. She was the desolation of every woman who'd wanted to be a mother but had never become one. She was Liv's own mother screaming in agony as she gave her own life for that of her two children. She was all the hearts that had ever been broken, and all the tears that had ever been shed. She *was* woman, and woman was her. Their pain was her pain, and hers was unimaginable. And Liv saw all this and felt a yearning to just reach out and give her the simple comfort of her touch, as though she was the mother and the tortured child pinned inside the vicious cross was hers, lost in a nightmare too long to measure. But her unseen captor held on too tightly and her hand was not hers to command, so she reached out with what words she could muster.

'It's all right,' she said, blinking away tears that spilled unchecked down her face. 'Shhh. It's all right.'

Eve's limpid green eyes held hers for a moment, then she smiled the faintest of smiles and sighed like something released, then Liv felt something press into her hand. She looked down. Saw the thin blade of a dagger tapering away from her palm into the darkness.

'Fulfil your destiny,' the Abbot said, holding her hand tightly in his. 'Rid mankind of its great betrayer.'

Liv stared at the slender blade, the horror of why she had been brought here suddenly manifested in its cold point. She tried to drop it, revolted by its intended purpose, tried to twist it away but the hands that held her were too strong. Samuel's words rose up in her frantic mind as she struggled against the men who held her.

If others die for your sake then God has spared you for a reason.

She'd often wondered what her reason in life was, but she knew this was not it. This exquisite, tortured woman could not die. Not by her hand. She looked up into the pale, elfin face, felt the breeze flowing through her, the smell of toasted grass stronger now as the sound it carried changed to something liquid, like ripples on a shore, that seemed to wash through her, bringing strange comfort and a rush of memories.

She saw herself sitting by the lake with Samuel in the sun-bleached grass of her childhood, listening to their granny telling stories from their Nordic past.

It's not supposed to be obvious to just anyone, Arkadian had said about the message scratched on the seeds.

It was meant for you.

The smells and the memories it brought now made everything terrible and clear. 'Ask' had not been an instruction. It referred to the legend of Ask and Embla – the first two humans. The message Samuel had sent her was:

Ask + ?
Mala T

The Tau and the question mark both underlined because they were the same thing. The Mala cross – the Tau – was Embla. The Sacrament was Eve.

141

When Cornelius had seen the green eyes staring out at him from the slit in the Tau, he'd thought for a shocked moment it was the woman in the burkha, brought here by some miracle. Only when the Abbot had revealed her identity did he realize the true marvel of the Sacrament. She wasn't just the woman in the burkha, or the mother who had abandoned him as a newborn – she was the fountainhead of all female treachery.

Eve had to die, for the crimes she had committed against man and against God; it was the only way to rid the world of her poison, and somehow the squirming girl in his arms was the key. He felt her struggling, saw the dagger in her hand twisting away from the symbol of his hatred trapped inside the cross and, without thinking about his actions, he shoved her forward with all his strength, slamming her into Eve.

Liv gasped at the impact and breathed in an ancient smell, like rich earth, and the promise of rain. It was the smell of Eve and it comforted her. She could feel the dagger between their bodies, held tight by their embrace and rendered useless by it; but she also felt the burning sensation of pain. It was coming from her throat and her right shoulder where the force had driven them on to the spikes inside the Tau.

She heard angry instructions from behind her and felt herself yanked back as quickly as she had been shoved forward. She gasped as an astonishing pain ripped through her, felt wet warmth gush from her neck and spread down across her chest, then her legs buckled and she slid to the stone floor.

The Abbot watched her fall and saw his dreams topple with her.

He looked up at Cornelius with murder in his eyes and reached for the dagger in his Crux. Then a sound made him stop.

It was a soft sound, like surf on shells, and it had come from Eve. He turned to face her. She was sobbing. The bottomless green eyes were turned downward to the crumpled form of the girl and her slender shoulders shook. He watched a tear fall through the darkness and disappear into the slowly spreading puddle of the girl's blood.

Then another sound tore through the chapel, a scream so powerful both the Abbot and Cornelius clamped their hands to their ears to block it out.

It was like the splintering of a great tree, or the crack of a shifting glacier. It was the song of the siren – and it was filled with grief and anger.

The Abbot stared at Eve through the force of the scream, defying her fury. Then, just as the terrible howl started to sub-side, he saw blood begin to flow from her wounds. It started as a trickle but grew steadily faster, dripping from the puncture holes all over her skin and flowing from the deeper ceremo-nial cuts on her arms and legs. He watched in wonder as it ran down her body, flowing far more freely than he had ever seen it, into the stone channels where Liv's blood also ran.

She's dying – he thought with a swell of triumph.

Then Eve spoke, in a voice that was more air than substance.

'KuShikaaM,' she said, like a soothing whisper aimed towards the ground where the girl lay bleeding. 'KuShikaaM.'

The girl looked up from the floor, like a child looking up at her mother. Then she smiled, and as her eyes gently closed – so did Eve's.

142

Gabriel had just reached the top of the stone steps when the terrible shriek split the darkness. He was up and running as soon as he heard it, using the awful sound to cover his rapid movement. He ducked into the faintly illuminated tunnel it had come from, leading with his gun, scanning for movement, edging forward as fast as he dared. The pain in his arm was now almost unbearable and he was starting to feel sick with shock.

He reached the end of the tunnel just as the scream abruptly stopped. He pressed himself against the wall. Ducked his head round the edge. Saw the glowing furnace on the far side, the sharpening wheels in front of it and the large circular stone on the back wall with a Tau carved into it. A monk stood by, looking into the blackness beyond the partly opened door where Gabriel guessed the sound had come from. Liv was in there, and so was the Sacrament. He stepped into the room.

The monk turned, saw Gabriel, pulled his arm free from his cassock to raise his gun but never made it. Two bullets hit him in the chest, jerking him backwards against the large stone door. His finger tightened reflexively, loosing off a round that hit nothing but rock.

He was dead before he hit the ground.

The Abbot and Cornelius spun round at the sudden sound of the gunshot. It had been close. Right outside the door.

'Go. See what it is,' the Abbot said, then turned back to the figure of Eve, so pale now she almost glowed as her eternal life force deserted her. The weaker she got, the stronger he felt. The prophecy had been fulfilled after all. Now he would be immortal. By killing a god he had become one. But even as his soul swelled with the ecstasy of this thought he became aware of a prickling sensation on various parts of his body. He looked down at the deep ceremonial wound circling his left shoulder and watched the recently knitted scar tissue slowly start to open. He raised his hand and pressed it against the cut, feeling the sudden wet warmth of blood rising beneath it, forcing its way between his fingers. He glanced at his other scars, each one now opening up in the same way, and watched for a few moments like a detached observer witnessing something macabre that was happening to someone else. Then he felt weakness settling on to him, as if the energy and rapture of his recent triumph was draining steadily away with the blood that now dripped to the floor. He reached out to steady himself, his hand resting on the edge of the Tau, and for the first time in all his years of being in the presence of the Sacrament he felt fear.

Gabriel reached the entrance, blinking to restore the night vision the guard's muzzle flash had stolen. He pressed his back against the round stone and slid along it until he reached the edge. Whoever was inside the chamber would have been alerted by the gunshot so he had to do this fast, and he had to do it right. He took a deep breath to steady himself and felt a strange itching sensation beneath the skin of his broken arm. He flexed his fingers tentatively, bracing himself for more blinding pain. Instead he felt an ache deep in his bones and his formerly useless fingers now closed neatly together. It still hurt and the grip was too weak to be useful, but incredibly it no longer felt broken. He was so distracted by this discovery that he didn't see the blade flash through the darkness until it struck him high in the chest, scraping agonizingly along a rib. Instinctively he twisted away, paring skin from bone, and brought his left arm up to knock the blade aside, jarring fresh pain into the injured limb and a cry of pain from his throat. Then he saw his attacker, naked from the waist up and covered in blood. A waxy patch of skin on his face glowed in the firelight. Gabriel recognized the evil in front of him. He remembered the scream that had brought him here, and his grandfather's shattered body on the warehouse floor. He caught a glint of realization in the demon's eyes as he saw how Gabriel cradled his arm – the look of a predator assessing the weakness of its prey.

The knife flashed again as Cornelius pressed closer, aiming for Gabriel's good arm. Gabriel stumbled backwards, raising his gun, but the nightmare vision pressed on, slashing again, this time catching more than just darkness. Gabriel felt the impact of the blade like a punch to his wrist but felt no pain. He levelled the gun at Cornelius. Saw the demon's eyes over the sights of his gun and pulled the trigger.

Nothing happened. Then he noticed the blood dripping thickly from his wrist and in a slow-motion moment of battle clarity he realized exactly what had happened. He dropped down and twisted away as the demon flew towards him again. He hit the stone floor and rolled, cradling the gun against his body as it flopped uselessly in his limp hand. The blade must have cut through the flexor tendons in his hand. It was now as useless as his other. He was defenceless.

He rolled again, keeping low and gaining distance, coming to rest just short of the furnace. He looked up and saw Cornelius, already standing above him. In his hand he held a thick metal pole, like a branding iron. He looked down at Gabriel and smiled as he saw the gun cradled now in his two useless hands. Then something distracted him, just for a moment, and he glanced down at his body as blood seemed to well up inside him and spill through the neat cuts in his flesh. Gabriel pushed away with his feet, sliding backwards across the gritty floor, gaining himself a precious few yards as he slipped the finger of his broken arm through the trigger guard.

Cornelius came to attention, alerted by the movement, and raised the bar high above his head, grinning maniacally as he stepped forward, towering above his defenceless victim. Gabriel clenched his hand into a tight grip around the gun, all the pain suddenly gone, all the strength returned. He angled it up at Cornelius and fired three quick shots.

Cornelius stood motionless for a shocked moment then looked down at the holes that appeared in his body. He watched the blood begin to ooze from them, joining the torrent of red already cascading down him. Then he looked up at Gabriel, took one step forward and fell dead to the floor.

143

Liv felt like she was sinking deep into water that was warm and thick with memories that swam before her as she sank; images from her life, flashing and fading like glittering fish. The breeze she had felt rinsing through her was now a current, bringing whispers of forgotten voices and fragments of distant memories with its flow. She sank deeper and the images thinned out, drifting upwards and away as a much brighter light rose up beneath her.

This is death, she thought as she watched it rise from the darkness to meet her. The light overwhelmed her and new images crowded behind her eyelids.

There was a garden, green and lush, and a man walking through it, and the sun shining down, or something like the sun. Then the shadow of a tree rose up and cut out the light, and she was in a cave, surrounded by men with hate in their eyes.

Then there was pain.

An eternity of pain and darkness as her flesh was ripped, and cut with blades, and burned with fire and boiling oils.

And there was the smell of blood.

And an endless, desperate yearning for the sun, to feel it on her skin and walk soft across the cool earth.

And pain was everywhere, flashing out of the darkness, imprisoning and overpowering her, for ever and ever.

Then she saw a face, with eyes full of sorrow and compassion. Samuel's face.

She fixed on the image, not wanting it to flit past like the others, holding it with her eyes until more things appeared within it.

She saw his body, naked from the waist up, flowing with blood from cuts deep in the skin. Then a cave, crowded with other men who reached up as one to draw bloody lines round their left shoulders with sharpened blades. And she heard a sound. An echoing chant of low voices bleeding together in an ancient language she somehow understood.

'The first,' they said over and over. 'The first. The first.'

And pain flashed out of the darkness and exploded in her left side along with the sound of shearing flesh. And a new voice rang out, full of anguish and pain.

'Where is God in this?' Samuel cried. 'Where is God in this?'

Then the images fled. And for a moment all was silent, and all was dark.

Then she felt herself starting to rise.

144

Liv's eyes fluttered open.

She was back in the chapel, lying on the spot where she had fallen. As she focused she saw Gabriel's face filling her vision, smiling down at her like warm sunshine. She smiled back, thinking she was still in her dream, then he reached out, laid his palm on the side of her face, and she felt the warmth of him and realized he was really there.

She glanced across at the Tau. The blood miring the spiked interior was now the only sign that Eve had been there at all. Liv traced its flow, down to the floor and the wet channels where it mingled with hers. Then she saw the figure rise up from behind the iron cross, his body running with blood, making him look like a demon in the dim reflected light. He raised the burning flambeau he held in his hand, the flames throwing ghoulish light across his hate-filled face. Gabriel sensed movement and started to turn but the heavy torch was already swinging down, aimed at his head, the flames roaring as it fell. A thunderclap shook the room, knocking the demon away and back towards the altar.

Liv looked across at the entrance, to where the sound had come from. A slightly built monk stood in the doorway. He had a gun in his hand and from where she lay his smooth scalp seemed to shine like a halo in the candlelight.

Athanasius looked upon the slaughterhouse scene he had discovered. The gunshot had thrown the Abbot away from him towards the vile needles inside the empty sarcophagus that dominated the far end of the room. He took a step into the room, the gun still trained on the bloodied figure of his former master. The Abbot wasn't moving.

He looked at the other two figures, a man and a woman. They were both looking at him warily. He lowered the gun and moved towards them. The man wore a cassock but Athanasius didn't recognize him. He had a cut in his side and another on his arm, judging by the blood that stained the sliced material.

The girl was much worse. She had a deep slash across her neck from which blood still flowed on to the ground and into the channels carved in the floor. He bent down to look closer. Then froze as the flesh around the wound started closing up, watching in silence as the miracle unfolded before him. Within moments the blood that had flowed so freely became a trickle then stopped altogether. He looked up into the girl's face, saw something timeless in her eyes and remembered the words he had read in the Heretic Bible.

The light of God, sealed up in darkness.

He reached out a hand to touch her face, then a noise by the altar made them all spin round.

The Abbot had shifted position. They each watched as his head lolled heavily on his shoulders, turning towards them until his eyes stared straight at Athanasius. The flambeau lay where he had dropped it, smouldering against his cassock and shrouding him with smoke. 'Why?' he asked, a look of confusion and disappointment on his face. 'Why have you betrayed me? Why have you betrayed your God?'

Athanasius looked up at the savage opening of the Tau and the wrist manacles dangling at the end of the crosspieces.

Not a mountain sanctified, but a prison cursed.

He looked back at the girl, her slender neck now completely healed, her endless green eyes burning with life.

'I have not betrayed my God,' he said, smiling down at the miraculous woman. 'I have saved Her.'

VII

___

And he saw the One. Walking the Earth.
Never ageing. Never withering.
And he became jealous.
He coveted her powers and wanted to
    possess them,
He thought if he could capture the One,
He could learn the secret of her everlasting life
    and make it his own.
So he began to tell a story against the One,
    who he named as 'Eve',
A false history designed to turn all men
    against her,
The story told how in the beginning there had
    been a man
A man who had been her equal – her greater
    even,
A man called Adam.
Adam had walked as a god in the garden of
    earth,
Causing life to flourish as Eve did.

And the story told how Eve became jealous of
 him.
She hated his rough body and the hair upon
 it,
And believed him closer to the beasts than to
 divinity.
So she caused a strange tree to grow
And persuaded him to eat of its fruit,
Promising it would give him a great and
 powerful knowledge.
But the fruit was poison and made him weak,
Robbing him of his divine powers,
And filling his head with anger and fear.
This story was told and retold
Until all jealous men believed Eve was their
 enemy,
And her death the only way back to divinity.
One day as Eve came near the caves where
 the men lived,
She heard within the sound of a beast crying
 in pain.
She followed the sound deep into the cold
 heart of the mountain.
And found a wild dog tied to the floor
Cut and bleeding, and howling from pain.
When Eve approached it the tribe emerged
 from the darkness.
They beat her with clubs, and cut her with
 blades

But she did not die.
Instead life flowed into her from the Mother
  Earth
Healing her and making her strong.
In a panic the men made a fire and pushed
  Eve on to it.
But blood flowed from her blisters to
  extinguish the fire,
And again her body became whole.
Some of the men went forth into the world,
To collect the poisons of the land
Which they forced her to eat.
But still she did not die.
So they kept her weak.
The light of God, sealed up in darkness,
For they dared not release her, for fear of what
  might follow,
Nor could they kill her, for they knew not how.
And as time passed the men became chained
  to their own guilt,
And their home became a fortress
Containing the only knowledge of the deed
  they had done,
Not a mountain sanctified, but a prison
  cursed.
With Eve still captive,
A holy secret – a Sacrament,
Until the time foretold when her suffering
  would end

The one true cross will appear on earth
All will see it in a single moment – all will
   wonder
The cross will fall
The cross will rise
To unlock the Sacrament
And bring forth a new age
Through its merciful death

New Book of Genesis
The Heretic Bible
— TRANS. BROTHER MARCUS ATHANASIUS

145

Distant sounds began to penetrate the woolly numbness of Arkadian's head: muffled shouts from urgent voices; the squeak of rubber soles on hard floors. He tried and failed to open his eyes, the lids too heavy to shift, so he lay there and listened, letting his senses warm up while the dull ache in his chest and shoulder blossomed into pain.

He took a deep breath and concentrated all his energy on opening his eyes. His lids parted for a split second, then he screwed them back shut.

It was bright: painfully bright. A negative image of what he had seen was now seared on his retina: a chequerboard outline of a suspended ceiling; a rail over to one side with a curtain hanging from it. He realized he was in a hospital.

Then he remembered why.

He lurched forward, trying to sit up, but a firm hand held him down. 'Whoa there . . .' a male voice said. 'You're OK; I'm just checking your wound. What happened to you?'

Arkadian struggled to remember. Rolled a dry tongue round his mouth. 'Shot,' he said eventually.

'That's for sure.'

'No.' Arkadian shook his head and instantly regretted it. Took more breaths until the bed stopped lurching beneath him. 'Was given a shot of . . . something . . . Don't know what . . .'

'OK. We'll run some bloods; we might have to sedate you again before fixing you up.'

'No!' Arkadian shook his head again, the spinning less severe this time. 'Need to call in.' He forced his eyes back open, squinting against the glare of the emergency room. 'Need to warn them.'

The curtain swished open and a short, compact woman in a white coat marched in and grabbed a clipboard from the end of the trolley. 'Sleeping beauty awakes,' she said, the fringe of her ash blonde hair falling round her face as she read the paramedic's notes. A badge pinned to her pocket identified her as Dr Kulin. She looked up at the wound. 'How is it?'

'Clean,' the nurse said. 'Still wet, but nothing major was hit. Bullet passed right through.'

'Good.' She dropped the notes back into their holder. 'Pressure dress it and move him out. We're going to need this space any second.'

'Why?' Arkadian asked.

She looked puzzled. 'Why do we need to pressure dress it? Because you've been shot and you're still bleeding.'

'No, why do you need the space?'

Dr Kulin glanced down at the badge tucked into Arkadian's belt by the paramedics. It was standard procedure. That way, when casualties from both sides of any violent encounter ended up in the same hospital, the good guys got seen to first.

'There's been an explosion. We've got numerous incoming. And from what I've heard of their injuries, Inspector, they'll all outrank your gunshot wound.'

'Where?' Arkadian already knew the answer.

A commotion outside snatched the doctor's attention. 'By the old town wall,' she said, jerking back the curtain. 'Close to the Citadel.'

Arkadian caught a glimpse of a trolley rolling quickly past. On it was a man, drenched in blood, dressed exactly like the one he'd examined in the morgue two days previously.

Arkadian closed his eyes and breathed in the smell of blood and disinfectant. He suddenly felt more tired than he had ever done. Whatever he'd hoped to prevent had already happened. He wished to God he could speak to his wife and listen to her soft voice rather than the chaos unfolding around him. He wanted to tell her he loved her, and hear her say the same. He wanted to tell her that he was OK, that she shouldn't worry and that he'd be coming home soon. Then he thought of Liv Adamsen, and Gabriel, and the woman in the warehouse – and wondered if any of them were still alive.

146

Dr Kulin followed the first trolley into an examination space and stopped short. She had covered the emergency room for upwards of ten years, but never seen anything like this. The man's torso was covered in cuts, straight and deliberate, steadily leaking blood on to the bunched green material of the cassock that had been hastily cut away. There was so much blood he looked as though he'd been dipped in it.

She turned to the paramedic who'd wheeled him in. 'I thought it was an explosion?'

'It was. Knocked a hole through the base of the mountain. This guy came from *inside* the Citadel.'

'You're kidding!'

'Dragged him out myself.'

She reached down tentatively and shone a pen-light into the monk's eye. 'Hello. Can you hear me?' His head lolled from side to side, making the deep cut around his neck open and close obscenely, as if it was breathing. 'Can you tell me your name?'

He whispered something but she didn't catch it. She leaned closer, felt his breath on her ear as he whispered again, something that sounded like *Ego Sanctus* . . . The poor man was clearly delirious.

'Did you do anything to stop the bleeding?' she said, straightening up.

'Pressure packs and a plasma drip to keep him hydrated. He just won't stop.'

'BP?'

'Sixty-two over forty, and falling.'

Not dangerously low, but near enough.

The heart monitor beeped as a nurse stuck electrodes to his chest. It also sounded way too slow. Dr Kulin looked at the wounds again. There was no sign of clotting. Maybe he was a haemophiliac. The clamour of fresh arrivals forced a decision. 'Five hundred IU of prothrombin and twenty mills of Vitamin K. And type him fast so we can transfuse. He's going to bleed out if we don't hurry.'

She headed back through the curtain and out into the main corridor. Three more monks rolled past at speed, heading to the far end of the ward, each losing astonishing amounts of blood from wounds identical to the ones she'd just seen.

'Where do you want this one?' The paramedic's voice snapped her back to attention. She looked down and was relieved to see it did not contain a monk. 'Right here,' she said, pointing to one side of the corridor; the examination booths were filling up fast and this one didn't appear to be haemor-rhaging. The paramedic steered the trolley to one side and stamped on the wheel brake.

'What's the story here?' Dr Kulin asked, easing open the cracked, blackened visor of the motorcycle helmet and shining a light into the woman's right eye.

'Found her in the tunnel,' the paramedic said. 'Vitals are strong but she was unconscious when we found her and stayed that way on the ride over.'

Dr Kulin switched her penlight to the left eye. It dilated slightly less than the right. She turned to a nurse. 'Straight to X-ray,' she said. 'Possible skull fracture. Don't remove the hel-met until we know what we're dealing with.'

The nurse grabbed a porter and was already moving the trolley away when the entrance doors burst open and two more blood-soaked monks were wheeled in: same wounds; same massive blood loss.

What the hell was going on?

She followed the first into a cubicle, did a quick assessment then administered the same dose of coagulating compound. She heard another doctor hollering for five litres of O-positive from down the hall. She moved to the next cubicle in a daze, battering aside the curtain as she went. Beyond it lay another surprise. Another monk, only this one wasn't bleeding; he was standing beside a trolley, arguing with a nurse, and holding a young woman in his arms.

'I'm not leaving her,' he said.

He had a large amount of blood on his cassock, though not nearly as much as the others. The girl on the trolley was drenched, the soak pattern suggesting massive neck trauma. Dr Kulin stepped forward and pushed down the neck of her T-shirt. The skin beneath was stained crimson, but she could see no sign of any cuts. 'Delivery notes?' she asked, searching for the source of the bleeding.

'Vitals low but steady,' the nurse said. 'Blood pressure eighty over fifty.'

Dr Kulin frowned. It was low enough to indicate major blood loss, but she just couldn't find the source. Maybe the blood belonged to someone else. 'Keep her on a drip and monitor the BP.' She smiled at the girl, seeing her properly for the first time. 'Other than that, you seem fine.' She was momentarily transfixed by the almost unearthly brightness of the green eyes that stared back at her, then got a grip on herself and switched her attention to the monk.

He pulled his arm away. 'I'm OK, really . . .'

'Well, you won't mind me looking then.' She parted the bloody, shredded sleeve of his cassock to peer at the red smeared flesh beneath. The source of his bleeding was immediately apparent, a nasty deep gash right across his wrist that had obviously been quite deep. It looked a good few days old, judging by the extent of the healing, yet the blood was fresh. 'What happened?' Dr Kulin asked.

'It got knocked about a bit,' he said. 'I'll live. But, please. Has a woman been brought in? Looks about forty. Black hair, five six?'

Dr Kulin thought of the woman in the motorcycle helmet. 'She's gone to X-ray.' The high-pitched sound of a cardiac alarm sounded somewhere behind her. 'She's been knocked about a bit too. But don't worry: I think she'll be fine.'

147

Liv heard the squeak of shoes amongst the cacophony as the doctor and nurse hurried away. She also heard a thousand other sounds.

Since Gabriel had carried her out of the Citadel, every colour, every sound and smell called to her like living things, as if she was experiencing everything for the first time.

As they had emerged into the night from the endless, smoke-filled tunnel, and Gabriel had laid her gently down on a stretcher, she had looked up and glimpsed the new moon hanging in the sky. She'd cried when she'd seen it; it was so beautiful and fragile – and free. Yet her tears carried something other than this brimming joy; they also stung with loss. She had sought her brother, and, though the memory of exactly what she had discovered in the mountain chamber evaded her, she knew it was over, and that Samuel was gone.

Now she was in this bright and clamorous place – so familiar and yet so strange. She could hear the sound of death in the erratic breathing of the men lying around her, and the drip of their blood.

She felt Gabriel's arms close around her, sensing her distress, and the citrus smell of him engulfed her, pushing aside the antiseptic taint of the emergency room and the metallic tang of blood and fear. She closed her eyes and sank into it, focusing only on him, and the sound of his heart thundering in his chest, rolling across the landscape of other sounds until all she could hear was its comforting beat. It was a heart that beat just for her, and tears rose fresh again, for this was as beautiful as the moon had seemed.

Then another sound crept in, low and insistent, crawling at the periphery of her consciousness.

She opened her eyes.

A bunch of lilacs, still wrapped in cellophane, lay on a narrow shelf, amongst the thermometer holders and plug sockets, a forgotten gift for a previous occupant. Lilacs . . . the state flower of New Jersey. Liv thought of home, and the life she had been living just a few days ago, and how strange that seemed to her now. The sound returned and her eye caught movement amongst the petals. A bee crawled out from the velvet depths of one blossom, hovered for a moment then disappeared into another.

'What happened in there?' Gabriel said, his voice vibrating through her body where it pressed against his.

'I don't know,' she said, marvelling at the sound of her own voice. She held his question in her head, focusing on it until another memory fluttered past, fragmented and incomplete. She remembered her fear in the darkness, the tapering dagger, and her revulsion at its intended purpose. She remembered the green eyes that had stared into the depths of her soul, and divined her essential purpose. And as this memory flitted past it brought something else, whispering through the blood of the man who held her, shushing in her ear and soothing with its sound, just as the strength in his arms made her safe.

Ku . . . Shi . . . kaamm . . .

The whisper spread through her, giving birth to other ancient words that flowed and pulsed with Gabriel's heartbeat.

KuShikaaM . . .
Clavis . . .
Namzāqu . . .
κλάξ/ . . .
מפתח . . .

KuShikaaM . . .
Clavis . . .
Namzāqu . . .

And though she could not name the languages from which the words came, she understood them all, as if born with their knowledge, as if each was a fundamental part of her.

She held Gabriel more tightly as the sounds filled her head, shutting out even the beating of his heart. They clustered together, forming an image in her mind, an image which finally showed Liv who she was, and what she was.

'*KuShikaaM . . .*' the Sacrament had called her.

KuShikaaM . . .

The Key . . .

Then the desert warrior stepped into the room.

The interrogator turned towards him.

The fat man's face remained clenched in expectation of another blow. When none came he opened his good eye and discovered a second figure standing over him.

'Your daughters?' The newcomer held up the photograph. 'Pretty. Maybe they can tell us where their *babba* hides things?'

The voice was sandpaper on stone.

The fat man recognized it, and fear seeped into his staring eye. He watched as the desert warrior slowly unwound his *kef-fiyeh*, slipped off the sand goggles, and leaned into the shaft of sunlight. Pupils shrank to black dots in the centre of eyes so pale they appeared almost grey. The fat man registered their distinctive colour and shifted his gaze to the ragged scar that slashed across his captor's throat.

'You know who I am?'

He met the grey gaze and nodded.

'Then say it.'

'You are Ash'abah. You are . . . the Ghost.'

'Then you know why I am here.'

Another nod.

'So tell me where it is. Or would you prefer it if I dropped this engine on your head and dragged your daughters over for a new family photo?'

A hint of defiance surged up at the mention of his family. 'If you kill me you will find nothing,' he said. 'Not the thing you seek, and not my daughters. Do what you like to me, but I will never tell you where they are.'

The Ghost nodded slowly. He set the photograph down on the bench and reached into his pocket for the portable Sat-Nav he had pulled from the windscreen of the 4x4. He pressed a button and held it out for the man to see. The screen displayed a list of recent destinations. The third one down was the Arabic word for 'Home'.

'Last chance,' the Ghost said, tapping a fingernail lightly on it. The display changed to show a street map of a residential area on the far side of town.

All defiance drained from the fat man's face as his staring eye flicked across the screen.

He took a deep breath and, in as steady a voice as he could manage, told the Ghost what he needed to hear.

The truck bounced out into the chalk white desert, the fat man grunting each time his head bumped against the passenger window and the pain jarred through his bruised flesh. The Ghost ignored him, fixing his gaze on a hazy pile of rubble starting to take shape through the windscreen. It was too soon to say what it was, or even how close. The extreme heat of the desert played tricks with distance. It did the same with time. Looking out at the bleached horizon he could have been staring at a scene from the bible: same broken land, same parchment sky, same smudge of moon half melted upon it.

The mirage began to take more solid form as they drew closer. It was much bigger than he'd first thought, a square structure of some sort, manmade, two storeys high, probably an abandoned caravanserai serving the camel trains that used to travel through these ancient lands. At least a thousand years old, its flat clay bricks baked hard in a long-ago sun and now crumbling back to dust.

The fat man pointed to a small cairn of rocks a few hundred yards short of the main ruin. 'There. Stop there.'

The driver steered towards it, crunching to a halt. The Ghost scanned the horizon for movement. He saw the shimmer of air rising from hot earth and the gentle movement of palm fronds and in the distance a cloud of dust, possibly a column on the move, but too far away to be of immediate concern. He turned to the hostage. One side of his face was now grotesquely swollen and his white *dish-dash* had developed a livid red pattern where blood had soaked through from his puncture wounds.

'Show me,' the Ghost whispered, opening the car door and stepping out into the furnace.

The fat man stumbled across the baked ground. The Ghost and his driver kept a safe distance, following his footsteps exactly to avoid any mines he may have tried to lure them on to. Ten feet short of the pile of rocks the man stopped and pointed to the ground.

The Ghost caught up with him and followed the line of his extended arm to a faint depression indicating where a trapdoor must be. 'Booby traps?'

The fat man stared at him for a second as if he'd just insulted his family. 'Of course,' he said, holding out his hand for the car keys. He took them from the driver, pointed the fob towards the ground and pressed the button. They heard the muted chirp of a lock deactivating somewhere beneath them. He dropped down, brushing away dust to reveal the hatch. It was secured on one side by a padlock wrapped in a plastic bag. He removed the bag and selected a key.

Sunlight streamed down into the bunker. A ladder dropped steeply away into the darkness. The fat man went first, sending a shower of grit before him. The Ghost watched over the barrel of his pistol. He had already taken the keys in case he tried to re-arm the cave's defences. The man looked up, his one good eye squinting against the brightness. 'I'm going to reach out for a torch,' he called. 'It's on a shelf by the ladder.'

The Ghost said nothing, just tightened his finger on the trigger in case something other than a torch appeared in the fat man's hand. A cone of light appeared in the darkness below them.

The driver went next and took the torch from him. The Ghost did a final sweep of the horizon. Satisfied that they were still alone, he slid down into the dark earth.

The cave had been cut from rock by ancient hands. The ceiling was uneven and vaulted. Deep shelves lined each wall.

Thick sheets of polythene protected their contents from the dust. He reached over and pulled one aside. It was filled with neatly stacked AK47 assault rifles. Underneath them were rows of spam cams containing 7.62mm rounds. Stencilled lettering on their sides: Chinese, Russian, Arabic. The Ghost pulled back each polythene sheet in turn: more weapons, heavy artillery shells, brick-like stacks of dollar bills, bags of dried leaves and white powder. Finally, near the back of the cave, he found what he was looking for.

It was on a shelf all of its own, loosely bound in burlap sacking. He eased the bundle towards him, feeling the drag of the heavy object inside. He unwrapped it reverently, with the same care he would employ to peel dressings from burned flesh. Inside was a flat slate tablet. He tilted it towards the light, revealing faint markings on its surface. He traced their outline with his finger, like a letter 'T' turned upside down.

2

VATICAN CITY, ROME

Cardinal Secretary Tantalus looked down at the tourists swarming across St Peter's Square. Several groups were facing him, glancing at their guidebooks and then at the window of the fourth-floor room in which he stood. His black cardinal's surplice blended into the shadows, so he was pretty sure he could not be seen. He knew they were not looking for him anyway, and watched them gradually realize their mistake and shift their gaze to the Papal apartments to his left.

Tantalus drew deeply on his cigarette. Smoking inside the building was forbidden, but as Cardinal Secretary of the city-state he didn't consider the odd one in his private office an outrageous abuse of position. He generally restricted himself to just two a day; this was his fifth, and it wasn't even lunchtime.

He crushed the stub in the marble ashtray beside him and turned to face the bad news spread across his desk. Morning prayers and early meetings had kept him away from it until now, so he had only just caught up with the daily papers. As was his preference, they had been arranged in the same configuration as the countries on a world map – the American broadsheets on the left, the Russian and Australian on the right and the European papers in the middle. Usually the headlines were all different, each reflecting their nation's obsession with some local celebrity or specific political scandal. Today they were all the same.

He picked up the morning edition of *La Repubblica*, one of the more popular Italian newspapers, and inspected its cover. Beneath a picture of the dagger-shaped mountain known as the Citadel were photographs of three people, two women and one man, and a banner headline that yelled:

DID THEY LEARN THE SECRET
OF THE SACRAMENT?

The papers had been full of little else in the aftermath of the explosion that shook the sacred mountain and the emergence of survivors – the first people ever to leave the Citadel. He picked up an English tabloid showing a riot of harshly lit pictures of monks being stretchered from the mountain, blood running from the ritual wounds that criss-crossed their bodies. The whole thing was a PR disaster. It had made the church look like some kind of demented, secretive, medieval cult: bad enough at the best of times, calamitous right now.

He sat down heavily at his desk, feeling the weight of the responsibilities he carried. Like the Vatican, the Citadel was an autonomous state within a state, but since the explosion he had heard nothing from within it – nothing at all. It was this silence, not the clamour of the world's press, which he found most disturbing.

He reached over the sea of newsprint and tapped his keyboard. His inbox was bursting with the day's business but he ignored it all, clicking instead on a private folder. A prompt box asked for his password. An hourglass icon appeared as his server processed the complex encryption software.

Another mailbox opened. It was still empty. He left the subject line blank and typed one word into the body of a new message:

Anything?

He hit send and watched it disappear from his screen, then shuffled the newspapers into a neat pile and sorted through some letters that required his signature. The chatter of the tourists drifted up from the square as they marvelled at the majesty and wonder of the church, little knowing what turmoil boiled inside it. A sound like a knife striking a wineglass announced the arrival of the reply.

> Still nothing. Sources inside the hospital tell me the ninth monk is about to die. What do you want me to do with the others?

His hand hovered over the keyboard but he typed nothing. Maybe the situation was resolving itself. Of the thirteen taken from the mountain, there were just four survivors. But three of them were the civilians, and they posed the greatest threat of all.

He rose from his desk and drifted once more towards the window, distancing himself from the decision he was avoiding.

There had been signs of life inside the mountain over the past week – candles passing in front of high windows, smoke from the chimney vents. They would have to break their silence sooner or later, re-engage with the world and hopefully tidy up their own mess. Until then, he would be patient.

He reached for the pack of cigarettes on the window sill, preparing to seal his decision with his sixth of the day. It was then that he heard the sound of shoe-leather on marble in the corridor outside. Someone was coming his way, in far too much of a hurry for it to be routine. A sharp tap on his door and the pinched features of Bishop Clementi appeared.

'What?' Tantalus's question betrayed more irritation than he intended. His personal secretary's efficacy was beyond reproach, yet Tantalus found it very hard to warm to him.

'They're here,' the bishop said.

'Who?'

But Tantalus didn't need an answer. Clementi's expression told him all he needed to know.

He grabbed the cigarettes and thrust them into his pocket, knowing he would probably smoke them all in the next few hours.

He should have dealt with the survivors sooner.

3

ROOM 410

Liv Adamsen burst from sleep like a breathless swimmer breaking the surface. She gasped for air, her blonde hair plastered across pale, damp skin, her frantic green eyes scanning the room for something real to cling to, something tangible to help drag her away from the horrors of her nightmare. She heard a whispering, as though someone was close by, and cast about for its source.

No one there.

The room was small: a solid door opposite the steel frame bed she was lying on; an old portable TV fixed high on a ceiling bracket in the corner; a single window set into a wall whose white paint was yellowing and flaking as if infected. The blind was down but bright daylight glowed behind it throwing the sharp outline of bars against the wipe clean material. She took a deep breath to try and calm herself and caught the scent of sickness and disinfectant in the air.

Then she remembered.

She was in a hospital – though she didn't know why, or how she had come to be here.

She took more breaths, long and deep and calming. Her heart still thudded in her chest, the whispering rush continued in her ears, so loud and immediate that she had to stop herself from checking the room again.

Get a grip, she told herself. *It's just blood rushing through your veins. There's no one here.*

The same nightmare seemed to lie in wait for her every time

she fell asleep, a dream of whispering blackness, where pain blossomed like red flowers, and a shape loomed, ominous and terrifying – a cross in the shape of a letter 'T'. And there was something else in the darkness with her, something huge and terrible. She could hear it moving and feel the shaking of the earth as it came towards her, but always, just as it was about to emerge from the black and reveal itself, she would wake in terror.

She lay there for a while, breathing steadily to damp down the panic, tripping through a mental list of what she could remember.

My name is Liv Adamsen.

I work for the New Jersey Inquirer.

I was trying to find out what happened to Samuel.

An image of him flashed into her mind, standing on top of a dark mountain, forming the sign of a cross with his body even as he tipped forward and fell.

I came here to find out why my brother died.

In the shock of this salvaged memory, Liv remembered where she was. She was in Turkey, close to the edge of Europe, in the ancient city of Ruin. She also realized the significance of the sign Samuel had made – the Tau, sign of the Sacrament, the same shape that now haunted her dreams. Except it wasn't a dream, it was real. She had seen it for herself, somewhere in the darkness of the Citadel she had seen the Sacrament, though exactly what she had seen remained unclear.

She glanced up at the heavy door, noticing the keyhole now and recalling the corridor beyond. She had glimpsed it as the doctors and nurses had come and gone over the past few days.

How many days? Four? Five, maybe.

She had also seen two chairs pushed up against the wall. Men sitting on them. The first was a cop, but not a New Jersey trooper. The shirt was a darker blue and the badges unfamiliar. The other had also worn a uniform, but unlike the cop his was universal: black shoes, black suit, black shirt, a thin strip of white at the collar. The thought of him now, sitting just a few feet from her made her fear rise up again. She knew enough of the bloody history of Ruin to realize now the danger she was in. And whether she could recall what she had seen or not would make no difference to them.

For the priest standing vigil outside her door was not there to minister to her troubled soul.

He was there to keep her contained.

He was there to ensure her silence.

ACKNOWLEDGEMENTS

First books are odd things. They're kind of like massive parties you spend years carefully putting together without the slightest idea if anyone will turn up.

You know your family will be there at least because they get dragged into the preparation and get to read the invite – a lot. Chief amongst these was my incredibly supportive and wise wife Kathryn whose mixture of enthusiasm and occasional harsh honesty always made me try harder. Then there were my two children, Roxy and Stan, who always seemed to know when to slip into the study when I really needed a distraction; and the grandparents – John Toyne, Irene Toyne, Ross Workman and Liz Workman – for a mixture of proof reading, taking the kids off our hands when we were both working, and never passing on any concerns they may have had about me giving up a well-paid, secure job in television to go and do something so foolhardy as write a novel.

I'd also like to thank Becky Toyne for sisterly encouragement, insider info and the list of agents I would never get but were worth approaching. One of these was LAW where, contrary to all expectation, Alice Saunders plucked me from the slush pile, dropped me a line asking for the rest of the manuscript and all of a sudden I started thinking maybe some folks would turn up to the party after all. With the formidable trio of Alice, Peta Nightingale and Mark Lucas in my corner the book got much better, and much shorter. They also brought their team of uniformly lovely and brilliant people to the table to help send out the invites. These include George Lucas at Inkwell and Sam Edenborough, Nicki Kennedy, Katherine West and Jenny Robson at ILA.

Then, finally, the guests started to arrive: first the publishers, who all said such nice things and made me wonder whose book they could possibly be talking about; and now you, dear reader. So welcome to the party, and thank you – all of you – for coming.

START/STOP

THESANCTI.COM